THE *Chronicles* OF *Benjamin Prescott*

a novel

Robert B. Stone

The Chronicles of Benjamin Prescott
Copyright © 2023 Robert B. Stone

Produced and printed by Stillwater River Publications.
All rights reserved. Written and produced in the United States of America.
This book may not be reproduced or sold in any form without the expressed,
written permission of the author(s) and publisher.

Visit our website at **www.StillwaterPress.com** for more information.

First Stillwater River Publications Edition

ISBN: 978-1-960505-73-6

Library of Congress Control Number: 2023917095

Names: Stone, Robert B. (Robert Bailey), author.
Title: The chronicles of Benjamin Prescott : a novel / Robert B. Stone.
Description: First Stillwater River Publications Edition. | West Warwick, RI, USA :
    Stillwater River Publications, [2023]
Identifiers: ISBN: 978-1-960505-73-6 (hardcover) | LCCN: 2023917095
Subjects: LCSH: Orphans—Rhode Island—Newport—Fiction. | Fathers—
    Death—Fiction. | Inheritance and succession—Fiction. | Revenge—Fiction.
    | Newport (R.I.)—History—18th century—Fiction. | LCGFT: Historical
    fiction. | Christian fiction.
Classification: LCC: PS3619.T675 C47 2023 | DDC: 813/.6--dc23

1 2 3 4 5 6 7 8 9 10

Written by Robert B. Stone.
Published by Stillwater River Publications,
West Warwick, RI, USA.

*The views and opinions expressed in this book are solely those of the author(s)
and do not necessarily reflect the views and opinions of the publisher.*

For Nolan, Ada, and Aubrey,
...and all who dream.

The CHRONICLES
of BENJAMIN PRESCOTT

PROLOGUE

*S*ome might hold to the belief that it is life that makes the man. Others will hold it is the individual who makes his life. In telling the story of a life, the perspective from which it is told can make a difference as to how one answers this question. If one is still a youth, more weight may be given on the side of individual accomplishment. But the wisdom of age may shift the balance. Just as important in answering the question is who is telling the story. My name is Benjamin Prescott, and this is my story.

As I write these words, I am struck by the passage of time. I sit, now, in comfort, in my own well-appointed house in a fashionable urban environment. I have wealth, position, and the respect of many. I am considered by those about me an educated gentleman. And, in this year of Our Lord 1760, living in His Majesty's American colonies, it could be said there are few who have attained that position having been born here and not in England. Yet none know, or even suspects, the humbleness of my beginnings.

As a youth, I could never have foreseen the life I have lived. I have known adventure. I have had what some would call good fortune. I have also known fear and the terror of death. Did I make this life I have lived? Or have the winds of fate made me into the person I am today? Let me tell my story and leave it to you, the reader, to decide. It is important that you know all there is to know of me and, so, I must start my story with the earliest recollections of my youth. Even now, as I write these words, I am struck by the distance of that time from this. And I feel again the sheer terror I experienced as a young boy. This is where my story begins.

ONE

I am shivering from the cold of my wet clothes. I am alone and scared. I know if those who pursue me can find my place of hiding, my life will be forfeit. And so, I hide, here, within a place I first discovered while once at play. Now, it has become my refuge. Dark and dank, shaking from the cold that my wet clothes encourage, I hope the incoming tide will erase any trace of my arrival here. I pray the surging waters will obliterate my footprints from the sand and carry the small skiff I used to reach my hideaway far to the north. When it is found, my hope is it will throw my pursuers off my scent and send them hastening to search for me in the wrong direction.

I hear the water swirling and gurgling in the dark as it slowly rises, filling and blocking the only entrance to my lair. Once the tide is high, I will feel safer knowing that no one can reach me, no one can surprise me; no one can kill me. Then, only then, will I risk sparking a flame and lighting the stub of a candle, one of many I have brought here since first I found this place. But for now, I will lie here in darkness, shaking with cold, and clutching the small sailor's bag that holds all that is mine in the world.

You ask what is this place? It is a portion of the stern quarter of a sailing ship whose name I never knew that floundered in a storm many years before my birth and broke upon the sands. It lies half buried, keel to the sky and rudderless, and from a distance in the dark, its blackened wooden shape looks much like many of the rocks that line the shores along Narragansett Bay. It is only upon closer approach that the shape becomes discernible as the remnant of a once great ship. It lies in the tidal shallows of Shelter Cove about a hundred yards off the thin width of low-lying sand that connects Conanicut Island to Beavertail in the lee of Dutch Island. Many a time have I rowed the distance from the west shore of the bay to Dutch Island and to Conanicut, beyond. I have been a strong rower from a young age and could power a skiff from the shore across the West Passage to this location in a matter of a quarter hour.

My curiosity while at play had led me to explore the true nature of this shape. It had taken several investigations for me to discover the only way to enter its darkened interior. The ragged hole in the decking on the underside near the sand only allowed entry when the tide was out and made it my secret hideaway where I could spend the few hours that were allowed to me to dream of my future or revel in my fantasies. But the tides determined my visits and, if I tarried too long, my reward would be to arrive home in clothes that smelled of seawater. This would invariably be followed by a withering tirade at the hands of my aunt who always found displeasure in me.

In the time since discovering my secret place, I had spirited away from her home – for truly, it had not been my home for many years - things of use that I thought would not be missed: a small flint and steel, tinder, a small pewter plate and cup, stubs of candles, a small knife, a small amount of cured meat from the smoke house. Even though these things were of little real value, there were times I stood accused of pilfering by my aunt and beaten for her suspicions. Little did she know the truth of her accusations to which I could never admit; just as I had had no idea how important my petty thievery of these few things would now become.

And so, this night, I sit in stillness, entombed in this haven, saved by the rising water, listening for any sound of my pursuers, trying to come to terms with the horror I have seen this night. It is difficult enough to deal with death, but, for a lad of not yet fourteen years to witness such violence is something that should never happen. Even more difficult is when the victim is that boy's beloved father. Worse yet is when the killer is the victim's own brother, my uncle. But worst of all is to know that I am known to the killer and am the only witness to his heinous crime and now, he and his minions search for me to bury the only witness to his crime. Had I not fled quickly I would already be dead along with my father.

And run I did, as fast as I could. At first, in a blind panic, not knowing what direction would bring me to safety. It was only when I reached the shore and realized the tide was just beyond low that I suddenly knew where I could find safety. I pulled a small rowboat into the shallows as I could hear the alarm being raised behind me, I strained with all my strength to feel its bulk break free from the sand and begin to float. I vaulted over the side rail and fitted the oars in their locks. A few strong pulls on the oars and I could see the shoreline receding rapidly as I melted into the darkness.

The only pause in my hasty departure had been to snatch the few rude belongings my father had always cautioned me to keep safe: a small pouch of coins, a small dirk, a well-worn bible. These few belongings I now hold in my arms wrapped in my father's old oilcloth sailor's bag. And it strikes me as I sit cradling this package in my arms, feeling how small an amount it is, that this is the only legacy I will ever have from my father. Even so, I hold it close and begin to sob quietly. It is the first time that I have allowed my emotions expression this night.

I was born into a family of some note in the early days of Rhode Island. Grandfather Prescott had served with distinction in the time of the Indian war, now called the King Philip War after its leader, who is better known to history as Metacom. As a reward for this service, the great landholder, Richard Smith, granted a large parcel of land to my grandfather to the south of his trading post in the newly won land along the west shore of the great bay called Narraganset. Out of this unsettled wilderness, my grandfather carved a farming homestead that produced slightly more than it consumed. Crops of corn, vegetables, and flax were successful enough to acquire a herd of sheep and some hogs and provide large enough quantities for trade. Though it was certainly not productive to the level of Richard Smith's many farms, it allowed prosperity enough for the purchase of a few luxuries for this home at the edge of the quickly disappearing wilderness.

My grandfather Prescott had two sons who survived to adulthood: my father, William, and his younger brother, Matthew. They grew up beside their father working the land as he had. William, the first born and my father, was ruggedly handsome with a shag of black hair above a noble forehead. He stood a full six feet tall, and his barrel-chest and broad shoulders were powerfully muscled. He married in his late teens Eliza Carr, a cousin of the Royal Governor at that time, and brought his new bride to live in a humble cabin on the farm. They must have had a true love for this daughter of privilege to give up the life she had been raised in and agree to come to this homestead on the edge of civilization.

In one's earliest memory, a mother is the person that I am sure most children remember most vividly. My mother was all that was tenderness and love. She was always there with a smile or a warm soothing touch. She was the kindest person I have ever known. I can remember once a savage appeared at our cabin door. He was dressed in rags and obviously hungry. Most settlers' wives would have screamed in terror and run to the fields seeking their husband's protection, but not my mother. She made this poor native understand through hand gestures that he was welcome. She took soup simmering on the wood fire and gave it to him with a piece of cornbread. She showed no fear and her manner set the stranger at ease. When he had finished his simple meal, he took from a pouch he carried a small string of shells and gave them to my mother. She lowered her eyes in response and when she raised them, he had gone.

It was from her that I learned of my heritage. Sitting in front of our fireplace in the evenings, she would tell me of my grandfather and my father. She told me of how she had met my father and how he won her love. It was from her I learned of my heritage and how she had come as a new bride with her husband to his family's farm so recently established in the newly secured lands of the western bay. She spoke of their deep love for each other. She spoke of the days before my birth when my father, William, had worked on the family farm with his brother and aging father. How he had done so without complaint, yet hating every day of it, until my grandfather's death.

It was when she spoke of my father that a tender gaze would settle in her eyes. She would speak of his manly presence, his great strength, and his mass of thick black hair. She would describe the days of long hours of work and how my father would come back to the house, his skin glistening with sweat and his clothes soaked with it. He would lift me up and whirl me around tossing me into the air. I am not sure if I truly remembered him doing so or if it was a memory created through the stories from my mother after he went away.

Uncle Matthew was no less handsome with light brown hair with a physique that reflected the days of physical labor on the farm. He was quieter than his older brother and less forward in his manner. He was known for his religious piety in his youth, and some thought he might eventually seek a life following Christ in some manner. Matthew had been raised a Quaker, but, as he matured, he had found solace in the King James Bible.

"Your father loved the sea," she had said to me. "He worked the land out of respect for his father, but he was always drawn to the sea."

There was never a hint of bitterness or reproach in her voice when she spoke of his decision to seek his fortune at sea. It had been a decision my father had agonized over for it would mean leaving his true love and his infant son. She had encouraged him to go. She knew he would never be content until he had followed the yearning in his heart. She was a strong woman in her own right and would wait for him to return. He would be a better man and a better husband when he did.

My father, being the eldest, was by right of first-born entitled to inherit the land upon his father's death. My Uncle Matthew's fate would have been at the whim of my father. And, when my grandfather died in my first year of life, my father did legally inherit all that there was. It was my father's desire that Uncle Matthew stay on at the farm and continue to work the land with him. But, if the truth be known, my father had always been drawn to the sea. My Uncle Matthew was always more the one to stay on land. In fact, it was my Uncle Matthew who had put all his effort into improving the farm while my father had dreams of sailing to exotic places.

And so, an agreement was formalized and signed between my father and his brother, Matthew. My father's inheritance would be divided between the brothers. My father's portion would be leased to his brother for the duration of his sea journey and, my mother and I, would be entitled to live on the farm with a small stipend drawn from the profits of the farm and the remainder of proceeds would belong to my Uncle Matthew. If my father did not return within seven years to reclaim his share of the farm, he would be considered lost at sea and his property would become Uncle Matthew's permanently. Uncle Matthew would become Lord of the Manor and my mother, and I, would become resident extended family. My mother held the right to have a home at the farm as long as she lived.

I remember the day he left us. I was but five, yet I remember it well. It was after the spring planting when the scent of the warming soil promises a fruitful harvest. The day seemed unusually warm for so early in the season and sunlight flooded through the windows of the room. Even the breeze seemed warm and inviting. The chirping of the birds, newly returned with the warming weather, was carried on the wind through the open door and was crisp and distinct.

He stood in the kitchen of our cabin embracing my mother. The sunlight coming through the windows lit his clean-shaven face and showed the sparkle in his eyes. He smiled broadly, trying hard to hide the excitement he felt over the sadness in his heart for leaving. I can remember feeling the strength in his arms when he reached down to lift me into an embrace. He had raised me in the same manner so many times before: when he went to market, when he went to Newport across the bay, when he left for work. Yet, this day, I sensed a difference. Whether it was the extra moment of embrace, the strength I felt surrounding me, I cannot say. But, resting my head on his broad shoulder and seeing my mother's face, I knew that this day was different.

As he passed me to my mother's waiting arms, he straightened his waistcoat and reached for a rolled blanket bound at each end with a length of rawhide to form a sling. Little did I realize that this blanket held all my father's clothes. A last embrace of my mother, with I in her arms, and he stepped through the door. I remember watching him walking away from us toward the landing in the tiny cove that served as the dock for the small boats of the farm. I could feel the heaving of my mother's breasts as she silently sobbed. I saw him turn and wave to us and I felt the forced enthusiasm in the wave returned by her. Not really understanding, I returned my mother's lingering embrace the only way I knew. I hugged her about her neck with all the strength my small arms could manage and buried my face against her neck. Had my father known the fate to which he was abandoning us to, he might have hastened home sooner.

—————————— >< ——————— —— ———————

"Run, Benjamin!"

These were the last anguished words my father said to me as he lay on the wood floor with blood pooling around him from the wound in the back of his head. My shocked stare darted from my father's face of agony to that of my uncle who stood over him, the fire poker still in his hand, dripping my father's life to the floor. My uncle's expression frozen in a twisted, evil leer. His sudden realization that I was witness to his deed began to dawn on his visage and I knew his next intent. And so, I ran from the room, slamming the door behind me to gain as much distance and time from my uncle as possible.

Two

$\mathcal{I}$ awake in darkness shivering with cold. I listen intently to the sounds about me for anything of human origin. There are none: only the sounds of the water slapping against the exterior of my refuge and the water sloshing through the now filled entrance hole. I know not how long I have slept. In the pitch darkness, I feel along the wooden ledge where I have stored my pilfered flint and steel and reach above this ledge to the next and feel my box of dry tinder. I take my pewter plate and set it on the cross member that runs across the space and pull a small wad of tinder from the box. In the dark, I strike the flint with the steel and try to see where it sparks in relation to the tinder. My second strike will be better directed.

I try to control my shivering knowing that the cold is overcoming me and strike the steel on the flint rapidly several times. The bright flash of the sparks blinds my vision for an instant. But there it is, a small spark has caught the tinder and I begin to gently blow upon it. In a moment, it grows and bursts into a small flame. I turn back to my storage ledge, my hand seeking any one of a dozen stubs of candles lining the ledge. I bring it to the small flame and gently push the wick into the flame. The light from the candle fills the darkness and I smile at my success.

Since the water still fills the entrance, I can see the tide is still in flood and I have not slept for long. I know the smoke from the candle will vent without notice through the small cracks in the boards about me without significant light showing. But the light from its glowing wick and the slight warmth it supplies my hands cupped about it are worth any risk. I take another candle stub and light its short wick. In a few minutes, I begin to perceive some heat and my shivering begins to subside. It is then the gnawing in my belly reminds me I have not eaten since early morn, and it moves me to reach for my small slab of cured meat.

I peel a small strip of meat and begin to slowly chew it trying to soften it with the moisture from my mouth. Seated in this small, cramped space, I begin to think upon my life and what has brought me to this place and condition. My mind turns to the history I had been told of my grandfather, Josiah Prescott, hero of the King Philip's War that finally wrested control of the land from the native inhabitants. For his bravery, he had received as a reward some of the land secured from the natives along the west shore of Narragansett Bay to the west of the island called Conanicut. I had been told the stories of the hardships he endured to carve a successful homestead and economic enterprise out of the wilderness. I knew of the five children born to him and of the three who had died in infancy and now lay in the small burial ground in the lower pasture beside the mother who had born them and died with the last. How my father, William, the first born and the second born, Matthew, his brother, had worked from early youth beside their father forcing the land to bring forth its wealth.

In time, crops of corn, flax, and wool helped to establish the family wealth. Josiah's wealth lay not only in crops. As the farm grew, the need for labor outstripped what three men could do. It was at that point that Josiah began buying slaves brought in by traders to Newport across the bay. There were five in all. Josiah's Quaker leanings meant that he treated his slaves with great kindness. In truth he was thought of as a good master. He constructed small cabins with great fireplaces for each of his men and tried to provide them with mates. He had succeeded in finding women for three of them. Because of Josiah's kindness, no slave ever ran from him. They worked almost as bondsmen cutting wood for the winter, herding the sheep, tending the crops of flax and corn. One of these slaves, Cam by name, was a skilled blacksmith. My grandfather had sought out slaves who possessed certain skills useful to a farming operation. They lived on the farm, had their children, and grew old, as did their master. In my childhood ignorance, I knew them only as farm hands and their children as my playmates. It was the offspring of these first five slaves, now numbering a dozen, who knew me well, and now searched for my hiding place.

As I chew another piece of hardened meat, my thoughts begin to drift. The sound of one of my candles guttering out draws me back to my present condition. I reach behind me to the ledge where my supply of candles is aligned and take down a lengthy stub. I move it to the flame of the candle that still glows strongly and watch the wick begin to glow as the light begins to fill my cavern once again. I carefully tilt the slender taper and drip a few precious drops of melted wax on the place where its predecessor only moments before became extinct. I look at my cache of candles and try to estimate how many hours of light they will provide me and how long I may need to hide in this place.

As I look at the dancing flame, my thoughts return to other candles that burned on other nights, when my mother would smile at me from across our small dining table and ask me for my thoughts. There were nights when I would ask about my father, and she would tell me of the adventures she imagined he was having and the exotic foreign ports to which he had been. She would assure me of his return on nights that I feared otherwise. And she would tell me of the wonderful stories and experiences he would surely relate upon his return. She did all this without a word from my father in support.

For five long years, I and my mother lived in ever worsening circumstances. The first change to come was the marriage of my uncle. His new wife, a prune-faced widow older than himself with a brood of children from her first marriage, looked upon my mother and me as mouths to feed that added nothing to her desire for position for herself and her children. She would rage at my uncle and turn him against us as his true kin. At first, it was small things: the seating at table, my uncle's right to head of table; the order of procession on the way to market. Then it became our very presence in the house that became an issue. She treated my mother and me as below her in station as the wife and son of an absent owner who was contributing nothing to her husband's enterprise. In her mind, my father had been irresponsible and run away to sea, abandoning us as a burden to his brother, and now, her family. Even when my uncle demanded my mother move us out of the main house to one of the smaller cottages, my mother complied without complaint. She knew it was not his true want, but that he would have no peace from his wife unless she got her way.

I remember well the cold winter nights when the only warmth we had came from the kindness of the slaves who secretly brought us wood for our fire and shared their meager food with us. I recall my mother sitting by the firelight stitching the rags we both wore. And never a word of complaint; always optimistically looking to the day my father would return and set things right. I remember her last illness.

It came upon her quickly in the spring. She lay bathed in sweat and coughing heavily. The bloody flux appeared on the second day. I tried to cool her brow with spring water, but her delirium made her thrash about at unseen phantoms. In her moments of clarity, she would make me promise to wait for my father telling me he would come soon now. I pleaded with my uncle to help my mother, but his wife would not hear of it for fear of infecting her precious children. I could see that my uncle was changing, becoming as hard and unfeeling towards me as his wife.

My mother died after four days of agony. I thanked God she had been out of her mind most of that time and perhaps had not suffered as much pain as she seemed to have. There was no formal burial. There was no service, no one to say a few words as she was laid to rest. My Uncle, against his wife's wishes, gave two of the oldest slaves time from their labors to dig a shallow grave near, but not too near, the graves of my grandparents. And, so, I became a true orphan.

With my mother's burial, my last protection from the full fury of my uncle's wife had been removed. It was only now that I felt how deeply her disdain for me went. It was about this time my uncle acquired at the insistence of his wife an indentured servant. Maureen was quiet and worked hard to satisfy the requirements of her master's wife. Even so, she often felt the temper of her displeasure. You must remember that indentured servants held no real value. Slaves were better treated because they had value as property.

My treatment at the hands of my uncle's wife after my mother's death was worse than Maureen's. She begrudged me what food I was given. The clothes on my back were of poor quality and handed down from the slaves. My aunt felt anything given to me was something taken from her own. And soon, my uncle began to reflect similar thoughts in his relation to me. I suspected my aunt was looking for any excuse, any slight to her, that might force my uncle to make me leave. But I would not return her taunts and ill treatment with naught but a smile as my mother had taught me. And silently, I stored my anger and swore revenge upon my father's return.

THREE

The second summer after my mother passed had come with heat that was normally felt later in the season. My Uncle and his wife had virtually banished me from their lives and the life of the farm. My treatment was no better than the lowest of the low. Without the influencing shield of my mother, my uncle's wife had completed her domination of her husband. I was of no stature and my only value lay in my uncle's expectation that I tend to my chores. It was only my free labor that kept me in shelter and food, such as they were.

One day I was lazily tending sheep, as was one of my usual chores, in the lower field by the bay when I saw a stranger approaching from the direction of the landing. His halting gait and sack upon his back made me curious as he slowly stepped along the path to the farm. Although I was sure I had never seen him before, there was something familiar about him. As he came nearer, I could see his steps made him sway and his face and hands were tanned dark, darker than any I had ever seen, yet he was not a slave. He was dressed in sailor's brown slops with a loose-fitting shirt open at the throat and I realized his walk reflected much time on the rolling deck of a ship at sea. He paused on the path and leaned against the stone wall that ran alongside the path in the shade of a tree. It was then I could see his black boots and the cane he rested against his right leg.

I sat up in my pasture and startled a few ewes about me. Their commotion drew the stranger's attention to my presence, and he stood erect and stiffened as he strained to see what had caused the sheep to move. He pulled his cap from his head revealing long gray locks neatly tied to the back. Who was this stranger who appeared so broken and spent? It was then he stepped from the shadow of the tree into the road and the light.

It was him! My father! My protector! Returned from the sea! Not dead in some foreign port or lost to thoughts of home on some exotic island or swept overboard in some storm as my uncle and aunt had many times pictured for me. No, not him! He was here and all would be made right with his return! I stood without realizing it and raced down the slope of the field scattering the sheep in all direction by my flight. As I neared him, I could see his face, its expression questioning and unsure, but I had no such reservations. With each bounding step, I became more excited. I knew who it had to be!

I reached the stone wall on my side of the dirt road and, placing a hand on one of the larger top rocks, vaulted the wall onto the dirt track. It was only then, a mere arms-length from an embrace, I skidded to a stop.

Was this my father, this broken hulk of a man, old before his time, worn and beaten and looking years beyond his age? I searched his eyes and saw the glimmer that remained there still.

"Benjamin?" he asked. "Benjamin, it is I,...your father...."

It was the voice I remembered from so long ago.

I do not remember those last few steps I took to feel my arms about him and his about me. I only remember the feel of his rough shirt against my cheek and the scent of sweat as I sobbed into his shoulder. The strength of his embrace seemed weaker than I remembered, but it was the first tenderness shown me by another human being since my mother's death. More important to me was the feeling that all the wrongs I had suffered were now to be made right. Here was my savior, my champion, altered beyond anything I could have imagined, but, nevertheless, he would protect me and restore me.

I know not how long we stood there in the heat of the day. I feared if I released my hold, he would disappear, having been only a figment of my deepest yearning, that it was all but a dream on a lazy summer's day. For his part, as he stroked my head and returned my tears of joy with those of his own, he said nothing more. It was enough that he was home again, and his son had been the first to greet him.

Finally, he took me by the upper arms and broke my grasp of him and, pushing me back a bit, began to look at me. He smiled at me, and I could see his once perfect teeth were now stained. The stubble of his beard matched the streaks of grey in his hair. The skin of his face was creased and leathery and weathered. But his eyes still held a sparkle I remembered.

He looked me up and down and, standing back, leaning on his cane, motioned for me to turn about. He smiled as I did and yet I was embarrassed by my appearance. Even though he wore the clothes of a man of the sea, they were clean and neatly cut and came together of a manner. Here I stood before him dressed in nothing better than patched rags, barefoot and dirty. I hung my head, too embarrassed to look at my father.

He saw my expression and placed his weathered hand under my chin and raised my head, so my eyes met his. No words needed exchange.

He clapped his left arm about my shoulders and guided me to the shade of the tree he had stood beneath earlier. He carefully sat himself on a low boulder near the base of the wall and reached for his sack which still lay where he had left it against the wall. As he motioned for me to sit beside him, he withdrew from his sailing bag a small oilcloth carefully wrapped. Unfolding it, he withdrew with care a book. Its black leather binding was still supple and shined as if oiled regularly and lovingly. Next, he drew forth a small leather pouch tied with a drawstring. From the last fold of the cloth, he removed a small slender knife.

"Benjamin, know this well," he said with sudden intensity. "I have been places, seen things and done much over these past years all of which I will tell ye in time, but mark what I say to ye now. There are some who would look to do me harm should they find me. And there are some who would seek what you see here." He picked up the knife and grasping the handle with his index and thumb along the blade, raised it between them to the level of his eyes.

"This dirk I keep reminds me of those who have fallen by my side and under my hand. Yes, Benjamin, I have killed those who sought to kill me. But I have sworn upon this day of my return to never raise my hand against any man ever again." With his other hand, he caressed the cover of the Bible sitting on his leg before him.

He replaced the dirk in the oilcloth spread out on the ground beside him and flipped the small pouch quickly into the air and caught it before it fell. The sound of coins clinking emanated from it.

"These be coins I've saved from places I have been. I will teach ye about them so ye know which is which and how many of one be equal to another." He smiled broadly at me and turned to look at the Bible. He picked it up with obvious reverence.

"Mark me well, Ben, of all that ye see here, none be more important than this." His eyes examined the book as his hands ran over its smooth surfaces. "The dirk may one day save your life and the coins may do the like, but this..." He held the book on the flattened palm of one hand and placed his other hand gently on the top. "This is where your fortune be. Mind you! Ye must look within it carefully to find the way and I may tell you more someday when I am sure of my safety, and none are seeking me to do either of us harm. But always know, these things here are my most valued possessions and hold the key to your future and a king's ransom." As he spoke these last words, his hand suddenly grasped my arm, and I felt the strength of his hand and saw a look in his eyes.

"Should anything befall me, you must guard these with your life!"

The look was gone in an instant and he quickly, but carefully, rewrapped the articles in the piece of oilcloth and slid the package back into his sack. Was it fear I saw in that look?

"So, tell me of your mother," he said in a brightening tone. "Will she be surprised by my return?"

Without thinking of the impact my words might carry, I replied quietly, "Mother passed near two years ago now. She died of fever and is buried there." I pointed to the little cemetery not realizing my father would know where it was. "She called for you at the end and told me never to stop expecting you. She knew you would come back."

I threw myself against him and ran my arms around him again. I wanted to be as close to him as I could. It was really him; it was not a dream. My father had returned, and things would be different; things would be better.

He put his arm about me, and I could feel him weighing my words. He stared off toward the cemetery for some moments stroking my matted hair. He showed no outward sign of grief, but I knew what he was feeling. He had returned to her. He had returned to feel her loving embrace once again and to hear the sweetness of her voice. He had returned to grow old with her. And now, she was gone.

A gentle patting on my shoulder told me I had slipped into restful slumber lying against my father.

"Time to announce my coming to your uncle, Ben," he said in matter-of-fact voice, "Let me see what changes have been wrought under his hand."

I stood and took my father's proffered hand and helped him to stand. As he started to shoulder his sack, I took it from him and happily shouldered its considerable weight. He smiled at my effort and put his arm across my shoulders. As we began an uneven gait up the road leading to the main house, I began to tell him what awaited him.

"Uncle has a wife, Father. And a pack of young ones she brought with her." Looking up at him, I search his face for some reaction to this news. I trotted a few feet ahead of my father and began walking backwards so I could see him. His pace was slow, leaning heavily on his cane, with his feet wide apart.

"They have the big house, Father, and her word rules."

"How does the plantation, Benjamin?" he asked me.

"Uncle has every field planted," I answered. "The harvests have been plentiful the past few years. He bought two more slaves to do the work of Joseph and Old Cam. They kind of do a lot of watching now. His wife has a fine new carriage and the clothes she wears are fine stitched. Uncle has a horse he bought last spring."

I saw my father's face change to one of question.

"But, Ben," he said, "what of your poor dress? If the farm does well, why are you dressed so? Is this your dress to do chores?" My backward pace slowed as the smile on my face faded and my head bowed.

"I have no other clothes." My words were barely louder than a whisper.

"Have you no place in the big house?" he asked calmly. I shook my head no. I sensed a change in my father's presence as he stood before me. I raised my eyes expecting to see anger in his expression. Instead, I saw only sorrow.

He wrapped me in his arms and bent his head against mine and spoke in the voice of a comforting parent.

"I have done you a great wrong, my son. I felt I had to see the world and fill my own cup with life. I left the two people I held most dear to me in the world and left their fate to others. It has come with a cost, the greatest of costs; a cost that you have paid in value more than gold. I swear to you, my son, payment for my sin is more than made right by what is contained in my Holy book. But you must learn its secrets."

With those words, he kissed my head and again began his slow pace up from the wharf, passed the greening fields with his arm about me. As we walked, he began to ask me about what had happened since he had left, and he began to tell me of his adventures. My father was home from the sea, and I was no longer alone.

Four

Walking up the rutted dusty lane that led from the boat landing to the main plantation house that day, flanked by fields walled with piled stones culled from those fields over the years, with my father's arm around my shoulders, was the happiest day I had known in many years. I must have sounded the magpie as I happily chatted about the farm and the crops it was producing. I talked of the slaves I thought my father might remember. In return, he talked of his first time signing aboard a sailing ship and having to learn a whole new world of terms. We were a father and son in happy conversation.

As we passed the last field before the house that was planted with early flax, a heavily bent figure appeared from a break in the stone wall. It was Old Cam. He had heard my chatter and came to see who I was talking to. I knew the real reason for his interest was to catch me not at my chores. Old Cam had been one of my grandfather's slaves. He had had a close relationship with my father and had hoped to someday be my father's personal servant. And then, my father left, and Old Cam hated him for it. Since he could not vent his anger toward him, he turned that anger against me. I tried to avoid Old Cam as much as possible, for, given the opportunity he would report what he considered my laziness or misdeeds to my aunt. He could not have done so expecting in return to gain her favor. She favored no one she considered below her, and she considered everyone below her, especially a slave. I felt he gained some small amount of pleasure by seeing me in disfavor with her. Of course, I was always in disfavor. I think it was his vengeance for my father directed at the only object available to him.

As I reached the break in the stone wall where Old Cam stood leaning against the gate post, I could see by the look on his face he was about to take pleasure in catching me out. But a look of astonishment began to appear on Old Cam's face as my father appeared behind me. It was as if Old Cam was seeing a ghost. He timidly pulled his battered straw hat from his bald head that was fringed with white.

"Is that you, Mastah Will?" he stammered, "Is it really you?"

I still remember the benevolent smile with which my father greeted these words.

"Aye, Old Cam," he said smiling and clasping a hand on the old slave's stooped shoulder. "Home from the sea, I am. Home to stay."

"You've been gone for so long," Old Cam said with a note of what seemed to be repressed anger. I could see in Old Cam's glance at me the fear of what I might say to my father of his treatment of me while he was absent.

"So many changes, Mastah…so many." He shook is bowed head. "New Missus in dah house…"

"So, I hear from Benjamin," my father replied with optimism in his airy tone. "It's good to be home, Cam."

"I neva thought I see you again, Mastah, never in this life," Old Cam said in a voice that trailed off to a whisper.

With that welcome from Old Cam, I and my father began again the slow pace up the slight incline of the path on our way to the big plantation house.

As my father and I passed beneath the shade of the last tall sycamore at the end of the path, he paused. I remember the look on his face as he surveyed the house in which he had been born and spent his childhood years and which he had left nearly seven years ago. To my then young eyes, it had changed little over that time and was the grandest house I had ever known, in fact, the only home I had ever known. Yet, now, in retrospection, having seen the world, I can understand better the look I saw that day upon my father's face.

It was not a grand estate as might have been a plantation in our more southerly colonies. There were no great porches or grand verandas as plantation houses of the tropics displayed, nor were there legions of house slaves waiting on their occupants. It was a large structure built for functionality. It was not a stately structure, but a New England saltbox with a sheer front facing to the east and a long sloping roof line descending to the west with its huge central chimney. Even though its construction was better than many, it was still a rude structure in comparison to the palatial estates in distant places my father had seen, and I have since known. It was built to withstand the rigors of cold New England winters as well as the heat of midsummer days. It was a working farmhouse. It had been thirty years since King Philip's War, yet thoughts of being a defensible structure had been built into its construction.

As unchanged as its façade appeared to me, I could see him noting every change that had occurred in his absence. The attempts at small elegances were visible, if seemingly out of place. Gone was the deep red stain common on New England homes replaced by clean white paint. The horse rail to the side of the door for securing one's mount was a new addition. The front door now owned a brass door knocker; an iron boot scraper to rake the muck of the fields from the soles of boots graced the large rough shaped stone that served as a doorstep. The different curtains in the front parlor windows drew a squint from his eye, as did the perfectly tapered candles in brass holders in the windows.

The sound of activity, of children playing and voices raised, drew my father's attention to the back of the house. As we came around the far corner of the house, a group of older children could be seen climbing in a small grove of apple trees set behind the house. My father directed me toward the rear door of the house that stood open in the warmth of the day. As we drew near to the door, a haggard and care-worn woman appeared with a bowl held in the crook of her arm, holding what looked like a lump of dough. She was startled by our presence.

"What are you doing here?" she exclaimed, her voice booming in disapproval. "Why are you not at your chores? Certainly, you have not finished them so early! Your Uncle will hear of this, ye lazy good fer nothin'...."

"And who is this you've brought to my door?" she continued with increased venom as she noticed the figure behind me.

"No doubt looking for a handout by his dress.... Be off with ye! I have no time for vagrants at my door. You, boy, as long as yer here, go and fetch me a bucket of water. And be quick about it!" With her foot, she shoved a wooden bucket through the open door in my direction.

As I cringed from the tirade and turned to retrieve the rolling bucket, I felt a firm hand take hold of my tattered shirt.

"Hold, boy!" I heard a voice bark. Still in his powerful grasp, I turned to see my father standing tall and, repressing his anger, calmly he said to the banshee in the doorway, "His name is Benjamin."

The response, given in such measured tone, neither confrontational nor angry, caused the woman to pause, her mouth falling open in mute shock.

"I am William Prescott, his father. Is my brother somewhere about?"

Standing in stunned silence, she stood like a statue. Suddenly another voice was heard calling from a distance.

"Judith? Judith, what is happening? I say, Cook, what are you doing? Is someone there?"

The voice seemed to shake the woman from her torpor.

"Yes, Ma'am," she managed to stammer over her shoulder in a voice closer to the mew of a lamb to an unseen form. "There is someone here saying he is William Prescott," with a question in her voice.

The sound of a few short steps and an arm stretched before the form in the door, and she was pulled out of the doorway. The door was fully drawn open to reveal a woman in elegant dress. Buckled shoes peaked from beneath a full dress of rust color. The bodice showing fine stitch work accenting a pronounced waist under an immaculate white blouse. Her hair was long and with curls piled above the forehead and covered by a lace fontange.

It was the only time I ever saw this source of much of my torment unable to speak.

"Brother William? Is it really you?" she finally managed to say. "You have returned?"

The transformation of my witnessing that occurred at that moment has stayed with me all these years. The viperous, acid-tongued witch that was the progenitor of my misery was suddenly transformed before me into a fawning, sugar-tongued lady of presumed class.

"Matthew will be so pleased to know of your return," she cooed. "I am your sister-in-law, Margaret. Welcome home, Dear Brother." The effusiveness of her greeting betrayed the shallowness of its feeling.

"My husband is away this day on business that takes him to lawyer Updike's," she related with added gravity. "He should return before sunset. He will be so pleased to hear this news. Do stay for evening meal."

My father accepted all of this with good nature, but, at the last, he replied, "You mistake my visit, Madam. I am home from the sea. Home to reclaim what is mine by right and duc."

The smile gracing the face of my aunt stiffened yet did not fail completely. The hands she clasped before her began to whiten as their grip on each other grew even tighter.

"Well, then we shall have to make accommodations accordingly," she replied with some coolness. "Have you luggage to be tended to?"

"Nay," he replied, "I have all within this sailor's bag which, for now, I shall keep in hand." She acknowledged this with diminishing interest. "Since my brother is away, I shall look about the place a bit until his return, if you mind not?"

"Oh, it is yours to do so," she said with even less enthusiasm. "I shall send your brother to find you upon his return."

What had begun as an angry exchange with a servant of no station had escalated to my father's first encounter with his previously unknown sister-in-law and then crashed with the understanding by this woman that her self-deluded image of her importance as the wife of one of the wealthiest plantation owners along Narragansett Bay was about to change. It was clear, even to me as a youngster, that the news of my father's arrival was not as joyously received by others as it had been by me. The reality of his arrival represented the worst of situations for some, and possibly, an end to the peace of the plantation.

FIVE

s my father touched the brim of his hat and gave a slight bow of respect, he put his arm about my shoulders and smiled at me. We turned from the kitchen doorway and rounded the corner of the house. I still remember the feeling I had at that moment. My breast felt it would burst with the pride of knowing that I now had a protector. He had stood against the wicked one and lived. No longer would I need to fear this tormentor. And I was confident in his ability to tame its cohort.

As we came around the corner of the house, my father gave out with a laugh.

"So, this is the hen who rules the roost over my brother?" father asked smiling. I dared to give a nod of ascent, hoping it was not seen through a window by one inside the house.

We walked beyond the house to the outside well of sweet water. I quickly dropped the bucket in and eagerly pulled the rope to bring it back up to show my father the strength I possessed. As I did so, he gazed at the walled fields visible from our location. My father noted the two slaves repairing a wall in the pasture where Old Cam watched them in silence and where he kept a watch on us. I took the wooden dipper from its hook below the hood over the well and quickly filled it with cool water, offering it to my newly returned champion.

My father ceased his gaze at the distant fields and returned it to the ladle I proffered. As he took it from my hand, he looked into my eyes. We stood a long moment sharing a slow drink of refreshing water. When we had drunk our fill, he replaced the ladle, tapping the frame of the well with his hand and looking at it as if greeting an old friend.

"Show me where your mother lies," he said softly.

With me under one arm and his rude cane in the other, we started the slow walk to the field where the family cemetery lay. I proudly slung his sailor's bag over my shoulder.

As we walked, my father began to talk of things he noted had changed while he had been away. Fields that had been planted with flax and wheat had been given over to peas, beans, and corn. He pointed to the tree lines that had receded while he had been away. The fields extended much farther than he remembered and the stone walls lining the roads to them seemed to snake out of sight. The distance to the cemetery was not far to my young legs, but my father needed to rest against the walls a couple of times along the way. When he did, I would patiently wait for him to recover his strength.

My desire to begin asking my father about his adventures I held in check, knowing there would be time when he was ready to speak of it. And there was so much I wanted to relate to him about the time gone by. No, for now, it was enough to feel his arm on my shoulder and know he was returned to me and that my days without succor were ended.

When we reached the field from which I had first seen his approach, I easily vaulted onto the wall and dropped to the other side. My father's lame leg made his negotiation of the wall a bit more difficult. After hiking himself up on the wall and rolling his legs over it, he dropped heavily on his good leg and, losing his balance, rolled onto the green grass. I could not help but laugh at his awkwardness. As he rolled on to his back, I could see from his face he saw no humor in his situation. But, when he saw me, he, likewise, burst into loud roars of laughter. He reached for my hand and, upon taking it, pulled me to the ground beside him. And so, we lay there, laughing as two devoid of sanity. It was my first fit of laughter in many years.

Once we had recovered our senses, we rose as one and made our way through the flock of sheep still grazing in the lush spring shoots of grass to the far corner of the pasture. It was here that the small gate to the family burial plot was situated. As we approached, our mood became more somber.

The plot had been originally at the end of the tree line up on the hill just before it gave slope toward the bay. One could see the waters of the Narragansett to the east and the house on the crest of the hill behind us to the northwest. The burial plot was not large and held only a few headstones. There was my grandmother's, her name and dates carved in the unpolished gray granite. Small clusters of moss grew on the uneven surface on its top. Then, there were the three small markers for her three children bearing only the carving of a year. The largest marker belonged to my grandfather. It was a pyramidal spire constructed of polished sandstone on a flat square base. It was inscribed with the entire legend of his life...hero of King Philip's War...husband of...father of...When my father asked me to read the inscription, only then did he realize that I did not know how.

"No one has seen to your education, Benjamin?" he asked in disbelief.

"Mother was beginning to when she was taken, Father, and no one has taught me since," I replied ashamed of my failure.

"Well, we shall start tomorrow in earnest. A man can be easily cheated if he cannot read and write," he stated firmly. He then looked about the small plot and said, "Where is your mother's stone?"

"She has no marker, Father, but she lies here," I answered pointing to the furthest corner of the plot. The look upon my father's face was one of mixed sadness and anger.

"Oh, my Dear Son," he said softly almost in self-loathing, "what did I do to you and your dear Mother." Slowly he approached the area I had indicated. A small clutch of wildflowers lay on the otherwise unmarked ground.

"I bring flowers from the fields for her when they bloom," I said standing beside him. Though I did not recognize the slump in his stature and the bewildered look on his face at the time, I know now he was a man completely defeated; broken not only physically, but emotionally.

"Benjamin," he said in a detached way, "would you see to the sheep and give me a few moments alone."

I nodded and set the canvas sailor's bag on the ground. As I slowly closed the gate and heard its sharp pitched metallic creak, I saw him carefully sit upon the ground, his game leg straight before him. I watched as he removed the package wrapped in oilcloth from his sack, unwrapped it, and slowly, reverently, removed the bible from it. A pair of glasses suddenly appeared upon his nose, retrieved from some unseen pocket. Carefully easing the hooks of wire over his ears, he opened the book and began to read. As he read, he laid one hand gently on the ground. There would be many days I would see my father sitting alone beside this spot quietly reading his bible to my mother.

I walked a few paces along the wall of the pasture and chose a boulder fallen from the wall to sit upon. And so, I sat in the warm, waning afternoon sun and watched my father through the iron bars of the gate as he communed with his lost love and my mother. The sheep grazed and bleated quietly and the warmth from the sun seemed to be idyllic and for the first time in a long time I was unafraid.

I am not sure how long I had been sitting there enjoying the sun when its brightness was suddenly blocked by a form. I opened my eyes and brought my hand up to shade them. Standing in front of me blocking the sun was Caleb, a boy a year or two younger than myself, and grandson of Old Cam. He was a secret friend because of the enmity his grandfather directed toward me. Regardless, we would meet away from the house and run and play in the field and woods. We would fish when we could, but most times our friendship needed to be circumspect.

"Missus sent me to fetch you and the man," he blurted out, leaning close to me. "She said to tell you Mastah has returned." He smiled at me nervously as he eyed the stranger, my father, sitting on the ground in the burial ground.

"She and Mastah was in a big fight when I left," he whispered.

As I smiled up at Caleb, I heard the creaking of the gate as my father opened it. He had his sailor's bag over his shoulder and smiled in the direction of me and my companion.

"And who is this, Ben?" he asked. Caleb stood erect and stepped away from me.

"I am called Caleb, Sir," he said boldly. "Missus sent me to say Mastah Matthew has returned. You should come to the house."

"Thank you, Caleb," my father replied kindly. "Will you see to the sheep?"

Caleb broke into a broad smile showing his beautiful white teeth and nodded enthusiastically. This was easy work and much more enjoyable than the kitchen and housework he would normally be doing at this time of the day. Best of all, he could not be punished because he was following an order given him by a white master.

As Caleb happily rushed off in the direction of the grazing flock, my father and I began the walk back up the hill to the house. He seemed confident in his stride while I felt a certain ebullience.

Six

We had only taken a few steps from the cemetery when my father stopped and turned to me.

"Benjamin," he said softly, "is there a place here you can hide something, and it will be safe?"

I nodded a reply. He reached into his sailor's bag and, retrieving the oilskin wrapped package, handing it to me.

"Good. Then stay a bit after I leave and hide this." He gave me a wink of conspiracy. Because my look of confusion surprised him, he continued,

"Do you remember, at my return, when first I showed you the oilskin, I told you there were those who might want to do me harm? This is what they would be seeking. Should they come, I cannot tell them what I do not know no matter what they might do to me."

Having said this, my father faltered a bit on his bad leg and struggled a bit to keep his footing. I knew that his bad leg became stiff when held in one position for some time and assistance in getting to his feet he appreciated. I reached out and held him at his elbow to help him gain his feet. After he recovered, he turned to me standing just outside the cemetery gate.

"Tell no one where you place that," he continued pointing to the oilskin parcel I held under my arm, "your future depends on it."

I watched as he took the first few steps up the slight rise toward the house and saw his stride improve slightly as he went. My joy at having my father home overcame any concerns I might have had over his words regarding the package I held in the crook of my arm. As soon as I was sure he was out of earshot, I returned to the cemetery to the wall of the graveyard where I knew a hollow existed within the wall. I felt the fieldstones until I found the one that came free easily. Pulling the stone from the wall opened a small hidden chamber between the outer and inner faces of the wall. I had used this chamber to hide the candles and other things stolen from my aunt and uncle when I could not take them to my secret lair straight away. I placed the package with care into the hollow and replaced the stone. At that moment, I had no idea how many times I would be retrieving this oilskin and replacing it. All I cared about was the figure leaning heavily on his cane, now, well across the meadow and nearly to the shade of the big Sycamore tree at the head of the lane.

I moved to the cemetery gate and heard the familiar screech from the iron as it turned on its rusted hinges as I swung it closed. That was a sound I would always remember. I raced across the field and joined my father as he rested in the shade.

"We will be moving out of the big house, Ben, and returning to our cabin. Your mother would want that. We'll need to do a bit of cleaning to make it livable, but I think it will bring some peace to our situation," he said with a smile.

The late afternoon sun was beginning to lengthen the shadows as my father, with his ungainly gait, and I trudged up the dirt lane in the direction of the house. Ahead of us, Old Cam and his companions entered the lane carrying the shovels, pickaxes, and lever bars they had been using to repair the wall that edged the field. Behind us, Caleb was lazily guiding the flock into the road with a small branch in his hand.

Tied to the horse rail at the front of the house was one of my uncle's fine horses. It stood calmly in the shade cast by the shadow of the house looking more like a statue than living transport. As Old Cam approached the house, he separated from his companions just enough to casually untie the horse's reins. He gently tugged on them to get the horse to follow along beside him in the same slow, loping stride Old Cam and his companions displayed. Even his head seemed to bob in rhythm with the men.

The block of stone that served as the doorstep before the front door of the house was high enough that my father needed to lean more heavily on my shoulder to step up to it. He smiled at me and then noticed his boots were caked with mud. He raked them over the iron boot scraper and watched as the rich, dark brown earth curled off his soles. He tossed his cane slightly into the air and caught it about midway down its length and, disdaining to use the brass door knocker, rapped firmly, but politely, on the door before him.

We must have looked an odd pair standing there. I, a young boy barefoot, threadbare, hair unkempt and dirty with the strength of youth blooming beneath his clothes; and the bent, weather-worn sailor, broken in health, sea bag at his side, leaning on his cane of raw wood worn smooth from use. The few moments we stood there, side by side, I remember well. The arm about my shoulders was my father's. He was home and taking me back to our home.

The sound of the rapping brought a bevy of small faces curiously peeking around the corner of the house. It was the same group that had been playing among the apple trees earlier that afternoon. These were my uncle's stepchildren, all neatly dressed, with clean faces and dressed hair. Although they were younger than me in age, my practical experiences had given me a much wider education in worldly ways. It was in formal education that they held the upper hand.

In a few moments, a young dark-skinned girl I knew as Kara opened the door. She was not much older than me and we sometimes spoke when she was out of the house. But those occasions were rare because she was maid to my uncle's wife and, as such, was constantly on call. She was barefoot and dressed in a spotless white blouse and grey skirt covered by a bibbed apron of deep blue. Her long, straight dark hair was pulled back in a tight bun at the back. She quickly glanced at us, then lowered her eyes and curtsied slightly. I could see that she was surprised at my presence at the front door of the house.

"Master Matthew is in the front parlor," she said in beautifully accented English. As I attempted to follow my father over the threshold, Kara's arm flashed out to bar my way. "I was told only to admit the one," she said in a strong whisper with a slight scowl on her face.

I stumbled backward, back onto the doorstep, taken aback by her treatment of me. I then realized it had been many years since I had entered the front door and never since she had been a part of the household. I stood there, feeling embarrassed and ashamed, not really knowing what to do.

"What is your name, child," I heard my father say kindly.

"I am called Kara," the girl replied dropping her arm, stepping back, and riveting her eyes once more to the floor.

"Kara, I am William. This is Benjamin, my son. As I am a Prescott, so is he," my father said in soft easy tone.

"Yes, Sir," she replied sheepishly. In a single fluid movement, she reached out and took my father's sea bag in hand, then stepped back opening the door wider and motioned with her hand for me to enter. "Welcome Master Ben," she said as she again gave a slight curtsey. As she did, she lifted her head just enough to allow me to see the smile on her face.

My father, with me in tow, entered the parlor to find my uncle seated behind his writing table near the window where the late afternoon sun's rays were still streaming in the west windows. He immediately stood and crossed the room and offered his hand to my father. It was only then that he noticed me standing behind him.

Uncle Matthew was dressed as I had rarely seen him, but certainly to impress. His vest of brocade reached halfway down his buff-colored silk breeches; its silver buttons intentionally large enough to be of note. His white linen shirt betrayed not a wrinkle and his black riding boots were polished as if never worn. His light brown hair was pulled back and tied with a black ribbon.

Looking at my father's lack of finery in dress compared to his brother's served only to emphasize how different they had become and how time had changed them both.

"Brother," my uncle said his voice devoid of emotion. "Welcome home."

My father received his brother's hand almost mechanically. Even I could feel the coldness of the room. He said nothing, but the look I saw upon his face showed his confusion at what was happening.

"You must have had a difficult journey," my uncle said returning to his desk and leaning against it. "Please...sit," he said to my father motioning to the two high-backed wingchairs flanking the fireplace. "You will have to tell us of your adventures."

As my father settled himself in one of the chairs offered, he removed his hat and dropped it to the floor beside his chair. He sat quietly looking about the room.

"How have you been, Matthew?" he finally said calmly. "I see that much has changed."

"Yes, Brother...yes, it has. I must apologize for not being here when you arrived. Had I been able to anticipate your arrival, I could have put off my travel today," he said acknowledging my father's comment, but continuing his own thought. "I trust my wife made you welcome. Of course, she had no idea at first of you who were..."

Suddenly I became the focus of his interest.

"Nephew?" I was stunned to hear myself addressed by a title so foreign to our relationship. "Would you mind leaving us?" I heard my uncle say. "Your father and I have much to discuss and much of it probably of little interest to you."

My Uncle extended his arm in the direction of the door and made it known to me that I was to leave. I looked at my father and he met my eyes and gave a slight nod in agreement. As I quietly inched my way along the wall from where I had been standing and lifted the latch to let myself out of the room, I wondered what I was missing. As I closed the door behind me, I suddenly realized that sweat was pouring from me. I could hear my own breathing and I could feel a pounding in my head. I could hear commotion in the back part of the house where I knew dinner was under preparation in the kitchen. I did not want to be confronted by anyone at that moment and so I quietly stepped to the front door and opened it just enough to slip through it.

Once outside, in the cooling air of dusk, I took a deep breath and sat on the stoop. I was glad to be out of the house that did not feel like my home. Yet, I was angry that my uncle had asked to be alone with my father only recently returned to me. What did my uncle have to say to my father that was not for my ears to hear? As I sat drinking in the fresh scents of the dusky air, I realized the windows had been open in the room where my father and Uncle now spoke. My curiosity rising, I quietly raced around the corner of the house and, bending low, took station beneath the first window of the room I came upon.

I sat against the wall of the house; the rough clapboards heated by the sunny day, warm against my back. I drew my knees up under my chin and tried to shut out the sounds around me and concentrate on the voices emanating from the window above me. I swore to myself at the happy chirping of the small birds in the tree nearby. It took me a few minutes to begin to hear what was being said.

"…has grown much since your departure," I heard my uncle saying with obvious pride. "Last year, I shipped many hogsheads of rum, and the new cheese house has brought a tidy profit since I had it built two years hence. The flax and wheat hay have also given a surplus we are able to sell."

"Yes, I can see that much has changed, Matthew," I heard my father reply, "and I congratulate you on the success both of the farm and to you personally."

"Then you must understand that I have questions about your return, William."

"As do I of you, Matthew," I heard my father reply.

"What has prompted your return at this time? I see that you have sustained an injury. Does this make your life as a sailor not possible?"

The sarcastic touch to my uncle's voice betrayed the distaste he felt over the choices his brother had made for a life. "Are you returned as the prodigal son expecting welcome and to claim share in what I alone have worked to now make a success? I now have a wife. I have children. Am I now expected to reduce the living standard of my wife and mine with the burden of supporting a man with injury that impairs his ability to contribute fully to the work? Why now, Brother? The time allotted you had almost run and now you return."

I could hear the heavy steps of my uncle's boots as he paced the wide plank flooring of the room. I could only imagine the manner of my father listening to this tirade. I then heard my father speak; calm, measured words unintended to inflame the situation.

"There is much I have to tell you, Brother Matthew. Some of what I have seen would be beyond your most evil thoughts. Some of what I have done would have caused our Quaker father to denounce me forever. But it is as it is. And I will answer your questions of me in good time. But I also have questions I would ask you to answer."

"Very well, William," my uncle answered as I could hear a chair being pulled across the wood floor. "I am listening."

"Why does my wife lie apart from the others in our family graveyard and have no marker for her grave?" The words were said without emotion; no anger, no malice, nothing. "Why do I see my son dressed in rags and find his education so lacking he can neither read nor write?"

I strained to hear a reply, yet none came quickly. After what seemed a profound silence, I heard my uncle speak.

"Your wife, Eliza, died of fever nearly three years ago. The circumstances of her death required she be separated from others lest the sickness be spread." The words came quietly with much halting. "A marker of pure white marble was ordered. I was informed it cracked while being engraved and it would take time to quarry another as fine."

"LIAR!" I wanted to shout! Had my uncle not told me that my mother deserved no better than she was given, and the cost of her marker would be better spent seeing to my support? Had my uncle's wife not reminded me time after time with every crust of bread I ate that it came from what would have been expended on a useless headstone for my mother?

"As for your son, Benjamin...." My Uncle's voice trailed into silence. I strained to hear. The silence was broken by a knock on the door of the room. I could hear the scurry of activity as the door opened and the two men must have jumped to their feet.

"May I introduce my wife, Brother," my uncle said. "This is Margaret...."

"I have already had the pleasure, as you know, Matthew, Dear," I heard my uncle's wife's voice reply in lilting sweetness.

The sound of chairs being moved and bodies settling into chairs was followed by my uncle saying, "As for Benjamin, Margaret might be better at explanation regarding him."

I resisted my urge to rise enough to hear more clearly for fear my mop of hair might betray my presence.

"Well, I would certainly support whatever my husband has told you regarding his behavior," she began, as if to diminish the acerbic tone of what was to follow, "but, he has not been easy. Since the death of his mother, he has been nothing but problems."

I clenched my fists upon hearing these words. Who had banned me from the house? Who had refused me all but the lowest of means? Who had turned my uncle against me? Whose children were forbidden to play or even speak with me and were punished severely if they did so?

"His level of disobedience and disrespect toward your brother and myself, have earned him dismissal from our presence. His manners have made him an outcast from his betters. He is an embarrassment to us all."

Why did my father not speak? How could he allow my person to be blackened in such a manner?

"You asked of his education, William," I heard my uncle say. "He displayed little interest in studies and his disruptive conduct required he be banned from instruction."

"Please understand, Brother William, if I may call you that," her voice dripping conciliation, "we have tried our best with him, but he has become what you see from his own making."

I tasted blood in my mouth from biting my lip. I was enraged yet could do nothing. Finally, I heard my father speak.

"If all of what you say be true, then, tomorrow begins a new way. However, Brother Matthew, and you, Dear sister, I fear that all you have said is not Benjamin's fault alone."

I could hear attempts at rebuttal being thwarted and took the chance of rising high enough to quickly peer through the window, hoping the movement at the window would not be noticed. I saw my father standing, his hand raised to silence, my aunt seated by the fireplace and my uncle standing beside her. The only person who might have seen me was my father, yet he gave no indication he did so.

"It has not gone without notice by me that neither of you acknowledge my son by name. His name is Benjamin. And he IS my son and a full member of this family and this house." My father's tone was firm and even. He was not anticipating any reply.

"You, my brother, have done well. You are right to take pride in your success. You ask if I have returned to take from you in some way, to diminish what you see as yours alone." At this, my father's voice became graver.

"We had an agreement. I have returned within the appointed time, but not to be of detriment to you and yours."

The concern shown in the posture of my uncle and his wife visibly drained at these words.

"But you have failed to honor your part of the agreement, Matthew," my father then said.

"How have I failed?" my uncle burst forth.

"Our agreement gave you free hand with the plantation. It also made you responsible for the wellbeing of my wife and child," my father replied. "Of these two, the welfare of those I held dear was the greater responsibility to me. I return to find my dear wife dead and no marker bears her name and my son being treated little better than the slaves you own. I can bear you no ill will for what I have found upon my return. I hold much guilt for what has happened. What is past is past. Tomorrow, I ask we begin anew."

Having said these words, my father left the room, and I could hear his uneven steps fade as he walked down the hall to the front door. I sat transfixed. After I heard the front door slam, I was tempted to bolt from my spot and run to my father. It was then I heard my aunt.

"Husband," she said, "this may not be resolved without him and his son joining the one who has already passed."

SEVEN

"Benjamin?" I heard my father say. I looked to my left and saw him standing at the front corner of the house. The words I had just heard were still ringing in my ear as I moved from beneath the window, staying close to the wall.

"Have you been eavesdropping?" he continued. I nodded as I hung my head feeling ashamed of being found out.

Father," I asked anxiously raising my face to see his, "pray tell me, you do not believe what you were told. I know I am not perfect, but neither am I without some merit. Please tell me you are not persuaded."

"Benjamin," he said tenderly, "I may no longer have two good legs, but that has not affected my ability to see and to reason. My brother has become blinded by the pursuit of wealth and his will diminished by his marriage. Yet, little does he know what wealth I too could possess."

I threw my arms about his waist and buried my face against him not really understanding the words he had spoken, but grateful that he knew the lies he had heard. As we stood there in the deepening darkness, the front door opened, and Kara called out to us to come to table.

It was the first meal of many I would take with my father at the dining table. The ritual of going to the well and washing hands and face before sitting at table became the norm. Under my father's direction, I quickly learned table manners. Being the eldest child of the household, I was privileged to be allowed to sit with the adults for evening meals.

That first night, the conversation around the table bore no relation to the earlier exchange in the parlor. In fact, it followed more a pattern of reminiscing about younger days. Two brothers reliving shared past experiences and passing over differences. It was unfortunate that this fraternity would not continue.

For the first time in many years, that night I could have slept in a real bed with linens. Though I began the night beneath the covers of the bed, I slept most of the night on the floor unable to find comfort on the straw-stuffed mattress. My father had gently shaken me awake as he prepared to descend for breakfast and instructed me to dress and follow. I found a pair of hastily altered pants and a linen shirt, which was slightly small for me, left on the sitting chair by the fireplace in the bedroom. A pair of leather shoes, worn, but serviceable, were on the floor. I quickly pulled the shirt on, as I did the pants and shoes, and bounded down the stairs. A hearty breakfast was on the dining table.

As my father had promised, the next morning began a new regimen for me. It was not to be without consequence, but I was happily unaware of how serious these were to be. Instead of daily chores, I followed my father's awkward gait to the field where the family cemetery lay in the corner and, there, began my education. As we settled in the shade provided by the fieldstone wall beside the wrought iron gate leading into the hallowed ground, I retrieved the oilskin from its hiding place. My father unwrapped his oilcloth bundle before him on the ground and lovingly removed the bible. Its warped, well-fingered pages and worn cover and binding bore witness to its heavy use over the years. My father held the bible in the palms of his hands, his fingers reverently and tenderly cradling the edges. His face became suddenly hard, and his voice dropped to a tone that demanded one's attention in full. I can still hear his words.

"Hear me well and remember what I say," he said. "Between these covers you will find the wisdom of life and the map to find your life's fortune. To know the first, you must read what is writ. To know the rest, you must search."

"What does that mean, father?" I remember asking.

"Someday you will understand. But, for the present, it is best that I tell you no more, but teach you how to read so you can discover for yourself," he responded.

And, so, I began my education in reading. Each sunny day we would spend an hour or two in the shade by the burial ground or in the barn in inclement weather. My slate was a grassless patch of soft earth, my pen a stick. Much of what my mother had taught me, and what I had thought lost by years of disuse, quickly returned. But the skill of making letters and stringing their sounds together to form words took longer. As my skill in reading grew, I still lacked an understanding of much of what I read and so it fell to my father to explain the meaning of the words I read.

At the end of that first day of learning, my father carefully wrapped the bible back into the oilskin along with the small blade and the leather sack of coins, showing me how to wrap the oilskin so it would be watertight.

Week by week, as my reading skills grew, my father would sit quietly listening to me read portions of scripture and psalms to him with only occasional corrections of words. If I stumbled on a word, he would have me read it again. When I finished a section or verse, he would ask me what I thought it meant or I would ask him what he thought it meant. It was during these weeks and months of schooling that I began to understand part of what my father had said. Here, in these pages, lay a plan by which one could live one's life. It was a guide to living a God-fearing life in the light of goodness to one's fellow man.

One morning, as the leaves began to turn color and the air betrayed a nip of autumn, my father settled himself in his usual place on the flat rock by the wall. He opened the oilcloth I had retrieved for him from its hiding place, as always, but instead of removing the Bible, he retrieved the small leather pouch. He held it before me in the palm of his hand.

"Today I begin to teach you about numbers so you may know how to value these," he said as he gently tossed the pouch on his palm and made the contents within jingle. "He who knows his numbers cannot be cheated of his wealth nor will he ever be shorted in his worth."

He smoothed out a corner of the oilcloth and carefully emptied the contents of the leather pouch onto it. Out tumbled more coins of silver and gold than I had ever seen in my life. He then divided the coins into groups based on the country in which they were minted. One by one, he explained the value of each coin in relation to the others. There were pence, shillings, and crowns made of silver, gold guinea, two guinea and five guinea coins. Each could be related to the other by the value of shillings and pence. There were Dutch ducatoons, French ecus and livres, thalers from the Germanic states, cruzados from Portugal, and doubloons from Spain. Although I knew nothing of these exotic-sounding foreign lands, I marveled at the beauty of their creations. All had a value that could be derived from our own English coinage.

Finally, and most importantly, my father placed two coins before me. One had a double portrait etched on its surface. It was made of gold.

"These two you will see most often besides our own coins," my father said. "These are of Spanish making. One is a reale, known as a piece of eight. The other, he said, pointing to the gold coin, "is a doubloon. The man who possesses many of these has wealth beyond his dreams."

He handed each coin to me so I could feel the weight of each. The raised engravings and ridged edges and the cool feel of the metal made me behold each coin with care.

"Don't be afraid to hold them, son. Feel the weightiness. They will last long beyond all of us. The material is made to last unless..."

My father retrieved the reale from my palm and leaned closer in a conspiratorial huddle.

"Unless one takes a sharp blade and shaves the edge making the coin no longer whole. Ye can feel it in the weight and see it in the shape. The other way to change its value is to cut the coin into pieces. Gold is soft and can be cut if struck with a sharp blade. But gold is valued because it is a rare metal. If cut, eight pieces be most common and, thus, its name a piece of eight!"

Having said this, my father sat back with a smile of satisfaction I had not often seen. He proceeded to gather all the coins and deftly slid them from his palm, over his fingers, back into the pouch from which they had originally appeared which he held in his other hand.

He lingered a moment with the last two coins. As he turned them over, using his fingers, he said to me in a faint voice,

"It is time you know of where I have traveled and what I have seen and done when I was away at sea. I will tell you as much now as I feel I can."

"When I left you and your mother, I signed aboard a coastal merchantman known as a shallop bound for New York. I knew so little of sailing and there was much for me to learn. Fortunately, the captain and quartermaster were good teachers and their instruction helped me to learn the basic language of sailing. By the time we landed in New York harbor, I felt I was ready to sign on a bigger ship and begin my adventuring."

My father paused for a moment and smiled to himself as his thought fell back to that time.

"I signed on to sail on a three-master to the Caribbean. We would stop in some southern ports, then go to the sugar islands for a cargo to return to Newport. That was the planned voyage and because I could read and write and knew numbers, I was given duties other than regular crew. I began to learn navigation and keeping the ship's log. Where the quartermaster held responsibility for the general crew, my responsibilities kept me mostly near the captain. I made three such voyages and learned every facet of trade and sailing."

I watched this man I knew as my father as he warmed to his narrative. His words relayed what was, obviously, the most exciting time of his life.

"When I reached New York after our third voyage, we ported for two days, and, during that time, I was recommended to visit a church in the heart of the city. It was nearly finished and one of the finest stone structures in New York. As I stood admiring the workmanship, a well-dressed gentleman with some papers under his arm, deep in conversation with a companion, approached me on the walk. As he went to pass me, some papers slipped from his grip and fluttered to the ground. I quickly began to help him in retrieving his papers and noted that they were designs related to the church.

"As I handed him the plans I had retrieved from the ground, I made the remark that it was a fine building he was constructing. With that, he looked me over and asked my name."

"He said to me, 'You could tell that from what you saw here?' and I told him I could read. He scribbled a note on a corner of a sheet and tore it off. 'Come see me tomorrow.'"

"And that is how I met the man I would sail the world with for the next three years."

With that, my father clapped his hands on his thighs and reared back with a grin of satisfaction on his face.

"Next morn, I took myself to the address he had given me which turned out to be just off the dock area. The shop was filled with rigging stuff not only for fitting out sailing ships, but for building land structures such as the church. I asked for the gentleman and was told he would be at his home at this hour and was directed to a fine section of the city known as Wall Street."

"The address brought me to a fine home and a man servant answered my pull of the bell cord at the door. As the door opened, I saw my new friend coming toward me beyond the man who had opened the door, with his hand extended in greeting. He ushered me into a sitting room that was furnished in more luxury than I had ever seen. He bade me sit as he saw I was reluctant to in fear of soiling such fine fabric with my rough clothes. As I did sit, he offered me tea or coffee and began asking me about my family and where I was from and how I came to learn writing and reading."

"We talked and talked, and I realized that he was a well-to-do socially active person married to a woman, wealthy in her own right, who had already been twice widowed by the age of twenty-one. He was wealthy in his own right having been in the sailing trades for a dozen years. During that time, he had sailed the Caribbean, been pressed into service at Nevis by the English to defend against the French, and now was part of New York Society and a respected member of the Trinity Church congregation. In fact, he was providing all the block and tackle to lift the stone façade into place."

"He told me he had been approached by the new governor of New York, one Richard Coote, Earl of Bellomont, to receive a royal sanction and commission to pursue known pirates and enemies of England. He said a new ship could be provided and built at the expense of some interested local merchants and colonial officials, as well as some English lords and other subscribers on the prospect of gains that would be realized on the prizes that would be taken on the voyage."

"He felt he had little choice but to accept the expedition because of his previous experience and standing in the community. And so, he was preparing to leave for England to take delivery of this new ship. Would I be interested in a position of purser on his voyage?"

"Now, a purser oversees all the financial transactions aboard ship, Ben. He accounts for all cargo, pays for all supplies, and maintains the books aboard. So, it's a vital and important post."

I had never been prouder of my father. He had held a prominent position onboard a ship captained by an influential gentleman.

"I, of course, agreed at once and we shook hands to seal the bargain. He asked me to be ready to leave for England in a fortnight and, as I left, he pressed some coins into my hand and gave me the address of his tailor."

"You'll need a respectable set of clothes to make this trip'", he said, "and for the first time, I caught a slight Scottish accent."

"Over the next few days, my new Captain introduced me to several luminaries of New York society, not least of which was his close friend Robert Livingston. I met the Rector of Trinity Church, Reverend Vesey, and even the Governor, Lord Bellomont."

"The day of our departure arrived and I, and my newly purchased trunk of new clothes, came aboard the *Antigua*, owned by my Captain, ready to sail for England. Our passage was pleasant and swift with no summer storms, and we arrived in just over four weeks' time. If New York was a city, London would be much, much more. The docks along the Thames River went on for miles and ships of every design and many foreign countries crowded together. I spent most of my time at my Captain's side as he hand-picked every member of the crew. It was a solid crew of good, seasoned, experienced sailors and our ship was the largest I had ever seen. The *Adventure Galley* was above 280 tons with thirty-four guns, and capable of mounting oars which would give her a distinct advantage in the pursuit of prizes where the wind had died."

In less than a month, we were provisioned and crewed. We prepared to set sail for home to receive our commission. We were not even out of the Thames when our first bit of misfortune happened. It was tradition to salute with cannon fire when passing a naval yacht on the Thames. With the Captain and I below decks, our quartermaster, who should have known this courtesy, failed to comply, and we were made to heave to. The naval officer boarded and impressed nearly half our crew for naval service as punishment for our insult. And so, we sailed with half our hand-picked crew lost to our service."

"Our passage home was not uneventful. We happened upon a French merchant brig sailing from New France when almost to America and we managed to engage and take her as our first prize. It was during this engagement that I sustained injury to my leg," he said laying a hand against his right thigh.

"I had been told to stay below, but, since I had never seen or been in a battle, I wanted to see what it was like. We outgunned the brig by five to one and the 'battle' did not last but one round of fire. Yet, that was enough to cripple me for life. A ball from the swivel gun of the brig hit our quarterdeck and splintered into hot pieces of metal. One caught me here, just at the knee." He began to pull the leg of his loose pants up over his knee.

"The wound bled heavily and, when it ceased, the damage to the bones was evident. Then the infection set in. The surgeon had to take a portion of the muscle to save the leg."

As he uncovered his knee, I could see the crooked way the bones had knitted back together, but above this, where muscle should have been, there was a depression to the large bone of the leg and it bore a massive scar, ugly and red.

"I had much pain," my father continued, "and, had it not been for the rum I was given, I am not sure I would have stood it. It was the first of a very few times I had too much drink."

My father sat for a moment staring, I think at his healed, but mangled limb, then began to lower his pant leg. I dared not speak. The sight of his leg had sickened me.

"We won the encounter, even with a reduced crew, and brought that brig *Le Cygnet* into New York as a prize vessel. I was taken to my Captain's home on a litter and was tended to by his wonderfully caring wife for nearly four months until I could stand with crutches."

"During that time, a new crew was assembled. Though they may have been skilled and experienced sailors, they were not men of character. In fact, they were men of the worst sort. But, with time running short and demands from the backers of the voyage to be at sea, we packed our stores and munitions, received our commission as a privateer of the Crown and prepared to board."

My father shifted his weight and gave a sigh that was half discomfort and the rest pain.

"It is important for you to know that I saw the Royal Commission, certifying our status as a privateer under protection of the Crown, myself. It was a document bearing the signature and seal of the English King William III. As much as that document was supposed to bless our voyage and keep us safe, it proved to be our undoing in the end."

My father picked up a small pebble from the ground and, with a look of disgust on his face, tossed it against the stone wall opposite where we sat. I could see tears forming in his eyes.

"We sailed for the Caribbean and would then cross the Atlantic to the horn of Africa. We saw no pirates nor prizes in the Caribbean, only ships carrying slaves. Our commission gave us leave to attack 'enemies of England,' ships of foreign powers at war with Her and, in particular, known pirates of which we found none, nor any prizes worth engaging. Those ships we did board only provided stores of supplies we needed. And so, we set course for the Cape of Good Hope, the southern end of Africa, and headed into another body of water known as the Indian Ocean. We had heard reports of pirate attacks near a big island called Madagascar."

This was a vastly different land, my son," my father continued, "the heat was tremendous: the winds were light and contrary. Many different tongues could be heard about the wharves and odd dress and strange ship designs were everywhere. We did not stay long in Madagascar, but, sought out intelligence about what was known of shipping lanes and pirate activity in the area."

"We sailed from there to a group of Islands called the Comoros. We arrived amid a cholera outbreak that took a third of our crew. The remaining crew were growing restless to take some prizes and enrich themselves. Even our Captain was feeling the lack of prizes. The voyage was failing."

All appeared lost when suddenly, we began overtaking some small prizes. They were cargoes large enough to provide some small return to the investors of the voyage. But tempers were still hot and in a heated disagreement over attacking a Dutch trader caused our Captain to shed blood. We were making sail for a ship flying the Dutch flag. Our gunner's mate was sure it would be a rich prize. Our Captain was refusing to attack because our then King, William, was Dutch. In the ensuing shouting and swearing, our Captain picked up a bucket, struck the gunner's mate, and killed him with a single blow. It was the only time I ever saw my Captain lose his temper."

"This incident calmed the tensions aboard. Shortly after, we happened upon a huge ship of a strange and uniquely wondrous design. She was made to heave to and proved to have in her holds a king's ransom. She had barrels of spices, silks and satins, leathers, gems, gold, silver, and all manner of wealth. The ship herself was a worthy prize, ornately decorated with gild and fine carvings. She was named the *Quedah Merchant.*"

I could see my father's eyes begin to expand with excitement as he relived the taking of the ship. He described gold in coins and bars, silver ingots packed in chests, gems of amethyst, emerald, and aquamarines as large as his fist.

"It was my job to record every bit of the captured cargo. My record ran for fifteen pages. In the end, our voyage would be profitable for backers and crew alike. And, with that thought, we turned for home sailing the *Quedah* back to New York as a prize."

"But, Father," I interrupted, "If such wealth was in hand, why are we not wealthy?"

"Aye, Ben, t'is more to the story," my father said lowering his head slightly. "Things had changed at home while we had been away."

"Our captain had been accused of turning pirate and of murder. Those who had issued our letter of marque denied its existence," my father continued, his voice betraying his bitterness.

We sailed for home and discovered we would be imprisoned if we made port, and so we sailed for Boston in hopes of obtaining a fairer hearing. But, fearing we might not be received well, our captain decided to bury the treasure on an island along the way." My father smiled to himself as he said this. "This would be our bargain if needed: give us fair hearing and we tell where the treasure is hidden. Give us no hearing and the treasure stays hid."

"What of the treasure, Father," I asked?

"We did not know that Lord Bellomont had become governor of Massachusetts in our absence. The crew and officers were all arrested upon landing in Boston and to make an example of the officers and our captain, we were sent to London to stand trial."

The bitterness in my father's voice was strong.

"The court convicted the officers of piracy and sentenced us to three years imprisonment. The judges convicted our captain of piracy and murder of a seaman and condemned him to death." I could see tears forming in my father's eyes.

"Those who gave testimony against him lied unmercifully. They hanged him in late spring 1701 at Execution dock and hung his body in a metal cage at Tyburn in the Thames as a warning to others who might think to turn pirate." A tear fell from my father's eye.

"I, and the other officers served two years. Two of us died in prison. I saw the body of my captain hanging in that cage half submerged by the incoming tide when I sailed for home," his voice but a whisper.

"Father?" I asked softly, "you have never said his name."

"You may know his name. His name was William Kidd," my father said with pride as he straightened his back. "One of the finest, most honest men I have ever known. And I am the only person alive who knows where the remaining treasure lies buried."

EIGHT

he thought of food made me suddenly realize that my stomach was reacting to those thoughts. It was only then I became aware of my surroundings. I shifted my cramped position and felt my foot slip from its bracing. As my consciousness returned, I realized the light within my hiding place was no longer from my candles, but from the sunlight filtering through the cracks in my refuge about me. The jagged entry hole showed a roughly circular slice of dry sand. I was no longer safe.

I slowly unfolded my legs and felt my muscles remind me of their cramped condition. I cautiously slid off my perch and eased my weight onto them, feeling the pins and needles of returning circulation. This was my third day without a decent meal. My stores of dried meat and water were all but gone and the storm that lasted the entire preceding day kept me within my hiding place. I only hoped the rains and wind of the storm hindered the search by my pursuers. But the gnawing emptiness in my belly told me I needed to eat. I needed to find food, yet, doing so, might lead to my discovery. I would need to remain cautious in my search.

Once the feeling returned to my lower limbs, I crouched beside the entry way and tried to see in all directions. The water had retreated with the tide and left the tidal flat an unmarked surface strewn with shells and clumps of seaweed and with flecks of sand glinting in the bright sunlight. I knew that to move from my hiding place would leave a track upon this smooth ground that could lead any who wished to my haunt. But the grinding hunger I felt spurred me into taking risks.

Putting caution aside, I pulled myself through the hole and out onto the cool sand in the shadow of the hulk. I sat very still and looked toward the shore fifty yards distant. The shortest distance to the rock and brush-lined shore would leave the fewest tracks but would also leave no doubt as to their origin. If I were to run, it would take less time of exposure, but would make deeper tracks in the soft tidal sands. If I carefully walked, I could leave lighter footprints less easily followed by someone curious to know, yet it would mean being visible that much longer.

As I prepared to make for the shoreline, I suddenly remembered my father's bundle. I reached back into the inside of the hulk and felt for the oilcloth. My fingers felt the slick surface of the package and strained to grasp it. I pulled it to my chest and held it tightly for a moment. I made up my mind. The time had come.

I stood for a moment in the shadow of the upended section of the wreck that had been my refuge for the last three nights and took one last look about me. There was no movement save for the gently breaking waves a few yards distant and the gulls kiting on the wind. I stepped from the shadow and calmly walked toward the nearest point of the brushy shoreline. I fought the urge to break into a run. I tried to make my steps land as lightly as possible, looking for what looked to be the driest spots of sand. I kept watching in as many directions as I could to see if I had been discovered by anyone. I saw no one.

It felt like forever, but, it had only taken a few strides to reach the rising sand and short scrub of the highwater mark. I slid behind a large rock that had been the mark I had picked out on the shore to head toward. I could feel my heart pounding in my chest. I looked up the slope to the higher land of Conanicut Island. The rising slope was covered by scrub trees and shrubs just coming into leaf. Still, it would provide some protection from discovery if any eyes were watching.

For many years now, since it had been purchased from the natives, the island had been used by many of the larger farm holdings to pasture their sheep. My Uncle was among them. In the spring lambing, most farms would cull their flocks on the island removing those that would provide for the table during the summer. Such had been the small flock I had been tending the day my father arrived home. With the spring lambing mostly finished, I knew the few shepherds who stayed on the island to tend to the flocks would be off fishing or berry gathering. I had done so myself the spring before when I had come to the island for the spring lambing.

The only real settlement on the island was Jamestown on the southeast side of the island across from Newport harbor. If I could manage to avoid Jamestown and the shepherds on the island, I felt I would be safe. Eventually those who searched for me would doubtlessly come to the island. The presence of a young boy on the island would be noted and talked about whether I was known by name or not.

I knew the shepherds' huts lay north of where I had come ashore on the west side of the largest grazing meadow. If I stayed to the tree line along the ridge of the shore, I could see across the meadow for anyone approaching and I could see the water of the west passage for any boat approaching the island. While I might avoid detection from the meadow, I would be cut off from a return to my hiding place in the wreck if someone approached across the water. I could also watch for the incoming tide that I would need to beat to return to the safety of my haven.

I rose cautiously and looked around me. The black shape of the wreck stood silently on the sandy tidal flat, a trail of footprints leading directly to the shore. I realized I was still holding the oilcloth wrapped package under my arm. I knew I should leave it here near the edge of the water. I would need more speed and agility than to be carrying such a package. Yet, I was reluctant to leave it while I made my run. I remembered my father's admonishment. I decided it would be better to have both hands free and, kneeling next to the large boulder, scooped out a few handfuls of soft sand and placed the bundle carefully under the edge of the boulder. With both hands, I pushed the sand over it and placed three rocks each about the size of my fist atop the small mound. With a final sprinkling of loose sand over the top, I turned to the slope rising behind me and began to scramble up it.

The climb was easy and only about thirty feet. The slope crested into the edge of a grassy field that gently rose and fell across the flat of the island. I stopped at the last line of saplings and peered across the field for any movement. On the far eastern side of the field, I could see the white coats of a large flock. I knew a shepherd or two would be watching them sitting, or most likely lying, in the shade of the trees nearest to them. Other shepherds would be off fishing or gathering berries. If I moved with stealth as did the natives through the trees along the edge of the field, I would reach the shepherd hut at its back.

Keeping a wary eye toward the flock for any sign of my discovery, I moved slowly from tree to bush and sapling to shrub. As I moved along, I glanced back over my left shoulder and saw the dark image of the wreck sitting stark and silent on the tidal flat. More importantly, I saw no activity as I looked along the west shore of West Passage. I moved swiftly, but smoothly, just within the trees and was soon in sight of the hut that sheltered the island's shepherds while they tended their flocks.

It could hardly qualify as a hut. It was more a lean-to with barely more than a covering roof. Its open spaced slats on the side walls allowed cooling breezes off the water to pass through the structure during the heat of summer, but also allowed wind-driven rain to do the same. A fire pit on the open side of the main hut was always kept at least smoldering not only for its warmth, but for cooking and drying fish that formed the main part of a shepherd's diet, along with corn or wheat bread.

As I drew nearer, I studied the hut for movement from within. I saw none. But my attention was drawn to a rack of dried smoked fish next to the fire pit. With less caution than was prudent, yet driven by the hunger in my belly, I broke from the cover of the shrubs and reached for one of the dried fish. Fortunately, no one was about, and I quickly retreated into the tree line again. Squatting in the relative secrecy of a bush, I devoured my stolen fish with the ravenousness of one who had not eaten in over twenty-four hours. In a matter of a few bites, it was consumed. I do not even remember what kind of fish it might have been. I was only aware that more was within reach. I again stepped out of the covering bushes and this time swiped two of the dozen or so dried fish on the wooden rack.

As my hunger began to ease, I watched the open field for any sign of movement that might indicate my presence had been discovered. My caution returned with every satisfying bite of fish, and I began to survey the hut from where I crouched. On the far side of the fire pit, I saw a covered bowl like one I had seen many times sitting on the sill of the kitchen window at the farm. It would contain a freshly baked loaf of bread. If it did, I was faced with choices. I could take a piece of the loaf, but, since I had no knife, I would need to tear a piece from the loaf, or I could help myself to the entire loaf. Or I could leave without touching it. My hunger made the third option unthinkable and either of the first two would leave the shepherds to argue among themselves as to what had befallen them.

With time beginning to be a concern, for the tide would be surging again shortly, I decided to sacrifice a portion of the loaf to cover my presence. Once more I left the cover of the brush and reached the covered bowl. Lifting the cover, I saw a beautiful loaf of freshly baked bread. I picked up the loaf and kicked the bowl and its cover over onto the ground. As I backed away from the fire pit in the direction of the trees on the opposite side of the clearing from the direction of my departure, I crumbled off a corner of the bread and let it fall to the ground. A few larger pieces were also sacrificed to about a fifth portion of the loaf. My hope was the shepherds finding the mess would conclude some small creature had helped themselves to their freshly baked bread.

Once I reached the trees, I ceased the wasting of precious food and circled back behind the hut and started rapidly walking back along the edge of the field. At the first occasion where I could see the West passage, I could see that the amount of exposed tidal flat was shrinking. I would need to hurry to reach the safety of the wreck before the incoming tide made it impossible. As I walked quickly in a half-crouch in the saplings and trees along the edge of the field, allowing the new leaves to help hide my presence, I pulled a mouthful of bread from the loaf and ravenously consumed it.

The sheep still seemed to be grazing without taking any notice of me. There was no indication that the shepherd's mid-afternoon vigil had been disturbed. I could look to my right down the slope to the tidal flat and see the water rising along its edge. The tide would soon be in flood, and I would no longer be able to reach my refuge for the night. I could feel my pace quickening as I reached the end of the field. Only a few more feet and I would be sliding down the ridge to the level of the beach and out of sight of discovery. With a final look back across the meadow at the flock of sheep and a partially consumed loaf of bread securely tucked in my arm, I began to slip down the slope watching the sheep and the meadow disappear from my view.

I could feel the elation of my success and the fullness in my stomach as my descent slowed as I neared the bottom of the slope. I had shown myself worthy of surviving in my own mind. I smiled to myself to think of my cleverness. I pushed myself up from my seated position at the bottom of the slope with my hand and, at that very instant, my head exploded in pain and the world went black.

NINE

The roaring noise in my ears was slowly replaced with the pounding I felt in the back of my head. It was the noise of the gales that accompanied the fall storms coming off the bay. But the pain in my head was like none I had ever experienced. Instinctively, I tried to raise my hand to the place of pain when I realized I could not move my arm. In fact, I could not move either of my arms. With my arms bound in such a manner I rolled on my side and, unable to control myself, gave out a low groan of pain. With that, a pair of powerful hands grasped my shoulders and roughly shoved me into a sitting position. The rancid scents of sweat mingled with the sweet aroma of rum invaded my nose.

As my vision slowly cleared, I saw before me a small fire well hidden by a ring of rounded cobbles from the beach. In the surrounding darkness, its light was thrown against a small area near the upslope of the island and seated in that circle of light were three men I had never seen before. They were men of the sea, but not of the hired variety. The one who was returning to his seat before the fire wore the slops of a sailor and a rough tan cotton weave shirt with short sleeves and a knit stocking cap of wool. He was short and stocky and quickly wrapped himself in a piece of canvas against the chill of the early evening air. The hair that bushed out from beneath his cap showed a tight curl and his face had not seen a razor in some time. The growth of beard could not hide his youth. His eyes were twinkling in the fire light and his nose, though straight, was bulbous at the end.

The man sitting to the right wore a leather cap. His face was thin and long as was his moustache that drooped about his full-lipped mouth. He wore a collared shirt of linen with an open throat loosely laced under a leather jerkin. His pants were striped and disappeared inside his massive boots. When he turned his head to tend the fire, I could see an ugly scar running from beneath his cap nearly to his jaw line. He stared at me with eyes that held no life. They were the eyes of one who held life of little value. Across his chest a leather sash held a large pistol and at his waist a cutlass that looked as long as I was tall. He never took his eyes from me, and I felt myself withering under his glare.

"Now, who have we here?" I heard the man in the middle say in a gruff, but kindly voice. As he spoke, he removed is tricorn hat to reveal a yellow and green bandana tied tightly about his head. A large earring of yellow gold hung from his ear. His eyes were large and glinted in the fire light as he leaned toward me across the fire. He was younger than his scarred companion, but older than the other. His moustache and short beard were well trimmed and his smile, though friendly, seemed quietly sinister. His shirt was of white cotton and contrasted smartly against the dark green and gold facings of his military style coat. Beside him on the sand lay a sheathed saber and a leather sash with three pistols inserted in protruding loops.

In the flickering light of the fire, I could see all three of my companions were deeply tanned by the sun and all displayed a swagger and confidence that told me they were imbibing heavily from a small cask behind them.

As I attempted to answer his question, I felt the gag between my teeth.

"Would ye be a shepherd shirkin' his duty?" He squinted, still smiling at me. "No...me thinks not." He rubbed the chin of his beard between his forefinger and thumb as if deep in thought.

"Might ye be a young buck on an adventure from home, or a runaway or, worse yet, a thief?" he said holding up my loaf of pilfered bread, now much eaten.

The speaker tossed what was left of my bread to the youngest member of the group and turned to his companion with the scar.

"If he be a runaway, he'd not be missed," he said.

"If he be a thief, he would find a home among us," replied the scarred man, his voice ending in a deep laugh.

"So, who might ye be, boy," the leader pondered aloud returning his look to me.

He heavily pushed the shoulder of the youngest member and said as he did so, "Johnny, be a good lad and remove his gag. He'll not be yellin' fer help. Will ye, boy?"

From the malevolent look in his eyes and the tone of his voice, I knew his meaning and nodded my head in response.

The youngest sailor scrambled around the fire pit to my side and roughly unknotted the rag that prevented my speaking. His open sandals held on by slender ropes kicked up sprays of sand with every crouched step. I spit the foul-tasting cloth from my mouth and realized the dryness of my mouth.

"Give our young guest a draught of rum, Johnny," the leader again pushed the youngest sailor by the arm. He reached behind them and retrieved the small keg from which he poured a clamshell of liquid. Carefully holding the shell so as not to spill but a few drops, He rounded the fire pit again and poured the liquid into my waiting mouth. I swallowed greedily until the burn of the rum made me splutter. I had expected water for some reason. This made all three of my companion's roar in laughter.

"No taste fer the captain's best rum, boy?" the leader said. "Well, that tells me yer not one of the rough and rowdy boys," he continued.

I could feel the bindings at my wrists were light sailing line, and not the heavier rope of halyards. Feeling about in the sand behind me with as little movement as possible, I felt the long shape of a razor clam shell. As I faced my captors, I knew I needed time to free myself. Slowly I began running the twine binding my wrists on the sharp edge of the clam shell.

"Who are you," I asked feigning great fear. "What do you want from me?"

"Who are we, ye ask?" replied the leader. "Why, me boy, we be free men of the sea; members of the Brotherhood. As for what we want with you. We want nothing!" He smiled kindly as his scarred companion broke into a sinister sneer. The youngest member nodded in agreement.

"We might make ye an offer to come with us adventuring about the world," he continued, "but, all we ask of ye is a bit of information ye might have."

"But why are you here?" I asked.

"We are in need of some fresh meat fer our ship anchored in the cove yonder," the youthful sailor volunteered.

"A few head of sheep will serve our needs," the leader chimed in," t'is all we ever take when we shelter here fer a night."

"But that is stealing!" I heard the words escape my lips before I could stop them.

This brought gales of laughter from the trio of pirates.

"The lad has morals, Capitan," the scarred man spoke for the first time. His accent was foreign to my ear.

"Aye, Carlos. He be a well-bred, God-fearing, young country squire, I fear."

"Lad, a few sheep missing is to be expected. No one need know the reason for it. Drowned in the bay, eaten by those who tend them, as long as we keep within reason, it is a small price to pay to keep us at sea and not ashore in yer towns," the captain said smiling.

The youngest pirate had said a ship was riding at anchor in the cove. I tried to look beyond the rocks that surrounded me to see its shape in the cove. I could not turn far enough and there was no light to see its form against the black of the sky. But, as I twisted to look for the ship, I could feel the strands of rope loosen against my wrists. And now I needed a plan.

"What information might I have that would interest you?" I said, returning to my position facing the group.

"It is but a small thing," the captain said as the laughter died, and smiles faded from his companions' faces.

"We seek a friend of ours, a man dressed of the sea, who might have been coming home somewhere in these parts who has something we seek. Ye may have seen him. He limps with a cane for his game leg."

I tried to show no emotion in my face, no reaction of any kind. Were these the men my father had feared the coming of?

The leader of the group cocked his head to one side and his stare became keener.

"Why, it seems our young friend here knows of our mate," he said in a faint voice to his companions. "Might that be so, boy?"

All three of them leaned forward to the light of the fire throwing their features into frightening relief.

"Where have you seen him," demanded the man with the scar as he began to reach across the fire to grab my shirt. The captain reached out and stopped him.

"Have ye seen him, Boy? Do ye know him?" the captain asked firmly.

I could feel my stomach tightening and the muscles of my neck tensing. Should I tell these men the information they wanted?

"What do you want of him?" I asked.

"He knows him, Capitan," the scarred man said turning to his companions. "I am sure of it!"

The captain raised his hand in silence.

"You know of him, don't you," he said to me as if he already knew the answer. "Where have you seen him?"

"Yes," I stammered. I could not resist the gaze of the captain's eyes. It was as if he read my soul. "I have seen him."

"I told you, mi Capitan!" the scarred man exclaimed in triumph. The captain again motioned him to silence.

"Did you see him here?" the captain continued to question me.

"Do you want to do him harm?" I found myself asking.

"Do him harm?" the captain responded, almost carrying off the act of surprise. "Whatever gave ye to think that?"

He turned to his companions and the three began to laugh; his companions a bit nervously, at first, but more robustly with his encouragement.

"What would make ye think we would do him harm, me young Hearty?" the captain said as the laughter quickly died. "It is only that when he left us, he had something that.... er...well...something of value... to us, it has value..."

"He took it from us," the youngest sailor blurted out. The captain gave him a stern look of disapproval.

"What he means to say, lad," the captain attempted to explain, "is he left our company with something we highly desire. A paper, it were, a chart of a kind. Did ye see him with it?"

"I saw him," I said withholding the truth. "He had no paper that I saw."

"But ye did see him!" the scarred man spoke intensely.

"I saw him a few days ago," I stammered, attempting to be as convincing as I could. "He was passing here on his way to Providence. But I saw no chart."

I could not bring myself to tell them the truth. I could not speak the words of my father's death nor the circumstances under which it took place. Yet, the scene was still fresh in my mind. How my father and his brother argued that night as they had many nights about the land and the farm. How my father had pursued his own desires to take the sea and left his brother to the work of farming the land. My uncle becoming increasingly heated in his berating manner. How my uncle felt my father did not and could not contribute his fair share to the running of the farm since his return, broken in health and spirit. They had argued many nights: my uncle often fueled by the taunts of my aunt and his consumption of port wine; my father spurred to reply by the spirits of rum.

What had it been that final night of arguing that had finally led to such violence between them? Was it my father accusing his brother of failing to uphold his part of the original bargain between them? Had his raising the specter of his brother's treatment of my mother and myself been too close to the truth for my uncle to manage? Had my father's reference to the actions of my aunt to deny my birthright been more than my uncle could bear? Was it the drink? Was it all of these? Was this what had led to one brother raising a deadly hand to another? Was my uncle in his right mind when he raised that fire poker and struck his brother, my father?

The look I saw on my uncle's face when he saw me standing just by the door has stayed with me all these years. It was a look beyond anger. It was the blood-spattered face of evil realizing that his act of murder carried out in a moment of emotion had been witnessed by one who could undo all he had worked so hard to gain. It was a look of realization that the only way to continue his life would mean more blood on his hands.

"He lies, Capitan! He knows more," the scarred man said with increasing emotion. Pulling a small knife from its hidden scabbard, he moved it in menacing circles.

"Let me loosen his tongue for him," he said, again moving toward me from across the fire.

"Belay that!" The captain stayed the man's movement with his arm.

At that moment, I could feel the ropes that bound my wrists loosen completely. In fear for my life, I scooped a handful of loose sand in each of my hands. As my companions relaxed slightly, I quickly leapt to my feet and threw the sand I held into the faces of the three men.

Turning on my heels, I ran in the direction of the hulk that was my refuge across the small isthmus of sand and boulders. I could hear the spluttering and cries of the three seated before the fire as they tried to deal with the barrage of sand that had been flung in their faces. My eyes adjusted to the darkness quickly and I realized I was running directly toward the boulder where I had buried my father's possessions. I dropped behind it and quickly scooped the sand away. Feeling the package come free, I could hear the three men behind me beginning to search for me.

I had no option left to me, but to try to make a run to the hulk. I knew the tide was again coming in and had been. I would need to run through water that would become deeper as I ran. The noise I would make would give away my location. But, if I could reach the wreck, I could defend myself well, even with only a small dirk. I would need to guard only one approach.

If I stayed where I was, my discovery was assured. Not knowing how near my pursuers were, I jumped to my feet and ran. I ran as fast as I could and felt the dry sand beneath my feet become wet. I could make out the dark shape of what I knew to be the wreck with the onrushing tide breaking white around it. I corrected my direction toward it.

I knew the sound I made running through the water would attract the men. I could hear them as they began to chase me. I heard the leader's voice telling the others not to fire at me. I ran as fast as the rising water allowed me. My lungs felt they would burst as I gasped for breath.

The water quickly reached my knees and I tried to raise my legs higher and gallop through the water. My pace was slowing because of the rising water and my own fatigue. Yet, I could see the hulk coming nearer. As the water reached my thighs, I could no longer get above the water and began to wade against the incoming tide. It was then I turned to see who pursued me. I could see but one, the youngest of the trio, struggling through the water behind me. The wreck was nearing. With one last stride, I took as deep a breath as possible and dove beneath the water.

TEN

I struggled against the incoming tide clutching my package with one arm and pulling along the sand bottom with the other. I knew I had made my dive farther from the wreck than I wanted to, but with the depth of the water and gains being made by my pursuer, I knew I had no choice if my refuge were to have any chance of remaining secret.

My lungs burned as I began running out of breath. I slowly began releasing air and feeling for the rough hull of the wreck. I pushed against the small rocks on the soft sand with my feet, reaching ahead, hoping to feel the hull so I would not need to surface for a breath.

I could hold my breath no longer. With one last desperate lunge, I felt the hull of the wreck and the edge of the entry hole. As I surfaced in the black darkness of the wreck, I gasped to fill my lungs with the stale, dank air it held. I took two or three deep breaths exhaling as quietly as my straining lungs allowed. I quickly pulled myself fully through the hole and felt for the ledge of the cross member that normally perched my feet. Finding it, I placed the oilskin package on it and quickly felt for the tie that bound it. As I fumbled to untie the knot, I tried to listen for any sounds. Knowing that voices carry over water, it would be difficult to tell how close my pursuer might be or whether my attempt to escape had failed. I threw back the wrapping of oilcloth and felt the handle of the dirk. I gripped it and stepped back straddling the entrance, my legs mid-calf in the cold water.

I was ready. In my mind, I was ready to strike with lethal intent whoever or whatever surfaced through the watery entrance into my sanctuary. I tried to calm my breathing and make no sound. I waited; listened. The slopping of the water against the sides of the hulk seemed louder than ever. I strained to hear voices.

"Captain! He's gone!"

The nearness of the voice frightened me. He had to be just on the other side of the planking. I tense, preparing for the worst. I heard a distant voice respond.

"Find him! Stand still ye lout! Listen for him!"

It was the leader's voice. It was obvious he was some distance from me, most likely shouting from the shore.

"I think he's drowned!" I heard the young sailor's voice boom out in reply. "He's gone under!"

"Leave off, then," I heard the captain say, "The tide is running, we must weigh anchor. We'll be at sea before he finds any help, if he hasn't gone to the crabs and fishes. Come along, Lad!"

I dared not relax my watch. It could be a trick. I felt the knife in my hand and readied myself to strike. I heard the sloshing of the water about my feet and expected to hear someone take a gasping breath in the murky darkness as they surfaced through the hole. I waited. Time seemed to drag. Every limb of my being was tensed for the strike. I could feel the strain. And then...nothing.

The sound of the water's movement about my feet was rhythmic without interruption. All was silent. I have no idea how long I stood braced for the attack. My arms began to cramp, and my feet ached from the cold water. But fear is a strong master.

When I could stand the cold on my feet no longer, I pulled myself up to my normal perch as quietly as possible and continued to hold the dirk at the ready. I convinced myself that I could spring to defend the hole in a moment And so I waited with no sound other than that of the water.

><

I awoke to the sound of rain pelting down on the wood of my hideaway. I could hear the wind whipping through the cracks of the hull. The occasional roll of thunder punctuated the rat-tat-tat of the rain. The rank stale air of last night inside my refuge was being replaced with air cleaned and refreshed by the rain. It rushed into my small space through the entry hole now empty of water.

As my consciousness returned, I stretched my arms and legs, feeling the tightness of my muscles I realized that I still held the knife in my hand. I looked at the red marks on my wrists made by the ropes that had restrained me and suddenly realized how close I had come to; I knew not what. As I sat pondering my condition, listening to the falling rain and the peals of thunder, I knew it was time to leave the safety of the wreck.

I had never intended it to be my place of refuge, yet it had served as such admirably. It was time to escape further from my uncle's grasp. The inclement weather would help to reduce the chances of my discovery as few would venture out in such conditions. All that remained was to decide the direction my flight would take.

If I tried to make my way west to the towns of Connecticut, I would have to travel through some of my uncle's land. The advantage would be that I knew the land and could take advantage of natural hollows and vales to avoid being seen. I would know where water could be found and could possibly make it to the settlements of Westerly and Stonington in a day or two. If my uncle were still searching for me to the north where surely the stolen boat I had used would have been found, there might be fewer of his people I would need to avoid. However, should I be caught, the truth about my father's murder at the hands of his brother would forever be unknown and surely die with me.

For me to escape to the north to the Providence settlement, I would need a boat since travelling along the shore would most probably bring me into the teeth of those who searched for me. At least being on the bay would give me the chance to see any who might approach me and allow me some chance of escape. But, still, if I should fail to reach my goal and be taken by my uncle or his minions, the truth of what befell my father would again be forever hidden.

If I headed east across the island called Conanicut to Newport, the bustling seaport and capital of Rhode Island, I could lose myself in the throng of people there and, perhaps, find passage out of the colony to Boston or New York or some far place of safety. I had not been to the capital, but once or twice as a very young boy and was unknown to any there. I would be just a face in the crowd and difficult to find.

As I sat weighing my options, I reached across to the place where the oilskin lay open on the crossmember beam and turned another fold of the cloth to reveal my father's Bible. I picked it up and held it close to my chest. I could feel the texture of the leather cover and the smell of the tanned hide. As I sat holding the one possession my father held so dear, I felt a calm come over me.

Although I knew how to pronounce the words, my understanding of many were still unclear to me. My father had had little time to teach me. Learning to read with ease, and understand what I read, and to learn numbers, had been a tall order since his return. It had only been a little better than two and a half years that we had had to live a lifetime in. He had taught me to read a bit. He had taught me to sign my name instead of making an uneducated mark. I had learned my numbers and the alphabet and had begun to use the book I now held to build my knowledge of words. I knew, or thought I knew, why my father held this possession, his Bible, the words of the prophets, in the highest regard. It brought comfort in its words and wisdom in its thought. Even if I could not read the words to bring me comfort, I knew it was there for me to learn.

A close clap of thunder roused me from my thoughts and brought me to action. I carefully placed the book back in the oilcloth wrapping. I folded the much-creased cloth over it protectively and placed the dirk in the next fold. Carefully, I doubled-folded the edges to make the package waterproof and pulled the cord tightly around the sides. I tied the cord with fingers that were white with cold and wrinkled by water.

I looked about in the partial light leaking through the cracks between the boards at what had been my refuge the last five nights; the sparseness of it, my hideaway. The stubs of my last two candles still stood high on the ledge. The tin plate and flint and steel lay on the shelf below. The small piece of canvas I had used for a blanket lay folded in the corner. I thought to myself, if ever I needed refuge again....

ELEVEN

I slithered through the hole in the underside of the hulk onto the sand flat for what I felt might be the last time in my life, my oilcloth parcel securely under my arm. The sky was overcast with ugly slate gray clouds. The rain wet the sand just beyond the sheltering side of the wreck. I saw a flash of lightning to the north and soon heard the accompanying rumble of distant thunder. I sat for a moment and watched the raindrops making small circular indents as they hit the sand. I wondered if my uncle would be desperate enough to be out in this storm. I wondered if I would ever be safe.

After a few minutes, the rain slackened a bit and, taking one more look around, I left the shelter of the hulk and walked toward the isthmus of low sand where the night before I had run for my life. I did not hurry, nor did I dawdle. As I passed the first wisps of beach grass and the slight rise above the highwater mark, I passed the boulder where I had hidden my precious oilcloth package the previous day. The hole beneath the boulder was still visible. I looked across the narrow band of sand that connected the two highlands of Conanicut Island. As I looked at the cove on the south side of the low-lying sand beach, there was no evidence that a ship just the evening before had been at anchorage in this deep-water cove hidden by the elevations on either side.

I walked across the stretch of sand toward the spot where I had been taken prisoner by the three sailors. I saw the stones that had ringed their fire. They had been kicked apart and sand thrown over the ashes and coals of the fire. It would have been unrecognizable as a recent fire pit to anyone except the keenest of eyes. Just beyond the campsite, I heard the buzzing of a hundred flies and behind a series of rocks, close to the edge of the water, the entrails of perhaps a half dozen sheep. They were already covered by flies and the crabs that would make quick work of their discovered feast. I wondered how long these few sacrificed sheep might feed a ship's crew.

I continued to walk the shoreline below the heightening cliffs along the north side of the cove. The shore was littered with boulders, large and small, weathered out from the cliff above. Occasionally the wind would gust and blow the rain into my face. Yet, being wet was preferable to being discovered.

As I reached the east tip of the island, the rock began to outcrop in ledges and the amount of sand beaches diminished. Soon, there was no beach and I found myself picking my way along the rock ledges along the southeast point of the island. This part of the island faced the open ocean and was lashed most severely by the wind and waves. I rounded the point itself and entered the small cove just behind the point. The waters there were sheltered and calm and I could climb down to the small sand beach within the cove. A small dock and fishing shed stood at the far end of the cove. I crossed the rocky sand to the side of the shed. No one was about and the shed door was held closed by only a wooden peg through a metal hasp. I removed the peg and took shelter inside.

It was small, only a few feet across with a single window set in the seaward wall. The raw wood walls were hung with wooden floats carved and shaped to identify them. Some were painted. A set of oars stood in one corner. Piled in the other rear corner of the shed were coils of rope of varying thickness neatly stacked and ready for use. Hanging on the door were several coils of lighter sail line. On the sill of the window, a rusted knife was stuck into the wood. I measured out a few feet of the sail line and cut it. I quickly bound my oilcloth parcel with one end of the cut line and tied the other end about my waist.

I looked through the window and saw the tide had reached low. The current through the channel between Conanicut and Aquidneck islands would be slack for only a brief time. If I were going to swim the narrow stretch of water across to Aquidneck Island and Newport, it was either now or wait for another turn of the tide. I knew, if the weather improved, someone might very well decide to check the cove and shed. That would mean discovery.

I opened the shed door and carefully closed it, replacing the peg through the hasp. Holding the oilcloth package now securely tethered to my waist, I walked across the sand to the edge of the water and waded in. I did not shudder at the water's cool temperature as I was already cold from the rain that had soaked my clothes and without hesitation, I began to swim to the entrance of the cove.

When I reached the rocky ledge that formed the outer rim of the cove, it was time to make my final decision. The current appeared to have slackened between the tides. The far shore appeared so much farther from this point of view than it had from the sand beach on the inner side of the cove. I was sure I could swim the distance. I let go of the rock ledge and struck out for the island shore ahead.

I considered myself a strong swimmer, but I had never challenged myself to a swim such as this. I had always heard that the currents in the west passage were tame compared to those in the east passage. I was hoping not to find the truth of that statement. The east passage into the Great Narragansett Bay was the most heavily used by commercial vessels. It led directly into the harbor at Newport and the deep channel ran all the way to Providence at the head of the bay. On a normal day, the channel would be filled with all manner of ships large and small. But the rain and wind would keep smaller craft in port. Even though I would not have to worry about discovery by these smaller craft, the wind and rain were whipping the waves into white-capped swells that slowed my progress.

It seemed like hours were passing and the distant shore got no nearer. I could feel my strength ebbing as the cold began to invade my muscles.

I looked back toward my starting point at the cove. It was certainly far in the distance, so I was making headway. I renewed my effort, assured in my mind that I could make it.

I was nearly all in when my hand encountered something as I stroked down through the water. I stopped swimming and dropped my legs beneath me. My knee struck the bottom. I had made it. I began to wade toward shore, my exhaustion replaced by the elation of success.

I stumbled ashore inside the point of the island several yards from where I had wanted to land and collapsed in the tall marsh grass that hid me from view. The rain pelted my face, and I could not have cared less. I had made it across a channel of water made treacherous by currents, heavily traveled by ships, and in dangerous weather, without injury or discovery.

I knew not what awaited me in Newport, but I was still alive, and I felt, for some reason, safer from my pursuer. I knew my uncle would not cease his search for me. Safety was not mine to have until I either escaped out of the colony or brought him to justice for his crime. But, at this moment, all I wished for was sleep.

The chilly rain continued to pelt my face and the raw, gusty wind made me shiver and prompted me to seek shelter from the elements. I cautiously lifted my head above the grass and looked about. The wind-swept grass and the occasional rock poking its dark shape above the grass were all that met my view. A line of trees began about a hundred yards distant, and I watched as their limbs bent in the increasing wind. They were the only shelter I could see. I forced myself to stand, though my muscles ached and demanded rest, and started for the trees.

The storm continued its fury as I stumbled through the sharp blades of wet grass and the soil began to lose its sandiness and become brown. I reached the trees just as a sharp fork of lightning struck just off the shore and the accompanying crash of thunder instantly was heard. I fell to my knees unsure whether it was the concussion from the lightning or just my legs finally giving out. For a moment I was motionless on my hands and knees in the grass under the trees.

After a few moments, I crawled to the base of the largest tree I saw and sought shelter in its lee from the wind. As I placed my oilskin parcel on the ground, my hand brushed against what felt like a nettle. I looked and saw the most beautiful sight I had seen in days: raspberries. There was an entire patch of raspberries. I began picking them as quickly as possible and stuffing them in my mouth. Their sweet juice reinvigorated me, and I sat back against the tree having eaten my fill.

For that moment, I felt a contentment sweep over me. I was out of the wind and rain and my hunger had been sated with delicious fruit. Best of all, I was close to Newport and feeling I was safer than I had been, if for no other reason than by distance alone.

TWELVE

I awoke to the realization that the sun had risen. It was warm on my skin and the heat of the day was rising. Near me, I could see cows grazing in the fields I had crossed in the rain the day before. The sound of their lowing brought a calmness with it. Lying beside that tree with the warmth of the new day's sun on my back and my belly filled with raspberries, I felt a renewal of strength.

After a few more handfuls of berries, I stood using the tree to steady me and looked out across the waters of the East Passage and Newport harbor. The channel was choked with small sailing craft. At first glance, there appeared to be no order to the sails, each facing in their own direction. But it soon became clear that the dance of sails was to the beat of the wind. As each boat reached the same approximate points, their sails would shift as they tacked against the wind, while others were running before the wind with booms extended and sails billowed nearly perpendicular to their hulls.

Coming into the passage was a large three-master, her sails at half reef and using the tidal current to make way. Her masts would soon join the forest of masts crowding the wharves of Newport. Looking to the right, the bustling seaport was alive with activity on her docks. From this distance, only the activity of a few men climbing the rigging of ships in port was visible. Like ants they moved about in the tangle of masts and ropes that were invisible. Some looked to be hanging in midair in an unseen spider web. Some ships sat tied up at the wharves, their holds empty, holds awaiting the cargoes of rum, cheese, and wheat they would carry to foreign ports, I thought. Some would head to a place known as Africa to sell their cargoes of rum and load a human cargo to be taken to the islands of the Caribbean, slaves that would grow and harvest the precious sugar cane that would be brought back to our colony to the distilleries to turn it into more rum to again be shipped away for profit. The ships at anchor in the harbor were likely such vessels, their holds filled with molasses and goods to be sold in the colony.

As I stood in the shade of the tree looking at the seagulls screeching and wheeling in the blue sky and watching the white sails propelling the ships of commerce across the blue water of the bay, I knew a new chapter of my life was about to begin. I felt the rope still about my waist securing my precious bundle. I slowly untied it and picked up my precious oilskin. I checked to see that it was still sealed and dry. Slinging it over my shoulder by the sail rope, I began walking through the grass toward Newport.

As I walked along in the meadow grass, passing groups of grazing cows, I wondered what awaited me in Newport. Lost in my thoughts, I did not notice the ground softening under my feet. I was walking into what turned out to be a large salt marsh and it required me to retrace some of my steps and begin to skirt its edge. The birds flitted and chirped in the reeds and drowned trees. The air was filled with the scent of sea water and grass. Before long, I came upon a rutted dirt path that ran in the direction I wanted to go. I kept to one side where I could disappear in the brush along the edge should someone approach, but none did.

It was not long before I began to see the path was widening and becoming more worn as other paths joined. Soon there were small houses coming into view. I had reached the outskirts of town. These were the small houses belonging to the dock workers, the cooper's helpers, carpenters, and the rope walkers who loaded the ships and built the barrels for the rum that they would load aboard ships and the men who twisted the rope lines that would sail those ships. These were the homes of the people that made Newport run. These were the places where the heart of the city beat and allowed the wealthy to continue to build their growing estates in other parts of the city and the colony beyond.

As I walked along, the sounds of the city began to grow in my ears. The road I followed grew wider and more compacted, its hardness keeping any weeds that might try to gain a hold from doing so. A two-wheeled dray appeared behind me and rattled past. The man holding the guide rope dressed in non-descript clothes and a slouch hat walking at the oxen's pace paid me no attention. I wondered if I could remain so invisible.

As I rounded the last bend in the road, I passed a couple of small shops and a blacksmith hammering at his anvil and I was struck by a growing sound, a buzzing, but different in some way. Suddenly, there before me appeared a scene I can still recall, even today. At first glance, it appeared to be sheer chaos. I must have stood there where the road entered the edge of the paved waterfront as one depraved of senses when those senses were merely overwhelmed. The scene before my eyes simply staggering to a youth of thirteen.

A huge plaza stretched before me with structures larger than I had ever seen to my right and along the wharves to my left. The space was paved with cobblestones with iron grates set in it at irregular intervals. Most of the stones had been worn smooth from years of traffic; some bore deeper scars from the repeated passage of carts and wagons laden with heavy loads.

To my left was the largest building I had ever seen. Made of massive dressed gray granite, its four stories stopped me as I gazed in wonder. The masts of the ships along the wharves had grown immensely in size from where first I had seen them from the point where I swam ashore. The cross spars with canvas folded beneath some and others unfurled and luffing in the breeze and those figures of men moving among them seemed to be performing a dance along the rigging.

Crowds of people scurried about, each on some unknown mission, moving to and from the ships across the square. There were more people here in this one place than I had ever seen in my life. So many carriages and lorries pulled by oxen and horse alike. Men rolling large casks rumbling over the cobbles and carrying other cargo to be loaded aboard ships. Voices rose against the din to a level of shouting to be heard. The winches squealed under the weight of their loads as they stowed that cargo into the holds of ships. Other ships at the wharves were being unloaded with a second army of workers laboring to take goods to the warehouses along the docks. The level of noise I can still feel resounding in my ears even now.

The scent of canvas and pitch tar assaulted my nose mixed with the aromas of seawater, wood, and manure that lay in small piles across the cobbles. The entire scene seemed chaotic, yet somehow fascinating. I stood in awe taking in the scene.

Such was my introduction to Miles End at the south end of Thames Street. Thames Street ran the length of the port with wharves jutting into the harbor on the west side. Warehouses, both company and privately owned, lined the landed end. Opposite the wharves on the landward side of the wide plaza were the business offices and counting houses of the wealthy. The Custom House sat on one side of the city commons up the slope from the harbor. Here too were the government buildings of the colony. It was here that cargoes were traded, and commerce held sway. Most prominent at the top of the common was a church. I would soon know all the streets of the city and all the important people, if not in person, then by reputation. But, at this moment, the site before me was alive with activity. People, teams of oxen and horse everywhere, the sight, the smells, the noise; the beat of commerce. I could feel my excitement being tempered by the fear of the scene before me. It was a world unknown to a boy raised only a few miles distant, but this was where my future lay – for now.

I was a ragged looking, dirty street urchin in salt-stained clothes with no shoes and a rope-bound oilcloth package slung on his back cautiously taking his first bare-foot steps on the first paved street I had ever seen. Moving slowly along the waterfront, moving in and out of the knots of people going in all directions, gawking at the huge ships along the docks to my left and the buildings to my right, I made my way, unnoticed and unseen by all who passed me.

That rapture was likely the reason I was not aware of the approaching danger behind me. Suddenly I heard a bellowing voice and the clatter of hooves approaching behind me.

"Move aside, Lad," screamed an angry voice, "Move!"

With that, I turned to see two huge black forms rearing above me. Instinctively I raised my arms across my face in a gesture to protect myself from the flailing hooves in front of my face. It was at that moment I felt a heavy blow into my right side against my ribs throwing me off my feet and onto the cobbles several feet away. As I recovered myself, the driver of the wagon regained control of his team and looked at me on the ground.

"Good Gawd! Get outta' me way, Boy!" His tone showing only slight concern. "Watch yer back here abouts!" he shouted as he pulled away.

Lying there on the wet cobbles, my pride hurting more than the few scrapes the fall had caused, I wondered what or who had caused my sudden fall.

"Are you alright?" a voice from behind me asked.

"I think so," I managed to stammer out.

I turned to see a boy as old as myself with skin black as coal. He was in much the same clothing as me, in fact, better dressed, with short boots and striped loose fitted pants. As he ran his hands over my arms and legs to be sure nothing was broken, he spoke again.

"That was a close one, friend. You sure no big hurts? Just a few bruises? You be fine in a day or two, but we better wash d'em out."

He jumped to his feet and offered me a hand to stand. As I gained my feet, he reached behind me and picked up my oilskin bundle that had fallen and held it while he guided me toward the edge of the paving away from the wharves where the crowds were smaller. He held my arm and started chatting about the docks and how dangerous they were and Newport itself and how the city had grown.

Only a short walk brought us to a beautifully carved fountain at the edge of the plaza. The figure of a maiden holding a large ewer with water spilling from it into a basin was something new to me and beautiful beyond words. My new friend retrieved a clean cloth from one of his pockets and wet it in the basin. As he began to mop the scrape on my forehead, the cool water felt wonderful as I gazed at the fountain. The fountain stood before a wide, grassy plot leading up to an impressive structure with a small steeple. This, I would learn, was the city commons and Trinity Church.

A slight sting brought my attention back to my companion.

"Who are you," I asked.

"Perhaps I should ask who ye be," he replied as he continued to bathe the scrapes on my hands. With a small laugh and a broad smile showing his beautiful white teeth, he continued,

"I know all the lads in town, but I haven't seen ye b'fore. As for me, they call me Toby. If ye doesn't mind my sayin,' ye look a mess, mate. Best put some shoes on if you want to keep yer feet. These stones are rough to walk on for any distance without sumt'in' to guard yer feet. What happened to yer clothes, mate?" he asked as he inspected my shirt which was wrinkled and well salted from my swim across the channel.

"I…I had to swim to the point; across the channel," I said hesitantly. "I lost my shoes somewhere." I lied rather than tell this stranger I had none.

"Ye swum the point?" he said in surprise. "Bless me! I never met no one what's done that! Why would you need to do that?"

I knew I had to come up with a reason that would instantly be believed or be faced with more questions.

"I fell overboard in the storm last night from a schooner headed up the bay to Providence. That's why I have no shoes. They'll never miss me. I did not like the captain and he didn't like me. Besides, I was planning to leave the ship in Providence anyway."

"Jumpin' ship in any event, eh?" Toby's eyes widened at this news. "That's how I got here, meself! My Papa put me aboard a ship in Jamaica," his face took on a look of deep thought, "maybe…three year ago. He tells me I will be a cabin boy for the captain and to be a good worker until I reach a port I like." He straightened his back and sat bolt upright, his pride quite apparent.

"Once I find one, I like, Papa say run from dat ship and no look back. Get yerself hid and don't be found until dat ship has sailed. I know where dis ship sails and I will find you when I follow you in short time." Toby's mood darkened with sadness. "Dat was three years ago, and he has not come."

"Don't worry, he will come," the words seem to tumble out of me before I could stop them.

"So, you are waiting too for you Papa?" Toby said in joy at finding someone else who was in similar condition.

"No, my father is dead. He was killed."

It was the first time I had ever said those words, and the profound acknowledgement of what had occurred and my present condition as a true orphan, weighed heavily on my thoughts.

"I am sorry to hear such a thing, my friend. But I think we can be fast friends, if ye like."

Toby put an arm about my shoulders and leaning close to me said, "while I am waiting for my Papa, I will teach you about Newport and you can teach me too."

As the sun was now well past midday and warmed us as we sat by the fountain watching the crowds of workers shifting about and ships moving off the wharves and others that had been standing off now tying up as quickly as space was available, Toby wanted to know of me, and I found myself weaving a story in response to his questions.

"Ye look a bit hungry, Mate," Toby said, "and we should do sometin' about them clothes. Come with me. It's late enough in the day for me to leave the work left to do for tomorrow."

With that said, my new-found friend jumped to his feet and, grasping my wrist, pulled me to my feet. He then reached down and gathered up my oilskin. Before he could say anything, I reached out and snatched it from his hands. He was startled by the roughness of my move but continued to smile broadly and said nothing.

"It is all I have from my father, Toby," I said a bit ashamed.

"I understand," he replied, "and it be the dearest possession to ye. Come along now. We need to get to the big gray warehouse across the way."

We slowly made our way through the knots of people and horse-drawn drays and such with Toby expansively displaying his knowledge of the port and Newport, in general. I was more absorbed looking at each face that passed to see if there was any sign of recognition. Invisibility was my desire.

We finally reached the front of the huge gray stone building I had first seen when entering the plaza and Toby boldly walked right through the open double doors as if he owned the place. The man sitting at the door drawing on a long-stemmed pipe hardly raised his eyes.

"Good afternoon, Mr. Janick!" Toby called out as we swept by. "I have a new friend today. His name is...." Toby stopped in mid-step.

"What IS yer name, by the by?" he questioned me as he wheeled round to face me.

I knew instantly I could not give my true name. Not here, not now. I looked past Toby's questioning face and saw a crate with the name Thomas branded on its side.

"It's Tom," I found myself stuttering. Looking at the stone of the building, I stammered out, "Tom Gray, Toby."

"This be Tom Gray, Mr. Janick," Toby announced proudly as he turned to face the immobile man who puffed on his pipe.

"Pleasure to meet you, Mr. Gray," came the unenthusiastic response.

"He'll be stayin' with the boys fer a bit, Mr. Janick," Toby continued.

"Jest clear it with Mr. Henning inside," Mr. Janick replied finally looking up at me with a keen eye that made me fear there might be recognition there somewhere.

Thus, was born the name I would carry for most of my future. Benjamin Prescott would live behind Thomas Gray and only be known to a very select, trusted few for many years to come.

As we passed through the doorway into the cavernous space of the warehouse, one could feel an immediate change in the atmosphere and temperature. The air turned instantly cooler and drier. The high set windows along the walls could not let in enough light to allow for more than a hazy twilight. The voices of the men at work within stacking away cargo just delivered or moving cargo out to be delivered either to a ship or a merchant echoed in the vastness of the space. As my eyes adjusted to the semi-dark, candles could be discerned hanging in lanterns from every support beam. This decreased the twilight of the space but little. Manufactured goods were neatly stacked to the fifteen-foot ceiling in distinct sections, roped together and marked with the name of the shipper and receiver or the ship to which it was consigned. I heard Toby's voice as in a dream saying something about three floors all like this and the topmost being off limits to such as us.

As I wondered at what I was seeing, I saw a man slowly approaching us with what looked like a ledger held against his arm. He was tall and lean and dressed in a brown waistcoat with double rows of silver buttons. As he moved in and out of the piles of barrels and crates, he appeared to be checking various sheets against shipments. As he neared us, he looked at us with what I thought was a sour disdain.

"Good day, Mr. Toby," he said, addressing us in a friendly manner. "Who have we here?"

"'Tis me recently arrived new friend, Thomas Gray, Mr. Henning," Toby replied cheerily, removing his hat. "I thought he might stay with me fer a bit, if it be in keeping with ye, Mr. Henning?"

"Newly arrived, eh? From where, Boy? Looks like you been playin' in the briny lately." Mr. Henning looked down his sizeable nose and was clearly sizing me up.

"I'm from north of Providence," I quickly lied. "Fell overboard when the ship I was on sailed last night, I swam to shore."

It was a half lie I hoped was good enough to end the interrogation.

"He's your responsibility, Mr. Toby," Mr. Henning intoned, "See that he knows the arrangement and the rules."

"Thank ye kindly, Mr. Henning. I will see he does," Toby said in a half-bow as this figure of authority continued past us.

Toby tapped my arm and nodded his head to the side in a signal to follow him.

"Mr. Henning is the warehouse manager," Toby whispered, "he's not as stern as he presents, but he can be if ye breaks his rules. He lets a few of us stay in the warehouse as a kind of security force. He calls us his 'Dock Rats.'"

Toby and I walked to the back wall of the warehouse to a space beneath the wide staircase rising to the upper floors. Here, there were several stacked raw wooden bunks, most of which were inhabited. Toby walked between the sleeping spaces and slumped on one of the lower bunks.

"This is where I hangs me hat. It's not much, but it's dry and safe and warm enough 'specially in winter. If, ye want, ye can have that one next to me."

Toby indicated a rack with one end under the stair risers and its other end near the head of his bed if it could be called a bed. As I surveyed these racks, for truly that is all they were, I noticed some were slung with knotted rope while others were slatted with rough wood. None had anything resembling a mattress and, those that seemed occupied were, instead, covered with what looked like old sails overlying rags. The one pointed out by Toby for me was planked. As I looked the bunk over, Toby sat up on the edge of his.

"That was Jamie's spot until he made a mistake," Toby said somberly.

"Did he break one of Mr. Henning's rules?" I questioned.

"Nay, Tom. He boarded a ship what was ready to sail and never came ashore." Toby dropped his head to his chest. He murmured. "He was a good sort, a good friend, but was always taking chances."

"What happened to him?" I asked as I sat on the bare wood of my new bunk, "Was he killed?"

Looking sideways at me, Toby replied, "I dunno, but more likely he was popped with a belayin' pin and woke up miles from shore with a nice lump on 'is head and a new position aboard ship as a cabin boy."

A small smile broke on Toby's angelic face as he said, "He's seein' the world, Mate! But, serious now, there is a lesson fer you to learn here and most probably Rule One: never go aboard a ship what's readyin' to leave port. Don't take no message for the captain or deliver any last-minute instructions by goin' aboard. Make an officer come ashore to take it from ye. Otherwise, ye may be sailin' afar for the next couple of years."

"Enough of that fer now, Tom," Toby brightly said, "We'll get ye some cover fer yer rack and talk with Mistress Mary at the White Horse about some clothes fer ye. We might pick up some food, as well. And I can tell ye some of the warehouse rules on the way there."

Toby sprang from the bunk and, reaching beneath it, produced a shirt and pants.

"Here, put these on fer now. Yer about my size and they'll do until we find better."

I took my oilskin parcel and deftly slid it below my new bunk at the end nearest the stair riser. It was all but invisible yet easily retrievable. I quickly changed and we were off to see Mistress Mary at the White Horse. As we left the Dock Rats' rude sleeping room, I grabbed a sailor's knit cap that was hanging on the corner of the wood upright on the last bunk. As we strolled toward the doors, I pulled it down low on my head in hopes it might further disguise my identity. Even though I knew my uncle Matthew spent less time in Newport than Providence, I wished to take as little risk as possible of being seen by him or anyone who might know me. I still hoped the search for me was going in another direction.

The early evening weather was cool with a gentle breeze coming in off the water. The waterfront was still humming with activity even as the sky was foretelling rain with gathering clouds to the west. As we crossed the plaza, Toby began to explain the rules by which the urchins of the waterfront, of which I was now one, were allowed refuge in the stone warehouse. He explained that neither Mr. Janick nor Mr. Henning owned anything in the structure but were employees who ran the daily operations of the warehouse.

This was the central shipping and receiving warehouse of the various trading houses. As ships arrived, the cargoes were unloaded and brought to this warehouse where they were accounted for, logged in, and stored until the individual traders sent their men to pick them up. Likewise, shipments to be made could be brought to the warehouse ahead of a ship's arrival and stored until loaded. The warehouse was made for the orderly operation of the port. The Customs House representatives had a specific location to inspect cargo for duties, and the existence of a secure warehouse meant individual owners did not need to be on call at all hours to receive and ship cargo. The warehouse was the idea of some leading traders of Newport and had been built with funds from certain individuals of "questionable" character. These reputed "pirates" went by names well-known in Newport. A certain Captain Tews and William Mayes were considered silent partners in the construction of this central warehouse. So there would be no disputes about who owned the warehouse, it was under the control of Customs House and Mr. Janick and Mr. Henning were employees of the Commissioner. Of course, only registered cargoes were kept within. That was not to say that other cargo did not flow into and out of the port outside the knowledge of the customs officials. Vessels were known to unload cargo in the various coves within the bay, cargoes that were unrecorded and paid no tax.

Crossing the paved work area of the docks, we proceeded up one of the streets at the north end. Toby began telling me the "rules" that had to be followed that allowed us to have safe shelter in the warehouse. The structure was open from sunrise until ten of the clock at the Customs House. We had to be inside no later than half an hour before that time or be left out for the night. We were required to extinguish all candles on the three lower floors shortly after closing, leaving only the middle lanterns on each floor lighted. It was our responsibility to see the candles were of a length to burn through the night and, if not, to be changed as needed. All lanterns to be relit by opening each day. Of course, this gave us free access to candlelight – within reason.

We were to "lend assistance" to Mr. Henning and Mr. Janick by answering their call and running such errands as they required swiftly and without delay. It was our responsibility to keep the floors of the warehouse swept and any animal droppings cleaned up as soon as seen. We were also responsible for maintaining clean water in the horse trough in front of the warehouse. Its level was never to drop below a mark on the side.

"It seems like a lot, at first, "Toby said with authority of knowledge, "but with the eight or ten of us working together, it's worth a warm place to sleep. Plus, we can get paid from delivering messages and such!"

Within a block or two, we arrived at a building lit by lanterns on either side of the door and candlelight glowing through the windows. A sign hanging from the corner of the building showed it as the White Horse Tavern. The sounds of multiple conversations flowed from the open windows.

"This is our way in, Tom," Toby said softly, "follow me."

We passed the inviting front entrance and walked to the backside of the tavern. Loud voices and raucous laughter emanated from every window along with the bright glow of many candles. As we reached the back stairs, the door leading into what was the kitchen flew open and a woman about the age I remembered my mother to be stepped onto the small landing. A rush of super-heated air flowed from the interior through the open door. In her hands were two pewter plates of half-eaten food.

"Evenin' Mistress Nichol. Wonderful night, is it not?" Toby said, respectfully, removing his cap. He elbowed me to do the same.

"Hello, Toby," she replied in a kindly voice. "Who is this with you this beautiful night?"

"This is me new friend, Tom. Tom Gray. Newly arrived in town, he is, and first place I be taking him is to yer fine establishment."

All I could manage was a shy nod of my head. Mistress Mary Nichol stood above us with her auburn hair afire with light from behind her. Her round face was set off by dark eyes dancing with a glint of fun.

"Well, nice to meet you, Mr. Gray. Might I offer you a bit of that fine cuisine that we offer? Of course, there is a cost involved to it," she said looking full faced at me with a sweet smile on her face.

"I have no money, Ma'am," I said quietly. Toby quietly chuckled under his breath.

"Your money is no good here, young squire," she replied with a small laugh of her own. "We have chores here about that need doing and, in return, we keep your belly somewhat full. The floors need sweeping, fireplaces need ashes taken away, trash needs carting to the fill, and my husband can use a hand on occasion restocking beer and liquor, and there are always dishes to be washed, just to name a few. You look fit enough and, I would say hungry enough, to make a trade." Mary Nichols took a half step back with an intent look at the pair of us.

"How long has it been since you had a decent meal, Young Tom." She asked in a concerned voice?"

I suddenly realized the only sustenance I had consumed had been some raspberries early that morning and I doubted that counted as a decent meal. Prior to that had been what I had stolen from the shepherds two days prior. I was suddenly feeling light-headed.

"It has been a couple of days," I replied.

You sit yourself down right on that step and let me get you some stew and bread. Toby, you sit too."

"Gladly, Mistress Nichol," Toby said, smiling broadly.

With that, Mistress Mary disappeared into the kitchen leaving the door open. The warm air wafting through the door brought the aroma of food to me, especially newly baked bread. The voices of those inside were louder and more raucous than before. Someone was singing a shanty popular at the time while other voices argued politics and trade. In all, the whole seemed akin to a gaggle of geese gathered in a pond with one honk little distinguishable from another.

In another moment, Mistress Nichols swept through the door with a bowl in each hand topped with a large piece of that fragrant bread. She handed each of us a bowl and admonished us to eat slowly, the stew was hot. Payment could be arranged on the 'morrow.

I held the bowl close to my face and drank in the aroma of the stew. Memories of earlier days and better times flooded back to me.

My mother had made a lamb stew much like what I now held between my hands. Balancing the hot bowl on my knee, I slowly took a couple of spoons of the delicious mixture and savored the taste. I could feel it slide into my empty stomach and felt it warming me. I took a piece of bread and dipped it into the thick, brown liquid. I leaned back against the step above me and slowly consumed it to the last crumb. Sitting on that step with food in my belly, a new friend hungrily finishing his food beside me, a beautiful evening with the moon just past full riding heavy clouds high in the sky, and the warmth of people about me, I was, for the moment, content just to be.

It seemed like a long time, but I am sure it was not, the door to the kitchen swung open and Mistress Nichol stood with her hands on her hips with the light of the tavern behind her.

"Well, young men," she inquired, "are we feeling a bit better? Body and soul be safely together once again?"

Toby and I stood at her arrival and now proffered our empty bowls, wiped clean with the last of our bread. She accepted the bowls, taking note of their cleaned state and reach inside the kitchen door to place them on an unseen table. She turned back to us with two tankards of cider.

"I see you enjoyed my cooking. This will wash it down," she said handing each of us the drink.

"How do I repay you for your kindness," I asked innocently.

"Tomorrow is cleaning day. We will close an hour early to wash the floors and clean ashes from the fireplaces in the tavern room and upstairs. I expect you here by eight in the evening," Mistress Nichols replied with feigned seriousness.

"Mistress Mary," Toby piped up, "Seein' as my friend Tom, here, is newly arrived in town and how he lost all his clothes when he fell off a ship what sailed last night, could ye maybe keep an eye fer some clothes fer him?"

"We'll see what we can find tomorrow," she replied with a smile. "Now scoot, the two of you, before Mr. Henning locks you both out!"

Toby and I thanked her and promised to be there promptly at the appointed time. Slipping on our caps, we headed off for the waterfront just as the clouds heavy with rain began to blot out the moon.

We had been at the White Horse for some time and, as we passed the Customs House, the clock above the door read twenty to ten.

"Toby," I said, "we're late. Mr. Henning will have locked us out. What now?"

Toby laughed.

"Never fear, Tom. Mr. Henning knows many things, but not everything."

As we crossed the pavers and began to see the doors of the warehouse more clearly, it was clear they were shuttered.

"We'll have to use the Dock Rats' door," Toby whispered like some master burglar. "Follow me...and be quiet." He held his finger up to his lips and softly blew against it.

Toby looked up at the windows of the warehouse on the top floor. They were dark.

"Come on. Follow me," he said.

Toby rounded the corner of the warehouse with me in tow. Pressing close to the building on a narrow ledge between the building and the edge of the wharf on which the warehouse was built, he reached the back wall of the building facing the water. Feeling our way along the wall on the vertical boards of the wall as the clouds shut out the moon and the skies darkened, I was intent on watching my step. When I looked to see how far behind Toby I was. To my surprise, he was gone! There I was, all alone, plastered against this building and my guide, Toby, had disappeared.

I knew I could not yell for him. I did not know what I should do. Afraid, with rain beginning to fall, I bent my knees and crouched down and leaned back against the building wondering what to do next. Suddenly, I felt myself falling backward and next thing I knew, I was inside the warehouse with Toby standing over me with his hand extended."

"Welcome to the secret door," he said with a chuckle.

"What happened?" I asked. "How did that happen?" I stammered as I reached out to grasp Toby's hand.

"It's the Dock Rats' secret entrance. It's been there long as I know. It's a door in the low board that opens when weight is put against it. See that rope and pulley," Toby said, pointing to an innocent looking contraption against one of the upright beams against the wall. "That stands it back in place as soon as the weight comes off the board and no one is the wiser!"

The pulley looked as if it belonged where it was. and the rope running through it was attached to a metal ring fastened to a set of boards in the lower part of the wall. The other end was attached to a lead weight of some size. When the door was opened, the iron weight would rise as the rope was pulled through the pulley. As soon as the weight against the door was removed, the iron weight would pull the door back into position and close the door as if it were never there.

"Now yer a real Dock Rat, Mate," Toby said shaking my hand. "But ye must keep the secret."

The two of us broke out in laughter, then realized other Dock Rats were asleep nearby and the realization that the hour was late. We stifled our joy and headed to our bunks. Five sleeping bodies were already occupying bunks. As we reached our bunks, Toby looked at the one above his and saw no one asleep in it. He pulled a length of canvas from it and tossed it on my bunk.

"This'll do ye fer tonight, Tom. We'll find somet'in' better tomorrow.

With that, we settled down in the darkness, each under our piece of old canvas. The hardness of the boards beneath me did little to stop the onset of sleep. I felt with my foot for my oilskin parcel. It was still where I had put it. Though I felt a need to open the book within the oilskin and read some short verses, I had no light, and my body was begging for slumber. Soon the blessing of sleep overcame my thoughts and I slept deeply.

FOURTEEN

I awoke to the sharp shaking of my shoulder and Toby saying, "Time to rise, Tom, and meet some other Rats."

I rolled from my hard bunk and put my feet on the cool stones of the warehouse floor. Before me stood an array of dirty, ragged boys mostly about my age.

"Meet yer fellow Dock Rats," announced Toby. "This here is Tim. He's been here about the longest after yours truly," he continued cupping his hand on the shoulder of a tall, slender boy with matted light hair that appeared to not have been washed in months. He was dressed in a linen shirt untied at the throat with full sleeves and loose-fitting canvas pants. He wore a blue vest with brass buttons that might have been part of a military uniform at one time.

"Welcome to the Rats," Tim said in a voice deeper than I expected. "Good to have another pair of hands with us."

Toby moved on to the next boy in line who looked much younger than I yet held an air of self-confidence. His thick black hair fell to his eyebrows and was tied with a blue ribbon at the back.

"This is Jackie, but we all calls him Scupper," Toby announced with the last few words in a sly tone of voice, drawing a quick dark leer from the boy. "We call him that because this one over here," now pointing to another of the group, "he's Jackie, also! Can't have two Jackies, ye know."

Nice to meet you, Scupper," I said extending my hand.

Scupper looked at my hand with the same look of disgust he had given Toby.

"If ye need anythin', anythin' at all, I'm yer man," he said, seizing my hand and leaning toward me in a confident, conspiratorial voice. "I can get ye nearly anythin' on the waterfront, if ye get me meanin'."

I nodded acknowledgement, though not fully understanding, and in a slightly detached way.

"Scupper is our informal provisioner," Toby said, lightening the mood.

"Could ye find him some bedding and clothes, ye think, Scupper?" Toby said, turning to Scupper. "He left his aboard ship when he fell overboard."

With that, all the group turned their attention to me.

"What? Fell overboard, ye say? What ship? When was this?" The questions were coming fast and furiously.

Wait, wait," Toby cautioned with his hands raised, "all shall be answered in good time, Mates. But no time now. We need to be about. Who are runners today?"

"John and Ezra are already gone," Tim piped up. "I'm at Customs this morning. Luke is lighting lanterns and is on call for Mr. Henning today."

"Tom and meself will make the rounds of the shipping agents this morning," Toby announced. "Tonight, we have a debt to honor for Mistress Nichol at the Horse,"

"I'll be lookin' fer some 'provisions' while I check the arrivals," Scupper offered.

"I guess that leaves me the trough, again," Jackie sighed. "Honest, guys, I can do more than that!" Jackie showed his frustration by kicking the stone floor with his ragged boot. Jackie was diminutive and wore a coat that reached nearly to his ankles. It was holed in several places and worn thin, but, obviously, he wore it with considerable pride.

With that, the group broke up and Toby and I were left alone.

"Don't pay Jackie no mind. He's the youngest and was pretty ill when he joined us. So, we try to gives him light duties until he gets his strength back full."

"What did all those things they were talking about mean, Toby," I said with some confusion.

"That's how we call our duties. Don't worry, you'll catch on soon enough. Until then, you'll work with me to learn the ropes.

I threw on the pair of shoes that had magically appeared at the foot of my rack, noticing the skin was rubbed raw on my feet, and followed Toby to experience my first day in Newport. It would be the first of so many that would fill my future. Yet, as time went by, I did learn every job fulfilled by the Dock Rats and realized we also performed an important function on the harbor front.

Much of what we did was communications. We ran messages from the Customs House to arriving ships and from arriving ships to their owners or those who had cargo aboard. We ran messages, usually written, between shipping agents and town officials. And there were no worries that these messages would be read by the runner because dock rats had no real education and could not read the messages they carried. We ran all day long and everywhere and anywhere communications needed to go. At the end of the day, half of all payments received were paid into our "Rat pool" for the benefit of all of us. Honesty was never a question.

Toby and I crossed the waterfront to the shipping agent furthest from the port to the north. It made sense to start at the furthest shipper we ran regular errands for and work our way back toward the docks. Toby explained that the biggest cargoes consisted of barrel upon barrel of rum. In fact, the number one industry in Newport and surrounding country was distilling molasses from the West Indies into rum and the number two industry was making the barrels to ship that rum to be sold in foreign ports, notably for slaves that would be brought to the West Indies and sold for molasses. It was the largest part of Newport trade at this time, but it was not the only export.

As we left the din of the waterfront, we approached a two-story building on the North Road with a sign extended over the door reading

"Vernon & Vernon. Exporters and Importers." A much rougher lettered sign announced Coddington Cove with an arrow pointing down a wide lane.

"Let me do the talkin', Tom," Toby said before we entered the front door, "the Misters' Vernon can sometimes be a bit testy if they be distracted with business. T'is said many of their ships make land here in the cove before tyin' up in Newport proper," he said in a low whisper.

With that, Toby pushed down the lever above the door handle and strolled into the waiting room with me in tow. A clerk sitting on a high stool behind a high desk barely took notice of our presence. He was not above middle height and had only wisps of hair looking like a halo circling his balding pate. His face had sad eyes with cheeks that sagged into a jowly chin. Mr. Elliott looked very tired.

"Good day to ye, Mr. Elliott," Toby piped up in a light and airy announcement, "Any messages to be run this beautiful mornin'?"

"Morning, Toby," Mr. Elliott replied in a detached way. "Only two. One to the Dockmaster. We have a ship expected early evening today. The other to the Customs House Inspector to be ready to clear her cargo upon landing."

"Yes Sir, Mr. Elliott," Toby replied respectfully.

"Have one of your fellows come by this afternoon just in case." Mr. Elliott set his quill in the inkwell in front of him and folded his hands with fingers laced in front of him.

"We have a ship overdue from its last port. Should we receive word of her, we may need another berth."

"Aye, Sir," Toby replied. He knew a ship beyond her expected arrival could be for many reasons, none of them good. We turned and left through the front door and headed back toward town.

We spent all morning and most of the afternoon going from one office to another to the Customs House, to City Hall. Everywhere we went, Toby tried to remember to introduce me. Unlike our meeting with Mr. Elliott, almost everyone seemed in a better mood.

By mid-afternoon, we had delivered a dozen messages and decided to make it a short day since we were going to the White Horse in the evening. As the heat of the day began to climb, the coolness of the warehouse called to us. We headed for home, such as it was.

As we walked toward the warehouse, Toby stopped to buy a meat pie that we shared as we walked. It was hot and filled my emptiness well.

When we reached the warehouse, there sat Mr. Janick in his usually spot. He never moved as we passed by, yet you knew your passing registered with him. We hurried to our bunks and hungrily finished our pie. Toby pulled from his pocket all the money we had collected throughout the day in the form of "tips" for carrying messages and dropped the coins on the piece of canvas that served as his blanket. He pulled a badly dented tin box from under his bunk and opened its lid. Inside was an array of coins, mostly copper, to which Toby added about half of the coins on his bunk. The other half he quickly deposited in a dirty sock he pulled from its hiding place behind his bunk.

"This is my stash," Toby said to me quietly. "We all have one and you should start one."

With his hunger satisfied, and the day's earnings from our work accounted for, Toby leaned back on his bunk and yawned. I reached down to the foot of my bunk and retrieved my oilskin package. Lifting it onto my bunk, I began to unwrap it. I noticed Toby raise up one arm and take note of my action. As I carefully removed the Bible from the oilskin, I held it against my chest and remembered my father. It had been nearly a week since I had held his book. I opened it and began to read.

"Are you reading?" asked Toby in quiet amazement. "Tom, you can read?"

I nodded yes.

"My father taught me before he was killed," I replied slowly raising my gaze to see the surprise in Toby's face.

"Could you teach me?" he asked hesitantly. "Could you teach all of us?"

I sat back and had to think for a moment.

"I don't know why I couldn't," I said, "but we would need a book for each of us. The same book."

"I bet you anythin' Scupper can find them," Toby replied warming to the idea.

"I'll only teach those who want to learn, though," I said quickly, "and we'll need to set aside a time to learn."

"I'm sure the others will want to learn," Toby said. "Can you read aloud a bit," he asked.

It was the first time anyone other than my father had asked me to recite. I smiled and turned to the book of Luke and began reading. Toby listened intently. After a half dozen verses, he lay back on his bunk and said,

"You read good. My father used to read to me, but that was so long ago. Can you read more?" Toby asked.

I began again and noticed, after a time, Toby was peacefully asleep. I stopped my reading and replaced the Bible in its protective oilskin and retied the package. Securing it in its hiding place, I stretched out and fell asleep.

FIFTEEN

I awoke from the noise about me and realized that all the dock rats were milling about in the warehouse. Toby was at the center of the crowd of rats gesturing to the others and, in his hands, I saw a book. It was my Bible. I leapt from my bunk and tore into the group surrounding Toby. I ripped the book from his hands and shoved him hard to the floor.

"Don't EVER touch my things again," I screamed at him as he lay on the floor with a shocked expression on his face. The other rats stepped back as I turned and walked back to my bunk clutching the precious volume to my chest.

Toby bounded up from the floor with his fists clenched and an expression on his face for a fight. In another moment, he recovered himself and cautiously approached me.

"Tom," he said softly, "I'm sorry, Mate, I didn't realize...I was so excited to tell the others about learnin'..."

"I'll think on that," I spat out without thinking.

"It was my fault, Tom," Toby continued, "the others had no part in it. I did not realize.... I was wrong to go in your parcel. I promise it will never happen again." With that, Toby turned and motioned to the others to give me space.

As much as I knew my reaction to be more than wrong, I could not help feeling disrespected and violated. I felt Toby should have realized how important these few things were to me. Yet, I understood his excitement at the thought of learning to read and sharing that with the other rats. I slowly placed the Bible on the unwrapped oilskin sitting at the foot of my bunk and tried to gather myself. After a few moments I picked up the book and walked back to the group of rats standing slightly away from the array of bunks. I called them all together and apologized to all of them. I explained this was my father's Bible and it was the only thing I had left of him. I put my arm around Toby's neck and told him I had been wrong. I then saw Scupper standing behind Toby.

"Scupper," I called, "I have a job for you. Actually, for all of us!"

I showed him the book as the others all gathered round. I told him we would need a book like this for every person who raised their hand now. Hands shot skyward from all present. Smiles and cheers broke from every face.

"Might take me a week or so," Scupper said. "One or two of somethin,' heh, that be easy. A dozen might take a bit longer."

"It has to be this exact book," I cautioned him.

"No worries," he replied with a glint in his dark eyes.

Little Jackie stepped forward and asked in a very faint voice, "Tom, Sir, would you, I mean could you, read just a little for us. No one has read to me since my mum died over a year and some ago." His youth and his soft demeanor always would strike me deeply. I looked at the rest of the rats and saw the anxiety in their faces.

"Come, everyone, get comfortable on your bunks and I'll read a few verses."

Everyone clambered onto their bunks and fell silent as I opened my father's Bible and scanned the page on which I had opened. It was the Book of Joshua. I glanced up and saw the looks of expectation on my audience's faces. I cleared my throat and read starting at Joshua I:9.

"Have not I commanded thee? Be strong and of good courage: be not afraid, neither be thou dismayed: for the LORD, thy God is with thee withersoever thou goest."

I stopped and looked for the reaction from my audience. The look of amazement at my ability to read shocked me.

"Read more," Luke spoke out, "please?"

I flip some pages further into the Bible and landed on Matthew Chapter 4.

"I indeed baptize you with water unto repentance: but he that cometh after me is mightier than I, whose shoes I am not worthy to bear: He shall baptize you with the Holy Ghost, and with fire."

"But what does all that mean," Ezra asked, "What does baptize mean?"

"That is what we all need to talk about and try to understand," said I, "and that will take more time."

"Time, we hasn't got, now, Tom." Toby piped up. "We need to be away to Mistress Mary's in short order."

I slipped my Bible back into its oilskin and slid the bundle into its concealment. I saw the group begin to break up with much chatter and excitement over the prospect of learning to read. Toby was busily changing into his finer clothes, and I reminded him we would be cleaning.

"Well, I can start out lookin' me best," he replied smiling broadly.

We laughed, even when I realized I had no such change of clothes. The dock rats had faded off into the dying light of twilight along with their happy chatter. Toby and I strolled out into the night with our arms around each other's shoulders, appreciating our growing friendship and the beauty of the evening. The sounds from the direction of the docks and voices of those still at work carried on the light breeze. The whole area had a different feel at this time of day. The soft, yellow light given off by lanterns and the movement of torches going here and there lent to an almost dream-like scene; the occasional voice breaking above the murmur momentarily disrupted the calm.

Toby and I crossed the plaza fronting the harbor and headed up the street on the short walk to the White Horse. It was the first of so many countless times we would make this walk. Not all would be in such buoyant company and pleasant weather. But this night would mark the beginning of a new chapter of my life.

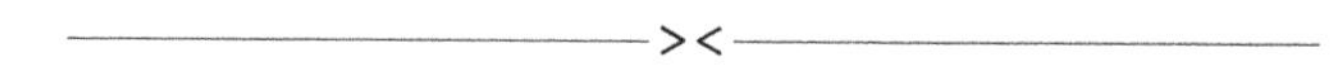

We arrived at the kitchen door of the White Horse Tavern just as the last rays of sunlight dipped behind the horizon. Unlike the previous night, the tavern was quiet with only a few lights visible. We knocked lightly on the frame of the kitchen door and heard footsteps approach from within. Mistress Mary Nichol unlatched the door and swung it full open. She stood before us for a moment before ushering us into the kitchen. Dressed in a plain, long gray skirt and crisply starched white blouse, covered by a similarly starched white full apron, Mistress Mary was a vision of beauty to be remembered by the two raggedly dressed urchins that stood before her.

"We're here and ready to work," the two of us managed to stammer out.

"Well, then, let's be about it," Mary replied to us.

Mistress Mary went about in the tavern room and dining room lighting candles with a taper she had lighted in the fireplace. As she did, she assigned tasks to each of us. We were sent first to fill buckets of water from the well on the north side of the tavern. These were added to a large caldron being heated over the kitchen fire. Next came the cleaning of the tabletops and chairs in the pub room and sitting room. While Toby and I scrubbed the tables with boiling hot water to remove food stuff, wax from candles, and rings left by tankards of spirits, our employer appeared with brooms and mops.

While the sweat on our shirts was evidence of our toil, the grumbling in our stomachs seemed to grow louder with each table we cleaned. But we complained not, as we knew food would be our reward. As we finished the tables and washed down the floor planks with buckets of hot water with some foul-smelling addition, we heard footsteps descending the stairs from the second floor. Since Mistress Mary was plainly visible behind the bar wiping down glassware, the sound startled Toby and me.

Striding into the sitting room came a man of above normal height dressed neatly in buff breeches and waistcoat over a linen shirt, knee high silk stockings and buckle shoes. His red hair was gathered at the back and tied with a ribbon. His features were chiseled yet held a countenance of kindness. In his arms, he held a pile of clothes.

"Good evening, boys," he intoned kindly, looking at us as we worked.

"Robert," we heard Mistress Mary say from behind the bar, "meet Toby and Thomas. They are the two young men I told you would be helping us this evening."

"Ah-h-h, yes," Robert replied, suppressing a broad smile. "I can see they have about finished in these rooms. Are we ready to attack the kitchen?"

He placed his burden on the nearest table and ran his hand across the top of the table checking his fingers for any residue.

"Well done, men," he said as he rubbed his thumb and forefinger together with a demeanor of feigned concern. "I see we still have ashes in the fireplace that need tending to, then off to the kitchen."

"Aye, Sir," Toby piped up. With that, Toby propped his mop against the doorway into the kitchen and disappeared for an instant, returning with a horsehair brush and dustpan. He placed himself on the floor in front of the hearth and carefully began pulling the dead ash from the low fire still burning on the andirons.

"Mind the hot embers, Toby," Robert reminded, "and be sure to drown the ashes in the small waste-water bucket at the back."

"Aye, Sir, I remember," Toby replied with a quick salute to his forehead.

"Thomas, come with me," Robert said addressing me for the time.

Yes, Sir, Mr. Nichol, Sir," I managed to studder out.

"Thomas, there is no need to be so formal with me."

Robert Nichol knelt to my level and put his hand on my shoulder.

"Would you be more at ease if I addressed you as Tom," he asked quietly.

"I think so, Sir," I replied in kind.

"Good!" He gently clapped my shoulder. "Now that we have that settled, let us go to the kitchen. "Toby, come when you finish," He called over his shoulder in Toby's direction.

"Aye, Sir," Toby replied waiving his hand over his head.

As I walked toward the kitchen door with Robert Nichol's hand on my shoulder, I caught a glance of Mistress Mary pleasantly smiling at the proceedings.

We were soon joined by Toby and Mistress Mary and our cleaning of the kitchen commenced. As we were working, a thought came to me.

"Mistress," I asked? "Is this a normal practice to do such cleaning?"

"It is not generally done, "Mistress Mary answered, "but it is the reason, we believe, our food and drink are so highly regarded. It may be part of the reason that the City Council and the judges from the court eat and hold meetings here. Our food is always fresh, and our taps are clean and spirits un-watered. Keeping order and cleanliness are next to godliness, Robert and I believe. We always try to keep sweet aromas in the rooms."

I have often remembered those words spoken that night and have tried to live by them.

As Toby finished dumping the fireplace ashes and washing down surfaces and the floor, Mistress Mary began setting out bread and honey, and Robert appeared with a ham from which he carved thick slabs of cured meat. As we sat before this feast, Mistress entered the kitchen with the clothes that had been left on the table in the sitting room.

"These are some things I thought might fit you, Tom." Mistress said. "Toby, you should look through them, as well. I know you have your own style, but you might find something to your liking," she continued glancing sweetly at Toby. "Remember, winter will be here before you know it, so do not dismiss the heavier items."

As Toby and I downed our well-earned meal, I could feel my pangs of hunger subsiding. The cider provided by Mister Nichol to wash down our supper felt cool in my throat. I quickly finished my plate and began looking at the clothes proffered by Mistress Mary. I held up some pants

I found against me to check their length. Mistress Mary stood watching my action with a knowing eye.

"If they be a bit long, Tom, I can turn them up," she said. "Try the sweater on." She continued pointing to the next item on the pile I was working through. The sweater was a bit long in the sleeves and waist, but Mistress Mary was insistent that I take it as well since, "You'll be filled out by winter."

Meantime, Toby was more than halfway through the pile in front of him and had found nothing of interest until he uncovered a smart looking long leather coat. It was worn on the elbows and neck but had been patched with brown flannel. He lifted it and let it unfold before him, Toby carefully slid his arms into the sleeves and snugged it up to his neck. He strutted about the kitchen seeking approval from all of us.

"I think that would look quite handsome with those striped pants you sport, Master Toby," Mistress Mary observed.

"I'll need to find a handsome hat to go with it, Mistress," Toby replied joyfully

I found an additional double linen shirt open at the throat and a pair of ankle-high boots. Toby and I exchanged piles and proceeded to ravage the new piles again. From this pile I found a pair of pants sewn from canvas in the style of sailor's slops that fit snuggly but had extra material at the waist that had been gathered and sewn. They could be adjusted as I grew.

"It's getting late, boys," Mister Nichols piped up, "you'll be in trouble with Mr. Henning if you don't hurry along."

Toby and I quickly gathered our piles of selected clothes, gave a hurried "thank you, kindly," to the Nichols and bolted out the kitchen door. As we made our way toward the harbor, we were lost in happy chatter about the evening. I asked Toby if he had met Mister Nichol before and he told me he had on several occasions.

"For some reason, Toby, I never thought Mistress Mary would be married, yet alone to such a handsome man," I said surprised at myself.

"He is well liked in the city," Toby shared. "He has a reputation for honest dealings and community service. It was because of him that the council meets at the White Horse. The Town Hall is not in the best part of town for late night meetings. He watches out for boys like us with little means, both he and his Mrs.," Toby continued.

As we crossed in front of the docks, we could see the great doors to the warehouse were swung closed and lights burned forth on the top floor. We skirted the front of the building close to the cool stone wall and worked our way down the side of the building to the hidden door. Toby, in front, reached the point in the wall and squatted back into the wall and disappeared. The door sprang shut silently and it was my turn to fall back through the door.

The Rats were all present and quietly talking amongst the bunks. The appearance of Toby and me brought cheers low enough to carry not too far in the still of the warehouse. As we walked through the group to our bunks, all were interested in seeing the clothes we held. Toby had worn his newly acquired leather coat home and it was duly admired by all present. I looked at the faces of the group and realized two were missing.

"Where are Scupper and little Jackie?" I asked the group.

"We ain't seen either since we left earlier," Luke replied, "They left us as soon as we was out of the warehouse and headed up East Street toward the hill."

"No worries, Tom," Toby leaned to me and said in a soft voice. "That part of town is pretty safe."

Thoughts of our missing comrades faded quickly as those present asked anxiously if I would read a bit to them. I tried to beg off, but the pleas were strong. So, I agreed to read a few verses if everyone settled down and got ready for sleep. Before I could retrieve my Bible, one could hear a pin drop with everyone in his appointed bunk. I opened to Genesis and began to read....

SIXTEEN

Morning arrived early. By the time I had reached Chapter six in my reading the night before, all listeners were lying still, and peaceful breathing came from every figure. I extinguished the last candle and joined the others in sleep. That sleep seemed to have lasted only moments when the crash of thunder and the pelting of rain against the windows awakened all of us from our slumbers. The flashes of lightning lit the interior of the warehouse with unnatural white light, followed by the sharp cracks of thunder that seemed to roll into the distance to die.

This would be a day of not much activity in the harbor. Ships in port would delay their sailing; ships arriving would stand off the point and ride out the rough seas in the passage into port. At least for now, we all could remain dry in the warehouse until the storm blew itself out or passed over. Our only problem was the empty growling of our stomachs.

We took a vote and agreed to spend some of our common funds to buy some bread and dried meat, a few pence to feed us all. Next, we drew straws to see who would brave the storm to get to the shop on John Street. Tim drew the short straw. With his shaggy blond hair stuffed under our only brimmed hat and a piece of canvas over his shoulders as a makeshift cloak, Tim looked more the scarecrow than one of us rats. Rather than risk his shoes shrinking from the rain, Tim elected to go into the storm barefooted. We all walked to the big doors and, as a group, offered encouragement, knowing full well, Tim would be soaked through by his return. The doors stood wide open with Mr. Janick only slightly shifted from his normal place to avoid the rain falling just beyond the threshold. He looked at the group as we approached.

"Sendin" one of yer own out in this storm?" he questioned in disbelief.

"We must eat, Mr. Janick," Toby explained.

With a clap on his back, and a final word of encouragement from members of the group, Tim trotted out into the storm.

"He won't be long," John said, and all agreed. As we watched Tim disappear up the street off the harbor front, we turned as one and headed back into the cavern that was our home.

"Can you read some more to us, Tom," Ezra asked.

"I can," I said, "but, it would be even better if we had the books Scupper promised to get us."

"Ask and ye shall receive," came a voice from the far end of the warehouse. It was Scupper with a sack over his shoulder.

"Scupper!" the group cried out as one. "When did you get here?" asked Toby, "and where is little Jackie?"

"I'm here," came an unseen voice from a shadow behind Scupper. It was Jackie. The two of them looked to be within an inch of being drowned.

Luke took the sack from Scupper's shoulder and John and Ezra pulled from a hook on the wall some dry rags used as towels by the boys and handed them to Scupper and Jackie.

"When did you get back? You two were gone all night. How did you get in? "

The questions were coming faster than answers could be heard.

"We just got back as you can tell from our condition," Scupper answered finally, drying his face, "and we got in while you was blockin' Mr. Janick's view across the doors. We just sorta eased our way through the open door and slid down the side of the warehouse, nice and easy like."

Scupper had a broad, sly smile as he spoke. He reached down and picked up the bag that was sitting at his feet.

"As ye requested, Sir Tom," he said as he handed the canvas bag to me. "Couldn't have done this much without little Jackie here. He's valuable fer his size.'"

Little Jackie beamed a smile as he peeled off his rain-soaked shirt and wiped the wetness from his chest with one of the rags.

"Slipped 'im through a window open ever so slightly," Scupper explained demonstrating with his hands a space of about a foot. "He unlocks the door and I walk in nice as ye please."

"It was easy, mates," Jackie spoke up among the cheers from the group.

I opened the sack and pulled out a new King James Bible. I looked at Scupper in amazement.

"Where did you get these?" I asked in stunned amazement.

"Where do ye think?" Scupper answered with a slightly playful ire. "Sorry I only could get six, but I figured any more might be taken as a serious thieving."

"This will serve quite nicely, Scupper," I said smiling at his cherub face.

Our attention was suddenly drawn to a figure approaching through the darkness of the warehouse. It was Tim; his hat brim drooped down about his face and water dripping off his protective canvas cloak. A streak of wet on the floor of the warehouse traced his path. The group, as one, turned their attention to the approaching figure. Tim stopped walking a short distance from the group and pulled from beneath his canvas cloak two loaves of crusty bread and a length of several dried sausages. A roar of approval rose from the group as they stripped Tim of his wet coverings and gave him approving hugs. Everyone then settled down to carve up the sausages and distributing hunks of the still-warm bread amongst our number.

As the rain continued to fall with thunder and lightning less prevalent, the dock rats enjoyed their repast and began to look at their newly acquired bibles. No more questions were raised regarding their source, nor was it ever mentioned again in my memory. Yet, watching these boys touching these books, fingering the lettering on their covers, opening them reverentially, and marveling at the unknown words within, made me appreciate the work my father had gone through to give me the gift of reading.

"What do the words say," Toby said breaking my train of thought.

"The words tell you things," I replied, "but, understanding what they are telling you is when you become educated."

I suddenly realized that I had spoken the words my father had spoken to me, and, for the first time, I understood the real importance of words and meaning.

And so, we began. As a group, we would spend the end of most days with a quick reading and discussion. On days when the weather was foul, we would take more time to read and discuss what we had read. Some of the boys were quick to sound out the words; others needed more time. Progression was at whatever pace the individual required.

Early on, we all came to the agreement not to let anyone outside our group know of our ability to read. Firstly, because we wanted to jealously guard our new-found ability and, secondly, we feared, if those we carried messages for knew we could read those messages, their trust in us might be lost. Once some words became familiar, a few of the rats wanted to be able to write in their own hands. If nothing else, they wanted to learn to write their names. So, we acquired some ink and pilfered a quill or two from somewhere – where was unimportant, but we knew it would not be traced to us – and paper from a few places. Each of the rats practiced making their letters and one or two showed great promise with clear, well-formed letters and Little Jackie even reached some simple flourishes, as did Toby.

Learning brought a tight-knit group of uneducated boys even closer. Attitudes began to change. They began to see themselves differently. A kind of pride in knowing they, too, could learn a skill that few of their station possessed. The questions that came early on regarding explanations of the meanings of words diminished as time passed, and proficiency in reading and increased exposure to words grew. Soon broadsides began to appear in the bunk area and were passed around to be read voraciously. Reading meant freedom to these young boys.

The seasons passed and the Dock Rats continued to perform their normal duties. The seasons turned into years and we, as a group, aged and grew into strong young men. And our days were filled in the same way, year in and year out.

Toby and I grew closer. We spent at least two evenings a week at the White Horse in service to Mistress Mary taking on more of the work as she and her husband aged. They took on the roles of the parents Toby and I no longer possessed. One evening, several years on, as we were restocking the bar, a city broadside lay on the bar and, absent-mindedly, I began reading an article aloud to Toby who was across the room.

"Thomas," Mistress Mary question, "What is this about? You can read? Who taught you? How long has this been so?"

I had forgotten Mary was in the room sewing.

"I'm sorry Mistress," I quickly blurted out. "I forgot myself."

"Do not apologize, Tom," Mistress put down her needle and turned to Toby.

"Am I to believe you can read as well, Toby?" she asked.

"Yes, Mistress," Toby replied meekly.

"How did this come about?" she questioned Toby.

"It was Tom what taught me to read and all the Rats, Mistress," Toby quickly stated. "Please don't be angry with him. He is a good teacher. He's teaching us to write."

"Well, Thomas, are there any other talents you possess I should know about?" Mistress Mary feigned displeasure.

"He writes well," Toby answered before I could, "and he can do numbers really good."

"Tom," said Mistress Mary calmly, "who taught you all this. Why did you not tell me you possessed this knowledge?"

"My father taught me, Mistress," I replied. "I did not have many years with him, but he taught me to read, to write, and to know numbers so that I might never be misled by words nor cheated of values."

"No need to be defensive, Tom, " Mary replied.

Without realizing it, my tone had changed in my reply to her.

"These are wonderful skills to have learned and will serve you well in life," She continued, smiling approvingly. "And to think you are sharing them with your friends!"

"By your leave, Mistress," Toby quickly spoke, "please don't say anything about the Dock Rats being able to read and write. It is a secret among us. We fear our ability to run messages might suffer if we are not trusted."

"I understand, Toby," Mistress Mary replied, putting to rest Toby's fear.

None of us talking among ourselves in the quiet of the White Horse Tavern could have imagined what the future held for our association. Here sat a still-young woman, greatly respected and beloved by two young men in their late teens, who would do anything for her approval and would stand by her through a coming storm.

SEVENTEEN

One evening in the warehouse after our reading session, and after most of the dock rats had retired, Toby and I wandered out into the sweet spring evening. It may have been four years since my joining the rats, but perhaps five. We sat down on one of the nearby wharves and were just enjoying the view. Without provocation, Toby suddenly asked, "Tom, we have known each other for some time now."

I nodded in agreement.

"I have never asked you about anythin' of yer past, and I know it is something you wish to keep secret. But I noticed the other day when we were at the White Horse, a man came in and you turned pale and left out the back."

I knew where Toby was going. It had been the evening of the town council meeting. As Toby and I were clearing and wiping down tables before the meeting started, the man I had feared seeing most walked through the door. My uncle, Matthew Prescott, strolled into the tavern. Dressed impeccably, he presented an air of superiority that was meant to impress all who saw him. I quickly headed for the kitchen even though my tray of dirty glassware was only half filled, being careful to keep my back to him. As soon as I went through the kitchen door, I placed my tray on the kitchen table and went out the back door. My heart was racing, and nervous sweat stood out on my face.

"Tom," Toby continued seeing my nervousness, "I don't know who he was, but that man scared you." Toby looked in my face with some concern.

"I know the story you told me when we first met about falling overboard from some outbound ship was a lie, but I have never questioned you for the truth until now. And I only do so now because of your reaction when you saw that gentleman the other night."

I thought to myself for a few minutes. Did I dare to share my secret with Toby? Was he asking me only out of curiosity? What would he think? How would he react?

"That was no gentleman. That was my uncle," I finally said quietly. I searched Toby's face in the dying light for his reaction.

"Your Uncle?" he said in quiet disbelief.

"Aye. The man who killed my father before my eyes," I continued feeling the anger rising within me.

"Had he seen me, Toby, had he recognized me, he would have killed me if he could, or would have me killed by others if he knew where to find me," I continued. "I am the only witness left to his crime."

"I have always noticed you constantly are looking about when we are out, but I never knew why," Toby said thoughtfully. "So, all this time you have feared seeing him?"

"Aye. I came to Newport because I knew he spent most of his time in Providence and the north bay," I said. "I wonder why he has suddenly come here?"

"I heard him speak before the council, Tom," Toby said after a few minutes. "Somethin' about askin' permission to ship directly from his docks across the bay, sayin' it would save him from having to transport goods to either Newport or north to Greenwich or Warwick. He was askin' to be made an associate of the Customs House so he could keep his own records."

"Are you sure, Toby?" I asked.

"Pretty sure. We can check with Mistress Mary," he said, "And Mister Nichol was also there and would also have heard it."

I nodded my head in agreement. If he were given what he had asked for from the town council and Custom's officials, his presence in Newport might have been an unusual, isolated incident. It was still the accidental nearness of him that I had feared.

"Do not tell me more, Tom," Toby said, "you are Tom and will be Tom until you decide otherwise."

We then stood and hugged and, arm in arm, walked back to the warehouse.

It was, somehow, uplifting to have unburdened myself to my closest friend. I had carried the frightening prospect of meeting my uncle, unexpectedly, some day on the waterfront or on some street in town by myself and being faced with the prospect of my eminent and swift death or, at least, the exposure of my whereabouts for my future disappearance. At the very least, it would mean my having to quickly leave the Newport area and the State for my own safety. At least now, someone would have an idea of what might have happened to me if I were suddenly to disappear.

As I now sat in my rack reading from the Bible by my flickering candle, without really thinking what I was reading, I looked at the tattered edges of the pages. I wondered about my father being able to carry this missive with him on his travels, where it had been, what it had seen. I closed it and held it against my chest as if it might answer my questions. My father had been raised a Quaker, yet a Bible is what he carried. Odd, I thought, that this would be his legacy to me. And with that thought, I fell asleep.

My life continued as before through the coming of winter. Snowfall was heavy that winter and the coves froze hard in early December. They said the upper bay froze, or nearly so, in January and the activity in the Newport harbor lessened for a bit. Fires were kept burning along the docks as sailors and dock men alike tried to shed the winter chill.

Toby and I continued to work at the White Horse Tavern. We were now trusted employees of Robert and Mary Nichol. As such, we were given judgement on feeding our fellow Dock Rats. With little need for our messaging services on the wharves and around town, Toby and I employed our group to shovel snow off the steps, spread sand on patches of ice, and, occasionally, to bus tables in the tavern. We were spending more time at the tavern as the new year started.

In January, Robert Nichol came down with a fever and heavy cough. Mistress Mary was concerned because her husband was rarely sick. Most of us thought it nothing more than a winter croup that would soon pass. As the weeks passed, the fever continued, the cough grew harsher. Mister Nichol's illness was worsening. He began to lose weight and color began to drain from his face. Then came the bloody flux and all knew that Robert's disease would waste him to the grave. It would only be a matter of time.

Meanwhile, his wife continued to run the White Horse keeping a smile for everyone and a buoyant attitude while, upstairs, her husband lay with a cough that racked his frame every few seconds. Whenever she could steal a few minutes, she was at his side, cooling his brow with a moist cloth and trying to ease his cough with honey-laced lemon or chamomile tea.

Toby and I began spending time daily at the tavern helping in any way we could. We would cover for Mistress often during the day as she would climb the stairs to spend a few minutes with her weakening husband. When the door closed each night, we would sit with Mistress Mary as she went through the receipts. Finally, one night when she was particularly tired, I asked her if I could do them for her.

"I have watched you do these so many times, Mistress, can I not do these for you so you can rest or be with your husband?"

She looked at me with tired, but loving eyes and asked "if I was sure".

"Should I have any question, you are only a stairway away, Mistress. And I promise to be careful."

Mistress Mary pushed the account books to me and standing reached across the table and placed her hand on my cheek. She swept past me with a whispered "thank you" and climbed the stairs. I sat in stunned silence, a sensation running through me I had never felt before. Toby, snapping his fingers in front of my face, brought me back from my reverie.

"Are you alright?" he was saying. "You are so pale I thought you were going to pass out."

"No. No, I'm alright," I stammered.

From that night on, I did the accounts nearly every night.

With the spring weather, Robert Nichol seemed to improve a bit. He was still very weak but would sit by the upstairs window that faced the harbor and watch the ships. Toby and I would run lunch upstairs and spend a few minutes conversing with him, his responses coming in a breathy whisper. Mistress convinced herself that all would be right soon enough.

On the fifth of May 1724, Robert Nichol died quietly in his bed at the White Horse. Mary bore her grief with a stoicism I have not seen since. The White Horse Tavern closed for three days. The funeral was attended by at least half the townspeople. Robert Nichol was well liked by those who knew him and thought well of by those who did not. It was one of the saddest three-day periods of my life.

After the burial on the third day after Robert's death, Mistress Mary, supported by Toby and me, returned to the White Horse.

"Should we plan to re-open tomorrow, Mistress," Toby asked gently.

"Aye," Mary replied, "and I think it is time you young men stop calling me mistress and call me Mary. After all, I am old enough to have had you both as sons and, if you are going to continue to work here, we need to restate this arrangement,"

Toby and I looked at each other not fully understanding what we had just heard.

"Well, don't look so stunned," she continued looking at the surprise in our faces. "Robert and I had been discussing this before his passing. If you have a mind for it, we, that is Robert and I, had some ideas to make some changes to this place. We wanted to expand the upstairs and add a couple of rooms to rent and become the White Horse Inn. Of course, that would require some full-time help. And, if you two have a mind for it, I would take you in for a share of the profits. What say you?"

"Thomas, you are excellent at keeping the books and ordering," She continued, "and Toby keeps the tavern neat and tidy and is learning to cook. Of course, having some rooms to rent to guests will mean more laundering and cleaning. We might need a laundress. But she will have to meet my approval," Mary said intently, deep in thought. "We will need to add a room for the two of you, as well. You will need to be living here permanently then. You will need to be the men of the establishment," she continued light-heartedly. "And you'll need to take more care of your adopted Mum."

The two of us were stunned into silence by what we heard. Toby and I had never really contemplated working only at the White Horse. It would mean leaving the Dock Rats of which we were now senior members. We would not be the first to have left. Luke had gone aboard a coastal shallop headed for New York. Ezra had left to try his fortune in Boston. Scupper and his pal little Jackie were still plying their elicit skills in Newport and surrounding towns. But Toby and I would be the first ones of the group I had first met nearly ten years ago to become gainfully employed in an establishment in Newport proper. In our minds, it was the end of the dock rats' group.

With summer coming on and improving weather in the offing, Toby and I knew we were faced with making the announcement of our departure from the group that had been our family before winter settled in. We knew we would have to tell the remaining members sooner rather than later. It would most likely be the end of a service that had grown along with the port.

"Well? What say you?" Mary questioned, knowing full-well the answer she would hear.

Toby and I looked at each other and in unison faced our beloved mistress and nodded our assent.

"Good! Then it is settled," Mary said with a smile. "I would like you both to move here as soon as possible. Robert did all the designs while he was ill, and I have already settled on a builder, and work will begin shortly on the expansion. In the meantime, we will find room for you here."

EIGHTEEN

*S*tanding outside the White Horse Tavern that evening, Toby, and I felt changed in some inexplicable manner. We were no longer boys who had worked for two people they loved and respected. Circumstances had changed markedly in a period of three days. We were now young men with new, added responsibility, new members, nay, owners in a business that had just suffered the loss of one of its principal owners. That evening, standing in the cool of a spring night, we pledged to one another to be the strength for our Mary and protect her and her business, for truly, it was still her business.

The doors to the warehouse were just closing when we arrived. Mr. Janick greeted us with a slight salute of his hand. I was suddenly struck by how he had seemed to have aged in a day. How many years, how many times, had I passed him, always at the door and always the same figure. Yet he seemed much older suddenly and I commented on it to Toby as we passed into the yawning darkness of the building. Had he really aged, or had I?

Our announcement of the events of the evening were received by our dwindling group of Rats with almost predictable lack of enthusiasm. Although happy for the bright future for Toby and me, the role of the Dock Rats as messengers along the port and town was rapidly disappearing as our numbers diminished. Neither Toby nor

I had realized this with our increasing activity at the White Horse. Little Jackie and Scupper wished us the best and hoped they might see us if they stopped in at the tavern. Ezra and John vowed to keep running messages as long as they could. Looking at the group in the light of the candles in the corner of the warehouse, it was clear we had all matured. We were no longer the young lads of a decade earlier. We were all showing the stubbly faces of aging into maturity. And we possessed the skills to read and write and the basics of mathematics, skills still rare among many in the town. We realized, then, that there were no more like us, no homeless wanderers, unsheltered, ill-fed children, shifting for themselves. The world we had grown up in had changed. The town had grown to a city and the city held little place for the sort we had been when we were younger. Our younger selves had no place in the prosperity of the growing community.

Toby and I began gathering our belongings in anticipation of moving to the tavern. As I pulled the oil skin parcel from its secure place as I had done nearly every night for so long, I turned to the remaining members of the group.

"Would anyone like to do a reading tonight?" I asked?

"I will read, if you like, Tom," said John. "I would like to read from my namesake, if all agree?" John was usually quiet and rarely took the lead, so I was somewhat surprised by his offer.

Each of the group retrieved their bibles and John announced, "Turn to John Chapter eight." John moved closer to the candle that was near to him and began reading. His voice was clear, and he read with little hesitation. When he read verse two, he paused.

"You taught us, Tom," he said admiringly. "You shared your knowledge with us and that is something no one can take from us."

I could feel everyone's eyes on me and could feel the nodded agreement from all present as John continued to read. I could feel the heat of blushing rising in my face, and I was proud of what I had done for these, my friends.

That night, I lay back on my rack that had become too short for my growing frame and opened my father's Bible. I noticed how worn the binding had become over the years; the page edges creased and frayed from being turned. It had been my constant companion and had taught me much as I had grown. As I read the verses, I thought to myself how a new chapter was about to begin for me and for Toby.

The next morning dawned clear and sunny, and Toby greeted me with good humor. We were excited about our prospects and ready to help with renovations of the White Horse in any way we might. Little did we realize the extent or the time it would take to complete the changes. It would take the entire summer and into the fall for the changes to be completed in the building, transformed, as it were, from a small structure into a substantial building. Since most of the construction was being added on to the original structure, the tavern and kitchen were able to continue to operate and bring in needed income, although on a reduced scale from the kitchen.

The addition of the rooms to be rented on the second floor required the roof to be taken down, which was done in such a manner that no area was left exposed to the elements for longer than a day or two. A new Dutch style roof allowed for a room on the third floor for Toby and me. The building of a new chimney with fireboxes for each of the rental rooms was the most disruptive construction of all, for the footing and stonework needed to set before completion.

By the third week of September, Toby and I bid farewell to the warehouse that had been our home for a decade. We shook hands with Mr. Henning and Mr. Janick and bade them to watch over the remaining Dock Rats with the same care and vigilance as always. With our belongings in hand, we walked across the harbor front and up the street to our new home at the White Horse Tavern and Inn.

As we walked in the cool early fall evening, I turned to Toby and said, "We are about to become known in a very public way."

Toby nodded in agreement.

"You need to have a last name, Toby," I said.

"I do not know what that is," Toby replied.

"Well, I guess that means you can pick anything you like," I said. "Where are you from?"

"My father told me it was called Trinidad," Toby replied.

"Toby Trinidad," I offered with a smile.

"I kind 'a like that. Toby Trinidad. Yes, I like it very much!" Toby said growing with enthusiasm.

"Tobias Trinidad," I suggested.

"Yes! Tobias! Even better," Toby stood a bit taller and smiled with self-satisfaction.

"Yes, Mr. Thomas Gray," Toby stopped in mid-stride and offered his hand with a beaming smile. "Allow me to introduce myself. I am Tobias Trinidad, at your service,"

"Pleasure to make your acquaintance, Mr. Trinidad," I replied taking his hand and together we laughed and resumed our walk.

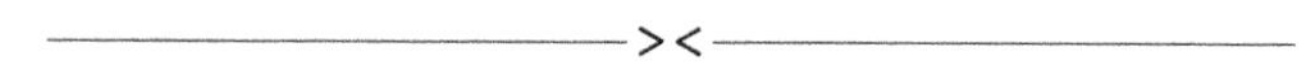

The changes that had been made in the White Horse Inn had paid off well. Over the next few years, it was a rare night when the rented rooms were empty. As Newport grew, so did visitors looking for a place to stay for a night or two while in town on business, as well as the occasional over-imbiber of the fine drink from the tavern needing a place to sleep off his indulgence. Along with paying guests came more sales from victuals and drink.

Toby and I devoted long hours to the business and became respected members of the community. The tavern and sitting rooms continued to be used by prominent members of the Newport community for meetings. The Town Council had learned of my ability to write and had asked me to function as scribe for some of their meetings. I never knew for sure, but my creation of a menu for the White Horse diners had raised great interest for its fluid, clear script. That is not to say that our Mary had not whispered in certain ears with praise for my ability.

Our reputation for hospitality and decent food grew each year because of Toby's ability in the running of the kitchen and tavern. Mary's small tavern had grown into a profitable business catering to the needs of a growing city, and Toby and I were a major part of that change and being rewarded with public recognition. While we appreciated what we were a part of, I kept careful watch for the one person I feared above all others. Toby attempted to allay my fears and would reassure me when my mood became black with worry. He would calmly remind me how long it had been since my last sighting of my uncle. Toby would tell me how changed I was from the youth who had run for my life all those years ago. And, though he was right, there were nights when the little boy would startle awake reliving in sweaty dreams the horror experienced as a youth.

As we had settled into our routine of hard work, some things had seemed to slip to a status of lesser import. Many nights the exhaustion from work had overcome any desire to open my father's bible. It sat beside my bed on a small stand. The oilskin rapping with its other contents sat below it on a shelf. One evening a year or two after moving into our room at the White Horse, I did pick up the Bible. As I opened the cover, it was obvious that the years had caused some heavy damage to the holy book. As I opened the book, I noticed the inside of the cover showed a definite crack from top to bottom. As I inspected the split in the inside leather, I felt an obvious thickness.

Bending the leather cover back a bit further exposed something small and folded concealed within. Pulling on the inside of the leather cover a bit harder, an edge of a folded paper became exposed. Carefully, I teased the exposed edge out from the leather. Finally, the entire piece slipped from its hiding place. I sat for a moment holding the Bible in one hand and my discovered prize in the other.

At that moment, the door to the room swung open and Toby entered our room.

"Another busy day," Toby started to say when, suddenly, he saw me sitting there on my bed with the Bible in one hand and something small and folder in the other.

"Tom? What is it? What do you have there? What look is that on your face?"

"I don't know," I replied, "I just discovered it in the cover of my father's Bible."

Toby tossed his bar vest on his bed and sat on the foot of my bed.

"Are you going to open it?" he asked.

Slowly, I began unfolding what I had found. It felt heavier and stiffer than the usual paper used for writing. As I unfolded the first crease, my heart began pounding in my chest. As I unfolded the second crease, a smaller paper dropped into my lap from within what I realized was parchment. I set aside the still folded parchment and picked up the paper that had fallen. I opened the paper and immediately recognized the writing as my father's hand. I began to read aloud.

> *"It is my hope this is my son who sees these words, for it means you still possess the Bible and I know you are capable of solving the clues and recovering the treasure so concealed. My only wish is that you ultimately use the wealth to benefit others."*

"What is this wealth of which your father speaks," Toby asked, his query showing on his face?

"I did not tell you much about my father, my friend, for I feared I could endanger you if you knew," I calmly replied. "I have always been afraid, if it were known that you were my friend and those who sought me could not reach me, they might reach my friends."

"I would never betray you no matter what," Toby replied firmly. "You are my brother."

"You do not know these people, Toby. I have seen what they are capable of doing."

I refolded the brief note and placed it among the pages of the Bible. I picked up the still folded parchment and proceeded to open the last two folds.

It was a map. Several placenames were noted: Newport, Narragansett

Bay, Orient point. It was a map of the eastern portion of Long Island and the lower Narragansett Bay, and all the islands scattered between and to Cape Cod. A circle on the western shore of Narraganset marked the family plantation. In the lower left corner of the parchment were two notes written in my father's hand. The first labeled what I held as Part One.

The second note was in two parts; both were bible passages. The first read Luke 3:21-22; the second was John 1:33. I looked at Toby and reached for my father's Bible which lay on my leg. I quickly found the first passage.

"Now when all the people were baptized, it came to pass, that Jesus also being baptized, and praying, the heaven was opened. And the Holy Ghost descended in a bodily shape like a dove upon him, and a voice came from heaven, which said, Thou art my beloved Son; in thee I am well pleased."

When I finished reading, I looked up at Toby.

"What does that mean, Tom," Toby asked completely bewildered.

"I don't know," I replied in similar confusion, "I honestly do not know."

"Of what treasure does your father speak?" Toby asked.

"There is much I should tell you, Toby," I said quietly, "perhaps, if we are to solve the meaning of this passage, you need to know more of my past."

With that I began to tell Toby much of what I had held back about my father, his association with William Kidd, his adventure at sea, my escape from the pirates before getting to Newport and the existence of Captain Kidd's treasure that was still buried somewhere, in my father's words, was worth a King's ransom.

"This is part one of a map to the treasure," I said pointing to the parchment lying on the bed. "I am sure of it. And this bible verse must be a clue to another piece and the second verse, a third." I could hear my voice growing with excitement.

"But what does it mean, Tom." Toby asked. "Is it a code?"

Toby went to his bed and pulled his Bible from its shelf and asked for the second verse sited.

"And I knew him not: but he that sent me to baptize with water, the same said unto me, upon whom thou shalt see the spirit descending, and remaining on him, the same is he which baptizeth with the Holy Ghost"

"Both of them speak of baptism," I said in thought. "I wonder if that means something."

"I don't think we are going to figure it out this night, my friend." Toby replied, breaking me from my thoughts. "Let us sleep on it and see what we think in the morning."

It was a restless night for me. My mind kept reflecting on my father and the scripture he had referenced on the map he had left for me. What did these verses hide in their meaning? Was it in their meaning? After tossing half the night, I finally fell asleep only to be awakened by the rising sun.

NINETEEN

During the second year of my tenure attending meetings of the Town, now City Council, acting as scribe, a person of some renown came to Newport and was quickly accepted for his charm, wit, and personae. His name was The Right Reverend George Berkeley. He was well-known in England and Europe for his writings and philosophy and his influence in education was well known. The Reverend had planned to begin a school for American natives in a location where they could not run away at the first educational discontent encountered. His thought was to establish this "college" on an island known as Bermuda.

Some tribal chieftains encountered so far in the Americas were already in opposition to sending their young to be educated by the European white men, saying, "why should we give our braves to you that they may be taught your ways and will forget our ways and language." Mr. Berkeley's dream of educating the savage lacked only funds to be realized. But Reverend Berkeley was staunch in his beliefs as an ordained priest of the Anglican Church that there was only one way to bring the blessings of knowledge and civilization to these people. He was now a Bishop of the Irish Church and was sure his mission was blessed by a "higher power".

He had been promised funds to begin his school from his powerful and wealthy friends in England and had come to Newport to await such funds.

No less than the King himself had promised such funds. Since Reverend Berkeley's anticipation of receiving his school's endowment was held so strongly, he decided to grace Newport with his presence while he waited.

It was my good fortune to meet the Right Reverend at a meeting of the City Council shortly after his arrival at which he was introduced with some fanfare and acclaim. As I sat making my record of the actions taken by the council, I was struck by this gentleman and his demeanor. His confidence, his explanations of his philosophical views I found of great interest. This man knew intimately many of the most imminent philosophers, authors, scientists, men of government, the elite of Ireland and Europe. I had never heard anyone speak as he did. Where I was educated in reading and writing and numbers, he was knowledgeable of the world, a world I knew little about.

As the meeting went long into the evening, I realized my notes would need to be heavily revised because of my interest in Reverend Berkeley. As the meeting ended and small groups began to have private conversation, I was called to a group having a discussion with the Very Reverend Berkeley. As I was introduced to him "as a secretary of the Council with a fine hand of writing", Reverend Berkeley inquired if I might be interested in being his secretary as he was seeking someone with excellent handwriting for his correspondence and knowledge of the region while he waited news of his funding.

I thought but a moment before replying most agreeably to his request. He asked what I did for an income since acting as Council Secretary paid little, if anything, he was sure. I told him I was part owner of the finest inn and tavern in Newport with my good friend Tobias Trinidad and our adopted mother, Mary Nichol.

"I am presently building a residence in Middletown, Tom, and would like you to attend me there when it is complete. Until then, I will be a guest of the head of the Council here in town. I can send word to this White Horse Tavern should I need your services?"

I assured Reverend Berkeley I would be at his service at any time and, yes, the White Horse is where I could be found.

As I walked home to the inn that evening, the full impact of what had occurred began to settle on me. I had been asked by a renowned world celebrity to join his circle of educated intimates and, what is more, to complete correspondence for him to rich and powerful people for his signature. The thought that I was capable of this honor because my father had had the foresight to teach me to read and write nearly overwhelmed me.

I opened the door of the White Horse a little beyond ten of the clock and saw no one except Toby and Mistress Mary shutting down the bar. I quickly sat at one of the tables in the tavern room and motioned for them to join me. I wanted to share with them what had happened. Excitedly, I related the events of the evening's meeting and my being introduced to Bishop Berkeley.

"Oh, Tom," Mary gasped, "how wonderful to make such an impression on one such as him,"

"Aye," Toby chimed in. "It can only bring you more recognition and more attention for the business."

"Mary, I will continue with my duties here, of course," I said turning my focus to Mary. "You and the White Horse will always be my priority."

We all sat there for some time talking and toasting, once or twice, thinking of all our shared experiences and how far we had come in our journeys of life. We spoke of the good; we spoke of the bad. We knew that there was much more ahead for all of us, and we all resolved to experience it as it came. We would be friends, always.

It was near midnight when we blew out the last candle and went up to bed. We each gave Mary our customary hug at her bedroom door and continued to our garret room. As we changed into our night dress, Toby asked what I thought my new position as Bishop Berkeley's secretary would entail as far as commitment of time.

"I don't really know," I answered. "I suspect a day a week, perhaps two. But I will still be keeping our accounts here and I won't let it interfere with that."

As we settled on the edge of our beds, we realized we were too fatigued, and it was too late to spend the normal hour or so once more reading the passages referred to on our map and attempting to figure out their meaning. And so, we extinguished our light and went to sleep.

As I lay in my bed thinking about Reverend Berkeley, and the group of learned men he had brought with him to form the core of his educational institution, I was excited at the prospect of interacting with them. What knowledge would they impart to me? What doors of learning would be opened to me?

As my thoughts raced about inside my head, I found restful sleep difficult. Then, my thoughts changed to the usual ideas about the treasure map and the two referenced passages on the section of the map I possessed:

"Now when all the people were baptized, it came to pass, that Jesus also being baptized, and praying, the heaven was opened, And the Holy Ghost descended in a bodily shape like a dove upon him, and a voice came from heaven, which said, Thou art my beloved Son; in thee I am well pleased"

I had read it so many times, I knew it by heart. But what it meant was as much a mystery to me this night as every night since Toby and I had first read it. Would we ever know its secret? I had begun to wonder. There had to be a cypher of some kind that my father believed I could solve. I could only hope his belief in me was not misplaced.

For the next few weeks as spring blossomed into summer, my normal routine took form. The Reverend Berkeley required my presence at his new home, Whitehall, usually two afternoons a week. If a ship sailed for England that week, correspondence would need to be ready to go aboard to the captain the day before. And many ships went to England every week and there was always some correspondence to which haste was attached. Since Whitehall was about an hour's walk from the city, I found myself making frequent extra trips nearly every week.

But I did so willingly because it gave me the opportunity to meet all the members of Reverend Berkeley's entourage. There was a Mr. Smibert and a Mr. James who were noted artists. Mr. James, I had gotten to know quite well from his very frequent visits to the White Horse, and his making use of our rented rooms only slightly less frequently when he was too impaired by his imbibing to return to his lodgings. Mr. Pachelbel, son of the famous composer, and Mr. Dalton were to form the faculty of music at the new college.

The greatest opportunity afforded me on these visits to Whitehall were the books in Bishop Berkeley's library. I could borrow these two at a time and Toby, Mary, and I would read them voraciously. These volumes covered many subjects beyond philosophy and widened our interests in a variety of ways.

It soon became apparent to all that Mr. John James had developed an affinity for strong drink and would be of little use as a member of any faculty of any school. The Reverend Berkeley dismissed Mr. James and he returned to England, thereby costing the White Horse Tavern one of its most profitable clients. However, we had many who frequented the tavern and dining room regularly. Mr. James's departure was unnoticed by most.

And so, as the days lengthened, Toby and I continued to run our routine of work and each night we would ponder the meaning of Luke 3:21-22. We would sit with our Bibles and read and re-read the verses. We would try to rearrange the words, find some hidden meaning. Then, one evening, as Toby sat to my right at the small table in our room, reading one more time the verses by candle, I laid my head on my forearms on the table in frustration and pushed my Bible toward Toby.

"Here," I said, "read it from mine and tell me it's different."

Toby smiled and gave a quiet laugh. He picked up my Bible opening it to the Book of Luke. As he lifted the page to read, I could see the light of the candle flame behind the page. As Toby began to read, I stopped him.

"What is that on the page?" I asked. "Do you see it? Those holes. See them? Is something eating the page?"

Toby looked at the page and held it up so he, too, could see the candle's light through the page.

"I don't think anything is eating the page," he said. "There are no other holes on the page other than our two verses," he continued with excitement rising in his voice.

I lifted my head as Toby pushed the Bible to me. He reached for his Bible and flipped the worn pages to Luke.

"Mine does not have any holes, Tom," Toby said quietly.

"Toby, get a piece of paper and copy out the verses," I said softly, trying to stay calm.

It only took a few moments for Toby to return with a blank sheet of paper and a lead. In that time, I had had a chance to look more closely at the arrangement of these mysterious holes. Some letters had but a single pin hole struck above them, and others held two holes.

Toby finished copying the versus and I read to him the letters with markings above them, telling him whether it was one hole or two.

"Ready?" I asked. Toby nodded. "Put the number of dots above each letter I call out."

We began.

"Put a single dot over the 't' in 'baptized', another over the 'r' in 'praying', another over the 'i' and 'n' following 'descended'. Put another dot over the 'i' in 'bodily', another over the 'T' in 'Thou', and another over the 'y' in 'my'. There are no more single holes.

I could feel the excitement welling up in my chest. My heart was pounding. How could we have missed these markings for so long.

"Tom, "Toby said cautiously, "it spells Trinity!"

We looked at each other in stunned silence.

"Let's go on," I said.

"Two dots over these letters. The 'N' in 'Now', the 'e' in 'people', the 'w' in 'were', the 'y' in 'praying', the 'o' in 'opening', the 'k' in 'like', the 'r' in 'from'. That is all there are. What does that give us?" I asked, my excitement now uncontainable.

"I think it says 'New York', Toby replied quietly. "I mean, it's misspelled, but all the letters are there!"

'My father once told me he had met his future Captain at a church in New York under construction. I believe he called it Trinity Church," I said unable to control my excitement any longer.

The two of us kicked back our chairs and embraced in a dance around the room. We had unlocked the location of the next section of the map. As we danced in delirium, it suddenly dawned on us that we had unlocked the general location, but where was the actual map piece to be found. Churches were large structures with many places where a piece of parchment or linen could be hidden.

Just as suddenly as we had celebrated our success, we suddenly realized how small our success really was. We knew there had to be more to the message. Had we missed something? But, what? We picked our chairs back up and sat back down. We quickly opened my father's Bible to Luke 3 and held the page up to the candlelight. There were no further marks of any kind around the letters in the two verses.

"Perhaps it is in the other verse, Tom," Toby offered.

I quickly flipped through the pages and found the reference made on our map in the Book of John. We anxiously held the page to the candle and, yes! There were the holes! As carefully made as in the verses of Luke. I read the verse to Toby for him to copy out. When he was finished, I began to read the letters.

"One pinhole over the 'n,' the 'e,' and the 'w' in the word knew. The one over the 'p' in 'baptize.' Then another over to 'o' in 'unto.' Another over the 'r' in 'Spirit.' The last one with a single pinhole is the 't' in 'baptizeth.'"

"Newport," Toby exclaimed! "It reads Newport!"

"Okay, okay," I blurted out. "Let's do the rest. Put two dots over the 't' in 'that'. The next is an 'r' in 'water', then the 'i' in 'said'. Next is the 'n' in 'Upon'. Put two dots over the 'I' in 'remaining'. Next is the 'T' in 'The' and, finally, the 'y' in 'Holy'"

"Trinity, Tom! It says Trinity right here in Newport! The Church at the head of the Commons!"

We again rejoiced for now we knew the location of the last two pieces to the map. We danced to exhaustion and then realized we still did not know where within these locations to search for our prize.

We decided not to share what we had discovered with anyone, including Mary, and continue to work on deciphering more information. We decided to sleep on it and allow our excitement to be tempered by what we still needed to learn. Even so, sleep came more easily that night than it had in many weeks. I finally knew that my father's faith in my ability was warranted.

TWENTY

Neither Toby nor I could sleep soundly that night. Our discoveries the evening before had given us a lift not only spiritually, but physically. As we sat with Mary for breakfast of tea and biscuits with marmalade, our smiles and light banter betrayed our new outlook to Mary.

"You two look like cats that swallowed canaries. What has the two of you so full of joy this morn," she said with a smile.

Toby and I looked at each other and decided without a word, we needed to share our secret with Mary, but we had to swear her to secrecy.

"Mary, we have something we want to tell you." I began.

"But we must have your absolute oath not to speak of it with anyone," Toby broke in. "It could be dangerous for any of us to speak of it."

"Aye, Mary," I continued, "there are those who have killed and would do so again for what we have discovered."

Mary's smiling expression suddenly changed. Her buoyant smile was swept away, and a more serious expression crossed her face as she sat between us.

"Oh, boys," she said in a low tone, "what have you done."

Toby and I burst into laughter at her assertion.

"We? We have done nothing wrong, Mary," I managed to stammer out. "No, no, it is something that may benefit all of us. However, Toby is right. There are those who have killed, and could do so again, if what we have discovered is true. We must not speak of it to anyone. Do we have your word on this?"

"I swear on Robert's soul," Mary responded solemnly. We knew this to be her most serious oath.

"Toby and I think we have discovered the whereabouts of a map leading to a treasure," I said to Mary. "We, of course, will need some time to piece it all together, but it appears to be genuine."

Mary's eyes widened and her jaw began to drop.

"This is the news you two have," she said in surprise. "A treasure, you say. And from which one of our sailor patrons did you 'acquire' this bit of information?"

"It is a map, Mary," Toby chimed in.

"Oh, beggin' me pardon. A map, no less? And I suppose it marks the spot with "X" and is just sittin' there waitin' for the two of you to go and dig it up? How much did you pay for this 'valuable' piece of fool's treasure? I expected better from the two of you!"

"No. Mary," I started to say, "it's not like that."

"Treasure...I suppose you're looking to go after this now and leave me all alone to run this place," Mary opined with tears welling in her eyes.

"No, Mary," Toby said as he sprang from his chair and held Mary as she rose from her chair. "Please. Let us explain."

A handkerchief appeared from some unseen source and Mary used it to dry her eyes. Calming herself, Toby helped her back to her seat. I then explained about the map I had found in my father's Bible and the fact that there were two more sections of the map yet to be retrieved. I told her of the coded message but stopped short of revealing our success in deciphering the code. I glanced at Toby at that point and got an approving nod.

"Why would your father have a map to a treasure, Tom," Mary quietly asked?

"My father had gone to sea for a few years, Mary, when I was young. He apparently fell in with a pirate crew for a brief period and it came into his possession," I offered in way of explanation. "He warned me before he died that there were men who might be looking for him if they ever thought he knew where the treasure might be."

Mary seemed satisfied with this explanation and took a sip of her tea.

"I do not know what fortune you seek, but this place could not be run by me alone at this point," she said thoughtfully. "So, I am happy to know you will not be off hunting this treasure and leaving me."

"Mary," both Toby and I said in unison, "we would never leave you here alone." We rose together and gave our heart-felt assurances and awkward hugs to Mary and a wink to each other.

With that, a knock at the back door made us aware of a messenger from Bishop Berkeley. He wished my presence at Whitehall as soon as possible. I finished my last sip of tea and was off in the brisk late spring morning to the Reverend Berkeley's.

The way to Whitehall was a pleasant walk. Newport was growing. It had already grown in the fifteen years or so since I had arrived. The roads had been greatly improved for carriage traffic and the number of cobblestoned streets in town extended farther and farther every year. I thought back to the days of the Dock Rats. They had ceased to exist some time ago. And yet, I wondered what had become of Little Jackie, Luke, Scupper, Ezra, and John. I wondered if their ability to read and write had stood them well.

I arrived at Whitehall to a flurry of activity. The structure was impressive and in a design that was new to the area. I found my way into Bishop Berkeley's study and waited by the door while he finished giving instructions to one of his footmen.

"Ah, Thomas," he summoned me. "I find I must make the journey to New York to consult there with a fellow academic this coming week. I, therefore, shall not require your services for the next couple of weeks or so."

New York! There must be some way to convince the bishop to take me with him!

"Sir, I have never been to New York. Would it be possible for me to accompany you on this trip?" I asked, trying to hide my desire to go. "I have heard much of this city and would like very much to see it for myself. I would be willing to pay my own passage and lodging, Sir."

"You seem keen to me to go and explore the big city of New York, Tom." He replied. "Come as my guest. You can travel as my secretary, in name at least. We leave on the packet boat a week from Monday at six in the morning. Meet me on the dock by quarter to."

"That is exceedingly kind of you, Sir. I shall be there without fail."

After completing a few short correspondences for the bishop's signature and preparing them for their trip the next morning, I was free to return to Newport. As I left Whitehall, I felt like my feet fairly flew above the ground. I was going to New York! I would have the time to explore one of the largest cities of the colonies and to find Trinity Church. Yes, Trinity, New York. The location of another part of the map. It was only fate that could have provided such an opportunity.

I was back at the White Horse in what felt like half the time it normally took, but I was neither more fatigued nor less excited about my trip. I came through the kitchen door of the inn and immediately saw Toby stirring a pot on the stove. I grabbed him by the arm and pulled him to the back porch.

"What if I were to tell you I am going to New York next week?" I said to him in a whisper. Toby pulled back from me with a look of disbelief on his face.

"I would say you were daft, taken leave of your senses. Or the luckiest so-and-so I know!" Toby broke into a broad smile and hugged me as I hugged him. "How," he asked?

I told him of the invitation from the Reverend Berkeley and the good fortune that he had agreed to my request to accompany him.

"Even so, I should have some money. I know he said he would cover expenses, but I should carry some coin with me," I said thoughtfully. "Do you think Mary will mind that I will be gone a few days?"

"It'll be fine," Toby reassured me. "Mary would want you to go, especially if it has to do with the treasure map." Toby placed his hand on my shoulder and gave a hardy laugh.

"This also gives us a bit more time to think about where I should search once I find the church," I said.

The next week was our normal routine with the tavern being busy every night until closing and food flowing out of the kitchen at a constant rate. With the coming of spring and lengthening days with mild weather, the wharves were constantly filled with shipping and commerce was booming. It was clear that Newport was an important port.

During the week, we sat down with Mary and explained about my going to New York for a few days. Her response, while enthusiastic, was more in the vein of getting this idea of treasure out of our heads by my failing to find any part of a map rather than hoping for our success. While we understood this response, we had hoped for enthusiasm in another direction.

Every evening, Toby and I poured over my father's Bible. Why had he chosen this passage? Why did both passages deal with baptism? What was the significance of the churches? All good questions that left us without answers.

I spent all that week before the trip to New York at Whitehall completing correspondence for the Reverend Berkeley under a title new to me of Dean of the yet unfounded college. Many of these letters were addressed to individuals of other institutions whose names I had become familiar with through my time with the Reverend. Most were seeking advice on establishing curricula and expressing some concern over the time it was taking to receive promised funds.

Finally, Monday morning arrived, and I was up before dawn and packing my small bag. Toby sat on his bed watching me. I picked up my father's Bible and stood with it in my hand, my fingers cradling the spine of the book.

"Toby," I said looking at him, "I am not taking this with me. I know the verses by heart. I am hoping I will have luck in finding that which we seek. Should anything happen, you will have this to carry on."

"Nothing is going to happen except enormous success," Toby replied.

I closed my bag, drawing the strings to close the opening and swung it over my shoulder.

"I'm off to the city," I announced.

As I came down the stairs to the kitchen, Mary was pouring a cup of tea for me.

"You will need this today for it will be a long one," she said with a note of concern in her voice.

Mary produced two fresh-baked sugar muffins and, wrapping them securely in a napkin, slid them into my bag.

"These are to keep you fed, even if you don't think you need them," she warned with a smile. "You be careful in the big city," she said with deep sincerity. "After all, you are like my son, and I will worry until you are back home."

I hugged Mary who was truly my second mother.

"Don't worry. I will be careful," I whispered into her ear.

I downed the cup of tea in two large gulps and headed out the kitchen door.

As I crossed the plaza toward the docks, I could see the Reverend Berkeley's carriage pulling up to the dock usually occupied by smaller sailing craft. I reached the door of the carriage in time to open it for my patron and greeted him properly.

"On time, as usual, Thomas," he responded pleasantly. "Let us get aboard so we can catch the morning north wind."

We hurried down the wharf to a small ship that might be considered a coastal schooner and hurried up the gangway, greeting the captain as we passed. The last of a small cargo was being brought aboard and we were ushered to a small stern cabin we would occupy on the trip. My small bag was stowed with the Reverend Berkeley's two trunks along one side of the cramped cabin.

The cabin was damp and dark with a low ceiling and two small windows facing aft. A bunk was built into the side wall of the cabin and a small table and bench filled the room. Against the remaining wall was piled the luggage we brought aboard. The Reverend and I hurried back on deck to watch the rising sun and the activity of the crew.

In no time our small ship had slipped her lines and we were backing sail out into the harbor. We soon caught the early morning wind coming down the bay and picked up speed as we headed out into the larger body of water known, in general, as Block Island Sound.

As the sun rose higher in the east in a clear and cloudless sky, the wind made its usual shift to the southwest and our little ship scudded along on an easy starboard tack. The Reverend and I walked about the deck and conversed about his trip to New York. He talked of his life in Ireland and the time he had spent in London. The Reverend had an eye for architecture and lavished praise on the great buildings of the city. Much time passed as we walked about the deck. We came to stand on the bow after several turns about the deck and were watching the coastline pass by when we saw the entrance of a large harbor and an obvious large town beyond.

"Ah," said Reverend Berkeley, "that would be New London I venture to say."

"It is quite a big city, is it not, Sir?" I asked.

It is perhaps larger than Newport, but nothing close in size to our destination," he responded with a smile. "We will be passing yet another city on our journey a bit larger than this, but it has Yale College to recommend it as an established city. And it is still much smaller than our destination of New York. As you know, I have corresponded regularly with Rector Williams over the months, and I will be making a visit to see the college."

Indeed, I did know the name Elisha Williams. I had completed many letters addressed to this esteemed gentleman. As Rector of Yale College, he was already leading the curriculum to a return to its former guidelines. He had increased the scope of the college, having awarded honorary degrees in medicine. Only recently, a letter from Reverend Berkeley had congratulated Rector Williams on the new residence built at a corner of the college property.

Our captain approached us and interrupted our discussion.

"We'll be portin' 'ere overnight," he relayed with a heavy accent. Feel free ta' walk the town but be back by night. We'll sail at sunup ta' make New York by just past high tide."

"Might we have time to visit the college here," the Reverend asked? "Could we delay New York for a day?"

"Reverend, I got a schedule to keep and a day's delay ain't no part of that," the captain replied sharply. "If ye want me to leave ye 'ere, you'll have to foind another ship to take ye the rest of the way to New York. Ye paid me fare to New York and that I be willin' ta' do. But I'll keep to me schedule. It'll cost ye a new fare for another ship. I make no return on monies paid."

The ship rounded the point east of the harbor and dropped most of her sail. The captain barked orders and the man at the helm deftly spun the wheel and slid alongside one of the wharves.

We decided to leave the ship and continue walking that part of town within a block or two of the harbor. The Reverend continued speaking of Rector Williams and the success of Yale, and the hopes he held for success equal to that institution for his own endeavors. He explained his philosophy of education, his desire to educate both academically and in religion, those he saw as lost without instruction. I did not make argument to the contrary but merely made the point that the students attending Yale were hardly the natives of the frontiers, but sons of colonists. While this was acknowledged by my mentor, his determination to spread the benefits of education to those who had not been given the opportunity, was his paramount belief.

Our lively discussion and the Reverend Berkeley's obvious interest in Yale College continued until we realized the chilling air of evening had come and the narrowing light of sunset had long disappeared. It meant we should return to our vessel. We were late for supper which was a simple meal of a stew of unidentifiable meat, perhaps lamb, and crusty bread. The captain and first mate were already at table and ate in deafening silence. The Reverend attempted a conversation once or twice and was meant with one, or two, word responses. Only when he asked about the vessel did the captain speak with some interest about her history and his time as her master.

He was English by birth and had grown up in a small village on the Irish Sea. He no longer had family in England and had been at sea starting as a boy of eight. The sea was his home, and his crew were his family. And that was that. The ship was one of many he had commanded over the years. He considered her a fair sailor, not the best he had ever been master of, but certainly not the worst. She sailed well into the wind and lost less than most when tacking. He had commanded her for almost three years.

Supper finished, we had little to entertain us and so we retired to our cabin and slept. I was happy the Reverend had nothing more to relate about Yale or Rector Williams and soon found myself asleep.

I was awakened by the sound of feet moving on the deck above me. The weak light coming through the small cabin window told me the sun was about to rise. I looked at the Reverend still asleep in his bunk. I quietly dressed and left the cabin, closing the cabin door as quietly as possible.

I came on deck to see a whirlwind of activity. Crew were pulling lines, raising sails, orders were being shouted. We were already away from the dock and heading to open water. As we left the harbor, the sun crept over the eastern horizon.

We passed into the river known as the East River just as the sun lowered over the horizon formed by the island. We had been under sail the entire day. It had been a magnificent day. The salt air, the consistent wind had allowed us to make an excellent time of our voyage. We sailed with the current, admiring the northern wilderness of the island of Manhattan. We would soon reach its southern end and our destination of New York.

TWENTY-ONE

We landed in a gathering darkness at a wharf on the west side of the river just where the river entered the huge harbor of New York. The streetlamp lighters were busily going about their duties shedding light upon the darkening streets. Arrangements were made with the captain to have our trunks delivered to our lodgings in the city. These were to be on Pearl Street. With this done, The Reverend and I started our adventure into the city seeking a place for dinner.

I was astounded by the number of people out in the evening air, far more than one would see in Newport. The level of noise just in the street was equal to that of the waterfront in Newport at the busiest of times. The feeble light cast by the streetlamps was bolstered by light coming from windows facing the street. Yet, the quantity of light could hardly be considered bright enough to see clearly. One had to watch their step so as not to inadvertently bump into fellow walkers.

We soon found a tavern that advertised a menu in its window and decided it was respectable enough to enter. By name, it was The Rose, appropriately enough on Rose Street, just off Bowery Lane. As we enjoyed a hardy meal, the Reverend told me of his plan for the next day and then asked me what my plans for the day might be?

"I have a desire to find a certain church my father once spoke about,"

I replied, trying hard not to be overly enthusiastic. "I believe it is called Trinity Church."

"I know of this church," Reverend Berkeley said setting his fork down and leaning enthusiastically toward the table, "It is well known in the city and beyond. It is the Rector I know well! He is Will Vesey, an old friend I met when he was at Oxford, as was I! He was a protégé of Increase Mather at that time and I believe he has been Rector for some time here in New York. I would be happy to make introduction to him for you, Tom," the Reverend waxed warm in his speech. "Had I thought of him, I might have made it a point to see him on this visit. I am scheduled to meet the headmaster of Collegiate School in the morning, but if you will delay your visit to Trinity until midday, I should like to join you and see my old acquaintance."

"It is a large city with much to see," I replied, my mind bursting to say no. "I can certainly wander the city and meet you at the church at noon."

"Excellent!" was the reply from the Reverend. He seemed buoyed up by the anticipation of meeting his past friend.

We finished our meal and our most delicious ale and headed off to our lodgings at an inn on Pearl Street only a block or two from where we were. We arrived in good order and went to our room on the third floor. Our luggage was in our room and no time was wasted changing into our night dress and getting to bed. Tomorrow would be an exciting day and I hope one that would get me one step closer to my father's secret.

Sleep was difficult on the unfamiliar mattress I found on my short bed. And, alas, the snoring of my roommate did not aid my quest for sleep. No sooner had I finally closed my eyes than the early morning clatter from the street awakened me again. As I wiped sleep from my eyes, I realized the Reverend was already gone. I quickly got up from my bed and washed at the basin on the stand in our room and pulled on my best set of clothes from my bag and headed downstairs.

Reverend Berkeley was nowhere to be found. I asked the innkeeper if he had seen my companion. In reply, he handed me a note. All it said was we would meet at Trinity Church just before noon. I asked the innkeeper if I might have tea and some breakfast and if he knew in what direction I might find Trinity Church.

"It's only a short walk down Pearl and turn left onto Wall Street. Stay on Wall and you'll find the church at Broadway right in front of ye."

I thanked him for his directions and within minutes a scone and tea were on the table before me. I sat there sipping my tea and enjoying the fresh scone with a bit of jam that had come with it and thinking about the verse from my father's Bible. I was so close to where I knew the next piece of the map had to be, but with no more idea where to look for it than I had when I left Newport.

"Pardon, young Sir," I heard the innkeeper's voice as it broke into my thoughts.

"Yes," I replied, a bit startled.

"Am I given to understand, you and your traveling companion will be staying one more night?" the innkeeper inquired.

"I believe so," I replied absently, "I will be seeing him this afternoon and will be sure to confirm that for you."

That reply seemed to satisfy the innkeeper and I finished my breakfast in silence. I rose from the small table I was seated at by the front window and, bidding the innkeeper farewell, headed out into the street.

It was a mild spring morning, and the warmth of the sun made a coat unnecessary. As I strolled along the street taking in the sights and smells of the city, I was struck by the variety of dress and languages that I could hear. The carriages that passed on the street were a mixed variety of farm wagons, many drawn by oxen, and more elegant carriages being drawn by horse. By far, the most preferred form of transport was horseback. All along the street were hitching posts and the clip-clop of hooves on the cobbled streets echoed about the buildings, as did the rumble of carriage wheels. Pedestrians had to mind themselves attempting to cross the streets.

I turned the corner onto Wall Street and headed west. The sun warmed my back as I continued my leisurely pace. Very soon, I could see a spire rising before me. As I drew nearer, the gambrel roof of the structure came into view and the stone façade of the rear of the building, along with the spire, clearly identified it as Trinity Church.

When I reached the corner of Broadway, I realized that the front of the church was ahead of me facing the much larger Hudson River to the west. I crossed the street known as Broadway and walked the length of the building rounding it to its front. I stopped for a few moments and admired Trinity Church. It was impressive to the eye. A rectangular structure of considerable size with a soaring steeple in the middle of a bustling noisy city: it seemed to almost emerge as a place of calm. The sounds of the city seemed not to be quite so raucous. The picturesque shade trees in the graveyard beside the structure rustled in the gentle wind coming off the river.

Since it was still well before the noon hour, I decided to continue my walk south to the section of the city I had been told was called The Battery. Returning to Broadway, it was obvious the wide expanse was well named and one of the busiest roads of the city. Within a few short blocks, I found myself standing at the southern end of the island looking out on the immense harbor of New York. It was magnificent to see the amount of commerce taking place upon these waters. Ships of all sizes and varieties, some scudding over the waters toward unknown destinations, while others stood drawing in their nets catching the fish that would feed this great city. Lost in my reverie, I did not realize how much time had passed. I turned from the pleasant scene I was enjoying and started to climb the slight hill of Broadway back to Wall Street and Trinity Church.

I was a bit late arriving at the church and cut through the tombstones to reach the front doors. To my surprise, I found Reverend Berkeley had already arrived and was engaged in animated conversation with a gentleman in the black dress and white throat bib of a churchman. He was shorter than Reverend Berkeley with a longer face and pleasant smile. Like my mentor, his eyes captured your attention when he spoke.

"Ahh, Thomas," I heard Reverend Berkeley say as I approached. "Allow me to introduce you to William Vesey, an old acquaintance of mine, and rector of this fine church and congregation. Rector Vesey, allow me to introduce Thomas Gray, my secretary."

"Your Servant," I replied to Rector Vesey.

"My pleasure, young sir," Rector Vesey replied in a wonderfully full voice.

"I understand from Reverend Berkeley here that you have a special interest in this church," the Rector continued.

As we stood on the walk leading into the church in the warmth of the day, I was suddenly unsure how to approach the subject of my interest.

Well, Rector," I awkwardly began, "my father once stopped in this church many years ago while it was under construction and the impression it made on him stayed with him until his death."

"Is that so," Rector Vesey replied with his chin cradles in his hand.

"While he was here," I began again, "he spoke with a man who was building the church, a person of some merit within the city, I understand, who was erecting the actually stonework."

"I believe you are describing Mr. William Kidd," Rector Vesey said quietly.

"Now there is a name I know," Reverend Berkeley inserted.

"Yes, George, I would think you might," Rector Vesey said in a knowing voice. "Why do you ask of him, Mr. Gray? What is your interest in him?"

I was beginning to feel cornered and unsure how to proceed. What I said next might determine if I received any information helpful to me in finding what I sought or exposing the truth of my history.

"It was long ago that my father spoke of him," I began, "but, I believe that could be the name."

"You speak of one who was a great supporter of this church and lent much labor and personal treasure to its construction," Rector Vesey spoke in very measured tones. "He put much effort into this, his parish. When it was finished being built, he made gifts to furnish it and make it a proper place of worship. And then, he was lost to us."

Rector Vesey cast his eyes toward the ground.

"You see, Mr. Gray, your father spoke of a man who was once part of the city's elite, a prosperous merchant, married into wealth and with children. As a prominent member of the city, it was incumbent upon him to accept a commission from the governor as a privateer in the conflict late of the last century."

The Rector shook his head, not lifting his eyes.

"All was well until...."

"Tom, Captain Kidd turned from privateer to pirate," Reverend Berkeley broke in. "If I recall correctly, he heard he had been declared pirate and attempted to sail into the port of Boston to avoid apprehension. However, he was arrested and taken to London where he was found guilty of piracy on the high seas."

"He also was found guilty of murdering a crew member," Rector Vesey added having recovered himself.

"England decided to make an example of him," Reverend Berkeley continued. "They hanged him and gibbetted his tarred body at Tyburn as a warning to others who might think of turning pirate. I saw his body hanging there in that iron cage perhaps a year after the event of his hanging."

"While he was part of this church, he was a righteous man," Rector Vesey opined. "I cannot speak to what occurred after, but it was a great personal disappointment to me."

"You spoke of his dedication to this parish," I began again, "of gifts he bestowed?"

"Oh yes," Rector Vesey brightened, "beside the work he did on the construction, he paid for a family pew, gifted a beautiful carved baptismal font, and made the first donation to the organ fund."

A baptism font! Did my ears deceive me?

"When the news reached us regarding Mr. Kidd's demise, we, the trustees and I, felt it best that we should retire the font and remove the family pew," Rector Vesey intoned.

"Retire?" I echoed. My heart was sinking with these words.

"Yes...yes." The Rector said shaking his head, "we petitioned our good Queen Anne and the church in England to supply us with a new baptism font which arrived within a year."

My mind was screaming; my heart felt as if it would cease to beat.

"So, there is nothing remaining of Mr. Kidd's generosity other than the gift of his work on the structure itself."

"Well, I am afraid we had to remove reminders of his connection to this parish community from the apse and nave to satisfy our members," Rector Vesey said with a wry smile. "I did not say his gifts were discarded."

This last statement stunned me. And the look on my face must have betrayed my lack of understanding.

"As I said before," Rector Vesey continued, "Mr. Kidd was a good supplicant when a part of this parish and, while his later life may have changed that, I believe what he did for the establishment of this church community deserves recognition at some point in time. His family pew and the baptismal font are stored in the church crypt until such time as his memory is no longer of consequence."

I felt as if I had been stabbed in the heart and suddenly revived.

"Rector Vesey," I asked quietly, "my father died many years ago when I was young, and I have little of his to remember him by. Do you think I might see these items of a man my father spoke so highly of and meant much to him?"

"I can see no harm in doing so," Rector Vesey smiled warmly. He reached in his pocket and withdrew a ring of keys. Picking through each, the Rector held one up and said, "The door is just beside the sacristy. Take as much time as you need. The Reverend Berkeley and I have much more to discuss."

I took the proffered key and, trying not to walk too quickly, entered the church and made my way toward the sacristy. The lock in the door next to the entry to the sacristy accepted the key smoothly and the door, itself, groaned on its hinges from lack of use as it swung open. A thick candle in a holder with a finger loop sat on a shelf just inside the door. I retrieved it and turned to the candle burning on the wall just behind me and caught a flame.

I began descending the stairs and could feel the cool air of the crypt rushing up to meet me. The flickering flame of the candle I held limited the area I could see to only a few feet. The crypt was cool, but not damp, and the air was not stale. As I made my way down the length of the crypt, I inspected some piles of long unused items. Rounding one of the massive columns, I spied a canvas cloth carefully placed over something about four feet tall. Only the base was visible, and it appeared to be made of stone. I placed my light on a ledge formed on the column for that purpose and I pulled back the tarp.

There, before me, covered in cobwebs, was a beautiful hand carved baptismal font. The font itself was a bowl for the blessing water held up by three leaf-carved arms folding down and melding into the body of the column. Each of these arms bore the engraved initials "WK." The whole of the column-shaped body was intricately carved with vines down to the footing. As I stood there admiring the beauty of the artwork, I nearly forgot my purpose.

I started thinking to myself, "Where would I hide something on, or in, this thing before me?" I started at the base wiping away the cobwebs as I went, checking the foot, looking for any kind of crack or crevasse large enough to insert a map. Nothing showed itself. I moved on to the column. I looked at each carved vine and leaf for something, any-thing that would provide space to hide a map. Again, nothing. I began checking the supportive arms under the bowl which would be filled for baptismal rites.

I noticed that the arms connected slightly below the baptismal font, so only the rim of the bowl was supported by the arms and a small space existed between the rest of the bowl and the arms. As I explored the arms, something had been folded and forced into this space on one of the arms. It was almost invisible from the dirt and discoloration with age. I looked about for something thin that might force the folded item from its hiding place.

I found on a shelf nearby what appeared to be a metal strainer with a very thin handle. Hurrying back to the font, I pushed the end of the handle into the space forcing the folded form out far enough for my fingers to grasp it. As it dropped into my hand, I felt my heart pounding in my chest. I had found it!

I had no idea how much time I had spent searching. I just knew I had been gone long enough to raise some suspicions. I quickly put the small, folded packet in the pocket of my breeches and threw the tarp over the font again. No one would have been able to tell it had ever been moved. I quickly hooked the candleholder on my finger and found my way back to the stairway leading up from the crypt. Although it was cool in the crypt, I was dripping with sweat.

As I threw the bolt locking the door to the crypt, I heard the voices of Reverend Berkeley and Rector Vesey echoing in the nave. I turned to see the two of them seated in the last row of the church in deep conversation. I quietly slid into a pew next to me and waited silently.

"Thomas?" I heard the Reverend's voice question. "How long have you been sitting there?"

"Only a few moments, Reverend," I replied bubbling over with joy inside.

"Come and join us, Mr. Gray," Rector Vesey's voice was light and inviting. "We have some thoughts on your future."

I walked back to the pew where Reverend Berkeley and the Rector were seated feeling a lightness in my stride that I hoped did not betray the excitement I was feeling inside.

"First, let me ask if you found what you were looking for in the crypt?" Rector Vesey asked innocently. My breath caught in my throat, and I felt the blood draining from my face.

"Yes, I did Rector Vesey," I replied trying hard to keep an even tone. "It was somehow comforting to see something my father might also have seen. I hope you don't mind that I said a small prayer for Mr. Kidd and my father."

"Not at all," the Rector replied jovially, "I'm glad you found something that eased your mind and gave you peace. But now, on to other thoughts."

"Tom," Reverend Berkeley began, "I have shared with Rector Vesey as much of your history as I am privy to and have told him of your ability to read and write and your good knowledge of mathematics." The Reverend was beaming with pride.

"Rector Vesey and I feel strongly that you should pursue a more formal education at a recognized institution," the Reverend continued, "Of course, our preference would be for Yale, and, with our combined recommendations, we believe your acceptance would be assured! What do you say?"

The look of shock on my face was not for the question that had been posed to me regarding my future, but for the relief that further questions about what might have occurred in the crypt were not to be asked.

"But am I not too old?" I managed to stammer out.

"Never too old to learn, Mr. Gray," Rector Vesey intoned, "education should be a pursuit throughout one's life, I believe."

"But I am no son of a gentleman," I protested meekly. "I have some funds, but I must work to earn my keep,"

"You let us worry about that, Tom," Reverend Berkeley said with an unconcerned flip of his hand. "You think about our offer. You have until late summer before acceptance to the new term would begin."

"We are offering you the chance of a lifetime, Mr. Gray," Rector Vesey said looking into my eyes for some sign of assent.

"I will think on it, Sirs," I stammered. "It is a very kind and generous offer."

With that said, the two men rose from the pew in which they were sitting and, with me following behind, began to walk arm-in-arm toward the open church door and the bright sunlight of late afternoon.

TWENTY-TWO

*A*s Reverend Berkeley and I walked down Wall Street toward our boarding room, I was aware of the Reverend's voice as if in a dream, not really hearing his words. My thoughts were on the folded piece of information in the pocket of my breeches. What would this section of the map tell me? How would it match up? Was it really a piece to the map or just an errant piece of leather stuffed into a space created by an error in the production of the font? I longed for just a few moments of privacy to be able to unfold what I held now in my hand and answer my questions. Suddenly, I became aware of Reverend Berkeley's voice.

"What do you think of that, Tom," he was asking?

"I'm sorry, Sir, what do I think of what?" I replied completely unaware of the meaning of the question. "I am sorry. I was thinking of Newport and how Toby and Mistress Mary were faring."

"Understandable," my companion replied. "What do you think of the Rector Vesey and I sponsoring you for Yale?"

"I feel I need to think on it, Sir," I responded, "I am not the only one such a decision would affect. There are my duties with the city council, and I need to speak with Toby and Mary about the effect my being away would have on the White Horse...."

"Yes, yes, I understand all of that is important," The Reverend replied, discounting the importance of such concerns considering a chance at real education, "but this could elevate you in the eyes of the community!"

"I really feel this is a decision I must consider most seriously, Reverend," I said trying to muster as much gravity as possible in my words. "I would be much older than others attending and already much schooled in real life. I am sure you understand."

"I do, Tom", the Reverend replied. "I realize it is a huge decision and one that should not be taken lightly."

We had reached the intersection of Pearl Street and crossed to our inn. The sun was beginning to sink below the western hills, and the gathering darkness felt cool on the skin.

"What say you to an early dinner and a good sleep before we leave tomorrow?" Reverend Berkeley suggested.

"Aye," I replied, "but let me first reassure our innkeeper that, indeed, we are staying this night, and I will grab my jacket against the cool of evening. Shall we dine where we did last evening?"

"I don't see why not," the Reverend replied with a smile. "Let me go on ahead and secure a table and you can follow."

I smiled at this suggestion and bounded up the two steps and into the inn. I found the innkeeper in his office and confirmed our room for the night, then bounded up the stairs two at a time to our room. No sooner had I shut the door securely, I reached into my pocket and retrieved the folded form. I paused for the slightest of seconds, fearful of what I might hold. What if it were nothing? What if I had retrieved nothing? When might I ever have another opportunity to search the crypt of Trinity Church in New York?

I steeled myself for what I might find within the paper in my hands and slowly tried to open the stiff folds. I quickly realized the form in my hand was made of parchment like the piece of the map I already possessed. The creases were deep showing the parchment had not been unfolded in many years. Slowly, I unfolded each fold and tried to flatten the deep creases on the table edge. When it was finally open, it was about the same size as the map I had found in my father's Bible. Only two things were written on the page in the lower left corner: the word "Bible" and the passage "John 1:33" one above the other.

The page itself was blank except for a hole purposely cut through the parchment. The hole was not centered. I had no time now to ponder the meaning of this strange message for my companion was waiting for me at dinner. I quickly refolded my new clue and stuffed it back in my pocket. I grabbed my jacket off the back of the chair and made my way quickly down the stairs and out into the gathering darkness. I trotted to Rose Street and entered the Rose Tavern not at all winded and found the Reverend seated in a comfortable booth near the fireplace.

I slipped off my jacket and slid onto the bench opposite my mentor and friend.

"I checked in with our friendly innkeeper, and he has not let our room out to anyone else for this evening," I said playfully.

"He seems a good gentleman and runs a clean establishment," Reverend Berkeley replied in the same light-hearted mood.

Dinner was passed with much good-humored conversation and laughter, along with a couple of pints of good ale. The shepherd's pie I consumed was quite satisfying, and the Reverend enjoyed his mutton stew. As we ate, the discussion turned to education and the offer that had been made to me to attend. The Reverend asked me about how I had become an owner of the White Horse Inn and my position there. Though I owned a tavern and inn, I was not in the habit of drinking, and two draft pints were not enough to seriously impair my thoughts. I was careful though in choosing my words.

I related to Reverend Berkeley how I began working at the White Horse when it was much smaller. I told him of Mary and her husband Robert whom Toby and I admired greatly. I spoke of his death and Mary's grief. The Reverend wanted to know about my father and how I learned to read and write and perform mathematics. Again, I tried to be vague when it came to my father. I did relate that he had traveled extensively as a young man, and, when he had returned, he took my education in hand. The lie was small and did not materially alter the truth. I then explained that my father's lessons had sparked my desire to learn and after his death, I had read every book I could and practiced my lettering and math exercises. I told him I had taught these skills to a group of young boys and that had spurred me to learn even more.

"Tom," the Reverend said as we paid our bill and began to gather our things to leave for the inn, "I believe your life experiences will qualify you, most likely over-qualify you, to receive a degree from Yale with little need of exposure to more learning. But the fact that you will have a degree in hand," he paused as if grasping for the words, "it puts you on a respected status with other educated elite."

We made the short walk back to our beds on Pearl Street under the orange glow of the streetlamps in an uncomfortable silence.

"Let us not have this discussion of your education affect our friendship, Tom," Reverend Berkeley suddenly said as we approached the Rose Inn. "I have profound respect for you and admire the knowledge you have. I believe that your knowledge may already be worthy of recognition by an educational institution to earn a degree, especially an institution with the reputation of Yale."

"Reverend," I replied, "I appreciate your guidance and opinion always. However, this is a decision that does not abide only with me. There are others to whom I have obligations and who would be affected by my absence in their lives, and I must consider that in my decision. Please, fear not that I could ever allow a discussion such as ours have any effect on our relationship."

This seemed to satisfy Reverend Berkeley's concerns, and we proceeded up the stairs and entered the Rose Inn.

I knew that sleep would not come easily this night. All I wanted was to get back to Newport and see how the new piece of the map related to the first section. My mind raced between thoughts of the map and the opportunity of education presented by my mentor, the Reverend, which I knew to be of great import to him and made with the best of intent. Yet, I still believed I would be a misfit among landed and wealthy fellow students, some half my age. I knew the offer had been made with only my future best interests at heart.

It seemed not long before the light began coming through the window in our room and I was still tossing thoughts within my mind. I rose unrested and poured a small amount of water in the wash basin. I bent over the basin and splashed water on my face attempting to wash my weariness away, at least temporarily. My companion lay soundly asleep as I slipped on my travel clothes and crept out of the room and down the stairway.

I was sitting at the table near the front window in the breakfast room enjoying my second cup of tea when the Reverend entered and took the seat opposite me.

"How did you sleep, Tom?" he said cheerily. "Are we ready to travel home today?"

"Aye, Sir," I replied. "I did not sleep well, too many thoughts running through my mind. When are we due at the boat, Sir?"

"About ten, I believe. We should probably get a move on," he continued. "I've already made arrangements for my trunks to be taken to the ship."

The sip of tea I had just taken stuck in my throat for an instant. I swallowed and said, "My bag is still upstairs, Sir?"

"Oh yes, Tom," came the reply, "I assumed you would carry it since it is so small."

A sigh of relief escaped my lips. While I had taken my prize from my new dress clothes and placed it securely in what I now wore, I wanted to make sure all my possessions were packed.

"We had best be off," Reverend Berkeley said as he finished his last bite of crumpet and jam and downed the last of his tea.

I quickly ascended the stairs to our room and picked up my bag, taking one last look about the room to be sure nothing was left behind. I arrived at the front office as the Reverend was settling our bill with the innkeeper and, bidding him good day, we went out into the street.

We had arrived in warm sunshine but were leaving in overcast with dark clouds to our west. We walked the few blocks to the waterfront where the boat was docked and found a hive of activity. The captain was standing at the head of the gangplank directing members of the crew handling cargo. He greeted us as we came aboard and noted the dark overcast.

"Do you think the storm will catch us," Reverend Berkeley inquired of the captain?

"Nay, Sir," he replied, "if we get underway on time, it should be behind us and blow to the north."

The Reverend nodded his understanding and headed for our cramped little cabin. We soon heard orders being given on deck and felt the roll of the hull as we left the dock and began to sail. We came on deck and watched the shore for a brief time. We passed the wilderness at the north end of Manhattan Island and turned east at the connection of Long Island Sound at a place called Hell's Gate. We watched as the shorelines to the north and south fell away and the body of water expanded. The wind was cold, and the lack of sun made it unpleasant to stand on deck. I excused myself saying I had not slept well the night before and felt the rocking of the ship might help me to gain some sleep.

"A thought, Tom, before you leave," the Reverend said as I turned to leave. "Since we are passing New Haven, I wondered if we might spend a night there and see Yale tomorrow and take another boat for Newport the day following?"

I was about to answer when the captain of our ship spoke.

"Did I hear ye say a stop at New Haven, Reverend," the captain asked politely?

"It was a thought, Captain," the Reverend replied.

"I would prefer not to chance it with the storm behind us. I would rather port for the night in New London. It be a bit farther on, but it would make for a shorter haul tomorrow," answered the captain.

"I was only wondering about dropping us off," the Reverend replied, "but, if you think best, Captain...."

"I do, Sir," came the captain's reply. "It will be unfit weather for traipsing about the muddy streets of New Haven for at least a day or two."

At this point, I excused myself and headed for the cabin. I had not expressed my lack of desire to delay returning to Newport. There was no need since the captain had intervened. I wanted to take the folded parchment from my pocket and thoroughly examine it, but I had no assurance of privacy in the cabin. With no lock on the door, the Reverend could enter at any moment, and it could be difficult to explain what I was holding without disclosing more than I wanted to at this point. So, with some disappointment, I lay down on the bunk built into the side of the cabin and felt myself slip into oblivion with the motion of the waves against the ship.

I was awakened by the sound of a loud thud and the heavy roll of the ship. The cabin seemed noticeably darker when a bright strike of lightning lit up the cabin through the small window, followed by the loud crackle of thunder. I could hear the wind whipping through the rigging and rain pelting against the window glass. As the boat pitched and rolled, I sat on the edge of the bunk getting my bearings and began to wonder where my traveling companion might be. He certainly would not still be on deck. Measuring the roll of the ship, I staggered across the short distance to the cabin door and waited for the ship to right herself before trying to open the door. Once outside the cabin, I grasped the railing of the stairway to the deck and called out for Reverend Berkeley.

"In here, Tom!" came a reply to my left where another cabin door stood shut.

I reached for the handle of the door just as the ship lunged once again and held tightly to the handle as it swung open and catapulted me into the cabin. The Reverend was seated in a chair that must have been bolted to the floor of the cabin as it was not rolling about with the motion of the ship. Before him was a table suspended by rope from each of its four corners from the ceiling. This allowed it to stay level by freely swinging with the motion of the boat.

"Are you alright, Sir," I asked of the Reverend who looked the color of early growth grapes.

"I felt much better crossing the ocean on a much bigger ship," came his reply. "I think the captain's prediction for the course of the storm was a bit off."

"Why did you not come and get me," I asked?

"When I looked in on you, you appeared so deeply asleep, I thought I would leave you to your slumber," the Reverend replied.

I took a seat in a chair opposite the Reverend, and we sat quietly experiencing the rolling movements of the ship as she rode the waves pushing ever forward toward her destination of Newport. The intensity of the storm seemed to wane after another hour. The wind dropped and the rain slackened. The movements of the ship became more predictable and the table before us swung much less.

"Shall we go on deck," I asked hopefully.

"I think that might be a great relief," the Reverend replied.

We slowly rose from our seats and regained our sea legs as we climbed up on deck. The air was sweet and clean, and the gentle creaking of the yards and rigging were comforting. The dark skies were well astern. The sun was still up in the western sky shining through the last of the storm clouds, its rays forming what is known as stairs to heaven. The undersides of the clouds showed hues from gold to bright orange and deep reds. As we stood at the railing, it looked as if the remainder of our journey would be very pleasant indeed. Little did I realize an entire day had passed as I had slept.

TWENTY-THREE

e had passed New Haven during the storm and were well east of it now. The winds that accompanied the storm had pushed us quickly eastward. As we stood at the rail looking at the shore of eastern Connecticut in the quickly fading light, our stomachs began reminding us we had not eaten since our light breakfast the previous day. We could see the captain by the helm at the stern and decided to ask if any food might be available by the time we arrived in New London.

"Ye might find an ale house near the docks that might still be servin' by the time we get there," the captain replied. "We're still a good four hours out from New London."

With that, he called one of the crew and gave him an order we did not hear. Within a few minutes, a sailor appeared before us as we stood by the rail and presented us each with a slice of crusty bread and a tankard of grog. As we began enjoying the small meal, the captain approached from the helm.

"Sorry for the poor vittles," the captain said after the sailor had walked away.

"How much farther do we have to go for Newport, Captain?" the Reverend asked.

"We should make port well before sundown tomorrow," the captain replied. "We've made good time with the gale that pushed us," he added with a smile.

We finished our crusts of bread and washed it down with the weak rum. The ship was running smoothly through the small swells, and we stood by the rail watching the shore pass and remarking on the gulls wheeling on the wind above us. In my mind, all I wanted was to get back to Newport, back to the White Horse and up to my room to match up the two parts of the map I now possessed. I wanted to urge the boat forward and have it gallop over the waves. I knew I had to summon patience, and so, I concentrated on making small talk with my companion.

"Reverend," I began, "do you honestly believe I have enough life experience to pass much of the requirements Yale would make of me?"

"My boy," he replied, placing a hand on my shoulder, "I believe you can pass any exam put to you by the present faculty of Yale. Yes, you need some formal exposure to higher math and a bit more exposure to languages. But your exposure through reading of many subjects has prepared you well, and the love of learning instilled in you by your father is a great tribute to him. But let us worry about such matters later. Let us just enjoy the cool, salty ocean air and the coolness of the evening."

A shift of the sails told us we were rounding to the entrance of New London harbor. Soon, the lights along the waterfront were visible. We eased up to Long Wharf, as we were told it was called, and secured for the night. The Reverend and I came ashore and set out along the promenade of the waterfront to find some food.

Not far along, we found an ale house that was quieter than some of the more raucous pubs. We stepped inside and asked if food could be had. A positive reply had us seated in a booth instantly, and our food orders given before our pints reached our table. It was a delightful meal with little conversation until our hunger had been satisfied. The hour being late, we returned to our ship and were soon asleep in our cabin.

I was happy to let the time pass the next morning as we stood silently at the railing of the ship and felt no impulse to continue to converse. I was anxious to get back to Newport. I had much to tell Toby and Mary. Four days was about the longest I had ever been away from the inn.

We had passed the northern tip of Long Island by mid-afternoon and were bearing down on Narragansett. It would not be long before we reached the entrance to the great bay and would land. As we approached the entrance to the great bay, the tide was in flood, and we swiftly slipped into the east passage and into Newport harbor. We went below and gathered our belongings. The Reverend's trunks would be delivered to Whitehall by members of the crew.

As we came back on deck, the ship eased into the dock as the last of the sails was lowered. Standing on the dock was my dear partner, Toby. Never was I so surprised and happy to see him. He was dressed in a new suit of clothes and looked all the world like a true gentleman of business. As soon as the gangway was secured, I hurried down the way and embraced him warmly.

"I am so glad you met me," I said. "I have it, Toby!" I whispered in his ear, "I have it!"

I suddenly realized that the Reverend had left the ship and walked up to us. I released Toby and introduced him, formally, to the Reverend.

"Reverend Berkeley, I said, smiling broadly, "allow me to introduce my good friend and business partner Tobias Trinidad."

"Oh, come now, Tom." Reverend responded. "I have met Mr. Trinidad on many occasions, but I thank you for the formal presentation."

"It is an honor to meet you again," Toby said with a knowing smile. "I think our friend, here, is a little excited about his trip to the city of New York."

With a slight amount of embarrassment, I nodded agreement.

"I am sure he will have much to tell you, Mr. Trinidad," Reverend Berkeley said clapping his hand on my shoulder.

"We should be away, Tom," Toby said, "things will be getting busy at the inn for supper, and Mary has but one helper until we return."

This statement from Toby stopped me for a moment, for I had no idea who this helper might be. But rather than question him, I agreed we needed to get to the inn.

"Could we interest you in coming with us for some supper, Reverend," I asked.

"As much as I am tempted by the thought, I believe that is my carriage coming toward us as we speak," the Reverend replied. And so it was, and we bid each other good day with the agreement to meet next morning to discuss our unsettled questions of education.

Toby and I walked onto the waterfront plaza and began the short walk to the White Horse Inn. As we did, I commented on his attire.

"I must say, Mr. Trinidad, you appear to have become quite the grandee in my absence," I chided laughingly.

"Well, Mr. Gray," replied Toby in the same jocular vein, "I felt it was time to have at least one dandified outfit for special occasions. And what could be a more special occasion that welcoming my friend back home after a long voyage."

With that, both of us burst into laughter. Two friends, one dressed in new pants, shirt, and vest, the other in fashionable traveling attire strolling arm-in-arm in the late afternoon from the docks in Newport. Neither of us could have imagined this scene when we were members of the dock rats not so many years before.

As we walked, I suddenly thought of something Toby had said.

"You said someone was helping Mary?" I asked Toby.

"Oh, yes. About that," Toby smiled. "While you were away, I, I mean Mary and I, hired someone."

"Oh?" I replied.

"Yes," Toby replied. "You can certainly fire them if you like. But I think you will be pleasantly surprised."

With that reply, we turned the corner, and the lights of the White Horse Inn came into view. I was home and just in time to serve out supper to our hungry and thirsty customers. Our maps would have to wait until later.

As Toby and I entered the inn through the tavern door, I heard his voice boom out, "Home from the big city is our traveler!"

A cheer went up from all present and Mary peeked around the bar and joined in. She was still strikingly beautiful in her white sleeved blouse and long, dark hair beyond her shoulders. As I made my way toward the kitchen, I felt many a pat on my back from those enjoying themselves. Here were Toby and I among the best dressed in the room and about to tie on aprons and start serving food and drink. It just seemed wrong, somehow.

As we passed into the kitchen, feeling giddy from our reception in the bar, Toby placed a hand on my shoulder and turned me toward the cooking fire.

"And here is our new employee that I think you should meet," Toby said.

Bent over a pot hanging on the cooking spit was a crouching figure wearing an apron. As he backed away from the fireplace and began to straighten up, I realized this was a person of some stature. As he wiped his hands on the apron he wore, I heard a deep voice say, "Is this the bloke I still has to meet?"

The voice was unfamiliar. And then I saw the face.

"Jackie!" I shouted. "Little Jackie!"

"Not so little no more, Tom," came the reply.

I crossed to him in a stride or two and we embraced. He was full as tall as me, if not an inch or two taller. This figure that I had last seen as a young boy was now fully grown into a strapping young man.

"It's so good to see you," I stammered out as we hugged. "Where did you come from? Where have you been? What have you been doing?"

"So many questions, Mate," Jackie rebuffed with his hands up in front of him. "You have hungry customers out there that need serving, and I will be here to answer all your questions when they are done eating."

"Come on, Tom," Toby chimed in. "We have orders here to get out." With that, Toby disappeared through the door into the dining room with a full tray of plates. I finished putting my apron on and hefted the second tray waiting to be served. I smiled at Jackie as I went through the dining room door.

"We have much to talk about later," I called to him as the noise from the outer room flooded the kitchen.

The evening seemed to move along quickly and, before I knew it, we were making the last round call in the bar and clearing the last dishes from the dining room to the kitchen. Toby relieved Mary at the bar and she came to the kitchen to help with closing down. With three of us in the kitchen, we had tamped down the fire, washed and dried the dishes, and stowed all the perishable foodstuffs in the pantry in no time at all.

The three of us came into the tavern room as Toby was finishing wiping down the bar. We sat at a table near the bar and Toby poured a sherry for Mary and a tankard of ale for each of the remaining three.

"I have so many questions for you, Jackie," I began after a toast and a drink from my pint.

"I have probably answered all of them for Toby already, but have at me, Tom," Jackie said relaxing back into his chair.

"Where have you been?" I asked.

"I've been to many places and seen much," Jackie replied. "Spent time in Providence: actually, a lot of time doing a little of everything and not much of anything. Scupper and I was together for a few years, but he wanted to see more of the world. Last I heard he was in Philadelphia trying to earn an honest dollar as a cloth merchant."

"Scupper?" I exclaimed, "a textile merchant? You mean like a tailor?"

"Oh," said Toby, "I hadn't thought of that." We laughed heartily.

"I think more like drapes and rugs," Jackie offered.

"I am late of Boston where I spent more than three years learning about the printing trade; remarkably interesting," Jackie continued.

"So, what brought you back to Newport?" I asked, taking another sip of my ale.

"I thought I might see about setting up a printing business here," Jackie said quietly. "After all, this is a place where a great deal of printing should be required. And I have it on good authority that the printer I apprenticed with in Boston is preparing to set up a shop here in Newport. You may have heard the name: James Franklin."

The older brother of Benjamin," I suggested.

"Aye. That he is," Jackie replied. "James has spent a bit of time in his majesty's accommodations for his writings, and Boston has begun to suppress some of his printing. I believe he has a brother here in Newport and he plans to leave Boston shortly and begin publishing here."

"We could use an experienced printer in Newport," Toby interjected. "He should find fertile ground for his talents here."

"We are fortunate to have a famous philosopher residing here, at present," I responded. "I would be happy to make an introduction. I have functioned as his secretary for some months now."

"In fact, Tom just returned this day from a trip to New York with Reverend Berkeley," Toby added as he finished his ale.

"Is that a fact," replied Jackie, with feigned surprise. "Must be quite the heady experience to know such a prominent personality." He laughed in jest.

We had all finished our libations and were ready to head to bed.

"Where are you staying," I asked Jackie?

"Oh, did I not say," he replied. "I'm staying at the warehouse by the dockside. You know, the one with the secret door?"

Everyone burst into good-hearted laughter.

"He is staying right here with us," Mary said through the laughter. "He'll be in one of the guest rooms for now. We will fix up the storage room in the garret for him in short order. I think Jackie will be with us for the near future," Mary said in her most motherly voice,

Toby and I gathered the tankards and sherry glass from the table and wiped the tabletop clean. We bid Mary and Jackie goodnight and went into the kitchen to put the barware at the washboard.

"Let us give everyone a chance to settle into bed before we look at the maps," I said to Toby barely above a whisper.

"You have the New York section?" he replied in a like tone.

"Right here in my pocket," I replied. "But it does not look so much like a map."

I reached into my pocket and felt relieved when I felt the folded parchment with my fingers.

We finished extinguishing the remaining lanterns and, checking the doors were locked, headed to our room in the attic. All seemed quiet as we passed the rooms on the second floor. As quietly as possible we mounted the stairs to the third floor. I entered the room and went to the table to retrieve my father's Bible as Toby quietly closed the door and jammed a chair under the doorknob. I opened the cover of the Bible and retrieved the first map from within the cover. As Toby settled on the bed, I pulled the second parchment from my pocket and unfolded it on the table next to the Bible section of the map.

As we stared at the two pieces of parchment, Toby intoned, "What kind of map is that?"

"I think it is meant to overlay what we have from the Bible, Toby," I replied.

Studying the New York parchment, it was slightly larger than the map itself. The corners had been clipped off at an angle and there were small holes at various places cut through the parchment and the one larger circular hole. Looking at the map from the Bible of Long Island and the lower coast of Connecticut and Rhode Island, there were small black marks spaced around the map, the meaning of which had meant nothing previously. I took the blank parchment and laid it on top of the map trying to line up the black marks to the holes in the overlay. The first attempt left the larger hole over water. I turned the overlay ninety degrees and, again, the prime hole lay over water. One more ninety degree turn of the overlay and all the smaller holes showed black beneath. The main hole showed land.

"That's it," I said under my breath, "Toby, that's it! That is where the treasure lies," I said, my excitement rising.

"Sh-h-h! Quiet, Tom," Toby cautioned. "You'll wake the household."

"But we have it, Toby," I said, forcing myself to control my excitement.

"Yes, Tom," Toby cautioned. "We now know what island. But, once on the land, where do we find the treasure?"

TWENTY-FOUR

"That must be the third part of the map, Toby," I said quietly. "It must be the actual directions to finding the treasure," I continued quietly, "and I know where it is!"

"John 1:33," Toby said in a whisper. I nodded in agreement.

"Let me tell you how I found the second part of the map," I began. I then related to Toby the story of my trip to New York. I told him of Rector Vesey and his friendship with Reverend Berkeley. I related to Toby of my discovering that William Kidd had been a member of the congregation and had contributed to the building of the Trinity Church in New York.

"Most amazingly," I continued, "was discovering that Mr. Kidd had gifted a baptismal font to the church!"

"No! You are not serious," Toby replied in hushed excitement.

"I then was told by Rector Vesey the font was no longer in use and had been placed in the crypt because of the disgrace brought on by Mr. Kidd's supposed piracy. In fact, his family pew had also been relegated to the crypt," I continued. "I think the congregation tried to erase any visible association with Mr. Kidd."

"But you obviously found it," Toby said. "You found the parchment."

"I did, but I had to tell a bit of a lie," I replied. "I told Rector Vesey my father had known this Captain Kidd, which he did, and that my father considered him a righteous and God-fearing gentleman. I asked if I might see the family pew of the man my father had so admired."

"On that flimsy excuse you were allowed to enter the crypt?" Toby was agape with disbelief. "You must have been terribly convincing."

I told Toby of rummaging through the crypt, finding the font, and finding the map.

"And now, I know the meaning behind the two bible verses my father used," I said, "and I know where the final piece of the map should be."

Toby smiled broadly.

"The Trinity Church here in Newport has a baptismal font," Toby whispered with a broad smile on his face.

"I would bet my life on it," said I, smiling just as broadly as my companion. "And, tomorrow, after my meeting with Reverend Berkeley, we shall visit a certain church in town."

I quickly refolded the two sections of our map and replaced them inside the cover of my father's Bible. We shed our clothes and changed into our nightshirts. As we lay down in our beds, Toby turned to me, wished me goodnight, and extinguished our candle. I wished him goodnight, as well, and tried to sleep while thoughts of tomorrow raced through my mind. What would we find at Trinity Church on the morrow?

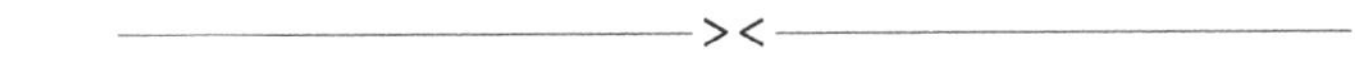

As the room lit up with the morning sun, Toby and I were already dressing, excited at the prospects of what today might bring. We hurried downstairs and found Mary already stoking the kitchen fireplace.

"Good morning, boys," was her cheery greeting. "We could use some wood for today," she said motioning to the fireplace.

"I'll get it," Toby said, "Tom has to meet with the Reverend this morning, so best to let him eat first."

"In that case, you had best sit, Tom, and I will make you some break-fast," Mary replied, directing me to a chair at the kitchen table. "Must be important to be meeting with him so early,"

"He made a very kind offer while we were on our trip to New York," I replied.

"You did not say much about your trip last night," Mary said looking at me with a questioning eye as she skillfully flipped an egg in the skillet.

"The Reverend offered to use his contacts to gain entrance for me to Yale to formalize my education," I said. "I don't know if I can do it."

"Oh, Tom," Mary gushed as she set the plate of fried egg with a slice of frizzled ham before me. "That is so wonderful! You'll be a proper educated gentleman!"

"I don't know, Mary. It would mean being away from here, and the inn, and my responsibilities here."

"Don't be silly," Mary admonished, moving her hands to her hips, and stepping back, "you can't pass up such an opportunity. Think to your future! You're still young and you could do important things with a good education."

"Well, I did not give an answer as yet," I said. "You and Toby, I think, need to agree on this."

"And don't forget," Mary added, "we have Jackie here now. And you won't be going for a few months, so there is plenty of time to get him acquainted with everything here. You must go, Tom, for your own future."

As Mary's words faded, Toby came through the kitchen door with an armload of wood for the fire. The look on his face showed he knew something had gone on while he was outside cutting wood.

"Did I interrupt?" he said questioning.

Mary looked at me as I finished my ham and egg.

"Tom has been offered the chance to go to Yale by Reverend Berkeley," Mary said before I could speak.

"Why, that is wonderful news," Toby said sitting on the other chair at the table. "Why did you not tell me this last night?"

"We had other things to talk over," I said without thinking.

"Other things?" Mary questioned. "What could have been more important than your future?"

"Are you going to accept, Tom?" Toby said, trying to keep the conversation away from other matters. "You must accept. It is an opportunity you cannot pass up."

"I will speak with the Reverend Berkeley today and find out much more about his offer," I replied. I took note of Toby's look: a mix of annoyance and disappointment caused by my inadvertent slip.

Mary slid a plate of eggs and ham in front of Toby and looked at me and nodded.

"I expect a full report tonight," she said, "and the details of when you will be leaving." The look on her face was one a loving mother would have for her son.

"You shall have it," I replied smiling.

I stood and reached for my shoulder satchel that was hanging on the peg next to the door. I looked inside to be sure I had my quill and some paper. Satisfied they were within, I shouldered the strap and bid farewell and left through the kitchen door for Reverend Berkeley's Whitehall. It was a beautiful morning for a brisk walk.

I arrived at Whitehall having walked for about an hour. I knocked respectfully at the front door which was answered shortly by Reverend Berkeley's butler. I was shown into the Reverend's library which was unusual as I usually was shown into his study. Thinking nothing further of it, I took a chair near the fireplace and quietly thumbed through a volume of the Iliad that was sitting on the table beside the chair.

I was so absorbed in the book I did not hear the door open and Reverend Berkeley enter the room.

"This is why I want to invest in your future, Tom," the Reverend Berkeley's voice interrupting my reading. He moved to the other side of the hearth and settled in the chair there dressed in his robe.

"How many would take the opportunity to pick up a book and begin reading while waiting for a host," the Reverend said with some degree of admiration. "Few, I would venture to say. But you, Tom.... You are that rare individual who has a thirst for learning and a curiosity that drives you to improve." I smiled in acknowledgement.

"Sir, this offer of education you have made, when would this require me to leave? And for how long?"

"First things first, I will write to Rector Williams at Yale today and request what he and his faculty might require from you to apply for admission," Reverend Berkeley began. "I am sure my recommendation will outweigh any requirement the faculty may desire, but we must follow the rules," he continued with a smile.

"But the cost, Reverend," I protested..."

"You leave that to me," he replied. "I am your benefactor in this matter."

His statement silenced my concerns.

"When would I need to be in New Haven," I asked.

"I would think you might plan for the early fall, perhaps late August," Reverend Berkeley replied, seeming unconcerned about the question.

"You will need my replacement to be ready by then. May I nominate my partner, Tobias," I asked?

"I would consider him should his writing be as clear as yours," he replied with a smile. "So, let us consider the question of your attendance at Yale settled for the present and get that letter to Rector Williams written and posted today."

I moved to the writing table that sat back from the fireplace and quickly addressed a piece of Reverend Berkeley's letterhead to the Right and Reverend Elisa Williams, Rector, Yale University.

"I wrote this out last evening hoping we would be in agreement today," the Reverend said as he stepped to the side of the table I was seated at and handed me a written note in his own hand. "When you are finished copying this, bring it to me in the study and I will sign it."

It was not unusual for the Reverend to 'rough out' correspondence he wished to send and to ask me to copy it into better form. His first drafts, as he called them, tended to show the free thoughts he manifested while writing, complete with words and phrases lined through in deletion, and alternate wording inserted above or below. This method of composing worked for an active mind, but required the talents of a steady hand to decipher the final draft.

It did not take long for me to finish the brief note and have it ready for my benefactor's signature. I packed up my satchel and headed to the study. I stopped at the door to the study and rapped lightly on the door. I was summoned to enter and found the Reverend Berkeley staring out one of the study windows.

"Your note, Sir," I said politely.

"Tom," the Reverend responded, "have you been to the renovated Trinity Church as yet?"

The question struck me dumb for an instant.

"Strange you should ask me that," I stammered out. "I had just made plans with Toby to go to the church this very day. Why do you ask?"

"I am considering making a gift of an organ to the new church," Reverend Berkeley said without turning from the window. "I would like you to see what you think while you are there today."

"I would be happy to look," I said, "but I am by no means qualified to judge."

"I do understand your reluctance," he said as he turned from the window, "I am just asking you to see what you think as someone coming to the church for the first time."

I agreed to the Reverend's request realizing it would give me a perfect reason to be requesting access to the church. I placed the finished letter to the rector of Yale on his desk which he promptly signed. Placing the signed and sealed letter into my satchel, I turned for the door.

"I will see it is posted this afternoon," I said as I began to leave.

"My thanks, Tom," I heard the Reverend say. "We will talk again soon."

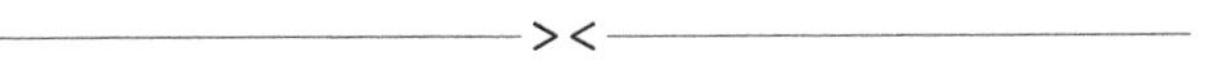

I reached Newport and the White Horse just past the noon hour. A goodly crowd filled both the dining and tavern rooms. Toby was busy at the bar, and I found Mary and Jackie hard at work in the kitchen. I hung my shoulder bag on the hook by the kitchen door and joined Mary and Jackie to begin serving in the dining room. As the afternoon wore on, the dining room emptied while the tavern began to see the usual afternoon lull before a crowd assembled for their discussions of news of the day while they enjoyed a beverage or two.

Toby caught my eye as he motioned for me to come to the tavern bar.

"We need to talk," he said quietly in my ear."

I nodded in agreement and went into the kitchen to see if Mary could relieve Toby for a few minutes. She dried her hands and followed me through the door into the tavern. As soon as Toby saw her, he began removing his apron and headed for the stairway leading to the upper floors. I took my shoulder satchel from the wall hook where I had hung it and followed.

No sooner had I closed the door to our bed chamber than Toby turned to me and said, "Mary suspects something is up more than just a trip to New York and talk of your education. I didn't know what you would want me to tell her, but she was at me all morning about why you were seeing the Reverend so early."

"I really did meet with him about attending Yale, Toby. I have his letter to the Rector right here," I said retrieving the sealed letter from my satchel and showing it to Toby. I then slipped the letter into my pocket. "But he also asked that I do something for him this afternoon that benefits us by giving us a different purpose for visiting the church."

I told Toby about Reverend Berkeley's thought of a gift to the church of an organ and his desire to have my thoughts after seeing the new structure that had just been completed.

"How did he know you were going to Trinity today," Toby questioned?

"I do not know," I answered. "His request came out of nowhere. I swear to you."

Realizing we had been away from the public rooms for, perhaps, too long, we agreed to try to function as if nothing had transpired and that Toby would tell Mary I would explain the morning visit with Reverend Berkeley directly but assure her it was about Yale.

As we came into the tavern, Toby returned to tending the bar and I went into the kitchen to help Jackie who was finishing the dishes. Before I could dry a dish, Mary came through the door from the tavern, hooked me by the arm, and escorted me out the back door onto the back stoop.

"So, tell me," she started, "what was this morning all about?"

"It was about Yale," I replied, "I swear. I have the letter Reverend Berkeley wrote to the Rector of Yale who is an acquaintance of his." I pulled the envelope from my pocket and showed Mary the wax seal. Her demeanor seemed to ease seeing the sealed letter.

"It had nothing to do with your treasure hunting?" she asked, looking straight at me with a silly squinted eye.

"You did not ask that," I replied coyly.

"I knew it!" she exploded. "Why did you not tell me?" She cried in frustration.

"Mary, Mary," I curled my arms around her in a hug attempting to reassure her, "That was not the primary reason for going to New York. The reverend had a meeting with someone in New York and it was an opportunity for me to see if another part of the map was where I thought it was. And it was Mary. And I found it!"

"You found it?" she uttered quietly.

"Yes," I answered, "and I know where the last part of the map is to be found."

"Oh Tom," Mary replied stepping back, placing her hands on my forearms. "Then, it may be real. The map? I am so happy for you."

"Let us wait and see," I cautioned. "We still need to keep the secret for now."

Mary nodded her understanding.

"When will you need to leave for Yale?" she asked.

"I am not yet even admitted, Mary," I answered. "That is what this letter is about. It will not be until the fall, I am assured. But I do have another task I need to perform for the Reverend today. He has asked me to go to Trinity Church to give him some ideas on a gift he is thinking of giving the new building."

"What kind of gift," Mary asked?

"He is considering an organ as a gift," I replied.

"And what expertise do you possess to make such a judgment?" Mary scoffed. "That is a likely story!"

"I swear it is true, Mary," I answered in my most somber tone.

"True or not, I know you are going to do as he has asked," Mary replied with a playful thump of my chest.

"I need Toby to go with me," I added.

Mary stopped with her hand on the kitchen doorknob and said, "You're sure that is the only reason you are taking on this task?"

"That was never the question," I replied with a slight smile.

Mary raised her eyes as if to pray to heaven and pushed the door she held in her hand and disappeared into the kitchen. I entered behind her and closed the door.

"I suppose the two of you should go on your errand now so you will be back for supper service," Mary said feigning disapproval.

"Yes, Ma'am," I replied complimenting her attitude.

"Don't you sass me, young man," Mary shot back with a smile.

Mary continued through the kitchen and into the tavern. In a couple of minutes, Toby appeared through the same door and announced Mary had relieved him so we could go on our 'errand.' I grabbed my shoulder bag from its hook and hurried up to our room. I saw the old oilskin lying next to the wall and picked it up and dropped it in the shoulder bag. Descending the stairs, I met Toby at the front door of the inn.

Trinity Church was only a few short blocks from the White Horse. The renovated building was larger than its predecessor and far grander, reflecting a growing congregation. Entrance was gained through doors on the west side where plans were to build a magnificent steeple. The church was cruciform in design with the chancery to the east. Walking through the graveyard, Toby asked when we would tell Mary about the map pieces.

"Should we find this piece of the map," I said, "it will be complete, and we can tell her our next move which will be to mount an expedition to find the treasure."

TWENTY-FIVE

In all my years in Newport, I had never entered Trinity Church. The Quaker beliefs of my ancestors had been sadly lost in my childhood. There was little time for religion in my circumstance. But I had picked up much of the High Church of England and Anglican religion from the reading of my father's Bible and my association with the Reverend Berkeley over the last few years. Yet I would not have counted myself among those with strong religious convictions.

As Toby and I approached Trinity Church, a certain reverence descended on me. The Church occupied a pre-eminent position at the east end of the rectangular city commons, better known as Queen Anne's Square. The green ran downhill west to the harbor promenade with shops along each side. The graveyard surrounding the building held many memorials of prominent citizens, some of whom had been founders of Newport, as well as many who had lived their lives with little note. The smell of fresh sawn wood and paint reached us as we approached the door. Though this end of the church was the oldest, the entire structure was undergoing painting after the addition on the east end.

We removed our hats and entered the vestibule cautiously. Just then, a rather small man with thinning gray hair and dressed in cleric robe entered the vestibule from the church proper.

"Can I be of assistance?" he inquired of us.

"Good day to you, Sir," I replied. "We are here at the request of Bishop Berkeley."

"Oh! The pipe organ," the man I assumed to be the Rector gushed. "Yes, yes. You will be wanting to see the area in the loft," he continued. "It is so very generous of the bishop to consider such a gift. And who is this with you?" It was his first acknowledgement of Toby.

"This is Mr. Trinidad," I said in way of introducing Toby, "and I am Mr. Gray, Secretary to the Bishop."

"Ah, yes," our new friend brightened, "Your reputation precedes you, Mr. Gray."

"Mr. Trinidad is here to inspect the space and take some measurements," I said.

"Oh, I see. And Mr. Trinidad," the churchman asked, "may I inquire as to your expertise?"

"Installing pipe organs is a specialty of mine," Toby responded giving me a side-long look. "I do the actual measuring for installations. You know, how many pipes can be fitted here and there. It is all quite complicated. Shall we begin?"

With that, the Rector led us into the church and turned to his right to a set of curving stairs. As he began to mount the stairs with Toby close behind, I spoke up.

"Since I have not been to your church before," I quickly said, stopping the Rector.

"Would it be asking too much if I took a few minutes to wander through your lovely structure?"

"Oh," came the enthusiastic reply, "by all means! You can join us when you are done."

The Rector turned his attention to Toby and motioned to follow him up the stairs to the choir loft. Just as Toby was about to disappear from my view, he turned toward me and mouthed the words "find it."

The church had three aisles leading to the chancel at the front of the nave. The center aisle ran to a unique free-standing pulpit. All three aisles separated into sections of boxed pews. I could hear the voice of our host expounding on the space that would be occupied by the grand organ, but I had little time to listen. If I could hear voices above me, I knew I could work to find the baptismal font and the hidden secret it held.

I scanned the front of the church as I backed up wondering if the font would be near the altar or a side of the chancel. I was not looking where I was going when my back suddenly bumped into what I thought was the wall. I had moved beyond the entry door from the vestibule. I turned to see what was behind me. There before me was a beautifully carved baptismal font!

I looked at the baptismal font. Unlike the one in New York, this font was made of wood painted a glossy white that from afar might look like marble. The base was a solid block of walnut or oak. The body of the font was all one piece of wood that had been intricately carved into cherubs and angels. The bowl to hold the holy water for a baptism was set into the top of the central body. As a piece of art, the font was lovely.

As I examined the font, there did not appear to be any place where a piece of parchment could be hidden. There were no joints in the body. The top of the font where the bowl was, was itself, wider than the base by several inches. I looked at the base again. The base was about six inches high. The four corners of the base were mitered, and an extra piece of wood had been added to the side of the font that would be against the wall, like a spacer to keep the font bowl at the top from resting against the wall. As I looked at this extra piece of wood, I realized it was not finished like the rest of the font. It was just a raw piece of painted wood covering one side of the base. It had been crudely added to this one side of the base and looked like an after-thought.

I looked about for something to pry this board from the font base. There were several workmen's tools lying just inside the door. I found a pry bar and, moving the font out from the wall, I applied the bar to the top of the added board. Giving it a sharp pry, it separated from the base and fell to the floor. I looked at the finished base of the font and saw nothing but the original finished base. I looked at the board I had pried free and saw the side that had been against the base of the baptismal font had been shaved out in such a way that a hollow existed. There, in the hollow, was a folded piece of parchment.

I quickly pocketed the parchment and pushed the piece of wood back into position. I slid the font back against the wall expecting the wall would help to hold the extra piece of wood against the font. I straightened my clothes, turned, and quickly began mounting the stairway to the gallery above. I found Toby in an animated conversation with the bewildered churchman. The poor man sat in a choir chair busily writing down the gibberish being expounded by Toby. For Toby's part, he had found a length of rounded wood and was calling out measurements based on the length of this 'ruler' of unknown length, all being duly recorded by our host.

As soon as Toby saw me, he gave me a knowing nod that I returned. Our host glanced up and noticed my presence and quickly turned to me as if I was his salvation.

"Did you enjoy the church?" he inquired hopefully, thankfully relieved of his prior scribbling.

"It is truly an amazing building," I replied.

"And, we have a growing congregation, I am proud to say," our host said seeming to beam with pride. "I am sure it is due in no small measure to Bishop Berkeley and Maestro Pachelbel."

"Are you done with your measurements, Mr. Trinidad," I said changing the focus to Toby.

"Indeed, I am," Toby replied. "I will need to take this rod with your permission," Toby said to our churchman who cringed a bit thinking Toby would begin throwing numbers for him to record again.

"Yes, yes! Of course," the churchman replied handing the paper with the recorded measurements on it to Toby. "I truly hope you will relay to the bishop our full compliance with his request."

I assured our host that we would certainly be sure the bishop would know of the cooperation we had received. As we started to descend the stairs into the back of the nave, I suddenly had a thought.

"Sir," I asked of our host, "might we pause a moment in one of these pews and offer a prayer for the success of this venture?"

"By all means," our host replied enthusiastically. "However, I will have to leave you on your own as I have a meeting in the rectory. But you know the way out when you are done." And with that assurance, the churchman opened the door of the pew nearest him and stepped aside so Toby and I might enter. He closed and latched the door in a single unbroken motion as I was sure he had done a few hundred times during his service to the church.

Finally, alone, Toby turned to me and in whispered voice asked, "What is this all about, Tom?"

"Where better to show you what I found than here in this sanctuary where we will be undisturbed," I replied in the same hushed tone.

"You found it then?" Toby said with controlled excitement.

I reached into my pocket and brought out the folded piece of parchment. As I started to unfold it, the creases showed it had been folded for a long time. When fully open, I recognized the handwriting. It was my father's.

The words flowed across the page with the measured pace of an experienced writer. They were written as a series of instructions. Toby and I began reading.

'Sail the southern shore east to the lowest point in the horizon north.'
'Drop anchor between the two pillar rocks and row ashore.'
'Strike inland to the edge of the pond you find.'
'Search for the lettered boulder.'
'Fifty paces in the direction opposite that of the 'arrow' you see.'
'Search to find a second lettered boulder.'
'Twenty paces as before and find the ring of cannon balls.'
'A fathom down lies what you seek.'

We looked at each other not fully understanding what we had just read.

"Is it a code?" asked Toby.

"I do not think so," I replied. "It is written so anyone finding it would have little idea of understanding it. It is time to put all three sections of the map together."

Toby nodded in agreement. I folded the parchment carefully and slipped it into my pocket. I unlatched the door of the pew and Toby, and I, slid out into the aisle, passed through the double doors into the vestibule, and left the church by the same path we had taken upon arriving. Neither of us said much as we walked back to the White Horse Inn. Our thoughts were centered on the instructions to be followed to find the treasure. Of course, it went without being said that, before these instructions could be followed, the island to which they applied needed to be known. And it was just as obvious that any one piece of the map was of little value without the others. The appreciation I held for my father's intelligence in constructing his map was proved, once again.

TWENTY-SIX

*A*fter a typical busy evening of diners and the usual imbibers in the tavern, our exhausted little group at the White Horse slumped into chairs in the tavern after ushering out the last of our patrons. The kitchen had been cleaned up and the tavern shut down and Mary, Jackie, Toby, and I sat down for the first time that evening. Between serving meals and serving the thirsty bar guests, Toby and I had attempted to talk about what should be shared at this point with Mary – and the possibility of including Jackie.

"How was your afternoon at the church," Mary began, "was it as successful as you had hoped?"

"It was," I replied. "I think Toby and I are in agreement that it may be time to bring Jackie in on our little secret, if you agree, Mary."

At the mention of a secret, Jackie's ears perked up. He leaned forward and folded his arms on the table we all sat around.

"I think Jackie should be brought in," Mary agreed. "That is, provided he understands that he swears on your father's Bible to say nothing of what he hears tonight to anyone outside of the four of us." Mary fixed a look on Jackie as cold as ice.

I had retrieved my father's Bible during the evening and now placed it on the table in front of Jackie.

Jackie looked around the table and saw the same expression on each face at the table. He slowly placed his hand on the cover of the Bible.

"I swear not to speak a word of what I am about to be told to any other living soul," he said solemnly.

"Now, can someone tell me what it is I just swore not to share with anyone?"

Toby and I started laughing and Mary smiled broadly.

"Jackie, it is a long story, but we are now in possession of a complete map to a treasure," I said.

"A treasure map?" Jackie replied in disbelief. "You have me swearing not to tell anyone about a treasure map? Are you serious? Are you all daft?"

"This map is the real thing," Toby offered. "Tom's father left it for him."

"This is not a laughing matter, Jackie," I said with as much gravity as I could muster. "We are reasonably sure the map is accurate."

The laughter had ceased, and I retrieved the Bible from in front of Jackie and opened the cover and removed the first section of the map from inside the cover. I turned to the back pages of the Bible and retrieved the second piece of the map. I then reached into my pocket and brought forth the third piece of folded parchment. Mary and Jackie seemed in shock.

"Forgive me," Mary said hesitantly, "I had not really believed you until this moment."

"I could not tell you more than I did," I replied to Mary. "There may still be those who would kill if they knew this existed."

"Tom," Jackie said with eyes wide, "you are serious about this? I mean, it really does exist?"

"I believe it does." I replied to Jackie.

"But you never said anything about this when we were all Dock Rats living in that warehouse on the docks," he protested mildly.

"I did not know of it then," I said. "My father had told me to always keep the Bible close, that my future was within. I did not find the first part of the map until Toby, and I had left the Dock Rats and were here at the White Horse."

"Why are there three pieces," Jackie asked now satisfied that I had not withheld this secret from the members of the Dock Rats.

"It's quite ingenious really," Toby spoke up.

"My father broke up the map into three pieces," I said. "Each piece is of little value without the others." I unfolded the first parchment and revealed what was a map of Long Island Sound and the islands and coastlines surrounding it. I reached for the second piece of parchment and began unfolding it.

"There is nothing on that except some holes that look like it was eaten by rodents," Jackie said with a look of puzzlement.

"Ah-h-h, but watch the magic," I replied as I placed the second parchment over the first lining up the smaller holes as Toby and I had done before.

"There is where the treasure lies," I said to the amazed faces of Mary and Jackie. "Fishers Island."

"That's brilliant!" Jackie exclaimed. "So, now we know what island. But where on the island?"

"That is contained in here," I said holding up the third piece of folded parchment. "These are the directions to the treasure. Only Toby and I have seen these, and I would like to keep them until needed."

"Your father was a bit of a genius, Tom," Mary said with admiration. "As you said, one piece without the others tells someone nothing."

"Our next task is to hire or buy a ship large enough to sail to the island and follow the instructions we have to find the treasure," I said.

"But what of the crew, Tom?" Toby asked. "None of us are skilled enough to sail to this island. We couldn't navigate our way out of the harbor, let alone sail in open water!"

"This is all too true," I said as all four of us nodded in agreement. "My preference would be to purchase a boat and hire as small a crew as possible. When we have found the treasure, we can pay each member enough in wages for them to quit Newport forever."

"They would need to agree to that before joining the crew," Toby hastened to say.

"Would there be enough treasure to be able to pay them that much?" Jackie asked.

"From what I know, there should be," I reassured Jackie. "Supposedly, there is more than we all could spend in our lifetimes," I continued with a smile, "but we won't know for sure until we see it!"

"We certainly get a goodly flow of ships' captains in here," Mary said. "I'm sure one or two might be looking to sell."

"I would bet from my experience most captains are not the owners of their ships," Jackie put forth. "Merchants own the ships; the captains run them."

"I think you are right, Jackie," I agreed. "That is why I am going to speak to Reverend Berkeley about obtaining a ship. I do not think he will be too inquisitive as to why it is wanted, and his contacts might ease the way for us to obtain such without any suspicion."

"So, there you have it," I said pushing back from the table. You are all a part of our little adventure now and know all there is to know."

Everyone nodded to each other in recognition of this fact and rose from the table. The last lighted candles and lanterns were extinguished, and all headed to bed. Tomorrow would be a good day to find a ship.

The sun was well up when I awoke the next morning. Toby was washing up in the basin on the chest of drawers. I groaned as I sat up and Toby turned to smile at my stiffness.

"Good morning, Tom," he said brightly. "It is a beautiful day."

I smiled to myself and replied, "Yes. I agree."

I reached for the vest I had worn the night before and pulled the piece of parchment from the pocket.

"Toby," I said interrupting his toweling off, "before we go down to breakfast, would you take pen and paper and make a copy of the directions written here? Only, alter some of the steps."

Toby stopped drying off and looked at me in an unspoken question.

"You want me to change some of the directions," he asked? "Can I ask the reason?"

"Our circle of people knowing of our quest is likely to grow larger," I said with thought. "Would it not be wiser to have as few as possible know the last part of the map? Understand, I do not distrust any who we have brought into our confidence at this point, but a slip of the tongue, the wrong thing said in an unguarded moment in front of the wrong person, could undo our hunt."

"So, as a precaution, we would carry a set of false directions just in the event..."

Toby voiced trailed off as he thought.

"I thought, as I slept last night, I had already made one, and possibly two, such slips of the tongue," I said quietly.

Toby looked at me in question.

"I mentioned the precise name of the island where the treasure should be found," I said, "and, I brandished the parchment with the steps to find the treasure."

"But, as you said, everyone is sworn to silence," Toby offered.

"I know," I replied, "but, if a slip can occur so easily, we must pay particular close attention and take more precautions,"

"Very well," Toby answered. "You wash up and I will find paper and ink and make a copy – with intentional errors," he said with a wry smile.

When I had finished washing up, Toby presented me with what he had written as instructions to finding the treasure. He had changed the directions to follow and the pacing so it would lead anyone using these instructions to find themselves wandering in a completely different location from the actual treasure. I took the paper and folded it just as the real parchment was folded. I pressed the folds tightly to make them appear to have been folded for a long time.

"What are you going to do with the real direction," Toby asked?

"Let's put them in John I:33," I suggested. "I think that is fitting, don't you?"

Toby smiled at me, and I gave a small laugh as we left our shared room and descended to the kitchen.

The aroma of sweet buns Mary had just pulled from the oven filled the air as we came through the kitchen door from the dining room. Jackie arrived with sweet butter up from the cool larder. The table was neatly set for the four of us to sit for breakfast. And my mouth started watering at the thought of those sweet buns.

As we all took our seats, Mary brought a basket of buns to the table and asked me what my plans were for the day.

"I expect I will hear from the bishop at some point today," I replied. "Our trip to New York will have put him back in his correspondence and he takes pride in being prompt with his replies. He may have heard about the funding for his college during his absence."

"What is the delay with that, Tom," Toby asked as he buttered another piece of bun. "Has it not been nearly two years the Reverend has been waiting for it?"

"Actually, nearly three, I believe, Toby," I replied. "The promise was made under our last king and this George does not seem concerned about honoring his grandfather's agreements. But the Bishop is an always hopeful man."

Another round of good British tea was poured by Jackie as we all devoured the luscious buns.

"I was thinking, should the Reverend ask for me today, I might be able to start a discussion about obtaining a vessel," I wondered aloud. "He wants me to go to New Haven and talk with Rector Williams of Yale."

"Would he want to go with you, Tom?" Jackie asked.

"He might," I replied thinking how I could avoid having the same thought. "Let me at least open the question with him and see what he says."

Conversation drifted into what could be expected this day at the inn. It was the weekend and usually a less busy time for food, but busy for the tavern. We were just clearing the table when I received a message the

Reverend would expect me about noon. I excused myself from clearing the dishes and climbed the stairs to put my shoulder bag together to be ready to leave for Whitehall.

The way to Whitehall I had walked more times than I could count. But it was a pleasant stroll in the late spring weather. It provided me with the opportunity to organize my thoughts, the time to reflect, time to think. How could I present an argument for me to visit Yale on my own knowing the Reverend's fellowship with Rector Williams? Surely, he would jump at the opportunity to visit Yale. I could see no straightforward way of proposing making the trip alone. Perhaps, it was better to be quiet about the subject of visiting New Haven for the present.

Now that I had decided not to pursue New Haven as a reason for obtaining a ship, I needed some other strategy, some other compelling reason that would find favor with my patron. My mind ran from idea to idea, and each was rejected as not having enough importance to require a ship. I thought about Toby and could think of nothing that would require him to need a ship. Jackie offered no real need for a ship, unless it could be related in some way to the White Horse Inn, or to the secret he did not want disclosed about the printing business. The printing business. The printing business required a press and large tables and type and paper in large volume. How would those things be transported? In crates aboard a ship? Over land by wagon on poor roads might damage a printing press, not to mention the time it might take due to harsh weather and road conditions.

These thoughts were turning over in my mind as I arrived at Whitehall. My knock at the front door was quickly responded to and I was ushered into the presence of Reverend Berkeley. He greeted me with his normal good nature and asked what I thought of his gifting the Trinity Church an organ.

"It is a fine organ loft with plenty of room for a fine organ. The sound should travel well throughout the congregation," I said. I reached into my satchel and retrieved the paper with the measurements written on it.

"I'm afraid I have forgotten the stick that was used to make sense of these measures," I said, handing the paper to the Reverend. "I shall bring it with me when next I come."

"Excellent," He replied. "I did not know Mr. Trinidad was skilled in engineering."

This comment caught me by surprise.

"He has many talents, Sir," I replied. "Toby did much of the design work when we enlarged the White Horse Inn a few years ago." I lied as convincingly as I could.

"Ahh, that is good to know," Reverend Berkeley replied, although I do not think he believed me.

"Let us speak of Yale," he began. It is important we do not let the subject drop but pursue it while the iron is hot. Tom, it is important that you are ready before the fall term. I must tell you I do not know how much longer I will wait for the Crown to fulfill the promise of funds made to me by the present King's grandfather."

This was the first time I heard a negative thought regarding the Reverend's great project of creating a school in Bermuda.

"My friends in parliament are suggesting I should present myself in person to the King to plead my case."

"I think I understand," I said grasping the seriousness of the situation. "Perhaps I can suggest a solution to the question of Yale. However, it might seem a bit round about."

Bishop Berkeley straightened in his chair and cocked his head to listen intently.

"I have been informed that a certain printer of some fame is planning a move to Newport to begin a printing business," I imparted. "I am not at liberty to share this person's name; however, he is held in some renown and has sent an agent ahead to Newport to secure materials for his establishment. These are to be acquired by ship from Philadelphia and New York."

"If I were able to acquire a vessel to assist this agent, it might be possible for me to arrange to leave the vessel in New Haven and meet with Rector Williams of Yale," I continued. "Would that meet with your approval?"

"That is an excellent idea, young man," Reverend Berkeley brightened. "How soon might you be able to arrange matters?"

"Possibly within a fortnight," I said without really knowing. "Getting a ship might be somewhat difficult. I am sure the agent would want the captain and crew sworn to secrecy," I put forth. "Of course, if someone of your stature were to let it be known you were looking for a ship to sail to Philadelphia and New York," I could see the Reverend's brow furrowing, and I changed direction, "it might raise some curiosity. It might be wiser for me to seek out a ship."

"Yes, yes, quite so," said the Reverend almost thinking aloud. "You must find the ship. And you can tell the captain that I will bear the expense. I will give you a letter to that effect. But you must find a ship quickly."

"Tell me one more thing," Reverend Berkeley asked looking up at me, "this printer, without telling me his name, does he have a brother named Benjamin?"

TWENTY-SEVEN

I left through the front door of Whitehall into the bright sunshine of the day, satisfied with myself and excited that I had solved the problem of how I would acquire a ship and secretly convey the treasure, once found, to Newport. No one would have concern about a ship sailing under the auspices of Bishop Berkeley. Going to New Haven, then New York and Philadelphia, picking up some crated cargo and returning to New Haven would raise no suspicions. A small stop at Fishers Island might seem curious, but, if only to make some repairs on the vessel requiring the unloading of a few crates of the cargo, who would care?

I was delighted with myself as I strolled along. My first thought was to approach a couple of the distinguished merchants of Newport. The Reverend was known to them and his asking for a ship might not only be quickly granted but would likely be considered a feather in their cap for providing such a distinguished personage the services of one of their vessels.

Buoyant with the thought of the plan, I reached the White Horse and entered through the rear door into the kitchen. Preparations were well underway for noon meal, and Mary was preparing small shepherd's pies for the patrons who would arrive shortly. Jackie was busy stirring the soup that was warming over the low embers of the kitchen fireplace. I smiled at them both as I entered, and they did the like.

I passed through to the tavern where a few of the daily regulars were in their usual places. Toby was behind the bar, a towel over his shoulder, pouring ale from a barrel. The stains on his apron showed it had already been a busy morning.

"Any luck?" he asked as I slid behind the bar.

"I have a plan," I said with a smile. "We will need to get Jackie a bit more involved, but I think it will work."

As midday approached, the tavern began to fill with people, and the throng of voices grew louder. Food started to be ordered, and I left Toby behind the bar to serve while I brought out food from the kitchen. While some food and drink establishments in town were rowdy and known for disturbances, the White Horse had a reputation for tasty food and friendly conversation. It was one of the reasons the Town Councilmen and lawyers and merchants preferred the White Horse, and we worked hard to keep the less desirable crowd away.

By late afternoon, Mary and Jackie could take a short break before setting up service for supper. The tavern crowd thinned enough that Toby could catch a minute or two from behind the bar. The four of us met quickly in the kitchen. Everyone wanted to know what had happened at Whitehall.

"Let me just say," I began in a hushed voice, "I have secured a promise from the bishop to support our obtaining a ship. We can talk about the details tonight after we close, but for now know, I have a plan how to get the treasure home."

With that said, everyone became somewhat giddy and had to be cautioned not to display such to the guests. We all nodded, smiles abounded, and we all returned to our duties. The evening seemed to drag on forever. Perhaps it was the anticipation of being able to discuss with the other members of our cabal how we might acquire a vessel. Perhaps it was the frustration of having to wait to do so. The hours until closing seemed endless.

Finally, the last of the regulars left the tavern arm-in-arm, supporting one another in animated discussion. Jackie quickly extinguished the candles on the tables nearest the windows that fronted onto the street and threw the bolt on the front door. Mary and I finished the last of the dishes and latched the kitchen door. Toby was coming out from behind the bar as Mary and I came from the kitchen, and we all joined Jackie at a table near the kitchen wall.

"I thought the crowd would never leave tonight," Mary said in exhaustion.

"Time just dragged tonight," Jackie agreed.

"Well, we might have been a bit anxious to be able to talk," I offered, "but it looks promising for the next step."

"How did you get the Reverend to support getting a ship?" Toby asked,

"I had to suggest I would go to New Haven and explore the possibility of attending Yale this fall," I shared sheepishly. "I also made a reference involving Jackie and his potential future plans. But I did not disclose any names," I quickly added.

"How did that come about?" Jackie asked.

"I intimated that an agent for a certain printer had been made known to me and that he had arrived in Newport to begin preparations for the arrival of his equipment."

"What possessed you to say that?" Jackie protested!

"Let me explain," I quickly began, "What would people think if we set sail and a few days later returned with eight heavy chests?"

Everyone at the table looked at their neighbor and their heads began to nod.

"It would be rather curious and probably the talk of the town," I explained. "Now think of this. Suppose a ship arrived with some large crates. What then?" I said with a shrug. "Would anyone even think twice? And if they did, if a rumor was circulating around town of a new printer preparing to set up shop, what then? Especially if the voyage was sponsored by so great a personage as the bishop."

"Tom, that is brilliant," Toby said in quiet admiration. "But we need a ship's crew that will keep quiet."

"Aye," I replied putting my hand to my chin, "that is the rub and one I need to resolve. I'll start making inquiries tomorrow with some merchants."

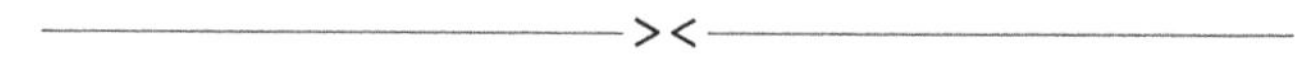

I was awake at the first light and was still the last one in the inn to descend to the kitchen. As I walked into the kitchen, it was obvious I had interrupted an intense conversation being had between Mary, Jackie, and Toby. Breakfast tea was on the table and, as I poured myself a cup, the tension in the room was overwhelming.

"Alright," I said calmly, "do we have a concern?"

Mary and Jackie both turned to Toby. He was obviously the reluctant spokesperson.

"It's not so much a concern," Toby began, "it's more of a need for us to understand a little more about the plan."

What did you mean about the crates?" Jackie anxiously broke in. "Where do the crates come from and what do they have in them?"

"The crates come from anywhere you like," I responded a bit flippantly, as I settled in a chair at the table in the kitchen. "New York, Philadelphia, New Haven, it really doesn't matter. As to what is inside them, they contain nothing. Or more precisely, smaller crates."

"Oh, well now," Mary said in confusion, "now you're really going to have to explain that one!" I smiled at her confusion.

"We have, say, a half dozen large crates ordered to be made for us." I began. "We then order eight crates each about half the size of the first crates. When we reach the island, we unload enough of the large crates with the smaller crates inside as we think needed. As we dig up the treasure chests, we put them in the smaller crates..."

"And put the smaller crates back inside the larger crates so the same number go back aboard, and they have weight," Jackie said thoughtfully, "like they contain heavy equipment like parts of a printing press!"

"As the other large crates left aboard DO contain!" Jackie broke in slapping his hand on the table.

"But won't the crew wonder why we stopped at a pretty deserted island and take some crates ashore?" Toby added.

"If the same number come back aboard as went ashore, should they wonder," I replied? "Sure, the ones returning aboard might weigh a bit more, but maybe not enough to cause a concern. And with the right crew, they will not question it."

"So, our real concern is the crew and not the vessel," Toby said.

"There's a half-dozen ships in the harbor right now that could easily be gotten," Mary said, "but would the crews be what we want?" We all quietly agreed Mary was right.

It was time to begin preparing another day of food and drink for our customers. As soon as I finished the morning book entries, I could leave for an hour or two and begin making inquiries of some of the merchants. I did not expect any of them would jump at the chance to make a voyage to as far as Philadelphia to pick up some crates with no description of their content. But the fact that the Reverend Bishop Berkeley was associated with the voyage might be of benefit in convincing one or more merchants to make a vessel available.

It was an overcast day when I left the inn and headed toward the waterfront offices of town merchants. The leaden clouds and northwest wind brought a chill to a summer's day. I began my search for a ship at the south end of Thames Street and was received with an enthusiasm equal to the weather of the day. I heard excuse after excuse. Ships were already committed; cargoes were behind schedule and every vessel was being pressed into service; cargo made profits and profits were needed to satisfy backers of the merchants.

I called in at most of the major shipping merchants on the waterfront of town and even to the north road. Even when I related the backing of Reverend Berkeley, little interest was shown. Obtaining a ship looked to be a distant mark at best. My time had run out and I was heading back to the inn as the noon hour was fast approaching.

Jamie, Toby, and I spent the next two days of poor weather spreading word about town to the merchants and shippers of our desire to find a ship and crew. Mary asked several of the patrons at the White Horse, as well.

On the afternoon of the third day as I walked back toward the inn, I had the collar of my coat turned up against the wind and, so, did not see the boy approaching me from behind. He tugged on my sleeve to gain my attention and offered a folded note with his other hand. Before I could say a word, he was off down a side alley and gone from sight. I unfolded the piece of paper and read the note scribbled within.

'I wil meat ye tonite at tavern close about a shyp'

The note was unsigned. The scrawl was difficult to read and yet its message was clear. Whoever had sent it would be revealed at the end of the day. Until then, I would be left wondering who I was meeting. But at least someone had responded to our inquiries. I folded the note and put it in my pocket. At least I would have something positive to tell the others. My first action upon entering the inn was to show the note I had received to Mary, Jackie, and Toby. We immediately agreed I should meet our unknown benefactor alone and see what the terms were to be for this 'shyp'?

The weather had promised to be cold and windy with rain occasionally spattering against the window glass. Yet, it was warm and cozy inside the inn. The fires in the tavern and dining room kept everyone snug and warm. Though the weather might be stormy outside, the inn was a happy gathering place filled with the aroma of food and the conversation and occasional laughter of imbibing men.

The poor weather brought with it a smaller number of patrons and an easier day of work. But even an easier day of work was tiring. Serving food and drink meant being on one's feet most of the day. It felt good to be able to finally sit at the end of the day.

Toby and I changed places behind the bar, and he quietly slipped into the kitchen leaving me alone in the tavern. As the small group of patrons began filing out that evening, I looked about the tavern at the faces of the last few people. Most of the faces were familiar to me. They were mostly the regulars. Was the sender of the note among them? How would he make himself known to me? I tried not to stare at any one face for too long, whether known to me or not. The minutes seemed to pass with no indication or approach to me from anyone.

As the last of the patrons passed through the door, a figure entered the tavern. His hat was pulled low on his brow causing the drops of rain on his hat to drip about his shoulders, and the wind had whipped the edges of his hair about his face. He was bent forward attempting to hide his face, and his great coat was pulled high and tight around his shoulders. His great boots clunked on the floor as he strode to a nearby chair.

"Madeira, if you please, Barman," came the croaking voice from the chair.

"Sorry, Sir, I'm afraid you missed the last call," I heard myself saying before I could stop myself.

"Very well," came the reply as the figure began to rise from its seat. "I'm sure another ship will come along."

"WAIT!" I cried sharply, "Madeira did you say, Sir? Coming right up." I fumbled with the glass as I went to set it on the bar. My stupidity at not realizing who this might be made me curse myself. I went under the bar and pulled our best madeira out and poured a full measure and a bit. I corked the bottle and placed the glass on a tray holding the stemmed base with my thumb.

I placed the glass before him on the table. My guest removed his hat which I recognized as a heavy weather hat worn by sailors. He shook it to remove the remaining water it held and tossed it on the chair beside him. He shifted the rain-slicked great coat he wore so it fell back on the chair and off his shoulders. He reached for the Madeira and downed half the measure in one gulp. He motioned me to the chair opposite him.

His face was heavily lined from years exposed to sun and wind. His eyes squinted like they had stared into sunsets and sunrises for far too long. His mouth was but a thin line below an aquiline nose that did not fit with his other features. The stubbled beard and long hair that fell in tangles from the rain framed his sea-worn face.

"Word is about ye be lookin' fer a ship," came the voice in a whisper.

"I am," came my reply.

"I have a ship newly launched," the man said, "she be a sleek schooner that needs a shakedown voyage before…" he paused searching for words, "before going to sea."

I was curious about his pause, but decided not to pry, as I hoped he would not want too many details about our voyage.

"From what I hears, yer lookin' to make Philadelphie," he continued.

"That would be the farthest point," I answered. "We would need to port at New London only to drop someone off. Then on to New York and Philadelphia possibly, unless our cargo has made it to New York by the time we sail.

"I can be ready to sail in three days," came the response.

"That would be most satisfactory," I said overjoyed by such news. "May I ask your name, Sir?"

"Cutler," came the terse response, "Captain Jamie Cutler of the schooner *Pelican*."

"Thomas Gray, at your service, Captain."

The captain raised his glass and drained the remaining Madeira.

"Until tomorrow," Captain Cutler smiled. It was an unexpected action on his part.

"I shall ask for payment in advance and specifics about the voyage at that time," he continued.

We rose from the table, and I offered my hand. Captain Cutler looked at my offered hand and smiled as he grasped it in a firm shake. He retrieved his hat from the chair beside him and, giving a heave of his shoulder, brought his rain gear into place on his shoulders. He showed himself to the door, and I stood for a moment before moving to lock it. I knew there were three anxious people waiting in the kitchen to find out what had happened even though I knew they had tried to eavesdrop on the meeting the whole time.

TWENTY-EIGHT

As I picked up the glass now emptied of Madeira and wiped the few drops of rain that had landed on the table, I tried to assess in my mind who this Captain Cutler might be and how he had learned of our desire for a ship. I was occupied by this thought as I was placing the empty glass and towel in my hand on the bar.

"What did he say?" Toby's voice behind me startled me. I turned to see Mary and Jackie at the table just outside the door leading into the kitchen, their faces reflecting the anxiety they were feeling.

"We will meet tomorrow to arrange particulars," I said.

"So, we have a ship?" Jackie said anxiously.

"I think we might," I answered. "I will know more tomorrow."

"Tom, you look worried," Toby said studying my face. "What is it? Something is not to your liking. Something has you concerned. What is it?"

"It is just," I started to say trying to form my thoughts, "how did he know we were seeking a ship? Who directed him to us?"

"He must have learned of it from someone you, or one of us, spoke with in the last few days, don't you think?" Toby offered.

"I do not believe the man I just met with wrote the note I was passed," I said.

"Who was he?" Mary asked. "I don't think I have ever seen him before."

"He called himself Captain Jamie Cutler," I answered Mary.

"I don't recognize that name, least ways, not that I recall." Mary said wrinkling her nose and twisting her lip. "I think I would remember his kind."

"Well, it's an offer of a ship and we should at least be thankful for that," Jackie said.

"And so, we shall," I replied. "But let us remember, it is the crew that is most important."

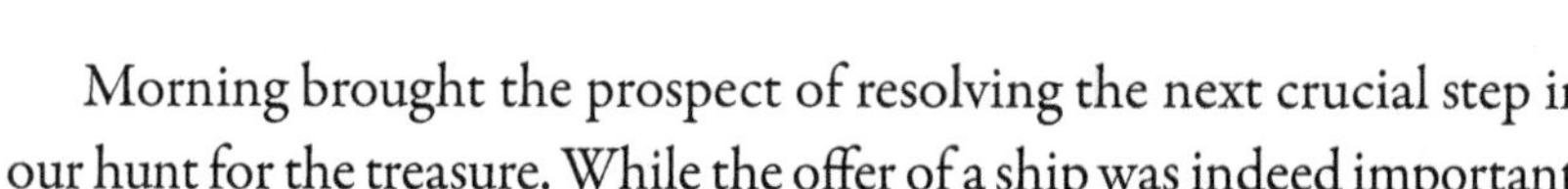

Morning brought the prospect of resolving the next crucial step in our hunt for the treasure. While the offer of a ship was indeed important, questions regarding the captain and crew needed to be resolved. Now that we had the prospect of a vessel, I needed to meet with Reverend Berkeley regarding Yale and discuss the costs he was willing to stand for the ship. Our tavern group would need to pay any additional costs.

Toby and I had saved a fair sum over the time we had been at the White Horse. Our confidence in our quest made us willing to commit all our reserves to funding the cause. We could not expect the same from Mary, and Jackie could afford to add little to the venture. Our standing and reputation in the city should make a loan a possibility if needed as a last resource. But we felt confident that we possessed enough funds to supplement whatever Bishop Berkeley was unwilling to fund.

As soon as my morning duties were finished, I bid Mary, Toby, and Jackie farewell and started for Whitehall. A little under an hour's walk found me knocking at the front door. Admitted to the study, I found the Reverend busy writing at his desk.

"Tom," he greeted me warmly, "so glad you came. I am just finishing your letter of introduction to Rector Williams. I explained to him, as you will see, my disappointment in not being able to accompany you and, therefore, not having the opportunity to see him. However, I will endeavor to see him in the fall when you return for instruction."

Bishop Berkeley was in an expansive mood this morning for which I was grateful. He sealed the letter with wax and his signet and passed it to me.

"How is the search for a ship progressing?" he asked.

"I have been approached by someone," I said trying to hide any misgivings. "We are to meet today to discuss details. I do not know if this person knows of your involvement. I have yet to disclose it."

"Good, good," the Reverend muttered leaning back in his chair. "Perhaps it is best that he learns no more than is necessary of my involvement. Sometimes the price is higher if a personage is known to have an interest."

"If we should agree to use this ship, I am sure he will expect payment in advance," I said.

"That is not to be, Tom," Reverend Berkeley said sternly. "I will provide payment when the voyage is completed. I might be willing to provide a third up front, but no more. There should be no profit to the venture until it is completed. We must be sure this captain and crew are honest."

"Very well, Sir. I shall speak with him today and arrange terms," I said.

"Who is this captain?" asked the Reverend.

"The man I met called himself Captain Jamie Cutler," I replied. "The name was unfamiliar to me."

"As it is to me, Tom. What merchant does he sail for? We should ask about..."

"I am not sure that is a wise course, Your Worship," I quickly cut in. "There is some secrecy involved in our voyage and we should probably feel out this Captain Cutler." Little did the Reverend realize the secrecy I spoke of was far different from the secrecy he knew about.

"Yes, I believe you are correct," the Reverend spoke after a moment of thought. "I leave it to you, Tom. I know you will use your best judgement. How soon did he say he could sail?"

"Three days, Sir," I responded. I realized I was still holding the Reverend's letter to the Yale Rector in my hand. I carefully placed it in my pocket.

"It will take all of that and perhaps a day more for your letter to reach New Haven," the Reverend said. "Hand me back the letter and I will rewrite it for a meeting a week from today. That should give you time to prepare and some time to negotiate with this Captain what's-his-name. I will send it by day's end by my own courier."

"Thank you, Sir," I responded. "I am off to meet Captain Cutler and shall inform you of the result."

Despite the Reverend's thinking, seven days was not sufficient time for all the moving parts of the voyage to be put in place. As I walked the road back to Newport, I was trying to determine what needed to be done and how quickly. It may have been why I did not notice the man leaning against the stone wall a short distance from Whitehall. As I approached him, I realized it was the Captain I was meeting in slightly different attire.

"Thought I would save you the trouble of looking for me in town by meeting you here," Captain Cutler greeted me. "I also thought this might afford us a bit more privacy for our discussion than we might expect in town, as well."

He was dressed in the same heavy sea boots he had worn the night before. His lace-trimmed shirt was covered by a blue double-breasted military-type coat with shiny brass buttons that fell well below his waist and covered his green breeches. The broad belt about his waist held a scabbard longer than his coat with an ornate sword hilt projecting from it. His hair was tied in a neat ponytail with a strip of red fabric just visible under his brimmed hat. His beard had been trimmed.

"I appreciate the accommodation, Captain," I started. "I do have a few questions to ask of you."

He made a short bow with a sweeping motion of his hat and said, "Ask away."

"By your speech and your demeanor, I do not believe you wrote the note that was handed to me," I said trying to show no judgment by it.

"That is true," he replied. "It was not I who heard of your attempting to obtain a ship, but one of my crew who is semi-literate."

"Do you have any knowledge of the nature of the voyage we wish to make?" I asked.

"Only that you desire a certain amount of secrecy," the captain replied, "and that is something I would also desire to have."

This reply took me back as I had not expected such a reply.

"I believe we may have a mutual agreement on the subject of secrecy," I said.

"Whether I disclose more of my reasons for secrecy depends somewhat on you sharing some of the reason for your secrecy," Captain Cutler replied.

"Very well," I started, thinking I would only need to tell him a portion of the whole secret. "We need to get to New York to pick up a cargo of crated manufacture, unless it has not reached New York from Philadelphia. If it has not arrived, we may need to wait a day or two for it to arrive. Before reaching New York, I will need to leave the ship in New Haven and be retrieved on your return. There might be one more stops on the way back to Newport."

"So, you want a ship to land you in New Haven on the way to New York to pick up a cargo, stop in New Haven to pick you up on the way back. And there might be another port made between New Haven and Newport," the captain repeated. "I suspect the possible unspoken porting is the real reason for secrecy," he said quietly. "But I understand and respect your request."

"Now I will be as open with you," Captain Cutler began. "My ship is presently under no flag. She was captured by my crew. We have renamed her *Peregrine*. She is a schooner that requires a cruise in local waters before entering the trade, as they call it. Since there is no Court of Admiralty here in Newport to grant her title to me, I must sail to a port like New York to have her awarded as a prize. Once she is clearly mine, we will sail for Africa with a cargo of rum and trinkets. You will not see us again and we will not see you."

"Now for the reason I desire some secrecy," he began again, "I need an out-of-the-way place for a day or two where I might change the appearance of my ship. She would still be a schooner, but a new color on her sides might make her less recognizable, if you get my meaning."

"I see," I replied. "So, making an anchorage in a secluded place, unexpected by most, for a day or two would be of some import to you?"

"Aye, it would," Captain Cutler replied.

"What would you say if I were to guarantee such an arrangement could be made provided our activity over those two days were never discussed beyond the ship to anyone?"

"I believe I could make such a guarantee," said the good Captain.

"Then I believe we have reached an agreement," I said extending my hand.

"There is one small matter to be determined," Captain Cutler said with a smile.

"A ship does not come cheaply and there is a matter of payment."

"I have been instructed by my silent partner in this voyage to authorize one-third of the total in advance of sailing and the remainder upon the safe return of cargo to Newport," I replied in full confidence of myself.

"Seeing as I have a pretty fair idea of who your partner in this venture is and knowing of his reputation," Captain Cutler said, "I accept the arrangement and will expect payment of one-third before sailing."

With that, he took my hand and shook it strongly. We bid each other a good day and I resumed my walking to Newport. I had taken no more than a dozen steps when I turned around to ask a final thought I had, but the captain was gone from sight.

I knew our next step for this plan to work was to somehow get the crates ordered, built, paid for, and ready for loading aboard our ship which might be arriving much too soon for this to all happen. There would be no time to have them arrive in New York. So, the voyage would need to go to Philadelphia. The costs were mounting. As soon as I reached Newport, I would need to set in motion getting the crates constructed.

When I entered the kitchen at the inn, it was late morning. I found Jackie and Toby preparing for the noon crowd. I quickly called them to the long table in the kitchen.

"We have just seven days before I must be delivered in New Haven,"

I said with some dismay. "I had hoped for more time. But nevertheless, we must begin getting the crates constructed. We need to have an agent in Philadelphia or New York who will be able to act for us."

"I know someone in Philadelphia," Jackie piped up, "Well, sort of know."

"Speak up, Jackie," Toby said, "we have little time and any person who might be willing to help us is better than none."

"I was thinking Mr. Franklin," Jackie said a little chagrined.

"Why not," I said. "Jackie, would you be willing to go to Philadelphia?"

"I, Uh...I don't know," Jackie stammered out. "I've never gone that far and I'm not sure Mr. Franklin would see me."

"Nonsense," I said in reply, "you know his brother and that should mean something."

Alright, I'll go," Jackie said emphatically.

"Good man," Toby patted him on the back.

"We will need a horse," I mused. "You do know how to ride, don't you, Jackie?"

"That is one thing I have learned," he said almost laughing.

"It is probably four days hard ride to Philadelphia, five if the weather is bad" I quickly calculated. "That does not give us much time to have the crates readied."

"You only need to be in New Haven in a week's time," Toby said. "We have no hurry to get to Philadelphia by ship. It will most likely take a few days longer just to get there and sail back. With the help of Mr. Franklin's reputation, I am sure the cargo will be ready."

Mary had been standing by the door into the dining room listening. I had not seen her appearance. Suddenly she came through the door from the dining room into the kitchen with a small leather pouch in her hand.

"Jackie," she said as she dropped it on the table with a thud, "there are twenty guineas in there for a horse and lodgings along the way and for the crates to be built."

"Mary, you don't need to..." I began.

"I know I don't," Mary said sternly. And, then to Jackie, "and just 'because you have 'em don't mean ye need to spend 'um."

"Yes, Ma'am," Jackie replied meekly.

"Tell Mr. Franklin we will make good any additional expense if he will stand it for us," I said.

"Go and pack some clothes," Toby said trying to hurry Jackie into action. "I will go see about a horse for you."

Jackie headed to his room with the leather pouch in his hand and Toby was out the door in a flash. Left alone together in the kitchen, I embraced Mary for I could see she was a bit upset.

"It's almost all I've saved," she whispered as I held her head against my shoulder.

"If I am right, Mary, none of us will ever need worry about money again," I said softly. "My father was a good man."

Twenty-Nine

Toby returned from the city stable with a solid-looking steed for Jackie. Within an hour of that, Jackie was in the saddle with twenty guineas of Mary's savings in his saddlebag and a letter written by me addressed to Mr. Benjamin Franklin introducing Mr. Jamie Saunders, the name Jackie had used when he apprenticed under Mr. Franklin's brother in Boston.

With all our hopes running high, I joined Toby and Mary for an evening of providing food and drink to our patrons. It was the first night in the last few that I felt relaxed enough to enjoy working. As the time approached closing, a familiar face came through the door accompanied by two rather swarthy-looking companions. As they took a table near the back of the tavern room where the lighting was dim, I approached.

"Good evening, Captain," I said quietly. "What can I get you and your companions?"

"Evening, young Squire," came the reply. "Rum all 'round and a moment of your time."

I went to the bar and served up three measures of rum and a short pitcher of water and, placing all on a tray, returned to the table.

"And now you have my attention for a few minutes, Captain," I said.

"When must you be in New Haven?" Captain Cutler inquired.

"A week from tomorrow," I replied, estimating that the Reverend's letter would arrive at Yale in two days.

"And there is the matter of expense," the Captain continued.

The Captain's two companions spoke not a word but took heavy draughts of rum as they listened.

"I am afraid we will need you to pick up cargo in Philadelphia. I am sorry for this news."

"I would prefer Philadelphia, actually," Captain Cutler said with a smile. "Less of a chance of raising any questions."

For the first time, this raised smiles of agreement from the Captain's companions.

"This will add a few more days to the voyage and I am sure you will increase the cost accordingly," I said. "I am prepared to pay seventy-five pounds for your ship and crew for the voyage with thirty pounds to be delivered in advance and the balance upon safe delivery of I, my companions, and our cargo to Newport."

At the mention of the payments, the Captain's two confederates began whispering with the Captain and gesturing as they consulted. Finally, all heads nodded, and the Captain spoke.

"Agreed," he said. I must have had a look of puzzlement on my face for he continued.

"These are my first mate and the crew's representative," the captain said. Each touched their hand to their forehead in a half-hearty sloppy sort of salute as their titles were revealed.

"In our line of work," Captain Cutler related, "we make decisions and agreements according to our pact. And these two associates represent the crew and are sworn to speak truth of our agreement."

"I see," I replied. "Then we have an agreement?"

"Actually, it is more generous than was anticipated," Captain Cutler smiled. "But we all have secrets to protect. And, at that price, they'll be well protected."

We shook hands all around and I offered another round of rum on the house to seal the arrangement. It was quickly agreed to, and I rose and went to the bar. I knew Toby had been watching with interest what was transpiring at the table. As I came behind the bar, he turned next to me and whispered. "Well, do we have a ship and crew?"

"Yes," I whispered back to him, "and for less than I thought we would have to pay."

I finished pouring the rum and decided to put the bottle on the tray, as well. The cost of the bottle was nothing compared to the savings negotiated on the cost of the voyage. As I approached the table, the sight of a bottle of rum, as well as three tankards of rum was greeted with grateful thanks from the table occupants.

"One other question, if I may, Captain?" I asked.

"Certainly," he replied as his companions began enjoying their seconds.

"I have not seen a schooner at the waterfront," I said.

"Nor will you," he replied. "She's docked north of town in Coddington Cove where it be a bit more private. She might be mistaken for another ship until we take measures to clean her up if you understand my meaning. We will sail from there in five days. Plan to be at the dock early mornin.' Eight will do."

"Very well, Captain. Enjoy your drinks," I said as I turned from the table.

Back behind the bar, Toby was anxious to know the details of my discussion, but the tavern was crowded, and we could not take the time to discuss what had occurred immediately. Closing would be that time. After a few minutes, I happened to glance in the direction of the table where the negotiations had taken place. The table was empty and all that remained were three tankards and an untouched pitcher of water.

The doors to the inn were securely locked and most of the candles and lanterns were dark as Mary, Toby, and I finally settled at our usual table for an after-hours libation. I told Toby and Mary of our sailing date and the charges agreed upon with Captain Cutler.

"I shall ask Reverend Berkeley for twenty-five pounds and tell him it is half the cost plus a day's lodgings in New Haven," I said. We will need to come up with more, but I think Toby and I can manage it."

"I have a bit more, if needed," Mary offered.

"You have done quite enough, my Dear," Toby reassured her. "Besides, with Jackie gone to Philadelphia and Tom about to go to New Haven, I will have to do the work of three for a few days."

"Toby, I will need you with me," I said. "You cannot think I would leave you out of the hunt!"

"Then who is to help Mary?" Toby shot back.

"Mary is going on holiday," I said with a smile.

"Holiday?" Mary repeated the word with raised eyebrows. "What holiday?"

"Mary," I asked, "how long has it been since you closed the inn and took a trip? Some time for yourself?"

"Why, never," she responded.

"Well, you are going on your first holiday to a large city," I said. "You will accompany Toby to Philadelphia."

"Oh, I don't know...," Mary stammered.

"Come now, Mary," Toby cut in, "it will be an adventure and I will keep you safe."

"We'll post a notice that the White Horse Inn is taking a holiday for two weeks to celebrate the proprietor's birthday," I suggested.

" But that was in April," Mary protested.

"So, it will be a belated birthday gift from your employees," I offered. "That will explain our absence, as well."

"But I can't afford to be closed for two weeks," Mary protested again.

"Mary, remember what I told you last night," I answered softly. "None of us will need to worry about money ever again."

Mary nodded in understanding.

We finished our drinks and headed upstairs to bed. In the morning, I would head to Whitehall to secure our funding from Bishop Berkeley. Until then, all I wanted was a good night's sleep.

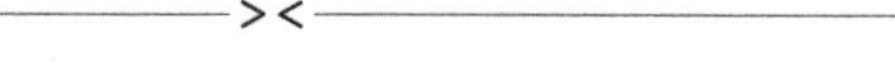

The next morning dawned with heavy fog rolling in on the waterfront. My walk to Whitehall, after a quick conversation with Toby and Mary, was quieter than usual because of the dampening effect of the fog.

Toby and Mary had tried to convince me to ask Reverend Berkeley for the entire thirty pounds. Their reasoning was solidly based on what I had told them of his willingness to only pay one-third of the total at the start with the remainder after the voyage was completed. I had decided to wait and see what his demeanor was when we discussed the voyage.

Whitehall appeared through the thick, damp fog like some large spectral façade, its windows like gridded rectangles darker than the rest. As I approached, the fog seemed to melt away, so the building took better form. I was taken to the study where Reverend Berkeley was at work at his writing desk.

"Ah-h-h, Thomas," he greeted me. "Are you ready for your voyage?"

"Yes, Sir. I leave in four days."

"Then you will be needing some funds," he continued.

He set his quill in the inkwell and opened a drawer on his side of the desk. He retrieved a box he placed on the desk. It was made of black metal with a lock. From his pocket, the Reverend withdrew a key and unlocked the box.

"How did negotiations go for the voyage?" he then asked me.

"I think we got a fair price, considering," I replied.

"Considering what, specifically?" Reverend Berkeley said stopping his motion of opening the metal box.

"I was unaware that Mary, our principal at the White Horse, had ordered some fittings for remodeling the inn and they will be brought aboard in Philadelphia," I said. "Since the cargo will now have some items for our own use, we feel we should shoulder the cost for those and any additional days of sailing," I explained meekly.

"What of the cost, Tom? What did you secure as a price?" The Reverend asked firmly.

"I secured a price of seventy-five pounds for the entire voyage with thirty paid at the start." I found I could not lie to this man I respected so greatly.

"Well done, my Boy!" Reverend Berkeley burst into a broad smile. "I was sure you would not be able to bargain for a fair price. I doubted you would get a vessel for less than a hundred pounds!"

The bishop opened the lid of the strong box and withdrew a sack that jingled as it landed on the desk.

"I would assume our fine Captain would prefer payment in gold rather than paper pounds," the Reverend said to himself. "And we need to provide some funds for your stay in New Haven," he said as he continued counting out gold coins. I had never seen so much gold in one place in all my life.

The Reverend opened another drawer and retrieved a small leather pouch into which he scooped up the coins he had counted out and funneled them into it.

"There you are, Tom," he said as he tied the strip of leather to the throat of the pouch with a double bow. "Two-thirds toward the voyage and another fifteen guineas for your trip to New Haven."

"But, Sir," I protested, "this is far too much!"

"Consider the rest a gift to Mary," he said jovially. "And tell her I shall be stopping at the inn to see those renovations when they are done."

I did not know the exact amount the Reverend had presented me, but I was not about to count it at that moment. I just knew it was more than he had originally promised. I thanked him over and over and assured him I would do all I could to justify his belief in me.

My return to Newport was disturbing. I had never walked this path with a heavy sack of gold in my possession before. It was an odd feeling. Suddenly, I was a person with wealth and yet, with that wealth came a certain feeling of dread. Should it be known I was in possession of such wealth, I could be the subject of an attack by some highwayman. I felt for the weight of the pouch for reassurance and quickened my pace.

I reached the White Horse in a dripping sweat and silently thanking God to have arrived safely. Toby met me as I came in through the kitchen door and asked if I was all right.

"Here," I said handing him the pouch, "take this upstairs and hide it in our room somewhere."

"Are you all right," he asked again? "You're white as a ghost!"

"I'm all right," I said, "really. I am fine. We need to look at this later."

Toby left through the dining room for the front stairs and after a few deep breaths I was feeling much better. I went into the Tavern, slid behind the bar, and began filling orders from the thirsty patrons there. When Toby joined me shortly after, we continued pouring whiskies and ales as if nothing had happened, which was as it should have been. Occasionally a call from Mary in the kitchen prompted us to serve an order of food, but, beyond that, it was a normal hectic day and night at the White Horse Inn.

The next three days passed in busy anticipation of our journey. A notice was tacked to the door of the Inn explaining its closure for the following two weeks. The evening following my meeting with the Reverend Berkeley, Toby and I had counted and recounted the content of the leather pouch. Fifteen guineas had been allotted for my expenses in New Haven, which was far beyond need. We counted fifty-five additional guineas, again, way beyond the amount the Reverend had originally pledged.

It was decided that I would take all the funds with me when I left the ship in New Haven. I would pay the initial thirty guineas to Captain Cutler. The rest would be paid once we were back in Newport. Even if the good Captain and crew decided to demand more from Toby or Mary, they would not have it to give them. It would be an incentive for all to abide by the agreement.

On the morning we were to begin our voyage, the three of us were delivered by carriage to the docks at Coddington Cove. It was the first time we had seen the schooner that would carry us to what we hoped would be our futures. She was tied up beside one of the short docks. Most of her hull was hidden by the taller and longer docks in the cove. At first, only her masts and rigging were visible. The carriage brought us to the end of the short dock. It was then that we could see the schooner's sleek lines. The hull was painted a deep blue with gray trimming. The masts were finished as varnished wood.

As the three of us unloaded our baggage from the carriage, a figure I knew to be Captain Cutler appeared on the gangway and came toward us up the dock.

"Good morning, all," Captain Cutler said boldly. "Welcome to my humble ship, the *Peregrine*." Looking at the ship tied up alongside the dock, it was clear new paint had been applied poorly to the stern and the name '*Peregrine*' had been painted over a shorter name.

As we shook hands all round and the Captain removed his cap and bowed to kiss Mary's hand in a show of chivalry, we were all anticipating a fine, uneventful voyage. Walking out along the dock toward the ship, the captain gave a shrill whistle and motioned two crew standing near the stern to come. They ran down the gangplank and, as they drew closer, the captain ordered them to bring our luggage aboard.

Just as we reached the gangplank, Captain Cutler caught my arm and held me back while Toby and Mary went aboard. I knew the reason.

"We have a small matter of funds to be exchanged, have we not, Mr. Gray?"

Having anticipated this request coming at some point, I had separated thirty of my guineas before leaving the White Horse from the total I carried and placed them in a smaller pouch. I reached into my shoulder bag and drew forth this pouch and placed it firmly in the Captain's outstretched hand. He proceeded to toss it slightly in the air so that it jingled when he caught it again.

"No need for me to count it," he said with a smile that ended cruelly. It has the feel of gold about it."

"The rest will be paid once we return," I reminded him.

"As agreed," he replied as he motioned me aboard with his arm.

As I boarded, Toby and Mary were coming back on deck having visited their accommodations below deck. Within ten minutes, sails were being raised and lines to the dock were cast off and we were underway. The schooner turned north up the bay and rounded the north end of Aquidneck Island. She then turned south and sailed down the passage west of the island. The Captain was standing by the helm and noticed me watching him. He stepped to the rail where the three of us were standing and quietly said to me, "We don't need to advertise our departure to the whole city. Besides, we'll have better wind on this side of the island."

We picked up speed from a freshening wind as we continued down the west passage. As we did, I saw the landing and dock to my family farm. The dirt path that snaked up the rise to the group of structures on the crest looked sadly worn. The buildings looked somehow old and worn, as well. The fields that had once grown crops were seen to be unplanted and fallow.

My Uncle Matthew was now elderly. Though I did not know exactly, I guessed his age would be well over fifty; perhaps even sixty. I had heard rumors over my years in Newport that Matthew had made some poor choices with investments and had gambled heavily. In that event, I told myself I would learn more of him and his plight when I returned.

We caught a fair wind when we left the bay and scudded along the shore tacking occasionally. The three of us sat atop the hatch amidship and enjoyed the warm sun and the breeze. We watched the crew of six move with agility about the ship keeping the sails filled with wind and watching the sky for changes in the weather.

After a few hours, Mary decided to retire to her cabin, while Toby and I continued to enjoy the afternoon sun. As we sat and talked, Captain Cutler approached us.

"We'll put in at Mystic tonight," he told us. "We'll get an early start in the morning and be in New Haven before noon if the wind favors us tomorrow."

"When do you expect to make New York?" I asked.

"We could make it there by evening the next day with a good wind and fair weather," Captain Cutler answered.

"It has been nearly a week since we ordered our cargo and I might have some word of it reaching me in New Haven," I said. "When we make port, I will speak to the master of the port which is where I asked word be sent regarding progress on our cargo."

"Very well," the Captain replied, "but be sure word gets to me by evening as I plan to cast off at first light."

"I will, Captain," I assured him. "It may shorten our voyage if we need not go to Philadelphia."

We landed in Mystic as the sun lowered in the west and went ashore to find food as we had not eaten since early morning. A fine inn just near the docks offered a full fare of food for hungry guests, and we sat together chatting about the next few days of our voyage. With little to do in Mystic, we all returned to our ship and bedded down for the night.

Upon our waking the next morning, the rolling of the ship told us we were already underway. The Captain was good as his word, and we were in port in New Haven as the sun was at its zenith. I left the ship and spoke with the harbormaster who had received a note by post for me from our fourth partner, Jackie.

I knew Mary and Toby planned to go ashore for food to the ale house that could be seen from where the *Peregrine* had docked. I hurried to join them. I shared the note with Toby and Mary. It was dated two days prior and reported that he had made exceptional time reaching Philadelphia and was fortunate to make contact quickly with Mr. Franklin. Upon hearing our request, Mr. Franklin had immediately employed a shipping firm to construct our cargo. It would leave Philadelphia this very day and would be in the port of Elizabeth in New Jersey in two days where arrangements would be made to transport it across the harbor to New York. According to Jackie's note, this could take another two days to arrange.

Mary and Toby both agreed, it was worth trying to send a reply to Jackie on the chance it might reach him in time to hold our cargo at Elizabeth and to expect our ship, the *Peregrine*, to arrive in two days, three at most, from this day. Pen, ink, and paper were obtained from the innkeeper, and I began writing. We found a postal rider who, by sheer luck, was headed to New York and would see our letter to Jackie delivered to the harbormaster at Elizabeth in New Jersey. Next, we composed a note to Captain Cutler identifying Jackie as our person in charge of our cargo and telling him that we anticipated the cargo would be in Port Elizabeth by his arrival. We then sent the note to the *Peregrine* for Captain Cutler. Finally, we were ready to indulge in some food which we all agreed was quite tasty.

The first food of the day being consumed, Toby and Mary returned to the ship while I began my search for a bed for three nights from an innkeeper with the promise it might be extended another day or two if I should require it. I had been told by people who had traveled to New Haven to seek out an inn known as Cook's near the City Commons. I had mentioned this to Toby before he left for the *Peregrine* with Mary. I found it with little trouble after directions from the proprietor of the ale house. I mounted the stairs to my room and shut the door exhausted from a long day. No sooner had I shut the door than a knock came. Cautiously I asked who it was and received a reply of "message from the *Peregrine*, Sir."

The note was in the practiced hand I would have expected from the Captain. It told me he appreciated the information regarding picking up the cargo in New Jersey rather than in New York. In fact, he preferred doing so. He did think it would take three days to reach the destination. So, with this information in hand, I prepared for bed and thought for the first time about my meeting with Rector Williams of Yale College.

THIRTY

My first day in New Haven, I decided to explore a bit of the town. I was not expected at Yale until the next day, and here was a city larger than Newport to investigate. I finished breakfast quickly, anxious to begin my adventure. I asked the innkeeper if he knew of a shop where I might buy a hat. He suggested a place called Pomeroy's about a block away in the direction of the harbor. I had noticed most people were wearing hats and I had none and so I decided to look about getting one.

I found Pomeroy's with no trouble and entered, tripping a small bell on a curled piece of metal above the door as I did so. The sound it made alerted someone to my presence and they appeared from a back room. It was Mr. Pomeroy himself. He was an older gentleman impeccably dressed and wearing a periwinkle wig. I inquired about a hat, and he proceeded to measure my head and suggested a fine-looking tricorn of black brushed felt or an identical one in deep brown. Since the best clothes I would be wearing the next day were brown, I chose the brown. At a price of two shillings, it was a bargain. I walked out onto the street with a new sense of myself in my new hat.

I struck off in the direction of the waterfront intending to stroll its length and then turn west into the city. The harbor was bustling with activity. Much like Newport harbor, it was obvious that New Haven's harbor was the center of commerce for the city. New Haven was a fine city with row after row of fine shops and homes. The streets were laid out in a more consistent manner than in Newport and the city was not done growing. I walked and walked and eventually found my way back to Cook's Inn. It had been a fine day and I had seen the better part of the city. I had seen the City Common and the building where I would be going the next day at the far end.

After a restful night of sleep, I arose to meet a fine, sunny day. I took extra care in dressing for my meeting with Rector Williams of Yale College. I had brought with me my best suit of clothes. While I knew them not to be of the latest style, I owned nothing newer, and I had taken great care of them having only worn them on a few occasions. The breeches and waistcoat were of good woven brown wool, a bit too warm for this time of year, but serviceable. My best linen shirt with lace cuffs sewn on by Mary gave a bit of fineness to the assemblage. A good pair of stockings and reasonable shoes completed my attire. I stood before the small mirror on the wall of my room and took great care to position my new hat to complete my attire. I took a moment to admire myself. The image I saw reflected cut quite the figure, I thought.

I descended to the breakfast room of my lodgings known as Cook's Inn. It had been well recommended by those in Newport who knew of my travel plans. The inn's location near the City Common also made it conveniently near the center of the city and close to the small campus of Yale. I took a seat near one of the windows that afforded a view of the Common. As I sat watching the activity on the Common, enjoying my morning tea and porridge, I felt quite the young gentleman. I only hoped I could conceal the nervousness I really felt in meeting Rector Williams.

Finishing my breakfast, I paid the proprietor for my next night's stay and headed out to the street. I was early for my appointment to meet with Rector Williams, so I decided to stroll through the Common up to the campus. The Common was much larger than that in Newport. Unlike Newport, a series of gravestones dotted the far end of the grassy expanse. As I walked about, the trees provided shade from the warming sun. I soon found myself at the entrance to a large wooden structure on the corner of Chapel and College Streets with its name prominently displayed above the door.

College House was an impressive, three-story building standing isolated at the west end of the Common. Bracing myself, I mounted the granite steps to the front door and pulled the bell cord. In a few moments, the door was opened by a man of taller-than-normal stature with a rather severe countenance, dressed all in black apart from the white bib of a cleric.

"How may I help you?" he said as he looked at my dress.

"I am here to see Rector Williams with regards from his old friend Bishop Berkeley," I replied. "I believe he might be expecting me."

"Your name, Sir?" he asked coldly.

"Thomas Gray," I replied.

"Please follow me, Mr. Gray," he said as he opened the door for me to enter. "My name is Dower, Geoffrey Dower. I am Rector Williams's assistant and Secretary of Yale Collegiate."

My first thought was how appropriately the name fit the personality.

"Rector Williams is expecting you," Mr. Dower continued as he showed me into a small reception room. "I believe you were not expected until tomorrow. Nevertheless, you are here, and he does have some free time today. Wait here while I introduce you."

The tone in his voice would have made ice seem warm. But I smiled at his request and seated myself in the chair he gestured to. I sat looking at the walls expecting to be called momentarily. The clock on the wall ticked off the minutes. Still, I waited. After twenty minutes by the clock, the door opened, and somber Mr. Dower motioned me to follow him.

He led me across the central hall to a set of double doors. Sliding both doors back into their pockets enough for us to pass through, he motioned with his hand for me to wait. Mr. Dower rapped lightly on another door in the room and a voice responded, "enter!" With that, Mr. Dower turned to me and motioned for me to come forward as he opened the door.

"Master Thomas Gray from Newport, Rector," Mr. Dower announced to a personage, yet unseen by me. "I believe you have correspondence from His Reverend, Bishop Berkeley, regarding a meeting with Mr. Gray."

As Mr. Dower stepped aside, I had my first view of Elisha Williams, Rector of Yale College.

"Mr. Gray," Rector Williams stood and extended his hand, "how genuinely nice to meet you."

Rector Elisha Williams appeared a man of slight build in his academic robe. He was much younger than I had expected him to be. His face was quite long and narrow and his expression friendly and open. His eyes indicated a lively intensity and his narrow nose beaked slightly over his thin lips. I reached out and shook his hand.

"How is my dear friend Reverend Berkeley?" he asked with a smile.

"He is well and wishes he could have been with me," I replied.

"He spoke quite highly of your abilities in his letter to me," the Rector said as he took his seat behind a large oak desk.

"He is quite kind in his praise," I said.

"He believes you are qualified for study here and should qualify for a degree in very short order," Rector Williams stated with a slight change in his expression.

"My education has not been very structured, Rector Williams," I began, feeling I should express something of myself. "Most of what I have learned is from reading and has been on my own."

"What subjects have you read on?" he asked.

"I have read a great deal of literature and poetry. Some of the classics, but I do not have a great grasp of Latin. I have read philosophy and taught myself algebra and geometry," I found myself spilling out words. "I have read a great amount of the Bible and works on the sciences, as well."

Putting a hand up and leaning forward in his chair, The Rector motioned for me to stop.

"I appreciate your enthusiasm, Mr. Gray," he said with a smile. "I am certain my friend George would not have sent you to me if he were not convinced of your desire to learn more."

"Would you be willing to meet with our First Tutor and have him assess your level of knowledge?" he continued.

"I would welcome the opportunity, Sir," I replied with a smile and relaxing for the first time.

"Excellent!" Rector Williams said excitedly. "Shall we begin tomorrow morning about nine?"

"I shall be here," I replied with equal excitement.

"May I ask where you are staying, Mr. Gray?" Rector Williams inquired.

I am at Cook's Inn just off the Commons," I replied.

"Ahh, yes. Let me contact First Tutor Edwards," Rector Williams said beginning to search the papers on his desk. "I have a syllabus of our degrees somewhere here. You know I have only been in this position for a brief period and things have been quite hectic."

I nodded agreement not really knowing of what he spoke.

"Uh, as I was saying," the Rector began again, "let me reach out to the First Tutor Minister Edwards and arrange tomorrow."

Rector Williams stopped the frantic search of his desk and bid me good day. I left his office and was shown to the front door by Mr. Dower. Once outside, I took a deep breath of the warm early summer air, crossed the street, and entered the Commons. I took my time walking through the Commons enjoying the feeling I had conducted myself well. While it felt like I had been only a brief time at College House, it had consumed most of the afternoon.

I soon found myself at the door of Cook's Inn and decided a late afternoon tea or an early dinner would be very agreeable. I entered and took the seat by the front window that I had enjoyed at breakfast. I ordered tea and toast and proceeded to watch the activity of the city from my window as I waited.

I was part way through my tea when I noticed a man in pastoral dress hurrying across the Commons toward the inn. At first, I thought it might be Rector Williams, but, as he drew nearer, I knew it was not. He crossed the street in front of my window, and I heard the door of the inn open. Moments later, First Tutor Edwards presented himself at my table.

"I understand we are to meet tomorrow," he began. "However, I thought this syllabus might help you to prepare for tomorrow." With that, he handed me a small brochure.

I asked Tutor Edwards to join me at tea and he accepted.

"I understand you are a protégé of Bishop Berkeley," he said as he lifted his cup.

"I have functioned as his secretary for not quite three years now," I replied. "I would not presume the honor of being called his protégé," I said.

"My responsibility here is to assess your academic strength," Tutor Edwards responded. "Tell me," he continued, "what is your interest in studying religion?"

"None," I responded surprised at the question. "I have studied philosophy, literature, mathematics, but not much of religion."

"You were not brought up in any church?" His surprise was genuine.

"My father was Quaker, but he died when I was young, as did my mother," I offered. "I have had little formal training in doctrine."

Tutor Edwards was deep in thought as he sipped his tea.

"These are troubling times for organized religion and doctrine," he said as he placed his cup on the table. "There are new thoughts, philosophies and ideas being expressed that some would say are enlightened. Others would call it heresy."

I could see Tutor Edwards was trying to choose his words carefully. We spoke pleasantly for several minutes on a variety of subjects while we sipped our tea. But Tutor Edwards kept returning to the subject of divinity and the recent controversies that had occurred.

"It has only recently impacted our college causing some division among the faculty," he finally shared. "I am happy to have met you this evening and look forward to tomorrow. Do read what I have left with you and let us explore things tomorrow."

Tutor Jonathan Edwards rose from his chair, shook my hand, and was away from the table in a matter of a minute. I watched through the window as he hurried across the Commons in the late afternoon sun. This man, whom I knew by reputation and his writings, was younger than myself and had already achieved so much. While I admired his writing, I did not necessarily agree with his ideas. I wondered how that might impact our meeting tomorrow.

I picked up the description of courses and degrees offered by Yale Collegiate Tutor Edwards had left on the table. With little thought, I paged through the slim booklet, for my thoughts were elsewhere. I expected the *Peregrine* would be nearing New Jersey by the time the sun set tomorrow. I could only hope the weather to the west had been clear and the winds favorable.

I ordered a light supper of bread and cheese and a pint of cider. I again opened the booklet and began to read with a bit more attention. As the time slipped by, I read the description of each degree awarded by the Yale Collegiate with growing interest. While I was less drawn to the degrees in divinity, those of philosophy attracted my attention. As the natural light coming through the window dimmed, I finished my repast and headed off to bed. I expected my sleep not to be restful this night as my thoughts ran from tomorrow's meeting to the present state of my friends aboard the *Peregrine*.

Morning dawned gray with fog. I washed up and dressed leisurely, being in no hurry to begin the day. I descended to the breakfast room and ordered a cinnamon bun and tea. I sat at my usual table by the window and looked out at the Commons wrapped in fog. I hoped my day would be brighter than the gray scene before me. By the time I had finished my meal, the fog was beginning to lift. I paid the innkeeper for another night of lodging and asked if he had received any messages for me. Upon his response of no, I left for my walk to College Hall.

Even though the fog was burning off, the air was still heavy with moisture. As I stood on the steps of College Hall, I ran my hand down the sleeve of my shirt and felt the wet fabric. Somber Mr. Dower opened the door, and I was led into, what I assumed was, Tutor Edwards's office. The room was sparsely furnished with a large desk and small chest of drawers at one side. A small chair in front of the desk was placed on a lower level of the floor while the desk and its chair were on a slight riser. The effect was one of minimizing anyone sitting in the chair before the desk. I took my seat.

The door behind me opened sharply and Tutor Edwards entered with the hurried strides I had seen the day before. He mounted the raised tier gathering his billowing academic robe and, pulling back his chair, sat heavily in it.

"Good morning, Mr. Gray," Tutor Edwards began formally.

I was made aware that much of the "examination" would be oral. Questions would be put to me to determine my current level of knowledge in several areas. Based on my responses, a determination would be made regarding my need for further study. This determination would be made by Tutor Edwards and Rector Williams who would also be asking me questions in some areas. We would have a break for lunch and resume in the afternoon until we were either done or it was determined we would need to continue into the next day. This news did not thrill me, but I digress.

The questioning began with a review of what I had recently read. As I mentioned each title, there were multiple questions about what I had read, what was my comprehension of what I had read, what was my opinion of it. Since my reading had been extensive, this discussion took quite some time. After what seemed an eternity, Rector Williams relieved Tutor Edwards and began asking me if I had read this philosopher and that philosopher. He asked many questions about Bishop Berkeley's writings and how they might have shaped my beliefs. While many of the questions forced me to formulate answers for the first time, it was an exhausting exercise.

Finally, Rector Williams announced we would break for supper to be served in the dining hall. First Tutor Edwards and two other first-year students joined us. As we ate a simple meal of stewed meat, potato, and carrots, a pleasant discussion was continued among the group. I discovered that both degree candidates were seeking degrees in divinity and anticipating calls by churches all over New England to serve as pastor. I was being left with the distinct impression that I was expected to have some type of religious awakening and seek out a career in divinity.

Supper completed; Tutor Edwards resumed what I was expecting to be a continuation of the morning's interrogation. To my surprise his questions became less intense and more general in nature. At about three in the afternoon, he asked if I would be able to write a short essay.

"Would you be willing to provide us with a sample of your thoughts on the direction of philosophical thinking as it relates to religion today?" Tutor Edwards asked.

I was taken aback by the request knowing, as Tutor Edwards already knew, I had expressed my lack of formal instruction in religious orthodoxy. However, knowing the importance of this meeting, I agreed to the task.

"You may have the rest of this afternoon and tomorrow morning," he continued. "And you may have access to the library of the college. You will find it just down the hall from here. There is paper and ink here in my desk and you may work wherever you are comfortable." With that, Tutor Edwards excused himself and stepped toward the door.

"I will plan to see you tomorrow. About midday?"

I nodded agreement.

Just as he was about to disappear through the door, Tutor Edwards stepped back.

" Oh, I meant to give this to you at supper. This arrived by messenger for you."

He handed me a sealed letter addressed to me at Yale College and disappeared through the door closing it behind him. I quickly broke the seal on the note and unfolded it. It was written in Mary's hand.

'Arrived New Jersey safely. Jackie met us with the cargo. Being taken aboard ship as I write this. We should be at New Haven in three days' time. Mary'

The letter was dated the evening of the day before. The news could not have been better. The *Peregrine* did not have to sail to Philadelphia, but only as far as New Jersey. The cargo was aboard, and the ship would already be under sail back to New Haven. I could now concentrate on the task at hand.

THIRTY-ONE

I withdrew several blank sheets of paper, a quill and inkwell from Tutor Edwards' desk and proceeded down the hall from his office until I found the library. I placed the writing materials on a table near the shelves and began looking at the sections of books. After several minutes, I realized I could not find the answer to Tutor Edwards's question in any book. He was asking for my own view. Yes, I could find arguments to support my views, but in the end, this was my philosophical outlook.

For what must have been several hours, I created an outline and began writing carefully and with deep thought attached to every word. Suddenly, my concentration was broken by a light appearing to shine from behind me. It was Mr. Dower carrying a candle come to inform me that it was near nine on the clock and the building was always closed at nine. If I desired to take my materials with me, I was welcome to do so, but I would need to leave.

"First Tutor did say that you may take any one volume you might like," he said in his flat monotone. "You should know that is highly irregular," was his final comment.

I thanked him, but I needed no book from the library and, quickly gathering the paper, quill, and ink into my shoulder pouch, I followed Mr. Dower to the front door and bid him a good evening. I heard the door close with more force than necessary and heard the lock thrown with force. I felt Mr. Dower and I might not have the best of relations.

I walked in darkness through the Commons feeling confident about the future. My answer to the question was well underway, and the prospect that I and my friends might soon be on our way to finding the treasure, if there were one, buoyed my spirits. The evening was pleasant and the short walk to my lodgings was invigorating, to say the least. I reached Cook's Inn in short order and took my usual seat in the dining room. I realized I was late to dinner and so, when approached by my server, I ordered only a pint of cider and some bread and jam.

As I sat waiting for my food, I pulled my written pages from my pouch and began reading. As I did so, the innkeeper approached and handed me a message he had received after I had left that morning. I thanked him and looked at the handwriting of the address. It was not Mary's. I quickly broke the wax seal and saw Toby's fine hand.

Brother, all is well here. There was a small delay loading our cargo and getting underway. We lost about a half day. I write this as we are casting off lines. We will not arrive in New Haven until evening two days hence, three days at most. We all hope you have been successful in your endeavor. There have been no problems with crew or Captain.

Toby

I pulled Mary's note from my pocket and read it again. This note indicated no time for its writing. Was Mary's note written before Toby's? What was the delay? Should I be looking for the arrival of the *Peregrine* the day after tomorrow, or the evening of that day, or the following morning? My bread and jam arrived, and I put both notes aside and continued mulling over in my mind these questions. This continued until the smell of the warm bread and the sweetness of the jam made me realize how hungry I really was. I decided to wait to address any worries about the arrival of a ship and enjoy my satisfying jam and bread instead.

I finished my supper without realizing the lateness of the hour. I gathered my papers and writing materials and headed off to my room. I changed out of my clothes and into my nightshirt and sat at the small table in my room. I began to read what I had written earlier to get my mind on track to continue. The hour was late, and the inn was quiet. The noise of the city had abated and the scratch of my quill across the paper was the dominating sound I heard. The thoughts seemed to translate into words that flowed easily onto the page.

The bright morning sun shining on my face woke me from my slumber. I had never made it to bed but had simply laid my head on my arms on the desk for what seemed only a mere second. As I wiped the sleep from my eyes, I saw before me on the desk ten pages covered in ink. Added to those I had completed in the library, my response to the Tutor's question totaled two dozen pages. I leaned back in my chair and nodded in self-satisfaction. It was time to dress for the day.

I took my time arranging the papers that could decide my future education. I carefully placed them in my carry pouch along with the quill and inkwell. I was looking forward to presenting my paper to Tutor Edwards. It was the first time I had written down these thoughts of mine. I was pleased with them. While it would be important that Tutor Edwards and Rector Williams found merit in my words and thoughts, the exercise of having me write my thoughts as concisely as possible had taught me much. And, for that, I was thankful.

I breakfasted at my normal table and enjoyed the view of the Commons in the bright sun. I was welcoming the thought that my time in New Haven was ending for now. I was anxious to be aboard the *Peregrine* and with my friends again. This final day of interview with First Tutor Edwards and Rector Williams might weigh heavily in their determination of my suitability to attend Yale, but I was determined to prove to them that Bishop Berkeley's belief in me was well founded.

I arrived at College House at the stroke of nine by the big clock in the entrance hall. Mr. Dower informed me that First Tutor Edwards would see me in the afternoon after supper so I would have plenty of time to work on my assignment. I told Mr. Dower he could inform Tutor Edwards I had completed my assignment and was ready to meet with him at his convenience. I asked Mr. Dower if I might wait in the library.

"I see no impediment to your doing so," he replied in his flat-toned voice.

I thanked him with a smile which was not returned and told him I knew the way.

Once I had closed the door of the library, I stood for a moment with my back against the door. The books, the sheer number of them, the enormity of the knowledge held within them, suddenly struck me. And this library was small in comparison to the great libraries of the world. I began going along the shelves just reading the titles and authors. I settled on a treatise by John Locke and sat down, beginning to read.

My mind kept wandering to thoughts of the *Peregrine* and my friends aboard her. Would she arrive tonight or the next morning or the night after that? How long would it take to locate the landing site on the south shore of Fisher Island? How long would it take to unload the crates? How many would need to be unloaded? Should one of us always stay aboard ship? How long would it take to find the treasure? How difficult would it be to dig it up? Was there even a treasure? So many questions soon to be addressed.

If the *Peregrine* arrived late in the day, it might be better to wait until the next morning to leave. Setting that aside, I was sure my companions would appreciate an evening on dry land before going back to sea. I would happily stay aboard in their place. It would give me the opportunity to speak with Captain Cutler, as well.

I could hear the clock in the hall strike one and knew that I would soon be called to my final interview. I would then be at liberty to head to the harbor in hopes of finding that the *Peregrine* might somehow have broken the barriers of time and arrived. I was still reveling in those thoughts when I heard the door of the library open, and the voice of Mr. Dower intoned that Tutor Edwards and Rector Williams would see me now. I thanked him and placed the book I had in my lap on the table before me.

I rose from my chair and followed him the short distance to Rector Williams's office.

"Mr. Gray," came the greeting from Rector Williams as both he and First Tutor rose from their chairs as I entered. I bowed and took my seat before them.

I opened my travel pouch and removed the treatise I had composed over the previous twenty-four hours. With some pride, I placed it on the table separating me from these men of learning and piety.

"Aah, yes! Excellent, Mr. Gray," came the response to my action. "I trust you found the exercise of merit," Rector Williams said as he took the pages and passed them to First Tutor Edwards.

"We are interested in your thoughts, of course," Rector Williams continued, "however, we can read this after. In the time we have left with you, we would like to speak of other things."

For the next three hours, the questions were friendly, but pointed. It became obvious the hope of these two venerable men was to convince me that spreading the word of God was a prime target of education at Yale. In the kindest of ways, I tried to convey my desire to achieve a degree in philosophy but had no desire to enter a ministry. At the close of our meeting, I felt I had stated my goal well, yet was unsure it had been heard. In any event, we parted with good wishes all around and with a promise from the Rector I would hear a decision within a month. I bowed and left the Rector's office.

I was relieved as I left College House. I had done all I felt I could to fulfill Bishop Berkeley's belief in my ability to measure up to Yale's admission standards. What happened from this point forward would be up to the powers that were at Yale. My concerns now shifted to a much more immediate and enticing prospect. And should this adventure bear reward, Yale might no longer be a concern, for, in these times, a man seemed measured more by wealth than station or intellect.

I quickly found myself at Cook's Inn and sought out the innkeeper. I secured my room for another night of lodging and requested if another room might be had for a woman who might arrive in the next day or two. I was pleasantly surprised to learn the inn kept such a room specifically for a lady and it would be available if desired. Having settled everything with the Innkeeper, I hurriedly changed my clothes into a less noticeable set of breeches, linen shirt, and vest and, taking my new hat, headed for the harbor.

I rounded the corner of the street leading out onto the waterfront. Ships were moored all along the waterfront and out the several wharves along it. I slowed my pace and began walking out the wharf with the sign which read "Long Wharf." This was a massive piece of engineering with a width of close to twenty feet and a hundred feet in length. The sides were finished flat with fieldstone and the top was packed fill with cobblestone carefully leveled and mortared in place.

I was admiring the various ships I passed as I walked along the wharf. Reaching the end, I saw the number of ships both leaving and entering the harbor. I wondered to myself where they might be going, what destination had these ships been to or where were they going to. The array of sails - all the different shapes, designs and combinations billowed in the wind. As ships entered the harbor, their sails disappeared as they were furled and those leaving suddenly displayed greater sails along their masts and spars. It was a fascinating sight to see.

I sat at the end of the wharf until the sun had nearly set. I watched the small fishing vessels return at the end of their day with nets drying on the deck. They swept past me as they ran further up the river to unload their catches. Ships were tying up all along the waterfront to await tomorrow's sunrise. The soft glow of their lanterns added light to the harbor. Though I could not admit it to myself, I was hoping I might see a certain schooner round the mouth of the harbor. I knew tomorrow held better prospects of that happening.

I arose late the next morning knowing I had free time to roam the city and wait for the *Peregrine* to arrive. It was only as I sat at my table by the window in the breakfast room that I realized there was much I could be doing in preparation for our expedition. There were provisions needed and a freshwater barrel, grog for the crew, and shovels, yes shovels! How foolish not to have thought of all this before now. With renewed purpose, I finished my repast and determined I should head to the waterfront shops. I quickly checked my funds and found I still held well over twenty pounds.

Bidding the innkeeper good day, I made the short walk to the waterfront and began looking for provisioners. As I walked the harbor, I saw a man seated on a barrel at the end of a ship's gangplank whittling with a small knife. He had the look of a captain about him, and I decided to seek this man's advice. He was short in stature with a weathered face from long days in the sun. His black boots nearly reached the edge of his coat which was double trimmed with shiny brass buttons. Beneath his coat was a plain linen shirt untied at the throat. He gave the appearance of having haphazardly thrown on the coat without consideration for his other clothing. But, above it all, he wore a hat turned up on one side with a huge plume running off the back. His hair fell in long ringlets he had pulled back to a great extent under his hat.

"Pardon, Sir," I said as I approached him. "Might you be Captain of this fine vessel?" I enquired.

"That I am, young Squire," he replied in an open joviality.

"May I ask a question of you?" I continued. "Are you ported here often?"

"Aye," he replied.

"If you were purchasing provisions for a voyage, where would you recommend doing so in this fine city?" I asked.

He cupped his chin in his thumb and forefinger and looked to the sky as if in deep thought. After a moment or two, he smiled to himself as if struck with an idea.

"Well, my young friend," he began, "there are a couple of good merchants you can trust."

He proceeded to expound on the virtues of two merchants, pointing in different directions with great animation as he spoke. I asked about shovels in a list of tools as not to raise suspicion. He was a wealth of information.

"Whichever ye decide to buy from, tell them Captain Bedloe rec-ommended them," he said finally, smiling broadly.

"I thank you, Captain," I replied returning a smile.

"Might I ask yer name, Squire?" Captain Bedloe called to me as I turned to leave.

"Gray, Captain! Thomas Gray," I shouted back with a wave.

As I passed the stern of the ship, I noticed the name lettered in gold paint. She was *The Mary N.* I paused in my steps and gazed at *The Mary N.* more closely. She was three-masted. Not being expert in ship design, I thought she might be classed a barque. Her lines were sleek, and she looked like she could make good speed even in a light wind. I knew at that moment; *The Mary N.* and I would meet again.

I spent the next few hours shopping for provisions. The recommendations from Captain Bedloe turned out to be accurate to a fault. I secured six days provisions to be delivered on notice along with a cask of freshwater and a keg of grog. The same provisioner was able to secure four shovels. My chore accomplished, I walked back along the waterfront so deep in thought, I was unaware of the activity in the harbor.

The hour was now well past midday. The heat of the sun caused my hair beneath my hat to sweat. I sat for a moment on a bench across from the water and removed my hat. It was the first time I had looked at the harbor since before speaking with Captain Bedloe. The building afforded some shade to the bench at its front and gave some relief from the midsummer sun.

I looked at the water and thought how cooling it would be to jump in. That thought was playing in my mind when I glanced toward the mouth of the harbor and saw a set of sails beyond the land. I watched as the sails approached the opening to the harbor. There was something about their arrangement that was familiar. As she cleared the point of land to the west of the opening to the harbor and her hull came into view, I knew her to be a schooner. But was she the *Peregrine*? There was something different about this schooner. As she settled from heeling,

I could see the hull was a sea green rather than deep blue. Other than that, she could be the *Peregrine.*

I stood and watched as she maneuvered through the ships in the harbor and headed for a smaller dock near the southwestern corner of the harbor. This dock sat slightly apart from the main waterfront and had less activity about it because it was short. I began walking toward her slowly, unsure if this was our schooner or not. As I got closer, I saw three people come on deck and stand at the railing as the ship was now being secured to the dock. It was Mary, Toby, and Jackie! As I drew closer, Captain Cutler stood out clearly on the aft deck. He raised his arm in recognition of me and waved. With that I saw my three companions waving from the main deck.

THIRTY-TWO

The schooner *Peregrine* glided up next to the short wharf amid shouts of greeting from my three companions on board. All of them seemed excited, as was I. The crew had the schooner secured to the dock in no time, and the gangplank was ready to convey passengers to the wharf. Mary was first to come off the *Peregrine* with a brilliant smile and her bonnet's ribbons fluttering in the light breeze. Jackie and Toby quickly followed her, and all of us exchanged embraces of greeting.

"How did the trip go?" I asked.

"All is well in New Jersey," Toby replied, "and Jackie did very well in Philadelphia."

"That I did, Tom," Jackie piped up, "and I even had a bit of funds left over."

I looked at Mary and she returned a smile and a nod acknowledging the truth of Jackie's statement.

"I will tell you of Mr. Franklin's suggestion over supper," Jackie said quietly. "I think it was brilliant," he continued.

"I was concerned you might arrive late in the day," I said to the group, "so I have reserved a room for you at Cook's Inn just off the Commons and an additional room for you, Mary. I have matters to discuss with Captain Cutler and will stay aboard the *Peregrine* tonight.

I have provisions ready to arrive at a moment's notice, and we should be ready to sail first thing in the morning."

"A good night's sleep will be much appreciated," Toby suggested.

"When you reach the inn," I said to Toby, "tell the innkeeper you are to have my room for the night which is paid, and the room for ladies is to be paid for when you arrive. The food is a separate matter and is quite good, in fact. I will meet you for some supper after Captain Cutler and I talk."

"If you are planning to stay aboard," Jackie piped up, "I would look to get your supper ashore. Much of what the cook aboard makes is tough as leather or thin as water."

Mary gave Jackie a heavy slap to the shoulder.

"That's an unkind thing to say," Mary said in feigned temper. "He tries his best and I will help him as best I can." We all laughed. It was good to be together again.

"I think you all had best be on your way to Cook's Inn," I said, "and I shall see you later."

One more embrace from Mary and a hearty handshake from Toby, and the group headed up the street toward the Commons and the inn. Captain Cutler had come to the top of the gangplank as our group departed. He gave me a salute of sorts and told me he needed to order supplies if we were to sail in the morning. I told him I had already ordered provisions and, if he were to send a crew member to let the provisioner know the ship had arrived, they would most likely be delivered this evening, but certainly by first thing in the morning. The supplies were ordered in the name of the schooner and were paid for already. Captain Cutler seemed much pleased by this news and dispatched the nearest crew on the errand.

"Permission to come aboard, Captain," I said with a smile.

"Granted," came the reply. "I believe we have some things to discuss, Mr. Gray," Captain Cutler continued, returning my smile. "Not least of which is where we are headed from here?"

As I walked across the gangplank, Captain Cutler extended his hand, which I took, as I stepped aboard.

"I believe a change has been made to the hull, Captain," I said feeling familiar with the Captain.

"Aye," he replied, "and more are about to occur. The *Peregrine* needs more changes to make her past identity disappear."

"So, you were unsuccessful pleading with the powers-that-be for formal title to the ship?" I inquired quietly.

"The crew decided the nicety of formal title wasn't a real necessity and that possession was all the title we required," Captain Cutler replied. "Let them's what wants to know worry about titles, as they say."

I was slightly taken back by the crudeness of his words, but the meaning was clear.

"Let us go below to my cabin and discuss matters," Captain Cutler said, returning to a more civil level of conversation.

"I would like to see the cargo first if you do not mind?" I asked.

"Aye," Captain Cutler replied. "That printing material was bloody heavy! Nearly broke our winch." His words stopped me mid-step.

"How did you know it was a printing press?" I asked with slight concern.

"Three of the crates have that printed on them," Captain Cutler replied with surprise. The rest are unmarked, but I have gathered they are for your business at the White Horse."

"I guess our Mr. Saunders has spoken of our business," I said with some disappointment.

"Don't blame him too harshly," Captain Cutler smiled. "I knew about the cargo before we left you in New Haven. Hard to keep secrets aboard ship."

I followed Captain Cutler to the main cargo hold of the ship. A canvas tarp covered the grate over the hold. Peeling back a corner, the section of the grate beneath could be lifted revealing a ladder into the hold. I climbed down the ladder and counted the eight crates assembled in the hold. Each one measured about five feet square and four feet high. They were lashed together to prevent their shifting when the *Peregrine* was heeling under sail.

"All seems to be in order here," I shouted up to Captain Cutler.

"There be two more in the rear hold," he informed me.

"Excellent," I replied as I made my way up the ladder and out onto the deck.

I helped the captain position the grate and replace the canvas. As Captain Cutler tied down the corner of the canvas, he asked me to follow him to his cabin.

The captain's cabin at the stern of the *Peregrine* was certainly not large. Its low ceiling did not allow anyone of my height to stand erect. Along the starboard wall was a bunk built hard against the hull. Next to it was a standing cabinet holding several muskets visible through the iron grating of the doors. A large padlock slipped through iron fittings on the two doors secured the cabinet. Across the stern of the ship was a map table. It was positioned against the series of small windows supplying the only natural light for the cabin. A rectangular table was hung from the ceiling on the port side of the cabin where it was free to swing with the motion of the ship. Two short chairs sat one on either side of it. We each took a seat.

"So, Mr. Gray, where are we away to?" Captain Cutler questioned as he slipped his hands into the enormous pockets of his coat.

"Do you know Fishers Island, Captain?" I asked.

"Aye. We passed it on the way from Newport to New Haven. We passed through the Race on an incoming tide to take advantage of the rip," the Captain continued.

"The Race?" I questioned.

"Aye," Captain Cutler replied. "T'is the outlet from the Sound to the greater ocean. It is narrow and the tides rush through at speed creating rip currents. Vessels try to time their passages to take advantage of the tide going in the same direction as they are headed."

"I am sure," I said not really understanding of what the Captain said. "My question is, do you really KNOW Fishers Island?"

Looking slightly puzzled, Captain Cutler said, "well let's look at a chart of it," and rose from his seat and walked to the chart table. A few charts were on the table while others were rolled and stood upright in a rack between the table and the stern. The captain shuffled through the charts on the table and pulled one into view showing Long Island Sound.

"Now, here is New Haven and here," he stabbed his finger onto the map on a small bit of land just off the coast of Connecticut, "this be Fishers Island."

I looked at the map and the place indicated by Captain Cutler's finger. The blob of island shown on the map showed no real detail.

"How well do you know Fisher's Island, Captain?" I asked again.

"I know well enough to avoid it," he said mockingly. "The only safe harbor is on the north shore and the island is mostly uninhabited."

"Suppose I told you there was a safe anchorage on the south shore," I said in a muffled voice, "one that offers a sand beach and privacy." Captain Cutler leaned his elbows on the chart table.

"A place where one might keel-haul a schooner to do a bit of hull cleanin' and paintin'?" he asked almost in a whisper.

"If one were so inclined," I replied with a slightly sly smile. "Of course, one might be too busy to care what his passengers were doing to pass the time."

"Aye," he muttered looking at the chart again. "There are one or two things of concern to be addressed."

"What might they be, Captain," I said pulling back from the table at this sudden change in Captain Cutler's voice.

"I'll need to get a tides chart from someone here in town," he said almost talking to himself. "We'll need to make our landing just past high tide as the tide is running to low slack tide.... Probably a good idea to bring aboard another dinghy and anchor," now he was speaking to no one, but himself.

"Do you know the location of this landing," he asked anxiously. "The south shore is pretty well known for rocks."

"I know it lies to the eastern end of the island,"

"Good, that is a bit farther from the race and should be easier to navigate," the captain said as he searched for a better chart in the rack behind the table. "I will see about a better chart tomorrow."

I did not tell him I held a better map. If Captain Cutler could find a more detailed chart, all the better.

"I shall stay aboard tonight, Captain," I announced to break the tension in the room, "but, for now, I must be off to meet my companions and gather my things to bring aboard."

"We may not sail tomorrow," Captain Cutler suddenly said. "It now depends upon the tides."

"I will be sure my companions are aboard at first light in any event, and I suspect the provisions will have arrived by then," I said.

"If the tide runs slack around midday, we might make sail by late morning," Captain Cutler replied. "It all depends on the tides."

I left Captain Cutler bent over studying the chart on the table and headed up on deck. The sun was setting, and I hurried off the vessel and up the street to Cook's Inn. I arrived just as Mary was descending the stairs to join Jackie and Toby at table. I greeted each warmly, and we took my favorite table by the window that looked out on the Commons. We exchanged some small pleasantries and ordered some light fare. I shared with them my conversation with the Captain about the tides, although I confessed to not really understanding all of it. I then turned to the cargo.

"Jackie," directing my first question to him, "you mentioned something about Mr. Franklin doing something with the cargo?"

"It was a stroke of genius, really," Jackie said enthusiastically. "Do you remember our conversation before I left about crates coming back aboard ship weighing more than when they were unloaded?"

"Aye, I do," I replied thinking back to the conversation at the White Horse.

"Mr. Franklin suggested weighting the empty crates with rocks of assorted sizes," Jackie said in a muffled voice. "That way, we can dump an amount of rock to offset any weight we put inside the crate. It will weigh about the same as it did when it left the ship!"

"That is brilliant," I said, as Toby and Jackie smiled and gestured in silent reverie.

"The rocks become a part of the landscape, and no one is the wiser," Toby offered.

"Captain Cutler did say the weight of the crates almost disabled his crane," I shared with the group.

"How long do you think it will take to find," Jackie's voice dropped to a whisper, "the treasure?"

"If the map is accurate and nothing has moved in twenty-five plus years, I think not long," I answered. "I am more concerned about digging it up and getting it ready to go back onboard," I continued.

"Aye," Toby chimed in, "I think Captain Cutler has other plans while we are occupied."

"I think he plans to further disguise the *Peregrine*," Mary added.

We all nodded in agreement.

"No matter what," I suggested, "the next few days will be difficult, but exciting."

We finished our light supper talking about the adventure already had by my friends in their journey to New Jersey and back to New Haven. They all agreed, Captain Cutler knew how to make the *Peregrine* fly. Soon enough, it was time for me to gather my belongings from the room that Jackie and Toby would now occupy for the night and head back to the waterfront and the *Peregrine*.

I made my way through the darkened streets and boarded the *Peregrine* without incident. The crew member on night watch acknowledged me as I came aboard. I headed below to the cabin that I had been shown was to be mine just before the captain's cabin on the port side and dropped my bag on the upper bunk. It had been a busy day and I knew the sun would be up before I wished to see it. But tomorrow could be the beginning of deciding all our futures. Or it might mean the ruin of us all.

It felt like I had just closed my eyes when I was awakened by heavy noises on the deck above me. I rose from my bunk and quickly threw on pants and shirt. As I came on deck, I could see the thuds that had awakened me were from the arrival of a second dinghy being brought aboard and tied down to the middle deck. The sun was breaking over the horizon and Captain Culver was standing near the helm supervising the securing of the rowboat. He strode to the railing above me.

"Morning, Mr. Gray," he said. "It appears the gods smile upon us this day! The tide turns in about three hours and we should make landfall before that. Your provisions are aboard, as are the extra anchor and, as you can see, the second dinghy. All we await are your party."

"They should be here very shortly, Captain," I replied. I returned to my cabin and finished dressing. When I came back on deck, I could see Mary, Toby, and Jackie coming down the dock.

"Morning all!" I greeted them. "We are good to sail shortly, so get aboard."

Captain Cutler interrupted his shouting of orders to the crew to acknowledge and welcome his passengers.

"Good morrow, Mi'lady Mary. Gentlemen," He intoned before turning back to the crew.

Within minutes, we were casting off lines and backing the fore jib to slide back along the dock into the harbor. Our small group found a place along the side rail amidship where we could watch the movements of the crew as they prepared to set sail, and yet, be out of the way. It was as if they were performing an orchestrated dance, moving through the rigging, and running the decks hauling lines. And then we would see the sails bloom into being and billow as the wind was caught within them. One could feel the surge of movement as the vessel strained to gain speed. It was exciting and exhilarating.

We were soon moving toward the mouth of the harbor as the freshening morning breeze began heeling the vessel. We stood together on the deck and watched as the sails eased off to port as we headed toward The Race. In a few hours' time, we would be running through the rip currents of The Race and rounding up on the south shore of Fishers Island. It felt almost surreal to be finally following my father's wish for me.

The vessel moved through the water buoyed by the current and pushed on by the wind-filled sails. We passed through The Race with the currents producing white-capped waves crossing at angles in our wake. Before we knew it, we were beyond the currents and sailing along the south shore of Fishers Island.

Captain Cutler called me to the helm. I tapped Toby's arm and we moved to the helm.

"What exactly are we looking for along this shore?" Captain Cutler asked.

"We are looking for a point where the island is so low, we can see the water across it to the north. There should be a small crescent of beach right at that place and two large rocks in approaching it."

"You have seen this beach?" Captain Cutler asked.

"No," I replied, "but I have it on good authority that it is there and mostly secluded."

Captain Cutler looked at me with a blank expression.

"You had best be right, my young friend," he said with gravity. "I spoke to several in New Haven who knew nothing of this beach and doubted its existence."

"That should tell you what a good secret it is," I replied with a smile.

Toby was scanning the shoreline trying to find the low point in the island's profile. He saw nothing but tumbles of rocks, some extending out into the water with waves breaking against them. Toby and I heard some shouted orders and felt the ship begin to slow as sails were furled. Toby knew from his talks with me that Fishers Island was nearly ten miles in length. But the height of the island was incredibly low, in general. We stood at the rail intently staring at the rough shoreline for what seemed an interminable time. I could feel the island slipping by and the eastern end nearing. Suddenly, Toby's hand was on my sleeve.

" There!" he said suddenly pointing the direction of the island with his finger. "See that dip?"

There it was. The break in the horizon was distinct. As we started past the spot, a small patch of sand came into view.

"Captain Cutler?" I called over my shoulder. In a stride or three, he was looking at the point where Toby was still pointing.

"Prepare to come about," Captain Cutler bellowed to the crew. "Furl the main! Genoa and jib to starboard!"

The schooner responded to the actions of the crew amazingly. The ship swung about under the two remaining sails and headed toward the sliver of a beach. As the vessel drew nearer to shore, the waves calmed.

"What is your plan, Captain?" I asked.

"The water is about half to low tide, so I plan to run her onto the beach," came the reply.

"On the beach?" I exclaimed in some distress.

"Have no worry," Captain Cutler said with a smile, "she'll be fine, and we'll be able to heel her over to work on her keel."

"But how will you get her afloat again?" Toby asked.

"You'll have to wait and see," the captain replied with a great laugh.

Captain Cutler turned to the helmsman and said in a loud voice, "Mind yer heading, mate. Keep to the clear water."

Our little group decided it was time to go below and gather our things in the event *Peregrine* decided the Captain's maneuver was not one she would tolerate. I wanted to be sure my father's bible was safely on my person or in a bag I had with me. Even though I had read and re-read the instructions many times and knew them by heart, I wanted to leave nothing to chance.

As we collected our things, we could hear a voice calling out numbers. Then we heard Captain Cutler bellow, "BRACE FOR GROUNDING! DROP SAILS!"

Within seconds, we heard the unmistakable sound of the hull crushing into the sand of the beach. The vessel staggered slightly and came to a halt.

The four of us rushed up on deck to see a full third of The *Peregrine* perched on the sand of the beach and her stern sitting in the receding water.

THIRTY-THREE

*S*he was sitting straight upright. All her sails were furled or lowered on top of the booms. Only her masts pointing to the sky gave any hint of her existence. Stripped of her sails her spars would be hard to distinguish from offshore.

"We have arrived," Captain Cutler's voice boomed from the helm. "We'll get your cargo unloaded straight away. That will lighten her so we can careen her a little easier."

"Aye, Captain," I shouted back. "We will disembark to the beach," I continued.

The crew had placed a rope ladder over the side of the starboard rail, and we clamored down its wooden slats with Mary coming second to last so we could help her in this most unladylike action.

The sand was warm with its fine grain running several inches deep. Walking was easier without shoes since the weight of the shoe buried your foot up to the ankle. The four of us walked with some difficulty to where the sand gave way to the shrubs and trees off the beach. Toby and I laid our coats on the ground and eased Mary down in a small shady area. Toby and I nodded at each other.

"Jackie," I spoke in just above a whisper, "Toby and I are off to follow the map. Stay with Mary and gather the shovels as soon as they come off the *Peregrine*. Make sure the crates are unloaded carefully and brought away from the ship."

"Aye, Tom," he replied. "They already have the first one off," Jackie continued pointing back at the ship. I patted his shoulder, and Toby and I were off into the underbrush.

We headed north more or less toward the pond we had seen from the ship. The underbrush grew thicker and the prickers and thorns began tearing at our clothes and any exposed skin. As we left the beach, we left the breeze that had kept the temperature cooler; the heat from the sun was making the temperature rise. Having braved the tears from the vegetation, we reached the edge of the pond in about ten minutes.

We began hunting for the stone marker described in the map directions. We did not know exactly what we were searching for, but, on faith alone, assumed we would know it when we saw it. I went in one direction, Toby went in the other, along the edge of the pond. The grass was knee high, but there were no thorns. I moved the grass with my arms and legs, brushing the long blades of marsh grass aside. How large was this marker I thought to myself?

"Tom! Tom, I found it," came Toby's excited call! I turned back and tried to run through the tall grass. I found Toby crouched in the grass beside a two-foot high, somewhat-rounded, boulder. Emblazoned on it was an incised "K." It was unmistakable.

"Where is the arrow?" I said to Toby.

"It is here, Tom," he replied excitedly. "See? Look here! Part of the letter forms the head of an arrow." I now saw it.

"We go fifty paces in the opposite direction," I said pointing. My voice betraying the excitement I was feeling.

Toby pulled a small compass from his pocket. He saw the surprised expression on my face.

"Something I picked up in New Jersey," he said with a smile.

We paced off fifty steps following the compass direction. It brought us to a small space shaded by a few trees. We began searching for another marker. As we found no stones as large as the earlier marker, we widened our search. We had no idea how long the "pace" of the person making the map might have been. A little further toward the edge of the trees, Toby found it. It was about the same size as the previous marker and carved into its side was what appeared to be an "M", or was it a "W" turned upside down? The carving looked as if it was done by the same hand as the first letter found.

"So, which is the arrow?" I said puzzled by all the possible answers.

"I think it would be the one in the middle, no?" Toby replied. "By the compass, that would be almost due south."

We began pacing in the direction the compass indicated. In twenty paces, we came into a clearing. We could look to the west and below us we could see the beach with the *Peregrine* now heeled over on her port side. The lower part of the hull seemed to be reflecting the sun in an odd way. Our crates were neatly stacked on the sand nearby. Without realizing it, we had increased our elevation perhaps fifteen feet. Turning from the view, we began looking for "a ring of cannonballs." We had no idea how large the circle might be. The two of us began walking in an ever-widening circle. We had about given up and were deciding it might be better to go back to the marker and try another direction, when Toby stepped on something hard near the edge of the clearing.

He knelt and saw the rounded surface of something buried in the ground. Pulling his knife from his belt, he began digging around what turned out to be a cannonball. He held the ball up with the broadest smile I had ever seen on his face. I then realized I was smiling just as broadly. I unsheathed my knife, and we began poking the ground around the edge of the clearing finding cannonball after cannonball. This was the place! We had found the location! The two of us embraced and danced for joy. After a few moments of excited exuberance, we realized there was still work to be done and time was precious.

We headed back to the beach but wanted to see if there was a way to avoid the area of the thorn bushes. This would make the trek to the treasure faster and less bloody. We retraced our steps back to the first marker. We found there were fewer thorns bushes if we angled back to the beach from this marker rather than going directly from the pond to the beach itself. There were also some trees along this route just off the beach that could shield our activity from the eyes aboard the *Peregrine*.

As we broke from the underbrush just beyond Mary and Jackie, the looks on our faces needed no explanation for our comrades. The tears in our shirts and stains of blood left from the briars did. Jackie had four shovels standing with their blades sunk into the soft sand nearby. A pair of pry bars and hammers lay on the ground next to Mary.

"You found it?" Jackie said softly with a half-smile. Toby and I nodded enthusiastically.

"Let's move a couple of the crates off the beach," I said.

The three of us walked to the pile of crates. They were stacked two high in a row. The three of us hefted the first one atop the nearest stack. It was not as heavy as I had expected. While it was not light, it could certainly be managed by any two of the strapping young men we were. We carried it to a point where it was just off the beach. Toby and Jackie went back and took the next crate by its ends and walked it back to place it next to our first crate.

"Should we open it here?" came the question from Jackie.

"Perhaps we should wait until we uncover the treasure," Toby suggested. "Once we know how heavy and how large the chests are, we can carry them down here."

"That was my thought," I said. "We only need to carry weight in one direction if we bring the chests down here." Everyone nodded in agreement.

The sun was now high in the sky, and the temperature on the beach was benefitting from the cool breeze coming in off the water. Each of us grabbed a shovel and, bidding Mary keep watch, the three of us headed back to the treasure site. It took only twenty minutes to reach the clearing where now the cannonballs littered the ground. The temperature was easily ten degrees hotter and there was no cooling breeze. Jackie and Toby stripped off their shirts and began digging in the center of the clearing.

I walked to the edge of the clearing to the west and peered down at the *Peregrine*. I could see the crew busily working on the hull and others working on the spars and masts. No one was paying any mind to what we were about. Mary was hidden from my view by the shrubs and trees to my right. I turned back to see Toby leaning against the side of a hole that was now about three-feet deep and five-feet wide. The sweat was rolling down his black body. Jackie continued to dig his shovel into dirt that was getting increasingly sandier.

"Toby," I said stripping off my own shirt, "take a break in the shade." Toby climbed out of the hole, and I slipped into his place. Jackie and I continued digging. The soil became increasingly sandy until it was almost pure sand. The sides of the pit began to cave into the hole and so the hole kept getting larger. Jackie suddenly stopped digging.

"How deep do we need to go?" Jackie said out of breath.

"About six to eight feet is my guess," I said stopping for a moment.

Jackie smiled and began digging again. Each shovel full was now pure sand, allowing the sides of the hole to collapse. The pit was now eight-feet around and five-feet deep. The sweat was falling from Jackie's face in a near stream. I suggested he take a break and Toby agreed. Toby and I kept digging. The shovels were sinking easily into the sandy soil and hitting nothing solid. The hole was now as deep as our shoulders and still nothing.

And then, THUD! Thud again. Our shovels were hitting on something solid. It was still not visible, but whatever it was, it was certainly solid. The sand in the hole was still deep enough to cover the blades of our shovels. Toby and I began taking shallower scoops of sand with our shovels.

We discarded the shovels and began using our hands to draw back the sand. As we did, a timber, or more accurately, a board began to appear. It was large and finished to some extent. The boards kept growing in length and number as we pushed away the covering sand. Jackie came into the hole and began sweeping aside sand with Toby and me.

Finally, we reached an end. We swept the top of the plank as clean of sandy soil as possible and began lifting. It was then we discovered this flooring was made of several individual wide planks laid down closely together. The first plank took two of us to lift and pull it away from the others. Leaning it against the edge of the pit, the three of us looked at each other, our bodies caked in sweat and sand, and we laughed.

I turned to the cavity under the remaining boards and dropped to my knees to see what I could in the dimness of the opening. All I could make out was a curved piece of wood. I reach my hand through the opening we had made and felt for I knew not what. Something I could identify. The object beneath was rounded up toward the planks I knelt on. I felt a strap with what felt like studs imbedded in it.

"What do you feel, Tom?" Toby asked quietly, but with excitement.

"I think it could be the top of a chest," I said cautiously.

Toby and Jackie hugged each other and clapped each other on the back.

"It's real!" Toby exploded with excitement. "Bless your father, Tom. He has made your fortune."

"He has made OUR fortune, my friends," I said as I stood and embraced my closest friends and my only family.

We quickly began getting the next plank free from the sand and tossing it out of the pit. This made an opening about one-foot wide and six-feet long. Another plank and we would be able to see what lay beneath this ceiling of wood. Getting the next plank out became easier as we had space to reach under it.

The sun was beginning to fall lower in the sky, but we would not be denied knowing what was beneath the planks. With a fourth plank removed, we could finally see one entire chest. Toby and Jackie knelt on the remaining boards and slowly felt their way down the ends of the chest. They looked at each other across the length of the chest and began raising it out of its resting place.

The chest was wooden. Hidden away for more than twenty years, it was in good condition. The metal fittings over its top and sides bore little rust or corrosion of any kind. The lock running through the two metal fittings at the front was large and only slightly rusted.

"Tom," Toby said catching his breath, "this must be close to two hundred weight." He was smiling as he spoke, and Jackie was nodding in agreement.

"We need to get this down to the crates," I said thinking aloud. "We should leave it in the low bushes until we have the crate open and are ready to put it in."

"What about our crew?" Jackie asked. "Suppose they find the pit?"

"We will have to keep a watch tonight to make sure there are no treasure hunting parties tonight," Toby replied.

"One of the crates contains three muskets, powder, and shot," Jackie related.

This news left me with a look of surprise as I looked at Jackie.

"Just a little something Mr. Franklin suggested," he said smiling back at me.

The three of us wrestled the chest out of the pit and decided to replace the four planks we had removed and cover them with enough sand to hide their existence. We hoped anyone looking in the hole would think whatever had been in it was gone. The three of us pulled on our shirts with no little concern over of the dried blood stains, sweat, and sand. Toby and I hoisted the chest by the strap handles at each end and struck out for the beach. Jackie went ahead to tell Mary what had occurred and to begin opening the first crate.

The weight of the chest staggered our ability to walk quickly. Our pace was further hindered by the bushes and the growing darkness. Just before we broke into the opening to the beach, we set the chest down just off the path that was now being made by our passage. We pulled a few branches from the shrubs around us and put them on top of the chest to hide its presence as much as possible. We then walked out onto the edge of the beach and saw Mary smiling at the two of us.

Jackie was busily opening the top of the nearest crate with one of the pry bars that had been lying on the sand. Toby and I picked up the other pry bar and began lifting the other side of the crate top. It came free with only moderate effort. Inside was a smaller crate that would easily accommodate our chest of treasure. Alongside the inner chest lay a small keg of black powder, three muskets, and a bag filled with lead shot.

"I had them unload this one first," Jackie said with a knowing smile.

"How did you know which one it was?" I asked him.

Jackie pointed to the end of the crate. I looked in the direction he pointed and saw lettered in black directly on the side panel 'LEAD TYPE." I looked back at Jackie.

"Well, it's partially true," he said smiling broadly.

Toby and I lifted the inner box out of the crate and took it back to the edge of the shrubs near the hidden chest. The weight of the inner crate was not excessive, and few rocks were inside it. We proceeded to toss about half the rocks into the shrubbery then lifted the chest from its hiding place and nested it into the small crate. It fit snuggly at the ends with plenty of space to the front and back. We checked the weight and determined it was close to what the weight of the crate had been. With that decided, we grasped the bottom edges of the crate and carried it the few feet to where Jackie stood by the larger outer crate. The three of us were lifting the smaller crate back into the outer crate when Mary said quietly,

"We have company coming."

We hurried our pace and slid the crates one inside the other and replaced the top of the outer crate. Coming toward us across the beach was Captain Cutler and three of his crew. Two of them were carrying another crate. The third carried a canvas sail in his arms.

"I see you're enjoyin' your time while we're here," Captain Cutler said brightly as he came closer. "We thought ye might like some shelter for tonight since the ship is hauled over."

"That would be very accommodating," I replied. I wondered if our disheveled appearance went unnoticed.

"We'll bring some more of your crates over and we can stack 'em, for walls and make a cover with a canvas," he continued. "I don't expect any rain, but we could have a heavy fog by mornin.' No need to have it soak us to the bone."

He smiled as he spoke and gave a deferential tip of his hat toward Mary who smiled at his cavalier action. While I am sure he noted our appearance, he made no mention of it, his attention focused on Mary. Meanwhile, his crew members were returning with another crate. In no time all our crates were laid out in a tight semicircle stacked two high and the canvas sail had been spread and tied down like a tent using the crates to hold it up. The one crate with our first chest inside sat inside the enclosure. The open side of the circle faced away from the water.

While this structure took shape, Captain Cutler amused himself pleasantly chatting with Mary about nothing. Had she enjoyed the sailing? Did she enjoy seeing New York from a distance? And was Jersey to her liking? Mary kept him busy while we watched the crew assemble the tented shelter.

"Cook will make some supper," Captain Cutler suddenly said to all of us. "We'll bring it to ye when it is ready. One of the crew will make a fire to give ye some light and a bit of warmth. All I ask is keep it banked from the shore. No need to make our presence known any more than necessary." He gave a knowing wink to the three of us.

"We'll move one of the crates to that side of the fire, Captain," Toby piped up.

The Captain nodded his approval and, once again, touching the brim of his hat with his fingers in a gesture of respect to Mary, started walking back toward the careened *Peregrine*.

"I think our Captain Cutler might be sweet on our Mary," Jackie said in jest.

"Away with yer smart mouth," Mary replied in feigned anger. "He's young enough to be my son." She laughed at the thought, as did we all.

The sun had nearly set, and a member of the crew arrived to make a fire as the captain had promised. Shortly after, a modest cooking pot arrived filled with a kind of stew along with shallow bowls and spoons. Mary took it upon herself to serve out portions. When only a small amount was left for her, we all insisted she take back some of ours.

"You are all working hard," she insisted, "and I am hardly doing anything but watching. You need food to keep up your strength for your labors."

She went on to insist that we all get some sleep, and she would keep watch and wake us as was needed.

Toby was soon asleep covered with a jacket against the coolness. Jackie sat beside me against one of the crates under the tent. Mary occasionally got up to stretch her legs and would casually look to the vessel beached and careened a hundred feet down the beach,

"Should we look inside the chest, Tom?" Jackie said quietly.

The question startled me from my thoughts. I had not even considered such an action. I was more involved in estimating how long it might take to retrieve the remaining treasure. Just then, Mary returned to her place just across from me.

"What say you, Mary," I said quietly. "Should we open the chest?"

Mary was silent for a few moments and then responded.

"I think it would settle our curiosity. I mean, it would be a shame if all your demanding work turned out to be for worthless rocks."

"Get a pry bar, Jackie," I said quietly.

"Don't open it." Toby's voice suddenly erupted. He had not been asleep.

"Has your father's word not guided us this far?" he continued as he rolled over and looked at us. "Can we not trust him a little longer?"

"Toby is right, Tom," Mary said with chagrin. "Your father's words have been true and guided us to this point. We shouldn't suddenly distrust them."

THIRTY-FOUR

The wind died just before midnight and the moon rose full. Its light replaced the dying embers of the fire. Shadows shifted across the light-colored sand of the beach as the moon rode higher in the sky. Mary had awakened me about this time as she could no longer keep her eyes open. She reported no activity from the direction of the *Peregrine*.

I looked across the beach in the direction of the schooner and saw only a lone figure standing watch near a small fire near the bow hidden from view of anyone at sea. Jackie and Toby slumbered peacefully under the canvas and were soon joined by Mary. Our three muskets stood leaning against two crates near where Toby and Jackie slept. As I settled in a spot where I could see the *Peregrine* clearly and keep watch of my friends, I realized it was the first opportunity to think about the future.

We were all about to become fabulously wealthy if the treasure was real. I realized I had no idea what each of my friends would want to do with such wealth. Would Toby want to travel? Would Jackie want his own business? Would Mary want to retire?

These thoughts were turning over in my mind when the report of a musket being fired made me aware I had dropped off to sleep. I looked around our camp and saw Jackie was nowhere to be seen and one of the muskets was missing. Toby awoke startled by the same sound of a rifle shot.

"Where is Jackie?" Toby said a bit confused.

"The pit, Toby," I said as I rose and grabbed one of the remaining muskets. We ran through the shrubbery up our newly made path and arrived at the pit calling for Jackie. Toby was in hot pursuit of me. Jackie lay face down near the end of the path up to the pit. A trickle of blood ran from a cut just above the hairline on his left temple. As I knelt by Jackie and rolled him on his back, Toby went around the pit with his musket at the ready. Jackie groaned as I moved him. I thanked God he was alive. I tore a cuff of my shirt and applied pressure to the wound.

"Did I hit him?" Jackie managed to say between moans of pain.

"Hit who?" I asked.

"The man looking in the hole," Jackie half-mumbled as he began recovering his thoughts.

"What man?" Toby said.

"The man I caught looking in the hole," Jackie said. "I told him to stay where he was, but he came at me, and the musket went off, and, and I don't remember what happened," Jackie said. "I felt a pain in my head and then you were here."

In the moonlight, nothing could be clearly seen. Certainly, no footprints would be discernible from our own.

"Well, whoever it was, he's gone now," Toby said. "Let us get you back to Mary."

We lifted Jackie from the sand and, putting one of his arms over my shoulder, followed Toby down the path in the moonlight to the beach. As we broke from the shrubbery onto the beach, we were met by Captain Cutler and three of his crew. Mary was standing against a pair of stacked crates.

"We heard a gun fire," Captain Cutler said excitedly.

"That you did, Captain," I said as I passed Jackie off to Toby and Mary. "It seems there is some curiosity from someone regarding what we are about while here," I continued restraining my anger.

"Is yer mate alright?" the Captain asked with concern, pointing at Jackie. "What happened to the lad?"

"Let us say, he had an unfortunate run-in with someone unknown," I replied intensely.

"I will tell you what I have told all my men," Captain Cutler began in a voice that would end in thunder as he turned to address the three crew with him, "our passengers have their own business here, as do we. They are to be left alone! You, here, are to tell the rest of the crew; no crewmember leaves the beach! If they do, they will suffer the punishment of the tides! Am I clear?"

"Aye, Sir," came a chorus of replies.

"Get away with ye," the Captain said gruffly. He then turned to Mary who was tending to Jackie.

"Is he going to be alright?" Captain Cutler said to Mary with some obvious concern. "I can send over some bandages and salve to clean the wound...."

"That would be appreciated," Mary replied with some ire.

The captain nodded at the chastisement and turned to go back to his vessel. Suddenly he stopped, whirled around and hastily touched two fingers to the rim of his hat in a gesture he knew he had forgotten to do, then turned and hurried across the sandy beach toward the *Peregrine*. Mary would have laughed had she not been so upset with what had happened to Jackie.

Toby reloaded the musket discharged by Jackie as, shortly, Mary met the emissary from Captain Cutler bringing bandages, water, and salve for Jackie's wound. We began to settle back down for the rest of the night. Mary dressed Jackie's wound and, after a couple of swigs of the rum sent along with the medical supplies, Jackie drifted off to sleep, as did Mary.

Toby sat across from me holding a loaded musket. The look on his face was intense.

"A penny for your thoughts," I said.

"I am thinking we should post one of us at the site of the pit," he said. "I do not trust our Captain any longer."

"You may be right," I replied losing all playfulness in my manner. "I doubt you or I will get much sleep this night." We both nodded.

We decided Toby would take the first watch at the pit and I would relieve him in three hours. I would whistle as I approached; he would reply like an owl. I would wake Mary before I left to relieve him.

Toby quietly rose and, gripping his musket mid-barrel, quietly slid into the darkness. I rose and gathered some dead branches from the small trees at the edge of the sand and tossed them into the embers of the fire. It would be a long night and, hopefully, with no further incidents.

As the moon began to set, I woke Mary with a soft touch and told her where I was going. I went up the path picking my way in the reduced light. As I neared the treasure site, I gave a light whistle. Nothing. I whistled again. There it was - the low hoot of an owl replied. I came into the clearing and saw Toby leaning against a stumpy little tree just off the clearing.

"Everything quiet here?" I asked Toby. He nodded.

"Why would Captain Cutler try to see what we are doing?" Toby mused.

"I do not think it was the Captain," I replied. "Remember, he is captain by consent. He might not have as much control as we would like."

"What was his warning about 'suffering the tides'?" Toby asked.

"All I know is it did not sound pleasant," was my reply. "You had better head back to the beach. Mary is expecting you."

"By the way," Toby said as he rose to leave, "I checked the pit, it does not look like any of the boards were moved. Whoever it was maybe believed we had already removed whatever was down there."

As Toby disappeared into the darkness, a feeling of satisfaction came over me for being clever enough to leave the boards covered with sand. As I took my place by the tree, I could feel the chill of fog rolling in. I knew the sun would be up in a couple of hours and the fog would begin to burn off. I also knew we would face a day of demanding work completing the transfer of the treasure chests into the crates.

The darkness around me soon began to shade into gray. Forms became clearer as the predawn sky to the east continued to brighten. The fog hung about the island like a drape that began to draw back with the heat of the day. I shouldered my musket and headed back to the beach.

As I cleared the brush and came out onto the edge of the beach, Mary was standing over a new pot of something like stew, serving it out to Jackie while Toby stood watching the schooner on the other end of the beach.

"Morning, Tom," Mary said cheerfully. "Stew?"

"Is that what it is?" I questioned in reply. Mary gave me one of her "away with ya' looks".

"Anything happening over yonder?" I called to Toby.

"Not that I can see," he replied coldly. "I still don't like what happened last night," he continued as he leaned his musket against the stacked crates in front of him and accepted a shallow bowl from Mary.

"We can't afford to dwell on that," I replied, "we need to get everything from the pit down here and into crates before the day is done. In case none of us have noticed, we are already gone over a week from Newport."

"Folks will think something has happened to us," Mary inserted.

"How do you feel this morning?" I asked Jackie noticing a small patch of dried blood on the linen bandage about his head.

"I've a good headache," he replied, "but it would take more than a knock on this head to make more than a dent."

"If you and Mary can manage to open the crates, Toby and I will go up to the pit and bring what remains there down here," I related. "We can load the crates and seal them again and be ready tomorrow to load them aboard and leave."

Everyone agreed to the plan. Toby and I finished our breakfast stew and, giving a nod to all, we set out for the pit. The leaves of the bushes were still wet from the dew, and we knew it would be another warm day. Upon reaching the pit, we both slid into the pit and began uncovering the boards. They more easily lifted from the sand now that they had been loosened. We pulled two more boards up and saw three more chests lined up beneath the boards.

The chests were all different; none were like the first one we had taken out. Their size was about the same three-foot long by two-foot wide as the first chest we had taken out, but these chests were about six inches deeper than the first. Two were flat topped with heavy iron fittings at the corners. One chest was closed with a hasp that ended in the shape of a circle with a hole cut through the middle that fit over a short round iron projection with a hole drilled through it. Through that hole was the hasp of a keylock that was impressive for its size. The second chest, though similar in size to the first, was closed by two lengths of heavy chain locked about it.

Toby and I were able to lift these two chests from their place beneath the remaining boards with moderate difficulty. With the two chests sitting astride the remaining boards and still in the pit, Toby and I flopped back on the cool sand exhausted from the exertion.

"Do you think we'll be able to get these down to the beach?" Toby gasped.

"We have to," I said trying to regain my strength.

"What if we had some rope," Toby said. "We could sling the chest and carry it with our shoulders instead of killing our arms."

"That is a promising idea," I answered. "Why don't you see if Captain Cutler would be amenable to giving us a length."

Toby nodded in agreement.

"Oh! And see if he might part with a bit of water," I added, "I will get the next chest out while you're gone," I said as Toby scrambled out of the pit.

Toby disappeared from my view as I sat in the pit. I turned my attention to the hole beneath the boards. The next chest was smaller than the first two. It measured perhaps two feet by two-feet square and two-thirds that deep. I could tell it was metal and its weight was substantial. I leaned over as far as I dared without falling between the boards and felt for something like handles down the sides. I finally found something I could get my fingers under to get a grip and pulled with all my might.

The chest lifted out of the hole and landed in my lap as I fell back. Its weight was considerable, and I struggled a bit to get it off my lap and onto the remaining boards covering the hole. I brushed some loose sand from the sides of the chest and began to see colors. The sides were gold in color. I knew it couldn't be gold; it had to be gold leaf. But set within the sides were gems. Some of them I knew the names of; others I did not. But they were amazing. The top consisted of two panels or doors made of the same metal as the rest of the chest. It was closed by a pair of double latches that formed circles. The right latch rotated to the right until it cleared the opposite panel. Then, the left latch rotated to the left until it cleared the other panel.

I opened the panels and saw leather pouches filling the chest. Nervously, I took out a pouch. I untied the draw strings and opened the top of the pouch. Out poured a handful of the largest emeralds I had ever seen. Deep green and flawless, to my untrained eye. I have no idea how long I sat there admiring their beauty.

"My God in Heaven!" I heard Toby's voice proclaim as he stood on the edge of the pit.

"They are rather magnificent, aren't they?" I said to him as he dropped the coil of rope he had on his shoulder and slid into the pit beside me. Toby carefully picked up one of the smaller gems and held it up to the sun between his thumb and forefinger.

"Just one of these," he marveled, "in the right hands could buy the finest house in Newport."

"There are many more pouches here," I said, sliding the handful of emeralds I held back into the pouch. "I am sure there are more and various kinds of gems in them. But we have no time to waste now."

As I started to put the bag into the chest, Toby tapped me on the shoulder and twirled the emerald he still held between his fingers.

"Let's keep this with its sisters and brothers," he said with a smile.

As I went to lift the chest, I said to Toby. "There must be something more in here. Gems can't weigh this much."

I proceeded to pull the pouches out of the chest. There were more than a dozen pouches of varying sizes. Beneath the pouches lay gold bars several inches long tightly stacked four or five deep across the bottom of the chest. Toby and I were giddy with excitement.

As quickly as we could recover ourselves, we replaced the pouches into the chest and closed the covers. Our excitement gave us renewed energy, and we lifted three chests out of the pit easily with the rope Toby had brought back with him. As I pushed the last chest up the side of the pit, Toby glanced back into the space beneath the planks.

"Tom," he said cautiously, "there are more chests under here." His voice was rising with excitement.

I slid back into the hole and watched as Toby dropped into the pit alongside me and pried one more plank out of the floor of the pit. With the plank removed, the shapes of at least three more chests were now visible. Toby looked at me in amazement.

"We need to get those out of the pit and hide them until we can get them to the beach," I said gasping for air.

We spent the next hour pulling away sand and easing the chests out one at a time from their hiding place. Again, the chests were of unusual sizes and slightly different shapes, but time was passing, and we needed to get the chests to the beach. Once we had removed all the chests and checked to be sure the pit was empty, there were a total of eight chests including the one we had already taken to the beach. Toby and I rested a moment and drank from the water bag he had also brought back from the *Peregrine*.

After a few moments, we took three of the chests out of the clearing and put them in some tall grass under some low bushes. The chest holding the gems and gold we placed behind one of the sapling trees and tore up some tall grass and completely covered it.

We took the rope Toby had brought and slung it under one of the larger chests. Together, we lifted it putting the rope over our shoulders and started down the path to the beach. Once we got in step, it was much easier to control the sway of the chest. It took about twenty minutes of walking to reach the edge of the beach where the underbrush thinned.

Jackie was waiting for us with three crates ready to receive chests. Mary sat in her customary place and kept an eye on the *Peregrine*.

The remaining stacks of crates hid what we were doing from any observing eyes aboard the *Peregrine* as Toby and I, with the chest between us, walked out onto the sand and placed the chest into one of the open crates with Jackie's help.

"How many are there, Tom?" Jackie asked.

"There are eight in total," I replied.

Toby and I gathered up the rope and started back to the pit. We did not run until we were out of sight of the beach. Then we broke into a trot. By the time we had delivered the third chest to the beach, we were exhausted, but we knew we could not stop. As quickly as we delivered chests, Jackie had open crates waiting to receive them. Each time we delivered a chest, Jackie would feel the weight of the chest and begin dumping stones from the outer crate until he felt the weight of the chest was offset. We kept placing the larger crates that had been filled in front of empty ones. This would make it appear from the *Peregrine* that we were doing nothing more than moving crates about.

It was now nearing midday. Toby and I could not rest but we feared a visit might come from the captain at an inconvenient moment. What if he decided to supply us lunch or just check how soon he wanted to be ready to leave? We could see that members of the crew were still busily attaching something to the hull and keel. The reflection of the sun upon it was intense as the sun rose higher, until the crew covered the side of the vessel with sail to stop the bright reflection. The captain must have realized the reflection might be detected by a passing ship that could investigate its source.

We now had half the chests securely placed into crates. Four more remained. Toby and I decided to make another run to the pit and carry all the remaining chests to the edge of the beach, leaving them far enough off the beach that they would be hidden well. Since we saw no one near the crates and heard no talking, we headed back for another chest. This one we left even a little further back on the path and, leaving the rope beside it, we casually walked onto the beach. As we broke out of the bushes, we heard voices.

Jackie was casually leaning against one of the crates when we appeared from the underbrush and heard Captain Cutler's voice in conversation with Mary.

"Ahhh, Mr. Gray," he acknowledged me as I came toward him. "I have good news to report," he continued.

"Good day, Captain," I replied airily. "And what might that news be?"

"Our repairs will be completed by day's end," he said clapping his hands. "The tide will be high tomorrow morn and we will be ready to get the vessel refloated."

"We should have our crates ready to be loaded by tonight, then," I said.

"Nay, Mr. Gray."

Captain Cutler waived his hand in front of himself in denial. "The ship needs to be as light as possible when we refloat her. We'll need all the labor we can muster, including the three of you."

I could feel Toby and Jackie looking at each other behind me as I assured the Captain, we would be more than pleased to place ourselves at his disposal when he needed us. This pleased Captain Cutler and, bidding Mary a good day, he headed back across the beach.

"He nearly caught us," Jackie said coming up behind me as I watched our Captain walk away. "I had just nailed the cover back on the crate when he approached.

"We have two more chests along the path," I said quietly to Jackie. "Did he say anything about bringing food over?"

"Yes," Jackie replied.

"Let us get another chest loaded," I said to Toby, and turning to Mary I said with a smile, "Keep a sharp eye out for that dinner pot."

With that, Toby and I left the beach to retrieve the remaining large chests at the pit and bring them down to the edge of the beach. We then retrieved the chest we had left farthest from the beach. We quickly secured it in a sling and headed for the beach. Jackie had a small crate open and waiting. We slipped the chest into the crate, placed it back inside a large crate and nailed the cover back on.

As we started to leave the beach to retrieve another chest hidden along the path, Mary called out, "someone is heading this way."

We gathered behind some of the crates and casually began a meaningless conversation as the crew member approached Mary carrying the, now familiar, pot of steaming stew. He acknowledged the three of us and set the pot down beside Mary along with the bowls and spoons.

Mary began filling the bowls with steaming stew. Toby and I decided to bring another chest from the shrubs just off the beach. Telling Mary we would return, the two of us headed into the underbrush. We chose the largest of the remaining chests since we had recovered a little of our strength. We slipped the rope under the chest near one end and then looped it around the other leaving enough rope on either end for it to be hoisted over our shoulders. It was the largest of the chests, yet it felt about the same weight as the others. We headed back to the beach and were greeted by Jackie with an open crate. The three of us lifted the chest into the crate and pulled the cover back into place and nailed it shut. The three of us looked at each other and gave a half smile.

"Time to eat, boys," Mary intoned.

THIRTY-FIVE

do not think any of us realized how hungry our work had made us. We ate ravenously and virtually licked our bowls clean.

"Only three to go," Toby said quietly.

"At least they are already down by the beach," I replied with a smile. "Let's get about it."

We stood and gave our bowls to Mary and headed into the shrubbery. We returned in only a few moments with one of the three remaining chests that were in the tall grass.

"I'm not ready," Jackie complained. "Give me a minute to catch up.

He pulled one of the upper crates off the stack and dragged it closer to where we had dropped the treasure chest. Taking a pry bar, Jackie slid it expertly into the separation of the side panel and the top of the crate and, pulling down on the bar with all his might, loosened the top in one attempt. Toby and I reached inside and lifted the empty crate inside out onto the sand. While we loaded the treasure chest into the crate on the sand, Jackie began pitching rocks out of the larger crate. In no time, we were ready to place the crate containing the chest inside the larger crate and nail it shut.

I picked up the rope and, making coils of it over my shoulder, Toby and I headed back into the underbrush once more. The beginning of the path to the pit was becoming more defined with every trip. Even so, I was a little worry that what we were doing would be discovered by members of the crew. Captain Cutler's response to someone attempting to see what we were doing had drawn a swift and severe response.

Toby and I pulled one of the two remaining chests from its hiding place and trussed it up in the length of rope as we had with the others. This would be the last of the larger chests. One more trip would be needed to retrieve the fancy gold-covered chest. We hoisted the chest and headed for the beach. Our shoulders were sore from the rope as we walked as much in-step as possible down the slight incline through the low shrubs. We broke onto the beach and Jackie was waiting standing next to another open crate. We unslung the chest and the three of us eased it into the small crate. Jackie nailed close the top and the three of us lifted it into the larger outer crate.

"Only one to go," I said aloud. "Certainly, the most unusual of all of them," I said with a smile.

Toby and I turned to make our final ascent. The path we had created seemed strangely long as we trudged in a single line up the slight grade. We reached the pit and uncovered the gold chest from its hiding place behind the tree. I stood holding the chest before me and saw Toby standing on the edge of the pit.

"A penny for your thoughts?" I asked as I came toward him.

"T'is not a pretty sight," Toby said sadly, looking at the destruction of the pit.

"I agree," I said, "but let it be a mystery to whomever should find it."

Toby shook his head and slid his fingers under the lamb's ear, half-circle metal grips on the sides of the chest.

"When my fingers give out, you can carry it the rest of the way," he said with a wry smile.

As we neared the beach, Toby's fingers buckled with the weight of the chest. I quickly gripped the chest with my hands under one end of the chest and Toby shifted his grasp to the opposite side. There was no way to hide the magnificence of the chest when we reached the beach. Its gold form and the brilliance of the imbedded gems on its sides caused an immediate reaction from Mary and Jackie. Toby and I walked directly to the open crate next to where Jackie was standing and placed the chest inside the crate. Before Jackie nailed the crate shut, I slid the locking mechanisms aside as I had before and opened the top panels. I removed one of the leather pouches from the chest.

"I've never seen anything that beautiful in my life," Jackie was gasping as he finished nailing the top on the outer crate.

"Come with me," I said to him as I walked to where Mary was sitting.

The three of us sat on the sand alongside Mary with our backs to the *Peregrine*. I produced the pouch which was about the size of a large pear.

"Open your hand, Mary," I said quietly. Mary looked at me with questioning anticipation.

The drawstrings closing the pouch grew shorter as I pulled open the top of the pouch. I took her hand and, turning it palm up, formed it into a cup. With my other hand, I lifted the pouch and poured some of its contents into her upturned palm. Out fell more than a half dozen sapphires of assorted sizes. Mary gasped in surprise.

"The other pouch we opened at the pit was filled with emeralds," Toby said with a smile.

Jackie's eyes were as big as marbles and tears were welling up in Mary's eyes.

"They're real?" Mary questioned in a whisper.

"I believe they are," I replied.

"Mary," Toby said hardly able to contain his excitement, "the entire bottom of that chest is filled with gold bars." She looked at Toby as if she were in a dream.

"I told you, Mary," I said, "we are all rich."

"They are so beautiful, Tom," Mary said as if she did not believe what she was hearing and seeing in her own hand.

I handed the pouch to Mary, saying, "this is for you to keep." I looked at Toby and Jackie and saw full agreement on their faces.

"We will be on our way home tomorrow and a new life," I said whimsically. "But first, we need to get our transport back afloat.

We spent the remainder of the day dismantling our makeshift tenting and lifting and dragging our crates nearer the *Peregrine* where we reinstalled our canvas cover. For the first time since we had landed, we were close enough to the vessel to see what changes had been made. Over the entire hull of the *Peregrine* up to the waterline, she had been sheathed in copper!

The *Peregrine* had now been up righted in anticipation of her relaunching. Captain Cutler sent word that he would like us to join him for our final supper on the beach. The two skiffs had been offloaded and now sat on the beach, along with the two anchors that had been onboard. The crew seemed busy removing other cargo from the hold and a couple of small cannons that seem to have appeared from nowhere and had not been seen previously.

A table appeared at the side of the *Peregrine* more hidden from the water and five chairs. As the sun began to set, Captain Cutler arrived dressed in his finest regalia and escorted Mrs. Nichol to the chair to the right of the chair at the head of the table. The captain seated Mary and then gestured to the rest of us to take a seat as he took the seat at the head of the table next to Mary. This was observed by all three of us with an exchange of some knowing smiles. It was obvious Captain Cutler was enamored of our Mary. Though she was in her late-forties, Mary looked no more than a woman of thirty. She could have passed as my sister, had I had one. It was amusing to see this salty dog of a captain, who fancied himself a swain, attempting to woo this woman who could have been his daughter.

We supped on the beach with the sun setting and the sand cooling beneath our feet. The crew of the *Peregrine* had caught a small wild pig and proceeded to roast it over a fire pit and the cook prepared potatoes and greens to go along. Several bottles of Madeira appeared, as well, and Captain Cutler regaled all with his stories, the bulk of which were told directly to Mary. As the sun disappeared under the horizon and dinner began winding down, it was time for Captain Cutler to address some questions from the rest of us.

"Captain," I began, "by what process do you intend to refloat your ship?"

"A very good question," came the Captain's response. This was his chance to impress Mary with his nautical skill.

"We shall use an old sailing method known as kedging," He proudly announced.

This was a term none of us were familiar with.

"Tomorrow morning, as the tide begins to rise, we will load the two anchors you see on the beach into the pinnaces, along with a second line tying the boats to the stern of the ship and row out beyond the breakers. The crew have cut two of the largest trees they could find, and they will be placed under the stern of the keel to act as rollers on the sand," Captain Cutler explained with great gravity.

"We shall then row the pinnaces out beyond the breakers and throw the anchors overboard, keeping the second lines secured to the small boats. As the capstans aboard the ship winch the ship toward the anchors, the men in the rowboats will row for all their worth."

"Will that be enough to get her into the water?" Jackie asked with concern.

"Oh, Heavens, Lad, no!" The Captain leaned back in his chair gesturing with his hands. "We will need to repeat the process over and over until she breaks free in the rising tide and begins to feel the water beneath her keel."

"But what if it doesn't work?" Jackie said with concern.

"I've never seen it fail, if it be done right," Captain Cutler said with a wry smile and a wink. "Between the two, and a rising tide, and our new sleek skin of smooth copper on her, I think she will slide into the waves slick as a newly greased pulley," Captain Cutler replied laughing loudly. Whether the laughter was from his clever reply or from the prodigious amount of wine he had consumed throughout supper might have been hard to determine.

"Once she's afloat, we'll ferry what we left on the sand aboard, restore your cargo, and we'll be off to Newport," he concluded placing the goblet he had been waving in his hand gently but firmly on the table.

"I think we should conclude tonight's merriment," Captain Cutler suddenly said breaking the mood he, himself, was feeling. "Tomorrow will be a difficult day for us all."

The Captain made a fumbling gesture at asking to escort Mary back to our canvas-covered retreat which Mary declined kindly and, taking hold of one of Toby's elbows and reaching for mine with her other hand, bid the slightly tipsy Captain a pleasant goodnight and turned the two of us toward our camp. Jackie dutifully followed.

As we walked across the beach, we could hear above the crunching noise our feet made on the sand the Captain giving orders to his crew to clear the table. Mary giggled into Toby's arm as she held tightly to both of us. It was a beautiful, but short, walk on that strand of beach with little wind to speak of and the moon just past full. It was a perfect night to be escorting our Mary to anywhere.

Sleep did not come easily. Jackie, Toby, and I took turns standing watch while Mary slept. The three of us had already determined that having Mary alone aboard the *Peregrine* as our crates were brought from the beach in the skiffs was not a wise strategy. We decided once the schooner was afloat, I would stay aboard and leave the loading of our crates to the supervision of Toby and Jackie.

I had taken the last watch of the night. The sun rose in a cloudless sky and activity was already stirring around the ship. The rowboats now stood at the stern of the vessel and lines were being rigged from the stern to the small boats. The anchors were carried to the small boats, as well, and placed inside. I woke Toby and Jackie quietly so as not to awaken Mary and pointed to the ship.

"It looks like we are about to try this kedging maneuver," I said. "We best be available."

The three of us shook the stiffness of the night out of our frames and started to walk across the beach in the direction of the *Peregrine*. We were met by Captain Cutler coming around the stern of the vessel.

"Good morning, Captain," I greeted him.

"Good morn, Mates," came his reply. "We may be in great luck today," he continued, "it appears this morning the wind is from over the island."

"What does that mean, Captain," Jackie asked quickly.

"We may be able to use a bit of sail to help move her. We can back the sails should the wind stay from the north," Captain Cuter replied eyeing the sky. "Might help to get her started."

"When do we start and where do you want us?" I asked.

"Tide just started coming in about an hour ago," Captain Cutler replied. We'll need to let it flood close to high before we start, so we have plenty of time for some food."

"How high will the tide come?" Toby asked the Captain.

"Last high tide was better than two-thirds up the hull," the Captain replied. "These full moon tides are higher than normal, so we should be able to float her without too much trouble, especially now that she has an empty hold and stripped of other weighty things."

We noticed Captain Cutler's eyes drifting to something behind us and turned to see Mary coming toward us across the beach. Each stride kicked up a small plume of sand and her long skirt brushed across the sand. Her white blouse beneath her bodice was beginning to show days of wear and her hair fell in dark ringlets being blown by the slight wind. She was a vision. Again, her beauty belied her age. Captain Cutler pushed past us and greeted Mary brightly. She shyly thanked him and accepted his invitation to have some food. He then took her arm and, acknowledging we were still near, began escorting Mary to the port side of the *Peregrine*.

Toby tugged at my arm as we rounded the stern of the vessel.

"We will be out of sight of the crates," he pointed in their direction. "I will hang back a bit and keep an eye." I nodded my agreement.

The table that had served for our supper the night before was now set in the shadow cast by *Peregrine*. Again, Captain Cutler escorted Mary to the chair to his right and saw to it that tea arrived and was served to her. A basket of biscuits and something akin to a scone appeared on the table. The growling in our stomachs would at least be calmed by ingesting these. The crew lounged on the sand and imbibed grog as all of us watched the waves advance farther and farther up the beach toward us and the beached ship.

Before long, the stern of the vessel was covered by several feet of water and the table we had been sitting at had to be moved for a second time as the water continued rising.

"It's time to begin!" Captain Cutler suddenly bellowed. "Get to yer stations, mates!"

THIRTY-SIX

In seconds, the crew reacted. Three scurried up the short Jacob's Ladder slung over the side of the schooner, followed by Mary and Captain Cutler. The remaining three crew and the three of us splashed through the incoming waves and tumbled into the two rowboats, now afloat, at the stern of the *Peregrine*. The oars slid into their pins and powerful arms and shoulders began pulling on them, drawing the ropes extending over the stern and secured to the schooner out of the water and making them taut. After rowing about one hundred feet, the anchors were heaved over the sides of the skiffs. The tide was rising quickly now, and the men in the rowboats waited for the signal to begin rowing to try to move the ship. As they faced the beach at the ready, a topsail suddenly blossomed atop the main mast. The lines to the submerged anchors snapped taut in the water as the capstans aboard the *Peregrine* began to tighten them, and the oars slashed the water in unison. At first, nothing was happening. A voice in each of the rowboats kept repeating, "PULL! PULL!" Still the schooner seemed not to move. Our hands on the oars cramped from straining.

Then, almost imperceptibly, *Peregrine* started to slide back into the water, ever so slowly, but moving. The log rollers beneath her stern were deep under water now. The topsail suddenly furled, and you could feel the wind had shifted so it no longer would help. A cheer went up from the rowers. The momentum of the ship as it moved farther, and had more water beneath her, was almost majestic.

A flag on a pole was raised at the stern of the schooner. That was the signal to recover the anchors and row them farther out and drop them again. Once we in the small boats were able to free the anchors from the bottom, we rowed out another fifty or so yards and dropped them again to the bottom. This had to be done quickly as the incoming tide was pushing *Peregrine* back onto the beach. When this had been accomplished, a member of the crew in the other rowboat raised a flag on a pole like the flag raised on the vessel. Again, we rowed hard, and the anchor lines grew taut again.

The entire process was repeated one more time. When the log rollers were seen to pop to the surface, we knew the schooner was now fully afloat. One of the anchors was brought aboard ship while the *Peregrine* rode at anchor from the other. The lines to the rowboats were thrown back aboard and one of the crew scampered aboard. With two crew in the other rowboat and three of us in our boat, we made for the beach. It was time to re-laden the ship with materials left on the beach and our cargo of crates.

We skidded the crate down near the water's edge and began loading our boat. We found we could easily fit two crates into the boat at a time. The other boat was loading items taken off the *Peregrine* to lighten her for relaunch. The cannons, the table, the chairs all fit into the bow of the second rowboat. We slid the small boats into the water at the same moment, and pulling on the oars with aching arms, headed for the *Peregrine*.

The other boat reached the vessel first and the winch aboard the schooner was used to hoist the table and cannon aboard. We held our position just astern until the crew aboard were ready to hoist our cargo. With two crates aboard, I told Toby I would go aboard *Peregrine* while he and Jackie retrieved the remaining crates with the other boat, as we had agreed.

I climbed over the rail of the *Peregrine* at the top of Jacob's Ladder onto the deck. I looked toward the beach and saw Toby, Jackie, and the other boat were already nearing the shore. Our crates were sitting on the deck and were ready to be stowed below. The winch made short work of transferring each crate into the hold. By the time these first two crates were safely stowed, both rowboats were coming back alongside the *Peregrine* loaded with more of our crates.

By late afternoon, the beach was cleared of everything. There were no signs of anyone having ever been on this beach. Toby and Jackie were exhausted and sought space along the rail to relax a bit. Mary stood near the helm next to Captain Culver who was now in his element.

"We'll stay at anchor tonight," Captain Culver said approaching Toby, Jackie, and me as we sat along the side of the deck. "You boys look like you need to recover, and my crew needs a bit of rest, as well."

To hear this from the captain was a relief, but also worrisome. We had already been away from Newport and the White Horse for nearly two weeks. We needed to get back as soon as possible. But a night of rest had an irresistible allure to it.

As the three of us sat on the deck of the *Peregrine* and watched the western sky turn orange and red with the clouds swirled in purple hues, no one spoke. Each of us was lost in his own thoughts, and content to be so. While our wealth was secured in the hold of this ship, our futures were just as unsure as ever.

It was not long before the aroma of the cook's special seafood stew wafted from below decks. Soon, one of the crew came by with bowls and spoons, followed soon after by another with a steaming pot of supper stew. It was only then we three realized we had not eaten since early morning. With little regard for the taste, we all downed the food and allowed it to warm our empty bellies. Mary was enjoying her meal seated on a short stair below the helm, listening respectfully to Captain Culver's stories.

We finished our meal and began talking among ourselves about how to pass the night. We all agreed we needed to stand watches. As we rode at anchor just off the beach, it was decided I would stand first watch and wake Toby at two bells and Jackie would relieve Toby at the next two bells. Staying awake would not be easy with the gentle rocking of the vessel at anchor, and I could see my two friends were barely awake even now. As I encouraged them to head below and get some sleep, Jackie quietly turned to me and brought his head close to my ear.

"I retrieved a musket from the crates and stowed it under the gunnel where we are sitting," he said in a whisper. "I noticed some of the crew are now carrying pistols. Our musket's loaded."

I glanced to the stern and saw the helmsman had a pistol tucked in his leather belt. I nodded my understanding as Jackie pulled away. He turned and went below. Shortly after, Mary swept past me and bid me "good evening" as she went to her cabin.

Activity on the deck slowed. Only the members of the crew on watch and I were left on deck. A damp fog began to roll in laying a moist coating on every surface. At the sound of two bells, I roused myself and shook off the stiffness of my joints and went to wake Toby. I rolled into the bunk Toby left and was immediately asleep.

The sound of feet scampering on the deck over my head woke me from my slumber. I looked to the other bunk and saw Toby stretched out and asleep.

"Time to rise, my friend," I said in a slightly louder voice that I hoped would penetrate any dream Toby might be having. His form soon shivered awake, and he sat up on the side of his bunk.

"I can't say I will miss these accommodations," he said sarcastically.

"I can't say the crew will miss where they have been forced to sleep since we have had their bunks," I replied. The two of us laughed softly.

We quickly dressed and came up on deck. The sun was just above the horizon and a light breeze was blowing.

"Good morning, mates," Captain Culver greeted us from above where he stood by the helm.

"Good morning," I replied as I mounted the short set of stairs to the stern. "It looks like a fine day!"

"Aye," the Captain replied. "We'll make Newport before dark if the wind holds."

As I stood near the stern, I looked back at the island and ran my eyes about the beach. Suddenly, I noticed something near the water's edge I had not seen before.

"Captain?" I asked, "Is there something on the beach? There! By the water's edge."

Toby mounted the stairs and looked in the direction of the beach. Soon Jackie was also looking toward the beach.

"Would ye like to use my glass? " Captain Culver offered politely. "It'll make it easier to make out."

I accepted the spyglass offered and put my focus on the object on the beach.

"Captain," I said as I realized what the object was, "Captain, it is a man's head!" I said with alarm.

Toby and Jackie grasped the rail and looked more intently at the object.

"Nay, Mr. Gray," came the cool reply from the Captain. "It is a man."

"I don't understand, Captain," I said more alarmed than ever.

"It is a man buried up to his neck in the sand," Captain Culver continued in the same cold vein.

"He's below the highwater mark, Captain," Toby added becoming agitated. "Surely, he will dig himself out before the tide rises as it is doing now!"

"I think not, my friend," the Captain continued with no emotion, "not unless he can untie his arms that are lashed behind his back."

"He's going to drown!" Jackie shouted.

"Precisely!" Captain Culver shouted back.

"Who is he?" I asked anxiously. "What has he done to deserve this fate?"

"He was one of the crew. Roscoe is his name," the captain related returning to his previous cold attitude. "This is the man who snuck up to your pit against my orders and attempted to cave in your young friend's head," he said pointing at the bandage still on Jackie's forehead.

"Captain," I said hurriedly, "there is no need for this brutality on our behalf. Nothing was harmed. Jackie will recover. We do not want this man's blood on our hands!"

"This has little, if anything, to do with you and your group," Captain Culver thundered as he turned to address the three of us. "This is about obeying your Captain's orders! It is about maintaining order and discipline aboard my ship! I gave a direct order that no one, NO ONE, was to leave the beach or interfere in your business."

"But, Captain," I began to plead.

"You heard me tell the crew when I repeated the order after the incident that the offender would suffer the punishment of the tides should he be discovered. This is not about you. This is to show the crew I will have my orders obeyed."

"The tide is reaching him," Jackie said quietly.

Captain Culver walked to me and snatched the spyglass from my hands. He then turned to the railing of the deck facing the bow of the vessel and bellowed to the crew, "Haul the anchor! Ready to make sail."

As we sailed farther from the beach, the small object now much nearer the water, disappeared. I think the three of us were in shock. We had seen a side of Captain Cutler none of us suspected he possessed. I was thinking to myself thank God Mary had not witnessed this affair when I suddenly looked along the starboard side rail and saw Mary standing about midship. Her expression told me she had witnessed everything. The sail home would not be lighthearted and pleasant.

We were soon scudding along in the main channel with a good southwest wind filling our sails. The crew went about adjusting sails to keep them filled with wind while the helmsman held his course. The four of us stood at the port rail and absent-mindedly watched the shoreline pass. The loss of one of their own seemed to have no effect upon the members of the crew. We, who knew the one lost far less than his crew mates, were stunned at the manner of his demise. Captain Culver made no apology for his action and the crew gave no sign of remorse for it. This was the punishment for disobeying the captain's orders aboard ship and it was tacitly accepted by all who might be subject to it.

As the sun set, we neared the entrance to Narragansett Bay, Captain Culver approached our group as if nothing untoward had happened.

"I propose we enter the bay and sail the west passage," he said in a friendly, calm manner. "It will be getting dark, and we need not announce our arrival. With any luck, we may not be noticed and be hidden a bit by sailing behind Conanicut Island."

I nodded in agreement with this plan and asked if we would be able to unload our crates upon docking.

"Aye," Captain Culver answered, "I would like to be sailing come midday tomorrow, if possible. If we can beg or borrow a wagon and team, you could be off with your cargo tonight."

"We might not be so lucky as to find such transport this evening, but we can try," I replied.

Until now, the captain had said nothing about receiving the balance of payment he was due. I knew this would soon occur. I turned to the group and very quietly said," We must be ready to pay the captain the rest of his money immediately upon landing."

"I don't know if we have enough left," Toby said.

"I'm not sure we do either," Mary agreed.

We quickly took all our funds and gave them to Mary. She counted it all and came up twenty pounds short of the balance we owed the captain.

"Do you think one of those bags in the fancy chest might have some coins in it?" Jackie asked.

"It might," I replied. "Jackie, do you know which crate that chest is in?" I asked.

"I marked each crate with something to tell me where every chest was," Jackie said with a smile.

"We will need to wait until as many of the crew as possible are busy. Could you and Toby then slip into the hold unnoticed, find the crate, and open it as quietly as possible?" I whispered. "Check the pouches, and, hopefully, one will have some coins in it. If we must wait until we dock, try to have them unload that crate first."

The crew were busy, yet there always seemed to be one or another watching our movements. Now that we knew our situation and realized we could do little to resolve it at that moment, all of us tried to relax until we docked. The passage of time seemed to slow as we were slicing through the water with good speed thanks to the sleek copper sheathing the *Peregrine* now sported. I attempted to strike up a conversation with the captain and ease any tension that might have been still harbored between us, I asked about the sheathing.

"Did you add that for more speed, Captain?" I asked.

"No, Mr. Gray," he replied, "for the worms."

The look of confusion on my face prompted the captain to continue.

"We will be taking the ship into warmer waters where there is a plague called the Teredo. They will eat through the wood of a ship and sink her," he said. "They can't eat through the metal, so it saves the vessel. They are in all waters, but worse in warmer waters about the equator and Africa."

Suddenly I realized Captain Culver was taking the *Peregrine* into the slaving trade!

THIRTY-SEVEN

I returned to our group standing at the port rail and shared with them all I had learned from Captain Cutler. None of our group was surprised having witnessed the brutality doled out by our Captain that very morning. However, realizing that our association with our Captain and his ship would be over in a matter of a few more hours, and what occurred beyond that was not our direct concern, we stood silently and watched the beaches along the Rhode Island shore slip by.

Before we knew it, the sun was well passed setting and darkness deepened. We heard the creak of pulleys as the ropes passed through them to tighten up the sails and felt the heeling of the vessel as we rounded to port and entered the mouth of Narragansett Bay. Hardening the sails further, the vessel swung into the West Passage behind Conanicut Island and away from sighting of Newport. We would again be passing painful landmarks from my youth.

As we sailed, I turned from the rail and looked to the west side of Conanicut. There, where the flats would soon be emerging as the tide ebbed, I searched for the broken stern section that had saved me that terrible night so many years before. It was no longer there. I suddenly realized that was an event some twenty-odd years passed. I turned back to the rail just as we began passing the clearing where my grandfather's house stood.

The silhouette of the main house stood out on the top of the hill with a few windows showing light. I knew it looked tired and old, unkempt, and ramshackle. It was no longer the proud estate house I remembered from my youth. The fields down to the water that had once yielded crops of corn and flax were fallow and overgrown. No sheep or other livestock existed. My heart sank at the sight, and I wondered how my uncle, who had been willing to kill for this land, could have cared so little for it as its sole owner.

We reached the northern end of the island with not one ship larger than a day sailor being in sight. We rounded the northern tip and headed straight for Coddington Cove just north of the main harbor. We landed at the dock late in the dark and work began immediately to offload the cargo. Jackie was first in the hold directing which crates to be lifted out first. The crane and winch on the dock was larger and stronger than that aboard the schooner and could manage two crates at once. As soon as the first two crates cleared the hold, Jackie was back on deck and making his way onto the dock.

Toby and I grasped the crates as soon as they were free of the crane and moved them to shore off the dock. As we walked back up the dock to retrieve the next set of crates, Jackie passed us with a wink of an eye. By the time we had retrieved the next two crates and walked them back to shore to be stacked next to the previous crates, Jackie was squatting behind the first two crates with the golden chest between his legs pulling out pouches and bouncing them in his hand listening for the chink-chink sound of gold or silver. Toby and I went back to the dock and retrieved the next two crates and when we returned to Jackie, he was standing beside the crates smiling confidently.

"You found it?" I asked with confidence.

"I found silver coins," Jackie replied handing a small pouch to me below the top of the crate that he stood behind. "I don't think they are English. Maybe, Dutch?"

"It will not matter to Captain Culver," I said confidently.

I opened the pouch and fished out a half dozen of the coins and gave them to Jackie. I told him to go to the docks in town and see if he could get a wagon and team. Toby and I went back to retrieving and stacking the crates being taken off the *Peregrine*. The sun was well down, and torches now lit the dock and lanterns appeared on the *Peregrine*. It was time to settle with Captain Culver. It was also time to find out why Mary had not come on deck since she had left us to go gather her things in her cabin.

I sent Toby to watch over the crates while I sat on the ship's rail and swung my legs around onto the deck. I scanned the length of the ship expecting I would see Captain Culver somewhere along its length. He was not to be seen. This seemed odd because he had always been on deck when the ship was in port, or at anchor. I asked a crew member as he hurried past me where he thought the Captain might be. His response surprised me. He was "entertaining" the female passenger in his cabin.

I hurried to the hatchway leading below deck in the stern and wrapped loudly on the Captain's cabin door.

"Enter?" came the response.

I burst open the door and saw Mary seated demurely on the edge of the Captain's bunk and Captain Culver sitting at his table under the stern windows, feet up, and a glass of red wine in his hand. All wore smiles. I approached the Captain's table and sat in the empty chair indicated by Captain Culver's motioning hand.

"Good you could join us, Mr. Gray," Captain Culver said jovially. "Our time together is nearly over once we settle your account," he continued. "I am assuming that is the reason you have joined us," he said as he took his feet off the table.

"Indeed, Captain. I have your payment with me. But surely, Mary need not be present for us to conclude our business," I said turning a hand toward Mary.

"Why, there is no need for her to run off just yet," Captain Culver replied with a slight edge to his words.

It was then I realized Mary was his last leverage to assure payment. Despite his attempts to be cavalier, Mary was really nothing more than a bargaining chip in the end.

"Very well," I said. "I am afraid we are slightly short in making full payment in gold, as agreed to, but we do have some silver to make up the difference."

"Double on the silver," came the cold, emotionless response.

"I'm sorry," I said a bit stunned. "Did you just say double if it is in silver?"

"The agreement was payment in gold," came the response as I saw the cold stare in his dead eyes. "Yer lucky I'm not makin' it treble."

"Very well, Captain," I said not testing further.

I retrieved the money pouch from my pocket and turned to Mary.

"Have you the funds, Mary?" I asked her. Mary slid off the bunk and walked the step or two to my side and handed me the gold coins I had entrusted to her. Captain Culver nearly choked on his sip of wine.

"You had it all this time," Captain Cutler sputtered out through his coughing and trying to take a breath.

"You never asked me, Captain," Mary said brightly.

I placed the gold coins on the edge of the table and proceeded to count out from the silver double the amount that was short. I folded the pouch which still had some coins in it and gave it to Mary.

"I would appreciate you seeing us off the ship, Captain," I said as I stood.

"As you wish," he responded.

Captain Culver bent down and retrieved a small strong box from beneath the table. He opened it and, glancing at them said, "Dutch, eh?" then deposited the silver coins in a cloth bag within. He picked up the gold coins and pocketed them in his coat. Taking a last sip to drain his wine, he extended his arm toward the cabin door and bid us exit. I opened the door and ushered Mary into the small hallway leading to the stairway to the main deck. I assisted her up the rail steps and onto the gangplank.

"Captain," I said turning around to confront the form behind me. "I thank you for your service and I wish you the best in your future endeavors, but I must say, I hope to never see you or this vessel again."

"We will be stocked and stowed by midday tomorrow and be leagues away by nightfall," Captain Cutler replied with a smile. "I may be somewhat of a rogue, Mr. Gray, but I do honor my agreements. I wish you also the best in your future enterprises, as well," he said, finishing with a smile and a sweep of his feathered hat.

By the time I had climbed onto the gangway and walked the dock to solid land, Mary was tightly hugging Toby. We had made it home. Now we needed Jackie to perform a small miracle by finding a wagon and team. We were discussing what to do if Jackie could not find transport for the crates when we heard the jingle of harness approaching on the road from Newport harbor.

Jackie appeared sitting atop one of the largest wagons I had ever seen, drawn by two enormous oxen. The smile on his face told us there was a story he was going to share. But, for now, all any of us wanted was to get our crates to a safe place and get home to the inn. As the wagon rumbled to a stop near the crates, Jackie applied the wheel brake and jumped down from his seat. Before I could speak, Toby took the lead.

"I know you want to tell us about where you got it," Toby said to Jackie, "but, please, let us get these crates loaded first?"

Jackie looked startled at Toby's request and the smile left his face rapidly.

"Okay, okay," Jackie responded, obviously disappointed at the rebuff of his story. "I just thought you might find it humorous that, not only did I get a wagon, but I also got us storage for the crates, and it was given for free..." Jackie's voice trailed off to a whisper at the end.

"What was that you said," Toby asked in a slightly raised voice.

"Oh, it was nothing," Jackie responded, feigning disinterest.

"No, no, Jackie," I interjected. "What did you say about storage?"

Jackie perked up.

"I said I was offered storage for the crates if we wanted it. But I guess...."

"Who is offering?" Toby demanded, "and don't be slow about it!"

"All right, all right," Jackie stammered raising his arms defensively. "I have a sort of friendship with the watchman at the old warehouse. Our old warehouse. He offered to let us temporarily store the crates in the warehouse with no charge because he knows who we are."

Toby looked at me for some sign of agreement. Thoughts were racing through my mind. There were more crates than we could easily secure at the White Horse, especially in the dark. We were all exhausted and, just for expediency alone, it was a suitable alternative.

"Let us get these crates loaded and let us all think about this while we do," I finally said. "Mary is dead on her feet, and we need to get her home."

The three of us muscled the crates into the wagon and helped Mary climb up to the seat where Jackie joined her. Toby and I each took a side of the oxen yoke and guided the animals in an about turn and onto the road to Newport harbor.

"Are we going to take Mary to the inn?" asked Toby as we broke onto the plaza at the waterfront. "This is as close as we will be." We pulled back on the oxen yoke stopping our progress.

"Toby, you take Mary home," I decided. "Jackie and I will take the wagon to the warehouse. At least for tonight." Toby nodded in agreement.

Toby turned to ask Mary if she needed help getting down from the wagon seat and saw she was asleep on Jackie's shoulder. Jackie gently nudged Mary and told her Toby would take her home. Mary nodded, still half asleep and, with Toby's help, got down from the seat. Held by Toby's strong arm, the two of them started up the side street off the plaza in the direction of the White Horse Inn and home. With my pull on the yoke, the oxen went into motion again, and we continued across the cobblestones of the plaza to the double doors of the stone warehouse. The doors were open, and a figure sat in that familiar spot once held by Mr. Janick.

As we drew near, I stopped the oxen and Jackie climbed down from the wagon. The figure at the doors made no movement as Jackie approached him. Jackie motioned for me to follow him. Jackie proceeded to have a hushed conversation with the man at the door who finally rose to his feet and pulled a glowing lantern from its holder and motioned for the wagon to be brought inside. Jackie took hold of the other side of the oxen yoke and helped guide the team through the warehouse doors and along the floor inside. We reached the back wall on the ground floor and stopped the team.

The area where the Dock Rats once roosted was empty space. But in my mind's eye, I could still envision the rough bunks that many years before had been our lair. Other than this, the warehouse looked much the same, even to the smells.

"I think we want to lay the crates along the wall here," Jackie said bringing me back to the present. "I don't think our secret entrance has been discovered," he continued in a lower voice pointing to the weight still hanging from the rope that activated the hidden door.

We carefully placed the crates to cover the secret access point and stacked them two high.

"Which crate holds the special chest?" I asked Jackie quietly. He tapped the corner of one of the crates.

"We can carry this one to the inn tonight," I said, "if you feel up to it."

"Let me talk to my friend and see if I can borrow a wheeled cart for the night," Jackie suggested. He walked to the front of the warehouse where his 'friend' had resumed his prior position by the door. While Jackie conversed with the man, I found a piece of metal I could use to pry open the crate Jackie had designated as holding the gold box. I tried lifting out the inner crate containing the treasure, but it was too heavy. I would need to wait for Jackie.

I then heard the rumble of a hand cart echoing in the cavernous space of the warehouse as it came in my direction. As it came closer, I saw that Jackie was not alone. A boy of about ten, dressed in dirty rags and shoeless, walked beside him.

"Who might this be?" I asked Jackie as the drew near.

"This is Andy, Mr. Gray," Jackie announced. "I have hired him for the night to watch over our cargo."

"Pleased to make your acquaintance," I said to the child as he doffed his ragged cap and gave an acknowledging head bob.

"Andy is the son of my friend at the door," Jackie added.

"I see. Well, we cannot have Andy work for us without pay," I said staring at the young boy who averted his eyes. "I say three silvers from this pouch ought to do." I reached for the pouched, then realized I had given it to Mary for safekeeping.

"May I pay you tomorrow?" I asked the boy. He nodded enthusiastically in agreement. We exchanged smiles and Jackie scuffled his hair.

"While my friend here may be short of coin tonight, I am not," Jackie spoke up. He reached into his pocket and retrieved the silver coins I had given him to pay for transport at the dock. Smiling, Jackie dropped three silver coins into the lad's upturned palm. The boy smiled in reply.

Jackie then helped me lift the heavy inner crate up and out of the larger crate and place it on the hand cart. We replaced the top of the larger crate and pounded down the corners with a few sharp raps of our hands. Our young security guard disappeared for a moment and returned carrying a piece of hole-ridden cloth. He settled his thin form in front of our crates, and wrapped the cloth, as best he could, around his form. Seeing him there, I remembered how cold the floor had been not all that many years ago.

With that thought still in my mind, I heard Jackie ask if I was all right and ready to go. I turned and walked to the oxen yoke and gave it a slight tug and the oxen began to move toward the doorway. Jackie walked on the other side of the ox team pushing the hand cart loaded with the smaller crate we had loaded. When we reached the doorway, the man, who had not spoken a word to me, rose from his seat and took hold of the oxen team.

"My friend will see to the wagon, Tom," Jackie said. "I will take care of him tomorrow," he continued. "I asked him to get his son a decent blanket for the night and gave him two coins to cover the cost.

With that, I thanked the silent man, and Jackie, wheeling the hand cart, and I started across the plaza toward the inn and home. It was then it struck me that the waterfront was strangely deserted and quiet. Only a few ships lay at anchor in the harbor and only two were tied up at the wharves. In a sense, I was relieved that our arrival and activities had been observed by so few eyes. Yet, it was still unusual to see so little activity on the docks.

We reached the White Horse with slight delay and carried the crate in through the back door. Mary and Toby were sitting in the kitchen with cups of tea before them on the table. Jackie and I set the crate against the wall furthest from the busy end of the kitchen and turned to join Toby and Mary.

"Would you like some tea?" Mary asked us.

"I would like something a bit stronger, if you don't mind, Mary," Jackie offered.

"Tea for me," I replied.

Jackie went into the tavern and poured himself a rum he then brought back to the kitchen. As the four of us sat at the kitchen table exhausted, yet happy to be home, Mary looked at us and began to laugh. The three of us exchanged looks that asked if Mary had gone daft.

"I am sorry, boys," Mary finally managed to say through her laughter, "but you are a sight. Two weeks since a razor has touched any of your sweet faces and you would scare your mothers' out of a year of life!" She burst into a round of laughter once again, and this time was joined by the three of us.

THIRTY-EIGHT

We finished our tea, and Jackie his drink, and decided to place the chest in Mary's room for the night. We would look at it more closely in the morning. Before we went off to bed, Mary and Toby gave us an assessment of the condition of the inn. The dust was thick on every surface. Our beer stocks would need to be replaced. Two weeks of no use might sour any ale. There would be plenty of work tomorrow to get the inn up and running for customers. But, for now, sleep seemed to call to all of us.

Toby and Jackie opened the crate and removed the chest within. They each took an end of the gold-colored chest and began muscling it to Mary's room. Mary and I left the crate open on the floor of the kitchen and double checked the locks on all the doors and windows before heading upstairs. Toby and Jackie were just coming out of Mary's room as we reached the top of the stairs. We all said goodnight and headed for bed. It had been a long day.

———————————— >< ————————————

The excitement of anticipation woke me at first light. I quickly dressed and quietly headed for Mary's room. To my surprise, I found Jackie asleep, curled up against Mary's door covered with a blanket.

I gently shook him awake and smiled at his willingness to spend an uncomfortable night standing guard. I gently rapped on Mary's door but received no reply.

"Mary has already gone downstairs," Jackie said as he yawned.

"In that case," I replied, "let us get the chest downstairs. Are you up to it?"

Jackie roused himself and, shaking off his achy joints, went into Mary's room with me to retrieve the chest.

We found Mary dusting off the tables in the dining room and humming to herself. The fire was already going in the kitchen, and it was clear she was already into her routine of cleaning.

"Good morning, boys," she said cheerily as we came into the dining room on our way to the kitchen carrying the chest. "Water is on for tea."

Mary dropped the towel she was using to clean a table and hurried to open the door into the kitchen. Jackie and I carried the chest into the kitchen and placed it on the floor by the kitchen table. Mary went to the fire and pulled the steaming kettle off its hook. Just then, Toby entered the kitchen stretching his arms and yawning.

Morning, everyone," he said sleepily.

"Everyone take a seat," Mary said as she poured tea for all, "I have muffins in the Dutch oven and sweet butter and honey. We must use it before it turns."

We all ate until we were stuffed. We had all had enough of watery stews. As we sipped our tea, I reached under the table and slid the closures of chest open. I pulled out a pouch for each of us, passed them around the table, and closed the panels.

"One at a time, let us see what we have," I said softly. "Mary, why don't you start?"

Mary slowly stood the pouch before her on the table. She carefully slid her slender fingers inside the top and pulled the pouch open. For some reason, she stopped and reached into her apron pocket. She brought forth a piece of fine black fabric and carefully laid it out on the table. Mary carefully tilted the pouch over the cloth. A stream of pure white, perfectly formed pearls flowed onto the cloth. They were nearly the size of a robin's egg and the dark cloth set off the creamy luster of their brilliance. The three of us gasped at the sight.

"I have never seen anything like them," Mary said breathlessly.

"I'm next," Jackie piped up.

He took hold of the pouch before him and pulled open the top. Cupping his hand over the opening, Jackie slowly lifted the pouch pouring the contents into his hand. Out came a flow of blood red rubies that sparkled in the sunlight filtering through the kitchen window. A collective 'o-o-oh' escaped each of us.

"Toby," Mary said, "you go next," excitement in her voice.

Toby carefully placed his fingers on the very top of the pouch and pulled it closer. Using only his thumbs and forefingers, he pulled the pouch open. Tipping the pouch over, he allowed the contents to begin pouring onto the wooden table. A pile of sapphires began building on the table, their facets catching the sunlight in the same way Jackie's gems had.

"Now you, Tom," Mary said sounding like a child on Christmas morning.

I looked at the pouch before me. I looked at the expressions around our table full of anticipation. I opened the pouch and, as Toby had done, tilted it over and allowed the contents to tumble out onto the table. A stream of gold doubloons spilled out onto the table, clinking as they fell. Everyone gasped.

"They are beautiful," Mary finally said.

"Aye," Jackie said, "there must be fifty or more there!"

"I've never seen that much gold before," Toby said in awe.

We all sat for a moment just gawking at the riches before us on the table.

"I think we might have a new problem," I said quietly.

Instantly, a series of questions erupted asking, 'what did I mean?'

"We will need to sell these beautiful stones for money, unless we plan to go into the business of selling jewelry. And we will need to sell them away from here."

What had been unbridled joy moments earlier now became a room somber in thought. Everyone expressed his or her idea for what to do about the gems: beautiful to look at, expensive to obtain, a symbol of wealth, but whose value could only be realized through pledge or sale.

"We need to think further on this matter," I finally said, "but now we need to put these beauties back in the chest and prepare for the day."

Reluctantly, each of us placed our finds back in their pouches and dropped them into the chest. Jackie and Toby lifted the chest and placed it in the pantry on the floor and covered it with a cloth and placed some pots atop it. Jackie was sent on errands to the brewery, the butchery, and the bakery. We would soon be getting deliveries that would need to be overseen and, in the meantime, there was plenty of cleaning left to be done. And, like clockwork, a few of the regulars started arriving in the tavern wanting to know where we had all gone for so long. There was some jolly fun had by customers over our growth of facial hair.

It took a week to get back into the routine of the inn. There were many questions put to all of us regarding where we had gone and what we had been doing. Every day or two, either Toby and Jackie or Jackie and I would go to the warehouse and open another crate. In the evening, we would gather in the kitchen, open a chest, and see the wonderful things within. The second chest contained a mixture of treasure and cloths: beautiful sheer silks and boldly colored embroidery, virtually undamaged from their time beneath the sand. Beneath these were a trove of gold goblets and jewelry, gold rings and bracelets, necklaces, and strings of pearls. At the very bottom of the chest was a layer of gold ingots each between ten and twelve inches long, two inches wide, and two inches thick.

The third chest, the lightest so far, held fabrics of many types. Since we had hinted that our trip was to shop for goods to redecorate the White Horse, we decided to leave these fabrics draped about the crate against the wall of the dining room so the curious could ask about them and be asked what their favorites were. In the bottom of this chest were four woven bags weighing several pounds each of gold and silver coins, mostly Spanish in origin, with some other coins having writing and symbols that were unknown to us. Each chest contained riches to make a person wealthy for life. These we consolidated as much as possible. We all realized it would be necessary to take much of this treasure far from here to convert it into usable funds. For that, we would need to find an honest agent who knew how to proceed. That might be a difficult person to find.

After a week of being home, I decided it was time to contact Reverend Berkeley to formally announce my return, although I was sure he knew I had returned. In fact, I was surprised he had not sent for me, my absence having extended longer than expected. So, one early morning a day or two later, I bid Mary farewell and headed to Whitehall.

As I walked the road north out of town toward Whitehall, I passed the docks where we had landed aboard the *Peregrine*. She was nowhere in sight. I realized I had not seen Captain Cutler, nor any of his crew, in the days intervening from our arrival until now. I hoped they were all on their way to some far-off port for whatever trade they might wish to conduct.

I arrived at Whitehall in good order, and my knock upon the door was greeted by one of the Reverend's servants who informed me the Reverend was away for a few days. He was off seeking advice and support for his position for funding from the Crown for his planned college in Bermuda. When asked when he might return, the footman had no idea other than he was expected daily having been away a fortnight. I left a message for the Reverend and, bidding good day to the servant, started back to town.

It seemed that every evening our group of four would gather after the inn closed and discuss what was to be done with all our gold, silver, and jewels. We certainly had more than enough coin and gold and silver ingots. It was the gems and semi-precious stones and the fine necklaces, bracelets, rings, and other fabricated pieces we needed to sell for their value. Certainly, there were some things we each wanted to keep, but the vast majority we wanted converted into money.

The other concern was even greater. Where could we keep such wealth? There were no banks in Newport capable of holding it. Gossip in town would surely expose our fortune to all. Was there an institution anywhere in the colonies capable of providing care of this much wealth and anonymity for us? Would we need to place our funds in London? It was Toby who proposed an answer to our dilemma.

"Why not start a bank of our own?" Toby mused. "We only need assets which we have, and their value can be in any form. We can have a jeweler appraise the value of the gems. Gold is certainly fine in any form, as is the silver. And we probably possess more minted coins now than have ever been seen in this colony."

"Not only do we have the funds," Mary chimed in, "but a soon-to-be Yale graduate to be our president!"

We all agreed the idea made sense and would allow the secret of the source of our assets to remain such: a secret. We would be able to use our wealth to help our community and still enjoy our good fortune. And so, the first private bank in Newport came to be an accepted idea, solely funded by our assets.

As we finished our inventory of each of the chests, we moved them to Toby's and my room on the third floor. It was evident just in the amounts of precious metals we were the wealthiest four individuals in Newport and in the colony.

Within a day or two of finishing going through the chests, word arrived that Reverend Berkeley was back in residence and wished me to come to Whitehall. I complied the same day and arrived at Whitehall mid-afternoon.

Reverend Berkeley greeted me in his library in his usual gregarious manner. He wanted to know how my trip had fared and what I felt was the result. I gave him my assessment and, when I had finished, he withdrew a letter from the desk at which he was seated.

"I have here," he began, "an offer from Rector Williams. Based on his meeting with you, your conversations with others, and the depth of understanding displayed in your written work, he is pleased to offer you a position to study at Yale this September with anticipation you might achieve your degree by the end of March or April." His expression showed his pleasure in making this announcement. I was, likewise, pleased, but less visibly so.

"Are you not pleased?" Reverend Berkeley asked.

"I am very pleased," I replied. "What is the degree he anticipates my completing?" I asked tentatively.

"Why, a degree in Philosophy and Divinity, of course," came the reply from the Reverend. I found it difficult to express excitement at this news.

"You do not seem pleased at this news?" the Reverend asked.

"Reverend," I began, "I am most grateful for your belief in me and your assistance in helping me gain admission to Yale. But I cannot see myself pursuing the church as a career and becoming a preacher. I feel my future may lie in business."

"My boy," the Reverend said very kindly, "I would not expect you to do otherwise! That would be a great disappointment to me! I believe you have much greater things to accomplish. A degree from an institution such as Yale can only provide you with more credibility no matter what course you decide upon!"

Hearing these words from this mentor gave me great relief. Without reservation, I accepted my good fortune and committed to spend the better part of the next year at Yale. Now, I would need to break the news to my friends and co-workers.

"There is one other matter we need to discuss," came a somber note from Reverend Berkeley. "I may not be here to celebrate your graduation," I heard him say.

My first thought was the Crown had finally funded Reverend Berkeley's plan for his Bermuda College.

"I have decided I must return to England and present myself at court in order to press my case for the funding for my college," Reverend Berkeley continued.

"When will you leave for England?" I asked.

"The weather will be turning soon enough to the fall storms," came the reply. "I will most probably leave in early spring since I have initiated one last attempt through a friend returning shortly to London who has promised to plead my case."

On that note, I promised to send an acceptance to Rector Williams at Yale and to be prepared to leave in a few short weeks. I again thanked the Reverend and wished him good fortune in this last effort to obtain his promised funding from the Crown and avoid the necessity of a personal trip back to England.

THIRTY-NINE

As I walked back to Newport in the late afternoon sun, my thoughts began to turn toward the establishment of our bank. I was formulating a plan that would allow us to prosper quickly and provide an explanation for our sudden wealth. The sun was warm in the late summer and the trees afforded dappled shade along the road. Tonight, would be the time to present my idea to Toby and Jackie.

I arrived at the White Horse to find it crowded beyond the norm. Word had spread through town that we were again open for business, and every one of our regulars, and a few of our occasional guests, had decided to come and celebrate our return. In the tavern, Mary was being regaled by the crowd with a concertina and a sailor's hornpipe. Toby was frantically trying to fill tankards of ale and grog behind the bar. Upon seeing me, he waved for me to come help.

As I tried to push through the throng of people to reach the bar, I received several well wishes and pats on the back. It was a happy crowd. And if Mary ever thought she was not liked and respected by her patrons, this celebration would put that to rest for a long time to come.

"Where is Jackie?" I asked Toby when I finally got behind the bar.

"Kitchen," came the reply. Toby directed my attention toward the entrance to the dining room with his eyes where I saw a young woman I did not know serving food to a table.

"Who might that be?" I shouted to Toby over the noise.

"I'll introduce you when it calms down a bit," Toby replied with a broad smile.

After three hours of raucous music, talk, and laughter, the crowd began to thin. It was getting late and most of those remaining would soon toddle off leaving us an unusually large mess to clean up. As Toby and I started gathering glasses from the tables in the tavern, I asked him again, "Who was that in the dining room before?"

"That is our new server," Toby replied with a smile, "courtesy of Jackie."

I stopped in mid-reach for a half-empty tankard.

"Say again?" I questioned.

"You will have to talk with him," Toby said with a good-natured shrug.

We finished wiping down the tables and bar and cleaning up the tavern. Each of us carried a tray stacked with dirty tankards and mugs into the kitchen where Mary was seated by the fireplace and Jackie was busy washing dishes that were then being dried by this young girl, who was still unknown to me.

"Well, that was quite an evening," I began as I set the tray of dirty glassware on the main table. "I think that is the biggest crowd we have ever had."

"Word got around that it was Mary's birthday," Jackie said half-turning around from the washtub. "You forgot, didn't you?" He was right. I had.

"So, Mary, how does it feel to be thirty?" I said, turning to address Mary and trying to maintain my serious expression.

"Aww, go away with ye," Mary said laughing with a wave of her hand.

"And who, may I ask, might this be?" I continued, turning toward the young girl drying dishes.

Jackie turned from the basin in the sink and wiped his hands on his apron.

"Tom, may I introduce Anna," he replied shyly. "She is new to town and was looking for employment." The young girl turned and gave a slight curtsy.

"Where are you from, Anna?" I asked, looking intently at her brown eyes and auburn hair gathered on her head.

"My family lives across the bay," she began, her cheeks flushing pink as she lowered her gaze. "We have fallen on hard times, Sir, and I left home to find work to help them and leave one less mouth to feed." Her response erased my smile from my face.

"What is your family's name, Anna?" I asked.

"Congdon," she responded confidently. "But my stepfather is Matthew Prescott."

"I've told her about you, Tom," Jackie quickly interjected. My eyes flashed to him.

"Told her what?" I said with an uncontrolled edge in my voice. Jackie was startled by my reply, as was Anna.

"Only that I have known you for a long time and that you are a good, kind man and friend," Jackie replied slightly shaken.

I saw Toby look at me from across the kitchen with a look of disapproval on his face. Mary sat completely still by the fire; her face showing shock at my reaction.

I regained my composure somewhat and felt the tension my reaction had sparked in the room ebb.

"I'm sorry, Tom," Jackie began apologetically, "I know I should have asked you before offering Anna employment, but you were not here. And Mary said we could use the help...."

"No, no, Jackie," I replied with my hand raised before me. "It is I who must apologize for my reaction. I am only tired. It has been a long day."

Turning to Anna who stood against the counter unsure of what had just happened, I said, "Anna, you are, of course, welcome. Thank you for your service tonight. We can talk more tomorrow." I turned my gaze to the group and announced I was going to bed and, again, apologized for my show of temper.

I was sitting on the edge of my bed when Toby entered our room.

"What was that all about?" he asked.

"Do you realize who Anna is?" I replied.

"She may be your relation by marriage, but she is not your blood," Toby answered. "The girl needs work, and we need the help. Jackie offered her a position. He did nothing wrong, nor does he know about your past."

"Yes, of course you are right," I replied realizing how foolish my reaction must have appeared.

How did your interview with Reverend Berkeley go?" Toby asked changing the subject.

"I have committed to attending Yale this September," I said unenthusiastically.

"I will need to spend eight months at study to obtain my degree, based on my experience and current knowledge."

"That is great news, my friend!" Toby said, excited by the news. He then noticed my darkening mood. "You are not pleased this has happened?"

"There is much to do here to further our plans for our bank," I began, "and I had to share with Reverend Berkeley that I had no interest in pursuing a degree in Philosophy and Divinity."

"Was he disappointed at that news?" Toby asked.

"That is the odd thing," I continued, "he was not! When I told him I wished to pursue business and possibly the law, he agreed with me and encouraged me!"

"So, what is the problem?" Toby asked, puzzled by my confusion.

"I was taken back by a response I was not expecting," I replied.

"Tom," Toby said, "it is important to all of us that you do this. We can begin the work of establishing our bank. You need to be the figurehead of our enterprise. This means you need the credentials to be seen in that capacity."

I looked at Toby's face and saw the earnest desire his words reflected there. I nodded in agreement and stood to embrace him.

"Thank you, my dear friend," I murmured in his ear. "You have been my true brother."

I slept well that night. There was much that we needed to do in the coming weeks before I left for New Haven, but I was confident in the ability of those I was leaving in charge to continue to pursue our dream.

Things would appear clearer with the coming of the new day. I knew the first thing I needed to do was to learn a bit more about our new employee. I felt well-rested as I descended the stairways to the public floor of the inn. Entering the kitchen, I found Jackie and Anna in playful conversation near the hearth.

"Good morning, all," I said in a light mood.

"Morning, Tom," came the reply from Jackie. Anna half-turned in my direction and did a half-curtsey, the smiling, happy face suddenly sullen and bowed.

"Anna," I said in the friendliest tone I could, "I do apologize again for last evening. I was extremely tired from the day. I am not really the ogre I might have appeared to be last night."

"It was partly my fault," Jackie piped up. "I should have told you about Anna as soon as you arrived."

"Well, it is probably for the best that Anna joins us," I said. "I will be leaving in short order for New Haven to attend Yale and an extra pair of hands will be of good use here."

"Thank you, Sir," Anna spoke for the first time. "I'm a good worker." She spoke looking directly at you. Her voice was strong and full-toned and her smile was sweet and showed a beautiful set of teeth.

"I am sure you will fit in just fine, Anna," I assured her. "Jackie, might I have a word in private?" Jackie nodded, wiped his hands on his apron and followed me onto the back porch where I asked Jackie to tell me more about Anna.

"She came into an office at a shipping company I happened to be at, looking for work," Jackie began. "After I talked with her a bit, I knew she knew nothing about business, and she was terribly nervous. The story about tough times for her family is not completely true. The fact is her mother threw her out because she refused to marry the man her mother had chosen for her. She had only met him once and he is thirty years her senior, but he is wealthy. I felt sorry for her and, knowing our situation at the inn, suggested she see Mary about employment."

"Anna has no idea about the treasure then?" I questioned.

"None," Jackie replied. "From my conversations with her, there is no love-loss for anyone across the bay, especially her stepfather."

Hearing this, I clapped Jackie on the shoulder and told him Anna was welcome.

Over the next six weeks, much needed to be done before I left for Yale. Toby, Mary, Jackie, and I spent every evening after the inn closed discussing our plans for establishing our bank. We determined it should be based as a trading bank. We could have the bank own ships, and cargoes could be the generator of income. Instead of calling it a bank, we could establish it as a trading and shipping company.

Mary was busy packing trunks with items to be sent with me to Yale. A few times she disappeared from the inn and proceeded to shop for all manner of new clothes. No matter how much I might protest about these preparations, Mary would not hear me. She was going to be sure I had everything she felt I would need while I was away. Anna continued to grow into the organization to the point of even trying to prepare a couple of dishes at Mary's direction.

As the time grew near for my departure, Reverend Berkeley was excited at the prospects for my future. While he was worried about ever receiving his promised funding from the Crown, he was happy at my prospects. In the last few days before I left, I wondered if I would ever see my benefactor again.

The morning of my leaving, a wagon arrived early, and my three trunks were spirited down the stairs from our attic room by Jackie and Toby and loaded aboard. I was dressed in clothes for travel and stood to say my goodbyes near the front door of the White Horse Inn. Toby and Jackie gave me bear hugs and whispered good tidings in my ear. I could see Mary holding back tears, her lip having a small quiver, as she put her arms about my neck and bid me farewell, admonishing me to return as healthy as I was leaving. Last to wish me well was Anna. As I offered my hand to her, she leaned on my forearm and, with a shy smile, gave me a soft kiss on the cheek and wished me luck and good travel.

I descended the three steps down to the street and climbed aboard the seat of the wagon next to the driver. The driver snapped the reins gently and we were off. I prayed all would be well while I was away.

FORTY

The ship to New Haven was an unremarkable coaster that smacked along on the waves of the Sound. I realized this was the first time I had been aboard a ship since our treasure hunt. As we passed the south shore of Fishers Island, I smiled to myself and said a small prayer for my father.

We sailed through The Race and continued to New London, arriving near dusk. The days had become shorter, and the night would be spent here in New London. The next day we sailed on to New Haven without incident. The captain tied up alongside Long Wharf, and I was able to obtain a wagon to carry my trunks to College House for a reasonable sum. My knock on the door of College House was answered by the aptly named Mr. Dower. I was allowed to stay in College House that night because of the lateness of the hour of my arrival. Mr. Dower was kind enough to assist me with my trunks. In the morning, I would be shown my quarters.

The next morning began an experience of eight months, fourteen days, and eight hours among the worst of my entire life. This was not due to the experience of formal education, but for the conditions under which it was provided, and the associates it was my displeasure to call classmates. Even to my somewhat inexperienced eyes, Yale was less than a shining example of higher education because of what it lacked.

My "rooms" consisted of a single room large enough to accommodate a narrow wooden-framed bed. My mattress, if it could be called that, consisted of a thin layer of fresh grasses covered by a coarse linen sheet that offered little comfort but at least began with a freshness. A small slit window and a narrow chest of drawers completed my furnishings. The window of four small panes bore one with a small brake in it and the frame was ill-fitted. It would leak copious amounts of frigid air during the oncoming New Haven winter.

As I had feared, many of my fellow students were much younger in age than I was. In fact, the youngest was no more than ten. These poor, privileged children had been shipped away to school by mostly wealthy families. Most were away from home for the first time in their young lives. Even so, most were of an under-educated, over-privileged variety whose parents saw some value to education, even if only for the status it might attach to their offspring or their family. At the least, it was one less mouth to feed and discipline at home. And, more importantly, they could afford the cost. Little thought was given to whether the child had any interest in the experience.

And most did not. Some of the older students, by older meaning sixteen and seventeen, took advantage of the younger students, making them fetch for them and function as young manservants. These older students felt they were insulated from reprisal and so they abused and belittled the younger group. They took pleasure in the abuse they inflicted and only demurred in my presence because they feared someone older.

What free time I found from my studies was little, while it seemed free time was boundless to others, especially the younger set. They had endless energy for racing up and down the halls, making noise, and pulling little pranks, not to injure, but to annoy. Even in class, the foolishness did not end. However, carried too far, it drew a rebuke from the professor and consequences beyond. Meanwhile, the older students considered lectures the droning's of boring old men relating information that would be of little use to them in their lives after school.

In a classroom with these two disparate groups, the harried professors attempted to impart knowledge, which may have taken their entire lives to master, to the few serious students that did wish to learn. I was among this group. And we were exceedingly small. And, of that number, the highest calling anticipated was to be called to a position in some small parish in some community to spread the word of God as interpreted by Yale. In truth, most of my fellow classmates had little ambition beyond the anticipated and supposed security of their own parishes or following in their fathers' footsteps.

As I had feared, I did not fit well into any group. The privileged group saw me as a threat to their lifestyle of intimidating the youngest and enjoying the benefits they saw as owed them. They quickly learned I would not stand for their foppery nor their treatment of the younger students. Some of the younger students saw me as a protector; others saw me as a threat due to their fealty to the bullies. Either way, for most of my time at Yale, I was the subject of many pranks and little thanks from any group.

Of the serious students, I found it impossible to have a conversation with any of them where the ultimate discussion did not become one about religious sectarianism, reformist doctrine, or piety. While these were all subjects in heated discussion at the time, none of these individuals showed the least understanding of the realities of the world. I feared a rude awakening awaited all of them.

I had decided to keep the secret of my sudden wealth to myself. I graciously accepted the payment of my tuition by Reverend Berkeley, even though I could easily have afforded the charge. While I felt dishonest in accepting the Reverend's largesse, to not do so might have raised some difficult questions. However, all my ongoing expenses for materials, books, clothes, and food, I paid for out of the funds I had brought with me. These funds I had quietly deposited in the Bank of New Haven upon arrival.

I received mail frequently from Mary and Toby keeping me informed of their progress with our plan and what was happening at the White

Horse. Toby related he had purchased a warehouse just north of the main harbor with a good wharf. He wrote how he had acted as the actual purchasers' agent so as not to draw suspicion as to where a Black man might have obtained such funds. He got quite the laugh from his deception. In the letter relating to this transaction, Toby's final sentence brought something to mind. He stated now that we had a wharf, all we needed were ships to tie up to it.

A few weeks later toward the middle of November with the first snow falling, Rector Williams suspended afternoon classes. The younger students bundled up and went to play on the Commons. The Snobbery went to their usual haunts to imbibe poor-grade liquors. I decided to take a stroll through town in the quiet of the falling snow. I soon found myself walking along the promenade at the harbor. As I looked at the boats in the harbor, my eyes wandered to those tied up along the walk. It was then I saw her. *The Mary N.* tied to the dock in the same location as when first I saw her. And sitting on an upturned barrel at the landward side of the gangplank was her Master, carving what looked like scrim while he puffed on his downturned pipe. He wore the same long coat with brass buttons and plumed hat as he had when last we spoke. The hat was pulled low, and the collar of the coat was turned up against the falling snow.

"Ahoy, Captain Bedloe! We meet again," I said as I neared. The captain stopped his carving and lifted his face to me.

"Why, Squire Gray, is it?" came the reply. Captain Bedloe deftly stuck his carving knife into a side stave of the barrel and offered his hand in greeting. "When I saw ye last, you were lookin' fer a provisioner fer a ship, if memory serves?"

"That I was Captain Bedloe," I said taking his hand. "And your advice was very helpful."

"And now yer back in port, here?" he inquired. "My guess is yer trip was a short haul," he continued with a deep laugh.

"Actually, I am here for another reason this time," I replied deciding not to tell him about Yale. "I might have a proposition for you, Captain Bedloe," I continued, "if you can answer a few questions for me."

"Well, I would like to try," came the response.

"Who is the owner of *The Mary N.*?" I asked politely.

"She belongs to me, Master Gray, and I am beholden to none," came the slightly heated response.

"I meant no offense, Captain," I quickly responded. "In fact, I am much pleased at your answer." Captain Bledsoe relaxed and seemed happy.

"How do you come by the cargoes you carry?" I asked sincerely.

"I have one or two trade merchants who will send cargo my way on occasion," the captain replied with a bit of suspicion.

"How many ports have you sailed to among the colonies?" I asked.

"Nearly all you would know," Captain Bledsoe replied, his suspicion growing.

"Here now, what is this proposal of which you speak?" he asked me.

"Captain," I began. "I would like to offer to buy your ship, *The Mary N.*, along with you as her permanent captain, and whatever crew you wish. You will retain full control of *The Mary N.*"

Captain Bedloe's lower jaw fell open, nearly dropping his pipe in the process. It was caught only at the last second by his weathered left hand.

"Here now," he said slowly, "are you havin' a go at me?" he asked in disbelief.

"No, Captain," I replied earnestly. "It is much to understand, I can appreciate. So let me explain."

"Please do," the captain stammered as he felt for the barrel to sit upon.

"I recently began a shipping company out of Newport. I and my partners are seeking ships to carry cargoes we contract for to various ports both here and abroad under our flag," I explained. "You would retain command of your ship but sail under our auspices, meaning, we would determine cargoes and destinations."

"Let me be sure I understand you fully," Captain Bledsoe said after a moment or two. "You have started a shipping business with no experience and no ships. You presently have no merchants giving you contracts. Do I have that right?" he said as he placed his hand against his chin as I had seen him do before.

"And you want to buy my Mary N. to start your fleet of vessels," he continued.

I nodded with enthusiasm.

"Why my ship?" he asked thoughtfully.

"Because one of my partners is named Mary Nichol," I replied, "and it is fate that your ship bears her name and should be found by me here not once, but twice. This ship is for her."

It was like a veil lifted before Captain Bedloe's eyes.

"I will guarantee a percentage of the profits from each cargo, as well as a set salary. That will be yours for as long as you desire to captain *The Mary N.*"

"Young Squire, Mr. Gray," Captain Bledsoe stammered unsure how to address me, "how is it that one so young as you can afford to make such an offer?"

"Captain Bledsoe, I have been blessed from my father with great wealth which must remain our secret for now. If you wish, I shall write a letter for you to take to Newport where you can meet my partners in this venture and know that I am in earnest," I said.

He nodded his agreement, and we continued to talk further about *The Mary N.* and his twenty years at her helm. In the end, Captain Bledsoe arrived at what he felt was a fair price for *The Mary N.* I agreed to return in a day or two with the letter and directions to our wharf in Newport. We parted in high spirits, and it was one of the best days of my dreary existence in New Haven.

I returned to my room at Yale campus, dismal as it was, with the snow beginning to fall more heavily. I was intent upon writing a full account of my conversation with Captain Bledsoe for Toby, Mary, and Jackie to review. I explained the reasons behind the offer to purchase Captain Bledsoe's vessel and hoped they would agree. She was a pretty barque, larger than the *Peregrine*, but with similar lines. She would hold a good amount of cargo and stand well in rough seas. I found myself writing more in support of approving my purchase of *The Mary N.* than explaining the plan to begin a fleet of vessels. I explained my agreement with the captain and hoped it would meet with the approval of my partners.

I sealed my letter and began writing instructions for Captain Bledsoe to reach the newly purchased dock and warehouse in Newport and his introduction to Toby, Mary, and Jackie. As I finished, a wisp of freezing air ruffled some papers on my desk which made me look to the window. The snow was falling hard and piling up on the window ledges and the ground. This first snow had turned into a real storm. I hoped it would not prevent my meeting with Captain Bledsoe on the 'morrow.

As I sat for a moment and watched the falling snow, I remembered how quiet it became when snow was falling. I suddenly realized it had been a long, long time since I had marveled at something as simple as falling snow. My thoughts went back to a time in my youth when I had cared for the farm animals. The horses, the mules, the sheep, even the pigs, all became quiet when snow began falling. Falling snow muffled all sound. It was then I realized I was hearing the call for dinner. I extinguished my candle and headed for the hall to share whatever meager meal was to be served.

I awoke the next morning to see a full foot of snow upon the ground. Mr. Dower announced that classes would be delayed until afternoon. Donning double stockings and pants, I dressed as warmly as I could and left to meet Captain Bledsoe. Along the way, I decided I should invest in a pair of boots for this was only the start of winter and snow would quickly ruin my leather shoes.

As I made my way to the waterfront, I slipped down a side street to Pomeroy's shop where I had previously been a customer. As the little bell above the door sounded, Mr. Pomeroy hurried from the back room to greet me. My request for footwear more appropriate to the weather brought forth a pair of knee-high boots of black leather that had been treated in some way to make them waterproof. I tried them on and found the fit was wonderfully comfortable. They were expensive and Mr. Pomeroy felt the need to apologize for the price. I assured him they were worth every penny and paid him without haggling about the price.

Mr. Pomeroy insisted I select a pair of socks at his expense so my feet would be dry.

Stepping out into the street in my new boots, I no longer felt the cold and wetness I had on my way to Pomeroy's. I gave a cheery 'thanks' to Mr. Pomeroy and, with a net bag he insisted I take with me to hold my wet shoes and stockings, I opened the door of the shop to the sound of the little bell.

Turning the corner, I was only a block from the harbor and *The Mary N.*. I walked along the waterfront to where the schooner was docked and asked the crewmember at the gangplank if Captain Bledsoe was aboard. He replied he was and directed me to the Captain's Cabin. I thanked him and, avoiding other crew clearing snow from the decks, made my way below to the stern cabins. I rapped on the door I believed to be the Captain's Cabin and heard a voice from within command me to enter.

"Good morning, Captain Bledsoe," was my greeting.

"Squire Gray," came the reply, "or should I be addressing you in some other way?"

"No, Captain," I answered feeling embarrassed. "I am quite comfortable with how you see me." I said with a smile.

"Here are directions to the location of our wharf just north of Newport harbor proper," I said to Captain Bledsoe as I retrieved the folded paper with my hand-drawn map from my coat pocket. "You can see it is really in Coddington's Cove actually."

"Aye," the captain said studying the rudimentary map. "There should be no problem finding this. I have ported in Newport many times."

Again, reaching into my pocket, I retrieved the sealed letter to Toby, Mary, and Jackie.

"This is your letter of introduction to my partners in this venture," I said with pride. "I think you will find them in agreement with all I have related to you and the terms we have agreed upon."

"I'll set sail for Newport as soon as the weather clears a bit more," Captain Bledsoe said taking the letter from my hand and placing it on the table before him.

"I must ask you," he began tentatively. "There is something different about you from the last time our paths crossed. I am not sure what it is.... Confidence? Maturity? Whatever it is, it suits you well," he concluded. I could not stop the color rising in my cheeks.

Captain Bledsoe rose from behind his table and extended his hand to me.

"I believe I will enjoy working with you," he said smiling and grasping my hand extended in response.

I strolled through the city from the harbor through the Commons to Yale hearing sounds muffled by the snow, pleased with the outcome of my conversation with Captain Bledsoe. As I got closer to College House, my good mood darkened with the dread of several more months of loneliness and boredom, poor food, and wretched living conditions.

—————————— >< ——————————

The days turned to weeks, and weeks to months, and still the trees remained leafless against the gray winter sky. The bare branches stretching toward the grayness almost pleading for the warmth of spring to arrive. The snow that was so welcomed late in the last year was no longer a welcome sight. It fell often and heavily this winter and the temperature kept it from melting. By all accounts, it was one of the coldest winters ever in memory.

Classes were by lecture and rote recitation, and I soon understood why the older students became bored by it all. It soon became evident that the limited number of professors required their lecture on subjects they had little, if any, interest in, and so their lectures were not enlightening beyond what could be gained from reading on one's own. There was little insight and even less enthusiasm. Combined with the dismal weather, a pall of gloom enveloped my days.

Only the letters from Mary and Toby brought some light to the gloom. When Captain Bledsoe presented himself, Toby was effusive in his praise of my actions. Mary wrote a note that arrived inside Toby's saying how touched she was about the name of the vessel. Toby related that Jackie was spending more time at our landing directing activity at the wharf and approaching various businesses for cargoes. Anna was now fully employed in the kitchen at the inn and was learning to prepare meals from Mary. Everything was going well in the real world.

It was not until the second week in April that the trees on the Commons began showing buds. It had been more than five months since winter had taken hold, and now, finally, the air smelled sweet like spring was coming. And that meant my time in New Haven was ending.

As the weather improved and the days grew longer, I had fewer lectures to attend and was required to complete what was referred to as a "thesis." This assignment was really an analysis of what I had "learned" during my time at Yale built around some philosophical or religious tenet. I would find myself frequently going to the Commons where I would sit and think about what the experience at Yale had really taught me.

It was on one such day that I suddenly knew the answer to that question. Education at Yale was not about learning in the traditional sense. I had already read more than any of my fellow students. No, the education here was more about the associations one could make attending. Friendships and acquaintances established here could be important for a lifetime. It was this that was the importance of higher education. And I had only just realized it as my time was ending. The various cliques of students I had disdained and discounted were the most important part of being here and I had nearly squandered it. It was the fellowships formed from the shared common experience that would surpass any "learning" gained from lectures. It would be the associative network created from school that would be the lasting benefit of obtaining a degree. And I had little time left to repair the damage I had done by not being a part of that network.

><

June had arrived in what seemed like a moment in time. It was time for graduation. I had worked hard to make associations with my fellow students over the last two months. To do so, I had had to overcome their suspicions about my motives. I had been so dismissive of many of them for my entire time at Yale, and, suddenly, I was seeking them out and attempting to establish relationships with them. I knew that I might never require anything from most of these fellow graduates, but one never knew for sure. Just as my circumstances had changed suddenly, so might theirs at some future point in time.

My final report accepted; I was going to receive my degree with honors. I wrote to Toby to tell him of my intention to take ship immediately thereafter for home. I received in return a note from him saying accommodation had already been made for me for a ship and it would be awaiting me in the harbor when I was ready to leave.

The day I received my graduation, I bid Rector Williams and Professor Edwards farewell and received their best wishes. I thanked Mr. Dower for his oversight of the students and piled my trunks into a hired wagon and headed to the harbor. As the wagon slowly moved alongside the Commons and drew away from College House, I turned around to look one last time at Yale. I hoped it would grow and thrive in the future.

The wagon rumbled onto the cobbles of the promenade along the harborside. I looked to see if there was a ship I might recognize. And there she was: *The Mary N.*

Sitting on an upright barrel at the end of the gangplank carving a scrim sat the familiar figure of Captain Bledsoe. But something was different. Gone was the brass-buttoned long coat and the feathered hat. In their place, the captain wore a proper Captain's brimmed cap with a slight metallic braid about the crown and a heavy weather coat of woven wool. He looked the part of a respected captain. He glanced up from his carving and saw the wagon approaching. He sheathed his knife and pocketed the object he had been carving and stood to meet the wagon.

The wagon stopped and I jumped to the ground and shook the Captain's hand as a broad smile came to his face.

"Well, Young Squire," he said brightly. "I hear congratulations might be in order," he imparted shaking my hand strongly.

"Your good wishes accepted, Captain," I replied. "But should you have made this voyage just to bring me home?"

"You think yer that important, do ye?" Captain Bledsoe laughed as he spoke. "Damn my soul if you think yer partners would send me to New Haven just to fetch yer hide home!" The captain saw the change in my expression.

"Pardon the curse, Squire, but that would be a poor bit of business on the part of yer partners," Captain Bledsoe continued. "I arrived in port two days ago with a cargo of nails and spirits and, this mornin' we loaded a cargo of wood, cloth, and fancies. If ye hadn't shown up today, ye might have been findin' other means of gettin' home," he finished with a smile.

"We'll sail on the tide in the morning," he added. "Tonight, we'll have a satisfying meal ashore and ye can tell me about what you've been doin' in New Haven."

"I would sooner hear what you have been doing and how things are in Newport," I said.

FORTY-ONE

The sun was barely above the horizon when Captain Bledsoe ordered all lines cast off and we headed out of New Haven harbor for Long Island Sound and home. We had spent a pleasant evening at Captain Bledsoe's choice of Mill's Tavern. The food was good, and the tankards were kept full. He expressed a genuine interest to know what I had learned over the past eight months. I gave him an all-to-quick review of what life had been like over the past winter in New Haven. I shared with him the dreary existence of a student, and the joy I felt leaving it behind me.

I then pressed him to tell me what he had experienced in Newport while I was away. His countenance brightened as he related his first meeting with my friends, whom he referred to as Mr. Trinidad, Mr. Saunders, and Lady Nichol. He had arrived at the White Horse Inn with my letter of introduction tucked in his pocket. He told me he wished to observe his prospective employers before introducing himself. He had been much pleased by what he saw: a tight-knit group who worked in unison much like the crew of a ship. He had intended to order some supper and a pint and requested if a "Mr. Toby" might be about. He was surprised when the Black man from behind the bar presented himself as Toby, but quickly presented my letters.

Toby immediately sat at the table and proceeded to read both the outer letter of introduction and the sealed inner note. Toby had been exceedingly gracious and offered food and drink to Captain Bledsoe. This would have given Toby time to alert the others and prepare them for introduction to the captain. Toby insisted the captain would be staying at the inn and could meet with the partners at the end of the evening. Captain Bledsoe asked if it might be possible for him to take leave to his room for a short nap and freshen up before dinner. When he returned to the dining room about an hour later, he was provided a tasty and filling supper and, as he finished, 'Lady Nichol' had approached him and introduced herself as one of the owners of the inn. It was evident that the captain was quite taken by Mary.

They chatted for some time about the inn and this new venture into trade and shipping. The swirl of activity in the public rooms began to slow and, as the last of the patrons left, the lamps and lanterns had mostly been extinguished in the public rooms. It was then that Mary, Toby, and Jackie seated themselves at the table with Captain Bledsoe. Jackie introduced himself as the junior partner which drew a slight chuckle from Toby.

Captain Bledsoe expressed his surprise that all my partners were completely accepting of him and *The Mary N.* and the agreements I had made with him. He accepted the offer to sign his ships papers over to the newly established Trinidad – Gray & Associates, Shipping & Trading Agents. In exchange for the sale of *The Mary N.* at the agreed price, Captain Bledsoe agreed to carry any cargo designated by the new ship owners for 5% of the profit from the sale of cargo in addition to his regular wage. It was more than the captain had ever imagined. By this arrangement, Captain Bledsoe would be set for life. In fact, he had already delivered cargoes to Boston and New York before sailing to bring me home. We returned to the ship in high spirits; he for his fortune and I anticipating my homecoming and being among my friends once again.

As we sailed eastward out of New Haven harbor, the wind was picking up and *The Mary N.* was riding the wave crests in fine fashion. Captain Bledsoe was sure we would make Newport by nightfall of the second day, and I would be home for the first time in nine months. I watched the shoreline pass and was exhilarated by the thought of being home with my friends once more.

We had passed New London by midday and Saybrook, where the Connecticut River spilled into Long Island Sound, by late afternoon. The wind remained steady and from the southwest and I lounged on the quarterdeck in the early summer sun. By dusk, we were sailing into Mystic Harbor to spend the night.

The next afternoon, I did not realize I had fallen asleep until a shift in the wind and lowering light of the setting sun made the air a little chilly. We were at the mouth of the Great Narragansett Bay and had jibed about Point Judith. *The Mary N.* heeled a bit as her sails swung to starboard, then settled back as Captain Bledsoe directed her course up the West Passage. I looked toward the stern where Captain Bledsoe stood by the helm. He knew I was questioning his choice of course. He came to the rail above me.

"Less ship traffic by this course," he said in his best Captain's voice. "Perhaps a bit longer, but less noticed."

As the light faded, we sailed up the west side of Conanicut Island and I stood at the rail watching the shoreline. In no time, I saw the small landing and the clearing beyond leading up the hill from the shore to a structure, now in shadow, that I knew to be the home that was, by right, mine. It was at that moment that I determined, someday, to have my revenge upon my uncle. But for now, I must deal with other matters.

A voice behind me ended my dark thoughts.

"I sense you are troubled by something, young Squire," Captain Bledsoe's voice was calm and inquiring.

"Oh, I am just thinking of those I am about to see after such a long absence." I replied.

"Mr. Gray," the Captain said," yer a man on the way up. You've a good head on those shoulders and you're bright enough to be important in this colony."

I blushed at his compliment but felt a bit of pride hearing it.

"You should read for the law," he continued. "Lawyers run the wheels of government, Squire, and I believe you would be an honest one, at least."

I thanked him for his suggestion but told him I had no interest in entering politics or the government service. But I could not forget his suggestion.

We rounded the northern end of Conanicut Island and made for Coddington Cove. It was dark now and the wharf was lit with torches to ease our approach. The captain ordered sails to be furled, and we glided the last hundred yards under single sail and landed at the wharf. I arranged with a worker on the dock who introduced himself as newly employed by Mr. Saunders of the shipping company for my trunks to be delivered to the inn and, bidding the captain farewell, struck out for the White Horse. It was a pleasant evening and I needed to regain my land legs after a long two days at sea. With my one bag over my shoulder with only my essentials, I took the short walk.

The dining room was empty when I quietly entered by the front door, the tavern, nearly so. As I stood for a moment inside the door and looked about, something was different, but I was not sure what it was. Then I realized what it was: Mary had changed the draperies on the windows. As I was admiring the change, the door to the kitchen swung open and, Toby dressed in his apron and carrying a tray of clean glasses, entered. It took a moment for him to see me standing by the door, but when he did, he quickly placed his tray on the nearest table and sprinted across the room to bear hug me.

"Welcome home, Tom!" he said in pure delight. The quiet conversations among the few in the room ceased.

Toby called out, "Mary! Jackie! Anna! Tom is home!"

The door into the kitchen nearly came off its hinges as the trio flooded into the tavern. All gave and received hugs. Last was Mary who, with tears in her eyes, gave the strongest of hugs and could only say," Tom. You're skinny as a rail!"

"Anna, there is some stew left from tonight. Fetch it in one of the bigger bowls...and bring the end of the loaf of good bread, as well," she called as Anna hurried to the kitchen.

"You sit right down here by the fire, and rest." Mary gently ordered me like an old mother hen.

Anna came through the kitchen door with a tray filled as ordered by Mary and placed it on the table before me. She smiled kindly and I thanked her. I had barely gotten a mouthful of the steaming deliciousness past my lips when the questions began flying too quickly to answer. How had it been? What did I learn? What was it like at Yale? What was it like in New Haven? On and on and on, the questions came, peppering me as I tried to enjoy the first food I had eaten in twenty-four hours.

"Let the man eat in peace!" Toby's booming voice came at last. The others fell silent. "There will be plenty of time for Tom to answer all our questions now that he is home," he continued without raising his voice.

The few patrons who had still lingered in the tavern had finished their drinks and quietly left as the celebration of my arrival commenced.

"Let us finish closing and give Tom a few minutes of peace to enjoy his meal. Then we can talk," Toby said smiling at me as I ate. "Mary, you can stay with Tom...but, let him eat," he admonished with a laugh.

The stew was warming to my stomach and Mary went to the bar and poured me a glass of our best Madeira, sliding it toward me across the table as she sat down.

"Did you miss us, Tom?" came Mary's first question.

"With all my heart," I replied. "Had it not been for Dr. Berkeley's encouragement, I would never have spent so much time away. But it is done, and I feel it has given me some new directions I may pursue." Mary placed her hand on my forearm and looked at me only as one who loves without restraint can.

I placed my other hand over hers and said, "Mary, my dear, you shall never want again for anything as long as you live. And, when this place begins to be too much of a burden, I shall see to it you have the little cottage on the bay I know you have always wanted."

My bowl of stew was not only eaten, but the dregs had been sopped up with the crusty bread, when Toby, Jackie, and Anna came through the door from the kitchen and sat at the table. Anna reached over and removed the bowl from in front of me and placed it on a nearby table.

"So," Toby began, "what have you learned?"

"I have learned what I need to do to serve our interests in the best way," I replied.

"Well, don't keep us in suspense," Jackie said excitedly.

"Yes, please tell us," Mary pleaded.

"I believe our trading business will require us to obtain certain documents from the maritime and colonial authorities and contracts for the performance...," I began looking about the table at the questioning faces of my companions. "I have decided I can best serve all of us by reading for the law."

The silence with which this statement was met was unexpected.

"Come now," I said in astonishment, "I do not mean to practice in any capacity other than contract law. I will apprentice under one of the local lawyers, perhaps even the colony's Attorney General, Mr. Updike. I will learn what I need to pass whatever I must only to gain the credential of a lawyer."

"So, if I understand you, Tom," Toby began cautiously, "you do not plan to practice law, only to have the status?"

"In a word, yes," I replied. The tension my announcement had originally created in the room dissipated instantly as everyone sighed in relief.

"How long will that take you, Tom?" Jackie spoke up.

"With consistent study and good guidance by a good tutor, I expect no more than two years," I replied confidently. "I shall attempt to meet with the colonial officers tomorrow to seek the guidance of the Attorney General."

Conversation began to turn to other aspects of my time in New Haven until I decided to change the subject.

"Enough of my experience in New Haven," I said. "Tell me what has occurred here in my absence?"

"Where should we start," Toby offered. "The inn has been as busy as ever. Anna, here, has become an important member of the household," he continued smiling as Anna turned her face to hide her reddening cheeks. "But I am sure you would rather hear about our other enterprise?"

"Indeed," I replied, "my conversation with Captain Bledsoe told me he is well pleased so far."

"He has been a great asset, Tom," Toby began, "he has spread word of our small shipping company to other captains of his acquaintance, and we have had a couple we have investigated."

"Investigated?" I questioned.

Let Jackie explain," Toby said with a smile. "It was his idea, and it is a good one, I think. He is becoming recognized as the agent and clerk for Trinidad & Gray Trading and Shipping." Jackie smiled at the recognition by his partner.

"When we are approached by a captain for a voyage, we do not immediately consign cargo," Jackie began, "we tell the captain we require some information about his ship and prior cargoes he has carried, and for whom. Most ask why we want to know such information about prior voyages. I explain we are a small company at present, and we intend to grow by only shipping cargoes with reliable ships and captains."

"I have not heard of this before," I said with surprise.

"It is not normally done because of the time it takes to obtain information," Jackie agreed, "but, I have developed a network, at least in New England, where it takes me no longer than a week to gain a picture of a captain's reliability."

"And it is working well?" I asked.

"Aye," Jackie replied with a smile. "We have found a half dozen ships with good reputations for captain and crew who have delivered at least one cargo, and we have managed to realize a modest profit in our first two quarters."

"Jackie is being too modest, Tom. He has managed to nearly keep the warehouse full of cargoes awaiting shipping," Toby interrupted, "and our customers are pleased by our caution in choosing the ships we employ."

"Our reputation is growing," Jackie said proudly. "Should this continue, we will be a force to be reckoned with in Newport."

I expressed my pleasure with all I was hearing and, amid a yawn, suggested we all adjourn to bed and continue in the morning.

FORTY-TWO

The next two years of my life were filled with activity. It was now 1735. The inn was doing well under the guidance of Mary with the help of Toby and Anna. Trinidad & Gray was prospering under the management of Jackie. Captain Bledsoe had become an integral part of the trading company working alongside Jackie, advising, obtaining cargoes, and clearing ships and schedules.

Shortly after my return from Yale, the Reverend Berkeley returned to Whitehall from his voyage to London to plead his case for funding for his college from the Crown. He had failed, being told confidentially by the First Lord of the Treasury that he would never see a farthing from the current occupant of the throne. His disappointment was total, and he had lost all future hope of fulfilling his dream. He had returned to the colony for only one purpose: to dispose of his properties and interests. His intention was to return to his home in Ireland and assume a new position within the Irish Church.

I spoke with him only once or twice during his brief time back in Newport. Our first meeting was joyful as he congratulated me on my success at Yale and I had shared my plans with him to study to be a lawyer. He offered at that point to make introductions on my behalf of his acquaintances in the legal profession in Newport and the rest of the colony. He asked what I thought he should do in disposing of his substantial holdings in the colony since he had no plans to ever return. I am not sure why he sought my counsel on this matter, but I was flattered by his request. Since I no longer required any assets, the thought that he might be considering settling any of his wealth on me never entered my mind.

Our second meeting was barely a week before his taking leave of the colony. In this meeting, Reverend Berkeley announced his decision to leave his holdings in the colony, including his beloved Whitehall and its library, to the university in New Haven. He hoped this might be the start of a new school within Yale. I assured him I would see to the orderly transfer on his behalf. The day of his departure, I met him on the wharf. He embraced me with great emotion before boarding the ship that would carry him back across the seas to his beloved Ireland. Knowing I would never see him again struck hard on me as he had been an exceptionally large part of my recent past. I owed much of my present maturity to him.

As he had promised, one of Reverend Berkeley's friends in Newport offered me a position with his firm to study the law. I spent many of the ensuing weeks and months reading every law book in his small library. When I had finished these treatises, I was allowed access to the library of the Attorney General. I would attend court sessions at least once a week and make notes of the arguments I heard and would go back to the libraries to clear up any points I was unsure about.

And so, summer passed into fall, and fall into winter. As I became more confident in my knowledge, I spent increased time attending court proceedings. I observed cases of civil suits and contract disputes, the entire spectrum of cases a lawyer would be expected to meet in his career. As the year came full circle, I became increasingly aware of civil cases involving my estranged uncle, Matthew Prescott. He had incurred a large amount of debt and was putting up parcels of land to secure debts he could never repay. There were liens being filed against him for failure to make payments.

By the following fall, I was ready to be examined to be admitted to the bar and become an attorney. The day came and Toby, Mary, and Jackie, all gave me their best hopes, and I headed for Government House where I would face a panel of lawyers, as well as a written examination. After almost four hours, it was over. I would know within a month if I had succeeded.

For a month I worked at the shipping company to learn more of the business and the inn just to take my mind off the waiting. All my friends were happy to have me back full time sharing the burden of running the inn. Once a week I would go to the courthouse and check the filings of new suits. Invariably there were more notices of debts owed by my Uncle Matthew.

My return to the White Horse left Jackie more time to manage the shipping firm and he was good at it. Within the two years I had been training for the bar, Jackie had turned a profit in the first quarter and doubled the profit every quarter thereafter. We had gained a dozen more ships and were now carrying cargo throughout the colonies and across the Atlantic. Our venture had succeeded beyond our wildest dreams. In fact, the treasure we thought would be our fortune was now growing faster by the profits from the shipping business than we could spend it.

Because of the success we had all experienced, our reputation and recognition among the people of Newport had grown immensely. We were personalities to one degree or another and, now that I was, hopefully, to become a lawyer, my name, within the city and beyond, was becoming well known.

In October I received word of my passing the review and was now able to practice as a lawyer. We had a celebratory supper at the White Horse with many a well-wisher offering future legal business. When the last of the partiers had left, the five of us, for Anna was now a full member of the group, sat at our usual table near the kitchen to relax with a final spirit.

"Well, Tom," Toby began, "what will you do now? Will you be leaving us for the loftier heights of lawyering?"

"Aye, Toby," Jackie chimed in. "He will be too good fer our company now! He will be wantin' to rub elbows with the swells from now on," Jackie allowed with a big grin showing he was kidding.

"What do you think, Mary," Toby questioned. "You think Tom will leave us?"

"Ooff! You two are terrible," Mary replied. "Tom is going to do what he wants and what he knows is best for him," she barked back, as Jackie and Toby laughed at their attempt to bait her.

"Seriously, Tom, what will you do?" Toby finally said in earnest.

"I have no plans to begin a law practice at the moment," I replied. "I have but one objective in mind and I will possibly need all of you to help in achieving it."

"The last time you said that" Jackie broke in, "it was the making of all our fortunes!"

"I think you might say we're all with you, Tom, no matter what it is," Toby said looking at the nods of agreement from all present.

"In order to achieve this objective, I will need Jackie to be my agent again," I said. "He will have to do so without divulging it is I who am behind this venture."

"I can do that," Jackie said earnestly. "What is it you need done, Tom?"

"First, let me explain to all of you," I felt the words tumbling from my brain, "I am about to do something I have waited a long time to do. I am about to seek my revenge for a wrong done many years ago." The group around me fell noticeably quiet.

"Tom, this is not like you," Mary said finally. "People who seek vengeance are changed in some way and you must not change."

Toby leaned forward on the table and in a quiet voice said, "Mary, I think I know what this vengeance is that Tom speaks of. He told me many years ago when we were both young." Toby looked at me, pleading with his eyes for me to say more.

"It is time for them to know your past, Tom," he urged.

I could not bring myself to speak of the plan that had formed in my mind.

"If you will not tell them," Toby said firmly, "I must, for them to understand." I nodded my assent.

Toby turned to the rest of the group and began his explanation.

"I believe the vengeance Tom is speaking of is for the murder of his father by his uncle when he was a boy." An audible gasp escaped the women's lips.

"Tom knows who he is," Toby continued. "Tom's true name is Benjamin, Benjamin Prescott."

"You mean the Prescott from the west side of the bay?" Jackie questioned. Toby nodded yes. Anna covered her mouth with her hand in disbelief.

"Why he owes everyone in town," Jackie spoke out.

"And that is why I have decided I must act now before there is nothing left of my birthright," I said gaining control of the emotions I could feel rising within me.

"He is a disgrace to the family name, a debtor and a drunk; a laughingstock to all who know him. And he is a murderer. I was witness to the act," I said coldly.

"But, Tom," Jackie spoke up, "he has nothing. You cannot avenge your father by exposing your uncle as a murderer after all these years. You even said you were the only witness. Your uncle has no money. His children have nothing..."

"He has the land," I responded under my breath, "land that belongs to me by right and he has burdened the property with many liens. If I can have nothing else, I want him not to have my father's and grandfather's land. I shall take it from him no matter what the cost."

FORTY-THREE

The first objective to be achieved in the future course of my life was determined by the conversation of that evening at the White Horse Inn. My friends now knew my darkest secret. I had sworn each of them to secrecy even though I knew I had no need to do so. All were willing to help me achieve justice.

A few days later, after I had begun to formulate my plan, I sat with Jackie and Toby at the Trinidad & Gray office. I explained to them my desire to buy back the property that was already mine by right of birth, but I could not act directly. I would need someone to stand as my agent as a buyer expressing interest in buying the property. I wanted Toby to realize he could not be that person for several reasons: he was probably better known in town than Jackie and, as a Black man, it might raise questions as to his ability to have access to funds to make such a purchase. In addition, I had a much larger project for him and certainly more important.

Jackie would present himself to Matthew Prescott as the agent of a wealthy individual interested in buying the Prescott holdings who wished to remain anonymous for now. He would begin negotiating but remain uncommitted as to price. Should my uncle begin inquiries on this prospective buyer, which I was sure he would, he would discover Jackie to be an up-and-coming prosperous owner of a shipping company.

"I want to see if my uncle is willing to divulge anything of the numerous parcels that are subject to liens of debtholders," I told him. "See what he tells you about what he would be willing to sell at what price, as well as the entire estate." Jackie nodded his understanding.

"He must not know at this stage that I am the buyer," I cautioned. "He will attempt to discover who you are, and in time we will allow him to discover the real buyer, Thomas Gray. But, for now, he must concentrate on learning who you are and not know whom you are representing."

I then turned my attention to Toby to explain his role in the plan. He would have the far more challenging task of assisting me in identifying the outstanding debts of my uncle. The two of us would need to search not only court records of liens filed against him, but assignments of property as collateral for loans.

"Toby, there will be other debts," I confided, "private debts, which are not yet registered with any court. We will need to know of these, as well."

"How will we know of these," Toby questioned?

"We will need to keep our ears open and ask questions of patrons of the inn who might have their tongues loosened by drink and might not remember giving information after," I replied. "We may need to make inquiries as far away as Providence, or farther. We must know the full extent of his debts. I know this may take some time, but it is critical to my plan."

"What part will Anna and Mary play," Jackie broke in?

"I wish to keep them out of this as much as possible," I replied. "I know Mary does not favor what I am planning, and Anna has ties to the Prescott household."

"Have no fear of Anna betraying you, Tom," Jackie reassured. "After she heard your history a few days past, she told me she, too, experienced similar cruelty from her stepfather."

"Even so, I think it best that she is not brought into the plan too deeply at this time," I cautioned.

"Let us begin in earnest tomorrow. Jackie, you should present yourself to my uncle in a day or two and make a general inquiry. We can talk about how before you go. Toby and I will go to the courthouse and begin searching for the legal notices of lien filings made against the property. I will show you how, Toby" I said finishing on a positive note.

"We keep this just to ourselves," I added cautiously. All nodded in agreement.

The next morning, I pulled Jackie aside as he came down from his room and, pressing twenty Spanish Reales into his hand, suggested he go shopping for a new set of clothes for his meeting with my uncle. After a light breakfast prepared by Mary and Anna, Toby, Jackie, and I left with a promise to return by the noon hour. As we made the short walk to the courthouse, Toby could not stop himself from commenting on the style Jackie should pursue in his new clothes: not too showy in lace or silk; more reserved English-cut business attire, something a high-level businessman might wear. All delivered with feigned seriousness, but very entertaining. At the courthouse, Jackie tipped his hat and headed further into town to find a tailor's shop. I could see from the expression on his face, he was glad to be done with Toby's humor.

I spent the first half hour introducing Toby to the personnel of the court records and showing him how to follow the recordings of property liens and collateralized loans. I stressed to Toby it was important that we find every transaction people had made with my uncle to whom he owed money whether it involved collateralization or not. I knew he would need to go back several years, and it would take time. I would help him every moment I could. But I felt the best way to gain information about my uncle's finances without raising suspicions might be to casually talk with other practicing attorneys who might have been involved in making filings on behalf of their clients. While Jackie might contact businessmen through his stature at Trinidad & Gray, my ability to be in the company of the wealthiest would allow us to be in contact with most of those who would be able to loan funds to someone who might appear to have the assets to repay.

The work was tedious and took many hours in addition to our duties at the inn. But, within two months, we had a fairly complete picture of the mountain of debt my uncle had created. It was something he would never be able to repay even in two lifetimes. He had borrowed two, and sometimes three times, against the same parcels of land. Those who held his debt would not know how worthless the paper they held as security was. It was time for the next step in my revenge.

Jackie had contacted my uncle, presenting himself as interested in buying my uncle's estate, hinting he might be the agent for another wealthy individual interested in buying his holdings. Jackie was eager to tell me of his meeting with Uncle Matthew. The path that had once led to the main house from the landing was overgrown and narrow. The fields on either side of the path that had once yielded crops of flax, wheat, and corn, and pastured sheep and livestock, were weed-filled and showed signs of having been so for some years. The outbuildings at the top of the path were weather beaten and in need of repair. No one seemed to be present.

The main house still presented a structure that had once been much grander than its present state. The wood about the windows was showing age, and several panes of glass were cracked and holed. The front door was heavily scarred from years without care. The metal hinges, door knocker, and handle were corroded to brown. Entering the front hall showed the toll the lack of care had exacted on the home. Jackie's first meeting with my uncle took place in the front parlor. Uncle Matthew had greeted Jackie in a disheveled state, slumped in his chair behind his desk in an obvious state of drunkenness.

Jackie was able to find out certain facts. My Uncle was alone except for a black house slave who waited on him and cooked his meals, and a mulatto field hand who had lived all his life on the plantation. His wife had died some eight or ten years past. He was unsure of the exact date. Two of her children had died shortly after from fever. The remaining children left as soon as they were able to either marry or find some form of employment.

At this first meeting, Jackie had expressed his mission on friendly terms, although he was not sure his message was received due to Matthew Prescott's condition. However, he was able to secure a second interview and left on amiable terms. It was at their second meeting that Uncle Matthew presented a better image of himself. He was freshly shaven, and his attire had obviously been cleaned and pressed for the occasion. His desk was cleared of the piles of papers that had covered it at their first meeting and fresh wildflowers adorned a vase in their place. Most importantly, Uncle Matthew was sober.

Jackie's rap on the front door was greeted by the servant girl in a freshly pressed apron who escorted him to the parlor. Matthew had risen from his desk at Jackie's arrival and taken a chair next to the fireplace, offering the other chair by the fireplace to his guest. I had instructed Jackie to begin exploring a price. How much land did the plantation have? What did Matthew believe his holdings were worth? How would he accept payment? Were there any encumbrances on the property?

Jackie knew the answers to most of these questions and was surprised at my uncle's responses. Jackie could hardly hold his anger as he related all to me. My Uncle had terribly inflated the value of the plantation. He insisted that no liens existed on any of the acreage and even challenged Jackie, or the personage he was standing for, to check at Customs House. He insisted he would only accept payment in coin to be received at the transference of the deed. None of this did I find surprising. I knew my uncle would want only to receive funds he could easily transport and leave the purchaser to discover the true status of his debt. I was now ready for the next step in my revenge.

I instructed Jackie to hold one final meeting with my uncle at which he would make an offer for the purchase of the entire plantation. That offer was to be a value of 3,400£ and not a penny more. It was important that the price be said in exactly that way, but without emphasis. I knew the price was greater than the value of the plantation. I also knew my uncle's level of greed. I told Jackie, should the price be accepted, a letter of intent was to be obtained and signed by both my uncle and Jackie as representative. The purchase would take place within thirty days.

Now came the critical part for Toby and me, and we would need to move quickly. Jackie returned within the week with the signed agreement from my uncle. Toby and I were ahead of schedule with our part in the preparation. I felt we would meet the thirty-day deadline without a problem.

The day arrived to meet with my uncle for the purchase of the plantation. Early that morning, Jackie, Toby, and I met on the wharf at Trinidad & Gray. We were dressed in attire suitable for the successful businessmen we were. Toby carried a small cashbox and a leather bag about his shoulder. Joining us was Mr. Worley from the magistrate's office of the Customs House at my invitation. Captain Bledsoe ushered us aboard *The Mary N.*, and we sailed for the west side of the bay in a light morning breeze.

I introduced Mr. Worley to Toby and Jackie and explained I had asked this member of the magistrate's staff to be a witness to transactions of the day. The four of us stood on the deck enjoying the sunshine and conversing about news of the day. Captain Bledsoe joined us once the ship was underway and spoke of his tenure with Trinidad & Gray.

Within the hour, we had rounded the northern tip of Conanicut and were making for the small landing of the Prescott Plantation. *The Mary N.* eased up to the dock and the crew made her fast as the sails were lowered. Our small party of five, Captain Bledsoe having joined at my invitation, disembarked, and made our way up the path leading to the house. Once again, we were greeted by the young woman in a pressed apron and ushered into the front parlor to meet Matthew Prescott.

Jackie introduced me as Thomas Gray of Trinidad & Gray Shipping and Toby as the other principal of the firm. He explained that it was I for whom he had been acting as agent and would be making the purchase of the property when all was determined to be in order. Jackie then introduced Captain Bledsoe as Captain of *The Mary N.* of our fleet. Mr. Prescott, dressed in his best, shook my hand, and made a bow to Toby, which was returned in kind, and made a like gesture to the captain.

"May I introduce Mr. Worley of the Magistrate's Office," I said in way of introducing the final member of our party. "I asked him to witness our transaction today to be sure all was carried out successfully."

"Your Servant," came Mr. Prescott's reply.

Toby and I settled into the chairs before Mr. Prescott's desk while the captain, Jackie, and Mr. Worley found chairs nearer the fireplace. And so, we began.

"So, Mr. Gray," Matthew began, "Mr. Saunders has expressed to me your interest in my lands."

"Yes, I have long had an interest in land on this side of the bay, especially this area," I replied.

"You are getting it at a very good price, you know," Matthew was about to begin expounding on the virtues of his holdings.

"Yes, yes," I said cutting him short. "Let us proceed to the matter at hand."

Jackie came forward with the signed letter of intent and laid it in front of me on the desk.

"The agreement is as follows," I began, "I have agreed to purchase your holding for a value of 3,400£ unencumbered in any way and free of debt. Are we in agreement?"

"That is the agreed upon price," came the response from Matthew Prescott.

Very well, then," I replied. "Considering your willingness to carry out the agreement, Mr. Worley has the transfer of deed for your signature."

Mr. Worley stepped behind the desk next to Matthew Prescott and directed him to the line for his signature. Mr. Prescott adjusted his glasses and, taking his quill in hand signed the document with a bold hand. Mr. Worley retrieved the document and moved to lay the document in front of me. I took the quill from Matthew Prescott and signed: Thomas Gray; born Benjamin Prescott.

I then passed the quill to Toby who signed as witness and Mr. Worley signed, as well. The document was then removed from the desk.

"And now for your payment, Mr. Prescott," I announced. This was Toby's cue to hand me the cashbox.

"Based on our agreement, I have taken the liberty to round up the odd amount and, for your convenience, I am making payment of the balance due you in pounds sterling, with that said, here is what you are owed."

I placed the sum of 25£ in a single stack of coins before him.

"What do you mean 'the balance owed to me'?" Mr. Prescott blurted out in his confused state. "Twenty-five pounds?"

I turned to Toby, who was retrieving a sizeable stack of papers from his pouch. Placing the papers before Mr. Prescott on the desk, I continued calmly.

"Yes, Mr. Prescott, the agreement was the sale of your unencumbered property. I have paid all your debts attached to the land, as I suspected you would not. I, therefore, already have title to most of what you thought you still owned. The balance owed to you after making good on all your debts is 23£.8.6d. I decided to round it to a convenient 25£."

"You can't do this!" Matthew Prescott blustered.

"Ahh, but I can," I replied with coldness. "I can and I have as Mr. Worley will attest, it is all perfectly legal. In fact, your attempt to sell what you no longer own, having already pledged it to cover debt, is a crime in and of itself."

"Is that not so?" I said, turning to Mr. Worley for his agreement.

I rose from my chair and leaning across the desk to be closer to his ear, I whispered,

"But, as we both know, Dear Uncle Matthew, this is not your first crime."

As I drew back to the edge of the desk, the look on my uncle's face was one of stunned awe.

"What did you call me…?" he stammered.

In my calmest, coldest voice I said softly, "Yes, Uncle, it is I, your nephew, Benjamin."

"But…. But you died. Years ago," he stammered in disbelief.

"No, Uncle. I am alive and well and what was mine by right is now paid for in full."

"Mr. Worley," I said turning to address him," please inform Mr. Prescott that, as of this moment, he is trespassing on my property, and I will give him until noon tomorrow to be gone."

Matthew Prescott sat with a look of confused disbelief playing on his features.

With that, I turned and left the parlor and the house, leaving the members of my party to follow. Once outside the house, I took a deep breath of fresh air.

"Captain Bledsoe," I said in a loud voice as he exited the house, "tomorrow at noon, burn it to the ground. I shall watch from *The Mary N.*"

"What if he's still here, Mr. Gray?" Captain Bledsoe replied.

"Then burn it with him in it!" I yelled back over my shoulder as I started down the path to the landing.

FORTY-FOUR

At precisely noon the next day, as I stood on the foredeck of *The Mary N.* as she rode at anchor just offshore from the former Prescott Plantation, I watched as flames enveloped the building on the hill and a great cloud of black smoke rose into the sky above it. I felt no remorse for my order to burn the old house. It held no good memories for me and was a place that carried all the worst memories of my childhood. It took no more than half an hour for the walls to collapse upon themselves and the chimney to be left standing naked against the sky. It was a relief to know it no longer existed.

Captain Bledsoe returned to *The Mary N.* to see me still watching the smoldering wreckage.

"As you ordered, Sir," he said to me as he approached. "It went up like a box of tinder."

"Thank you, Captain," I replied with no emotion. "Was he still there?"

"No one was about. I know you had your reasons, Tom, but, still and all, it was a shame to see such an old place go that way," Captain Bledsoe said shaking his head in regret.

"You have no idea, Captain, what my time at this place was like, what it cost me, how sad the memories of it are to me." I spoke as if to no one, but only to hear the words expressed to myself.

I stood at the rail a few minutes longer until the last wisps of smoke reached into the sky. Toby had been at my side the entire time, yet I only now acknowledged his presence.

"Are you alright, Tom?" Toby said softly.

"Yes, Toby," I replied looking at him. "I am better than I have been in a long time. Let's go home."

Toby put his hand on my shoulder and said to Captain Bledsoe, "Captain, time to set sail."

Captain Bledsoe gave the command, and the anchor was brought up and the topsails unfurled. *The Mary N.* slowly swung about and picked up speed as she headed out into the bay above Conanicut Island. Nothing was said as we sailed toward home, and neither did I look back at the smoldering wreckage on the hill.

I would not return to the property until six weeks later. Soon after our return from Fishers Island, I commissioned a new marker to be made for the family cemetery down on the hill. I had been informed the carving of it was almost completed and it could be ready to install at that time. Though I had no idea how, or where, my father's remains had been placed by my uncle, I hoped they were at least buried somewhere in the plot, perhaps even near my mother. But this marker would forever mark the place, and state the truth, of what had happened at this homestead.

We landed at Trinidad & Gray's wharf without incident. Toby and I began the short walk to the White Horse Inn discussing what should be done with the property I now owned. I told Toby I had no interest in becoming a gentleman farmer, nor leasing it to be farmed by others. Was he interested in the property? To my surprise, Toby responded with a desire I would never have thought to hear.

"We are none of us getting any younger, Tom," Toby began, "I would like to see my father once more if he is still alive and before I am too old to make the trip. I would not want to stay in Trinidad, you understand, but just to know if he still lives."

"I understand, my friend," I replied. "As I have finally put concerns of my father to rest, so you should do the same. Let us set to work getting the details worked out."

"There are many other details I do not think you have been aware of lately, Tom," Toby said with a wry smile. "You have been much distracted of late and have missed much of what has been going on about you. You have had much on your mind, and you cannot be faulted for not seeing what has been so plain to the rest of us."

Toby wrapped his arm about my shoulders and gently shook me as his smile grew to a full grin.

We bounded up the stairs to the inn and, arm-in-arm, entered the tavern room with wide smiles and good moods. Anna was serving behind the bar and gave us a smile as she saw us. The few patrons greeted us as we passed through the room into the kitchen. There, we found Mary sitting by the fireplace preparing some fresh vegetables for a pot. Toby quickly shed his coat and took an apron off the hook behind the door. Tying it around his waist, he excused himself and went into the tavern to help Anna behind the bar.

I seated myself at the kitchen table and looked at Mary. It was the first time in some time that I had really looked at her. I was surprised at what I saw. Mary was growing old. Her lace bonnet now covered auburn hair streaked with white. Her frame was slightly bent as she sat paring celery into the cooking pot. The hands that had once been so youthful and smooth were red and now beginning to show wrinkles. Her face was beginning to show creases, and those eyes that had always been so lively were a bit dimmer now. Mary suddenly realized I was looking at her.

"Is there a reason you're lookin' at me that way?" she said in a playful way.

"Just thinking, Mary," I replied, "how long have you been running the inn?"

"Why would you be thinking about that?" she questioned.

"Do you ever think of retiring, Mary?" I asked, trying not to betray my real meaning in the question.

"And what would you have me do with myself all day?" Mary shot back at me.

"Mary, would you not like being able to sleep late and not have the worries of the inn?" I suggested. "You know I promised to build you a cottage on the bay when you were ready. I now have a property on which to build your cottage if you are ready."

"So, now I should be ready to give up my business and become a woman of leisure, just because you can now fulfill your promise," Mary replied with a smile.

"You know you no longer need to work, Mary," I began, "you are wealthier than any other woman in this town." I rose from my seat and approached Mary. She stopped working with her knife and looked at my face as I knelt before her. "I'm just asking you to think about taking life a little easier. Will you think about it?" Mary patted the back of my hand.

"I will consider what you ask," she said tenderly.

"Toby has told me he would like to return to Trinidad to seek out his father," I shared with Mary.

"Yes." Mary replied, "he did mention it to me. You need to speak with Jackie, as well."

This last statement took me by surprise, but I tried not to show any reaction. I was beginning to believe Toby had been right. I had been preoccupied and I needed to get caught up.

That evening, as Toby and I retired to our room, I decided it was time to find out what had been going on around me, of which I was unaware.

"Can we talk for a few minutes?" I asked Toby.

"I was hoping you would want to talk," Toby said as he sat on the edge of his bed. "I know you have been fully absorbed in other things of late, and there are things that have been going on around you that you have totally missed."

"Yes, you are quite right, apparently, old friend," I replied. "But I feel like the huge weight I felt about my past has finally been lifted from me. So, please, tell me what I have missed?"

"Well. To begin, I already told you of my desire to find my father, if he is still alive," Toby began, "but there is so much more that has gone on. Jackie has made Trinidad & Gray into one of the largest shipping firms in Newport. He is devoted to the business, and he and Captain Bledsoe work hand in glove as smooth as any team you can name."

I smiled at the thought that little Jackie, the Dock Rat who ran errands years ago, was now among the most respected businessmen of the town. But that was not all of which I was unaware.

"You must know that Jackie and Anna have eyes for each other," Toby continued, "you can't have been blind to that? It has been evident to everyone who knows them for months. Anna spends every spare minute at the shipping office, and Jackie stays up after the inn has closed talking with Anna in the kitchen or on the back porch."

"Toby, I have been completely unaware of all of it," I said a bit baffled at my inability to see this love blossoming. "Has Jackie made any commitment to Anna, or she to him?"

"Tom," Toby said with a note of disappointment in his voice, "I believe they have been waiting for the opportunity to approach you to ask your blessing."

"Good Lord, Toby," I said in dismay, "I had no idea. They must think me a perfect fool!"

"And then there is Mary," Toby said to change the subject. "In spite of what Mary may say, I think she would not be opposed to selling the inn and getting that little cottage you promised her,"

"I asked her about that very subject just earlier today," I replied in surprise. "She insisted she would not know what she would do if she gave up the inn."

"I would have expected that response from Mary," Toby said shaking his head. "She is tough, but she is tired. I think she could be quickly convinced with the right incentive." I nodded my understanding.

"I am glad we spoke," Toby said, "and I have given you much to think about. While nothing is pressing, these are all things which will be coming up."

"I owe you much, my friend," I said to Toby. "And I need to see that you get to fulfill your wish to find your father as soon as possible."

"All in good time, my brother," Toby said with a smile as he climbed beneath his covers and extinguished the candle.

As I lay back on my pillow, I knew sleep would not come easily this night. My mind was racing with the things Toby had related to me. He was right that I had not been aware. But now having been enlightened, I would need to prepare for my response when I was finally presented with each situation.

In my mind, the most immediate concern was to fulfill Toby's wish to find his father. It was also the most personally distressing. The longest separation Toby and I had ever had since we met so many years ago was the eight months I had been at Yale. His travel to Trinidad would mean a separation of more than a year. I would be without my oldest companion and confidante. But I owed Toby the chance to make this journey and to help him in any way possible. I would begin in the morning.

FORTY-FIVE

*A*fter a day or two to consider the steps required for Toby's trip, I went to my office at the shipping company. When Jackie arrived, I was already involved in the first steps of preparing papers for Toby's journey to Trinidad. I quickly explained to Jackie what I was about and asked that he have Captain Bledsoe meet me as soon as possible. Jackie told me the good Captain had been on a short run to Boston and should be returning this day by midafternoon. I asked Jackie if there were any ships with cargoes ready to leave for the Caribbean. He looked at his schedule and saw only one ship scheduled. Was it possible we could schedule more vessels to the Caribbean, I wondered? Jackie assured me not only was it possible, but highly likely there would be more.

Upon hearing this, I returned to my task. I was writing letters of introduction for Toby to use on his journey. Would they be of value to him? I had no way of knowing, but I felt it could do no harm. My thought was to speak with other merchants and people at the Custom House to see if they could supply names to attach to these letters. Surely it would not hurt to have letters of introduction to planters and government officials in Trinidad and possible ports of call along the way.

I was intent upon my work when a knock came on my door. I could see through the glass in the door it was Jackie seeking admission. He had, I thought, an odd expression on his face. I bid him enter. Because of his demeanor, I asked him if there was something wrong?

"No, Sir," he replied tentatively. "Not exactly. Well, no, not at all."

Why so formal, Jackie," I said as he stood before my desk nervously shuffling his feet like a young boy who had something to confess. "What is it?"

"I've been meaning to speak with you regarding something very important to me," he began tentatively. "You see, Tom, I know you have been preoccupied with other matters and I didn't want to burden you with something more...."

"For heaven's sake, Jackie! Spit it out! We have known each other far too long for you not to be able to talk to me. What is wrong?" I said trying to be as understanding as I could be.

It's about Anna, Tom," he finally blurted out. "I mean it's about me..., us...I mean Anna and me." Finally, I understood.

"Sit down, Jackie," I said, finally understanding the sweat that stood out on his forehead. "Toby already told me about you two."

"And you made me stand there and look like a fool?" he said with a sigh of relief. I gently laughed at his fear.

"The two of you wish to marry?" I asked.

"I love her, Tom," Jackie confided. "It took me forever to get up the courage to ask her. I have already asked Toby to be my best man and he has agreed. Anna wanted to ask if you would walk her down the aisle."

I was unprepared for this request but instantly agreed. Jackie fairly flew from his chair and reached across my desk to shake my hand and attempt an embrace. His joy at my acceptance was totally heartfelt and genuine.

"I must tell Anna!" he said as he bolted out the door, "she's waiting in my office to hear!"

"But wait," I shouted as he disappeared. I sat back in my chair and smiled to myself that Jackie felt he needed to ask my approval. Was I suddenly a father figure? I sat for a moment shaking my head, not sure what to make of what had just happened. I then returned to completing the correspondence for Toby's trip.

Another knock on my door had me look up to see Captain Bledsoe's weathered face standing at my door. I motioned for him to enter and greeted him warmly. I congratulated him on his quick return from Boston, to which he replied that the sun had set an hour before. The entire afternoon had passed unnoticed by me as I labored.

I quickly addressed my concerns for Toby's voyage and was pleasantly surprised by Captain Bledsoe's news. He had contacted a fellow captain who would be leaving for the Caribbean at the end of the next month and had agreed to provide passage to Cuba. From there, Toby would need to seek another ship. This would mean Toby would be leaving sooner than I had anticipated, and though the news would delight him, it meant I would need to accept the pain of our separation more quickly. The captain had also agreed to sail to Newport to pick up his passenger.

$$><$$

Several weeks passed after the happy news of the impending nuptial. Mary and Anna threw themselves into planning. There was happy chatter from morning to evening with frequent trips for shopping. Jackie was more concerned with finding a place for him and his new bride to live. There was no suitable lodging at the shipping company building, and it might be awkward for the newlyweds to continue residing in the inn once they were wed. Acquiring lodgings or a small house was no easy task in bustling Newport. The wedding would need to be held before Toby left and time was growing short.

Toby was busy preparing for his departure. The transporting of a sizeable amount of his wealth to fund what might be a journey of two years or more presented a problem to be addressed. It was decided that several letters of credit signed by our company would suffice. Toby's excitement was growing as the prospect of finding his father grew closer.

While these events were in the middle of planning, another event was about to take place attended solely by me. The stone mason had contacted me to say he had completed his work on the cemetery monument

I had ordered. Arrangements had been made for its transport to the west shore of the bay and for installation in the family burial plot on the old farm.

I arrived at the family cemetery as the old sandstone marker was being removed from its base. It was the marker my father and uncle had erected to honor their father over half a century ago. It bore the scars the weather of all those years had laid upon its surfaces from rain and snow and freeze and thaw. It had been years since I had stood for any length of time near this spot.

The white marble of the new grave marker gleamed in the midday sun. I watched as the workers carefully set the new marker on its new permanent footing in the correct orientation. The three-foot square base, rising to a height of five feet, was to be placed so the side facing the old iron gate showed the oval relief bearing the carved inscription. It was here the legend was placed.

In Memory of
Josiah Prescott
Colonist, War Hero, Farmer, Father, Grandfather
William Prescott
Son, Father, Sailor
Eliza Carr Prescott
Loving Wife of William
And Mother of
Benjamin

I stood back to admire the three-foot, four-sided spire that rose to a point above the base. I could only hope that my father had been buried here by his brother. I would never know for certain, but I could hope that he and his beloved Eliza rested together within the stone walls of this small cemetery. As I leaned on the old, rusted gate, and looked at those walls that had now begun to fall because of neglect, and the length and dearth of weeds that were growing, I knew I had to make this small plot anew and I would spend whatever it took to make it the special place it needed it to be.

I was leaning on the railing of the boat on my way back toward Newport, looking back at the white spire shining above the tree line, when I was suddenly struck with the inspiration of what to do about the property I now owned. I was excited by my thought and could hardly wait to reach the White Horse and share it with Mary, Jackie, and Anna. For the moment, thoughts of Toby's departure were no longer foremost in my mind. At least for the moment, they would return shortly. But first I needed to go to my office at the shipping company.

I arrived at the White Horse shortly after closing and gathered Mary, Jackie, Toby, and now, Anna in the dining room. I was excited at the prospect of sharing my idea about the old farm with my friends.

"I must say," I began, "we have many things going on at this moment." Heads nodded all round.

"Toby will be leaving us sometime in the next month to seek his father," I continued, "we have a wedding being planned, and none of us are getting any younger." This remark drew a smile and quiet laugh from my audience.

"I have a proposition which I think will move all of us a long way toward resolving a problem our soon-to-be bride and groom are facing, and provide an option for our Mary, as well," I declared with a broad smile.

"As you are all aware, the property on the west side of the bay that I own is of no value to me as I have no desire to be a gentleman farmer or have a grand estate. However, it does have a beautiful view of the west passage and Newport beyond Conanicut Island." Turning to Jackie and Anna, I continued, "As my wedding present to both of you, I would like to give you the property and help you build your home there."

The look of astonishment on Anna's and Jackie's faces was one I shall never forget.

"There is one caveat to this arrangement," I added. "A parcel of the land facing the water must be provided to build a retirement cottage for our Mary."

I looked at Mary who had stopped in the middle of her congratulations to Jackie and Anna, stunned into silence.

"What are you suggesting, Thomas?" came her reply. "I am not ready to 'retire'? What would I do all day?"

"You can help Anna with the children, Mary," Jackie said half in jest.

"And Newport is just across the bay," I added enthusiastically. "You could always stay with me if you wanted to come to Newport and leave the next day for home. You have Jackie who will be running the shipping company and taking a boat several days a week, I am sure. Why, you and I could travel the world if you have a mind to?"

"You shouldn't have the worries of the inn at your age, Mary," Toby added. "We are all moving on with our lives, and I would not feel at ease leaving you with the prospect of new employees to train. Jackie and Anna will be busy with family and work, and it is time Tom was free to pursue his own career, whether that be the law or politics. Heaven knows he could do either!"

"I know this plan will take some time," I broke in, "the building on the property alone may take a year or more. That will give you time to get used to the idea of being free to do as you wish. All I ask, Mary, is for you to think about it. I know it is something we all want for you,"

FORTY-SIX

Toby left on his voyage to find his father just short of six weeks after my plan was presented. He was full of hope, and many tears were shed as he hugged each of us and bid us farewell. It would be two years before we would hear of him again, and even that word was one of uncertainty. Each day during those two years, I prayed Toby had found his father and hoped it was only due to the slowness of communication that prevented us from knowing of his success.

Jackie, who now wished to be called James, and Anna were married the following spring after what was considered a reasonable time of engagement. While Toby was not present to be Best Man, I, dutifully, walk Anna to the altar as she had wanted, she was still the most radiant bride and Jackie was every bit as handsome in his wedding attire. The day of the wedding dawned cool and sunny with little wind, and the reception at the White Horse was attended by dozens of our friends. It was a celebration that would be long remembered.

While work was progressing on their new home across the bay, they resided with Mary in the inn. It was to be a grand estate with seven bedrooms for the large family they were anticipating. Jackie had plans for a barn and several outbuildings. His plans included employment of field hands to return the fields to a working farm status, working either as tenants or indentured servants who were arriving late in the colony.

The wealth he possessed from his share of the treasure and his success in business meant he would pay his workers a good wage. The land for Mary's bayside cottage had been cleared, and the cottage was taking form based on Mary's design. I was pleased to see a new life beginning on the property and my own hurtful past swept away by the building of new structures.

It took two years to finish construction of James' and Anna's new home on the west bay. And it was a good thing it was finished when it was, for Anna was heavily pregnant with her first child. Mary's cottage was completed at nearly the same time. But before she would consent to move to the cottage, Mary insisted on selling the inn to someone of whom she approved. With some luck (and advice from her legal counsel) Mary found a buyer that she heartily approved of to continue the operation of her beloved White Horse Inn.

The momentous day for everyone to move across the bay came. James led the way aboard Captain Bedloe's vessel with great fanfare. Anna, in her present state, elected to sit on the cargo hold cover with Mary at her side for the sail across the bay. Jackie, now James, stood at the rail near the forecastle with me having a light conversation about nothing of importance. For a couple of weeks prior, several boatloads of furnishings and household goods had been ferried across the bay to make the house ready to be occupied. James had already employed a young girl from Newport as a maid for Anna and a cook with experience in midwifery. Likewise, Mary had planned for a companion to keep house for her and prepare meals.

Our ship rounded the north point of Conanicut Island, and we could all see the majestic white manor atop the hill and the small cottage nearer the water. To the south of the new house and halfway down the hill, the white marble spire in the graveyard glinted in the sunshine.

—————————————— >< ——————————————

The ensuing twenty odd years have held much to be grateful for and some things to be sad about. With everyone else pursuing their futures, it was time for me to see to my own. I decided it was time for me to travel. I wanted to see the major cities of the colonies such as Boston, New York, and Philadelphia. I was fortunate enough to meet many of the important personalities of our time. I traveled to the southern colonies, to Charleston and Savannah. I crossed the Atlantic and went to Ireland attempting to meet with my old benefactor the Reverend Berkely. I was sad to learn of his death in the year before I arrived. I visited London and was awed by its size.

When I had satisfied my desire to travel, I returned to Newport and purchased a comfortable residence just to the east of the city and settled into my active retirement. I established my law offices near the Custom House and became a member of the Philosophical Society of which Reverend Berkeley had been a founder. My travels have given me a wider prospective of the world. The legal community received my practice well, and I found myself being asked to hold positions in the Colonial Government. This employment allowed me to be privy to information regarding relations between the various colonies and Britain. The Molasses Act of 1733 had a chilling effect on shipping in New England, and cargoes began slipping into ports without paying the imposed tax. The increasing presence of the military after King George's War, for whom colonists were expected to billet and feed the troops, became an annoyance and a regular topic in governmental meetings. It was an interesting time. I could see the attitudes of those in colonial power moving away from what had been tradition. There were those who rankled under the onus of increasing taxation over which they had no say. The attempt by our mother country to interfere with our trade and commerce and to justify those taxes we paid for the protection of the colonies rang hollow when most of the fighting in George's war had been conducted by the colonists themselves. Since the dispute with France began in Europe before spreading to North America, and was over additional territory Britain wished to possess, it seemed unfair to expect her colonies to pay for a war that was not of their making.

Anna had given birth to another healthy child within the month of my return and Mary, now "Granny Mary," would climb the hill most mornings to help with the newborn. She would be named Louisa and be the first girl of seven children conceived by the happy couple. Two would not survive. But the three surviving girls and two sons brought immense joy to their parents.

I found love, in what some might say, was late in life. It was unexpected and my wife, though beautiful to my eyes, was delicate in form, and she was taken by a fever in only the second year of our union.

It is true that time and the years begin to pass rapidly with age. It had been three years since Toby's departure to find his father. I would find myself most Sundays in mild weather at Mary's cottage enjoying tea in the afternoon then strolling arm-in-arm up to the stately house on the hill to enjoy dinner with James and Anna and their noisy brood of children who called me "Uncle Thomas." Other days I would take my leave of Mary and go to sit peacefully in the late afternoon sun on the bench inside the cemetery plot.

One such Sunday, James announced he had news to share. The gaiety of the children was removed as they were ushered from the dining room by their governess. James removed an envelope from his pocket and, pushing his chair back, stood to read.

"I made inquiry regarding Toby since we have not heard from him in some time," James began. "I received the following message from a shipping associate in New York who reported Toby as having had passage booked aboard one of their vessels returning from Venezuela by way of Trinidad with stops in some other islands as well. The *Aurelio* was reported overdue at Havana, Cuba, and is assumed to have been lost with all hands aboard."

My Friend, my brother for over forty years, gone forever. I could see my tears falling silently on the table before me. I was immobile as this news resonated in my ears and my mind tried to comprehend. I could hear Mary choking back her tears. James dropped the paper he had been reading from and sat back heavily in his chair.

"As sad as this news is," I finally was able to speak, "we can hope that our brother Toby found his father, or learned his fate, and was returning to us."

I reached for my glass and lifted it to toast saying, "I would sooner know this of Toby's fate than always wonder what had happened. Good rest and God bless."

Everyone raised their glasses, and with a somber "Amen", toasted our deceased friend.

Toby's estate was settled according to the terms of the will he had executed before his trip. His stated assets made no mention of the treasure. It only spoke of his assets in general. Those were to be split between James, Mary, and me, as we had all agreed long ago: survivors would share. James asked that the name of the shipping firm be changed to include his name and I agreed. Trinidad & Gray became James Saunders & Sons, Shipping and Trading. I became a silent partner.

One of the reasons I ceased my travelling was my suffering an injury from a carriage accident that left me lame. And so, now, I walk with a cane as my constant companion. Injuries and sickness are a constant worry as we age. Sickness is the more worrisome for the pain one may suffer before death comes. Sickness is even worse when it sweeps through an entire population. During one such episode, Mary was taken. She was nursed by Anna through her fever, and, in turn, Anna became ill. They were both taken within a week of each other.

James and I saw that Mary was buried beside her long-deceased husband, Robert, in the north burial ground. Mary had passed nearing her seventy-third year. Anna was buried beside her two children, who had not survived infancy, in the new cemetery plot near the house. Louisa was twenty now and would be the lady of the house. She would be her father's comfort and help to raise her siblings.

I was becoming increasingly frustrated with the measures Britain was taking in their relations with her colonies in America. Should the colonies become united in their dissatisfaction, it could result in Britain losing control of them. I determined it was time for me to retire from public service and enjoy my later years. Since Mary's death some five years previously had left her cottage empty, James suggested "Uncle Thomas" might take residence to be closer to those who "loved him." With much prompting, and many pleas from the children who were aging before my eyes, I agreed.

I felt the winters more sharply than when I was younger. But for the greater part of the year, I was able to enjoy the weather, and, on most days, I would take a short walk with my cane to support my lameness to sit on the bench that sat within the walls of the cemetery plot and enjoy the sun. The repaired stone walls protected me from heavy winds, and I could read undisturbed.

Louisa became my near-constant companion. Every morning she would appear with some breakfast to be sure I was eating. One of the older children would find me to walk me to the family house for supper. Louisa had grown into a fine young woman who should have been married some years earlier. One morning, Louisa arrived as usual, but with a companion. She was introduced to me as Elizabeth, or Bess. Bess had been the wife of one of the farmhands on the estate who had died just a few months earlier. Would I accept her as someone who would see to my needs in future? Louisa would still visit, but she was going to be married to the son of a prominent person in Providence. And so, Bess became my housekeeper, cook, and companion.

That was four years ago. I have become very dependent on her, and our bond is strong. James retired from business last spring and passed the shipping business to his two sons. They had both apprenticed at the business and both had received excellent educations with our connections through Reverend Berkeley at Yale. I am looking forward to a few more good years, even though the political situation between the colonies and Britain is showing great strain. I fear war cannot be far off. I am content to only observe the worsening situation and spend my days enjoying James's children and the warmth of the sun as I sit on my bench in the family cemetery and read.

Epilogue

This entry in this chronicle is made by the hand of James Saunders, the friend of a great man known to many as Thomas Gray. Let it be said here that his true name was Benjamin Prescott. Mr. Prescott was discovered sitting in his favorite place on the bench in his family's burial plot having passed from this life quietly and peacefully in the light of day. He was found with his father's tattered Bible in his left hand. It was open to a passage in the Book of Luke. In his right hand, he was holding a gold doubloon.

He was a kind and gentle man, whom I knew only once to display anger and seek revenge, and that was with good reason. I owed him my life and my fortune, and I will execute the mandates of his wishes as contained in his last will and testament. Chief among those bequests is his desire to anonymously gift in the memory of the Right Reverend George Berkeley most of his substantial assets to the college that bears the Reverend's name at Yale University.

This manuscript, written in Mr. Prescott's own hand, was discovered among his papers. It is unknown exactly when Mr. Prescott began it. But it is a record of a time past and the adventure of his life that I, and others, shared with him. May he rest in peace.

Respectfully penned,
James Saunders
September 23, 1770

Acknowledgements

I wish to express my thanks to the following people who read early drafts of the story and, in some cases, offered critical review and opinions. I can never express to them how much their assistance and encouragement aided in the completion of the work.

Special thanks to Margaret (Maggie) Skenyon who read more than one draft with a critical eye for grammar, punctuation, and continuity. I thank Sheila Verdi and the late Robert Verdi, my good friend, for their encouragement of the project. Likewise, I thank Mr. David Devereux for his reading of an early draft and his enthusiastic reception to the story. I thank all my friends who read drafts of the story along the way, including Mr. Robert Wade, Mr. George Richardson, and, for reading a much later draft Ms. Nancy Nordquist. The reviews and critiques they provided were greatly appreciated. In addition, I thank my cousin, Ms. Elizabeth (Betsy) Brewster, for her knowledge regarding maritime information of Long Island Sound and Ms. Amy Folk, historian, for Southold Township on Long Island, New York, for leading me to Mr. Pierce Rafferty. His expertise of Fishers Island was of immense assistance. If I have been remiss in failing to acknowledge anyone who had input, I offer my sincere apology.

Finally, I want to thank my wife, Angie, for reading multiple drafts, her insights, critique, and patience. Most of all, for her understanding of the time it has taken to produce the work.